1695

JESSE

The Post-Death Adventures
of Elvis Presley

To Lorraine,

I hope you enjoy the book.

Best Wishes,

Bun DuVall

JESSE

The Post-Death Adventures
of Elvis Presley

Brian DeVall

Aventine Press LLC

This is a work of fiction based on historical facts and figures. The author of this book does not contend or imply a belief in any of the theories in this book, nor does he maintain that any of the characters or organizations mentioned herein played any part in any conspiracy.

Published by Aventine Press, LLC
2208 Cabo Bahia
Chula Vista, CA 91914, USA

www.aventinepress.com

ISBN: 1-59330-043-3

Printed in the United States of America

For my Mother

"To famous men all the earth is a sepulchure."

-THUCHYDIDES

CHAPTER I

FAME AND FORTUNE

The loving crowd strained to hear his voice, but instead of words, they could only hear an inaudible mess of slurred lyrics and labored breathing. The fans were undaunted, though. It didn't matter if they could hear him; they could see him, and for this mass of fervent followers, that was enough. Many in the crowd were seeing their musical messiah for the first time; none of them knew they were all seeing him for the last time.

As aging women squealed as they once had in their teens; flashbulbs popped and sparkled from the dark void of the audience. Sweat poured from the skin of the man's tanned forehead as the threads holding his white sequined jumpsuit together strained and pulled with every movement of the lumbering dinosaur.

Elvis Presley's hands shook wildly as his body once had as he mopped the sweat off his brow with a red scarf. Women clamored and pressed their bodies against the barrier, desperately reaching out theirs hands, praying that the scarf might end up in their grasp. Instead of bending down to hand it to some lucky lady, he dangled it haphazardly over the orgy of hands until it was ripped away.

Forgetting the next line of his song, he improvised an incoherent mumble. Elvis stumbled over his own feet as he saw a spectre staring at him from the front row. It was a young boy, his dead twin brother, Jesse. He had died at birth but throughout Elvis' life he had been a haunting presence. He was an imaginary friend as a child and the voice in his head as an adult. Jesse had an angry look on his face, a face that looked like Elvis' as a child. His eyes peered through Elvis, burning him with his gaze.

The microphone fell from Elvis' trembling hand as the vision disappeared as quickly as it came. The microphone hit the stage with a loud thud and a hiss of feedback. In that moment, he felt an eternity pass, as he searched the crowd for his twin brother. As the sound of his rapidly beating heart echoed through his head, a roadie ran onto the stage and picked up the microphone. He tried to hand it back to the King, but he could see that Elvis was too doped up to even hold it.

The roadie awkwardly remained onstage, holding the microphone up to Elvis' lips like a human mike stand while the living legend stammered and murmured through the rest of the song, oblivious to the pitiful display. The song ended and Elvis plodded off the stage. Despite the sad and pathetic nature of the performance, the crowd clapped and cheered for an encore.

Backstage, Elvis nearly collapsed. He took a few breaths from the oxygen tanks that were waiting for him and downed a packet of pills. Not feeling the relief he needed, he instructed his on-hand physician to inject him with Dexedrine. Feeling the surge of relief gush through his veins, he eventually hobbled back onstage as the packed crowd roared with approval. He had been gone for almost thirty minutes, but no one had cared and no one had left. After he finished his encores, his assistants helped him from the stage to his limousine, where he uncoiled in the backseat, reeling in his stupor.

The crowd still cheered and hoped he would return once more for one final song, but it was not to be. The news was broken to them by a booming voice that came over the speakers.

"Ladies and gentlemen, Elvis has left the building."

Graceland stood as a lavish shrine to excess, and was the shining jewel of Memphis, Tennessee. It was a hillbilly Shangri-La. Its gates were adorned with guitars and musical notes, giving passageway to a world of overindulgence. Behind the brown bricks and white columns guarding the front door was an exquisitely designed palace, fit for a king. The foyer was painted white and had a mirrored staircase with a massive chandelier above it. The living room was decorated in white, gold, and blue. The decor was elegant and comfortable, with mirrors on the walls and a white, fifteen-foot couch that stretched along one wall in the room. The living room connected to the music room, which had a black grand piano, and was where many impromptu late-night performances had occurred. Around the entryway to the music room were stained-glass windows with peacocks on them, windows that Elvis had decided to buy when the salesman informed him that peacocks symbolized eternal life.

The dining room had blue drapes and was painted white, with beige shag carpeting and a black marble floor. Above the glass table was another opulent chandelier. It was a room where Elvis and his friends would eat, talk, and often play cards.

The den, or the Jungle Room as it was sometimes called, was an excessive, if not gaudy salute to the tropics, with exotic plants, waterfalls and Hawaiian-inspired decorations all around. The excessiveness was topped off with thick carpeting on the ceiling. It was where Elvis would hold court with his friends, and where they would spend most of their recreational time.

The entire house was extravagant, ornate, and brightly colored, bordering on campy, with the exception of one room, the room where Elvis now spent most of his days. It was his bedroom, but it felt more like a sepulchre, a tomb for the walking dead, inhabited by a dying recluse, withdrawn from the world that adored him.

The room had black walls and ceilings, with black curtains pulled tightly closed around the windows, which were covered with aluminum foil to prevent any light from entering. Elvis Presley sat alone in his bed, pulling the sheets over the bottom of his face like a death shroud. He watched three televisions simultaneously as his mind drifted in and out of consciousness.

He grabbed a handful of pills and threw them in his mouth, swallowing them. His head was already swimming from some Valium he had taken earlier, and these additional pills put his mind beyond coherency. He took a sip of water to wash the Benzedrine down, but most of the fluid spilled out of the side of his mouth and onto his bed and silk pajamas. His hair was dirty and matted, and his three-hundred pound body smelled of week-old sweat.

This was not the same Elvis Presley who had electrified the world some twenty years earlier. This was not the same handsome young man who had scandalized the nation with a swivel of his hips on a new invention called television. He was not the same person who proved the critics wrong with a leather-clad comeback in 1968. This was a man on the verge of collapse, emotionally and physically. Despite his size, he was now a mere shadow of his former self.

His addiction to painkillers and sleeping pills had not only ravaged his health, but injured his mind and soul as well. He lived in a perpetual fog, a fog that he self-medicated to maintain. His spirit was reflected in his eyes -- a once smoldering intensity, now dull and lifeless. The demons that he had once harnessed to create a musical revolution had now saddled him and made him a slave.

Graceland had joined forces with his unprecedented fame to become his own decadent prison. Apathy and depression now ruled the man they called the King as he watched his televisions with the desire to do little else.

On one channel, a talk show recounted the horrific murders of a deranged serial killer who had been stalking the streets of New York City and called himself the Son of Sam. The killings were rapidly approaching their one-year anniversary and still the police were baffled. The murderer would approach parked cars with couples making out in them. He would then fire shots into the car window with a .44 Bulldog and disappear into the night like a ghoul. His victims were females, usually with long, dark hair, causing many women in the Big Apple to cut their hair short and dye it blond. To make things worse, the killer would send weird, taunting letters to the police, promising more murders to follow. The city was in a paranoid panic as the police scrambled to find any lead they could.

Elvis' attention to the story was distracted when he saw three familiar faces on one of the other televisions.

The faces belonged to Red West, Red's brother Sonny, and Dave Hebler. They were all former employees of his, turned traitors in his eyes. They had just written a book, *Elvis: What Happened?* It was a scathing tell-all, revealing to an unsuspecting public the truth about Elvis' sad, downward spiral into drug addiction. The betrayal by Red and Sonny hurt Elvis the most. They had been his trusted friends since the beginning, before the world had ever heard of Elvis Presley. They were members of his elite circle of friends, dubbed the Memphis Mafia.

The Memphis Mafia were an assortment of band mates, relatives and old friends who had fiercely protected Elvis and his image. They rode the crazy ride of fame with Elvis, sharing a deep bond and the spoils of super stardom with the king of rock and roll. They had been guarded and tight-lipped to the press about Elvis' sexual and drug excesses, and he rewarded them with expensive gifts and luxurious cars. They had toured and practically lived together for the last twenty years. Elvis had provided them with every creature comfort they could desire. He somewhat arrogantly likened their relationship to that of Jesus and his disciples. Red and Sonny of course, were now playing Judas.

Elvis had unceremoniously fired the two brothers and new member of his flock, Dave Hebler, when his father Vernon advised him that his fortune was disappearing and he needed to cut expenses.

When Elvis read an advance copy of the book, he was infuriated and deeply hurt. He feared how his fans would view him, and it sent him into a deep depression, one in which he was still engulfed. Elvis had once had an almost wholesome image. He openly criticized and spoke against drug use, but now the world would know the truth about his own addiction. It was a truth that he had yet to face.

As he watched Red and Sonny on a TV talk show, promoting their book and telling the shocked audience about Elvis' eccentric and self-destructive lifestyle, he pulled out a gun from his nightstand. He gripped the gun and pointed it at the image of Red and Sonny on television. His upper lip curled in anger as he tightened the grip on the gun but, in the end, he didn't shoot the television. Instead, in a moment of great pain and despair, he pointed the barrel of the gun at his own temple.

His finger squeezed dangerously on the trigger as his mind reeled with memories of a great life gone wrong. His thoughts, as they always did, journeyed back to his mother. Despite all the lovers who had come and gone in his life, she was the only woman who truly owned his heart. She had died twenty years earlier, but still he could not put the loss behind him. Prior to her death, Elvis had had the world at his feet. Though temporarily exiled from music to serve his country in the Army, he was still rock and roll's brightest star. It all changed for him on August 14, 1958 when his mother, Gladys Presley, passed away. He was so distraught that he could barely function, and the doctors gave him sedatives to control his grief. From that day on, neither the grief, nor the pills, ever went away.

The gun trembled in Elvis' hand, offering a solution to his pain and a way for him and his mother to be together. As his finger began pulling back the trigger, a young girl's voice interfered.

"No, Daddy. Don't!" the imagined voice of his daughter, Lisa Marie echoed through his head, pleading.

A solitary tear sliced a path down his bloated face. His lips quivered in silent anguish as he put the gun down and began weeping.

He cursed himself for not being able to pull the trigger. He so wanted to die and end the misery, to take his own life in one final, brutal act, as opposed to the slow, cowardly suicide he had been pre-scribing for himself. The thought of his daughter had saved him on that night, but it had not healed him. In desperation, he called the one living person whom he thought could help. He placed a call to Tom Parker.

Colonel Tom Parker was his longtime manager and almost a father figure to him, more so then his own drunken, bumbling patriarch, Vernon. The truth be known, Parker was more of a con artist than anything else. Through trickery and deceit he had acquired the contract of Elvis Presley, taking an unheard-of percentage of Elvis' earnings and working him like a circus animal, never once considering Elvis' wants or needs when making business decisions. Still, Elvis loved him blindly and obeyed his every demand, almost afraid to ever tell him no.

He tried to reach Parker but couldn't, only getting his answering service. In his drugged-out state, he left a sad, rambling message on the machine and then medicated himself back to sleep.

CHAPTER II

I WANT TO BE FREE

The next evening, Elvis awoke from his Benzedrine stupor to see the face of his manager, Colonel Tom Parker.

"Elvis?" The Colonel called to him, trying to break through the haze that had engulfed his mind.

The Colonel was a rotund, slovenly man who always had a cigar in his mouth and a scheme on his mind. A former carnival barker and shameless promoter, he had once had an act of dancing chickens. People would throw down their money and watch as his chickens inexplicably began dancing to music. What the spectators didn't know was that the chickens were standing on a hot plate that Parker would turn on when the music began. If only he had treated Elvis as well as he had the chickens.

"Tom?" Elvis murmured.

"Elvis, my boy, I came as soon as I got your message," the Colonel said. "What's wrong?"

"I'm losing it, Tom," Elvis confessed. "I can't go on any longer."

"Nonsense. You've got a big tour coming up. You can't disappoint the fans."

"I can't do it anymore, Tom."

"That's crazy talk. You just need to lose a little weight. What are you pushing now, about two hundred and fifty pounds?" Parker asked as he took a puff on his cigar.

"That's being kind." Elvis took a breath. "I can't let the fans see me this way."

"You've got to do the tour," Parker said. "You're nearly broke. In two months you'll have nothing left. Why do think you had to let those sons of bitches Red and Sonny go?"

"How is that possible, Tom? I've sold millions and millions of records."

"How? You're always buying Cadillacs for everyone. You own your own jet, and you've got a drug habit that I don't even want to guess on what it costs you. Son, you need to pull yourself together. Living up here in your ivory tower, popping pills all day, it's enough to make any man go insane," Parker said bluntly.

"Maybe I am insane. Last night I almost committed suicide."

"Suicide? Dammit boy, you can't go out like that. Get yourself together. You're Elvis Presley, the King."

"I don't want to be Elvis Presley anymore," he said. "I can't go anywhere without my fans mobbing me. I'm grateful for every one of them, but they all want something from me that I can't give them. Everyone wants me to be this spry, handsome young rock and roller, but I'm forty-two years old, fat, and washed up. That's not how I want to be remembered. Sometimes I think I'd be better off dead. God knows, I'm probably worth more dead than alive," he rambled in disgust.

The wheels in Tom Parker's head began turning. He knew realistically that Elvis only had a few dozen performances left in him, if that. The cash cow was dying, and he needed to figure out a way to milk as much money from it as possible. Elvis was indeed worth more dead than alive, and premature death was always a good career move, especially if planned in advance. Parker's greedy eyes lit up as he imagined what Presley's death would do for record sales. It was a thought that had crossed his mind before, a theoretical plan that he had fine-tuned in his head.

"This may sound weird, but have you ever considered faking your death?" Parker suggested slyly.

"What?" Elvis asked, confused by the idea.

"I'm talking about a carefully constructed ruse that would free you from the pressures of being Elvis Presley."

"How would I do that?"

"Oh, it's quite easy actually, if you have the money and the know-how, and I have both."

"You?" Elvis asked with surprise.

"I'll let you in on a little secret, Elvis. I'm not a colonel, and my name's not Tom Parker. It's Andreas van Kuijk. I'm an illegal immigrant from Holland who knows how to work the paper trail. My entire identity is a mirage. I have a fake birth certificate, driver's license, Social Security card, everything. Tom Parker exists only on paper, and I can do the same for you," the Colonel boasted.

"That's impossible."

"Son, never underestimate the power and blindness of bureaucracy."

"Okay. But what about faking my death?"

"Well, you're an expert on pills. Perhaps you can take something that will slow down your heart rate to a faint beat and then we call an ambulance. We pay off a few of the many Memphis doctors that you already have in your pocket to declare you dead, and have them fill out a bogus death certificate and autopsy report. We sneak you out of the hospital and put a wax dummy in your coffin. Then we get the coffin in the ground as soon as possible, while you take a plane out of the country before anyone even suspects a thing."

"It sounds pretty far-fetched to me," Elvis responded.

"Trust me, it's not," the Colonel assured him. "I can take care of everything."

"But where would I live?"

"Where everyone goes to hide out, Buenos Aires. I'll make the arrangements. It's the perfect place. Lose some weight, grow a beard or something, and you'll blend right in."

"It sounds like you've really thought this out," Elvis observed suspiciously.

"A good manager anticipates every possibility."

"What about Lisa Marie?"

"I'm sure Priscilla can handle her. She'll be well taken care of, I promise you that. Your death I expect will be very good for album sales, and she should inherit a fortune."

"How much of that money would I see?"

"Well, you're going to have to leave most of your money behind. It would look too suspicious if you didn't, and money trails are easy to follow. Hell, for years I've been overpaying my taxes just to prevent the government from investigating me and finding out I'm here illegally. You could take some cash with you, but just enough to live modestly off for a while, and I could always get more to you from time to time," Parker instructed.

"That would be okay," Elvis ruminated. "Money has yet to buy me happiness. I believe that one has to give up his wealth and earthly possessions to achieve inner peace," he preached.

"Are you actually considering doing this?"

"I don't know. I'm so confused right now."

"Before you decide, know that once you do this, it's as final as death. There is no turning back. You could go to jail for fraud and your fans would never forgive you," Parker warned.

"Well, I guess I should think about it before I decide."

Elvis left the room so that he could be alone and ponder the proposal; he retreated to the Meditation Garden, a beautiful outdoor area next to the pool, a sanctuary where he would sometimes go to clear his thoughts. It was a very tranquil place. Its sidewalks wrapped around a water fountain and were adorned with flowers and bushes and an enclosed with semi-circle wall with stained glass windows and Greek columns. He tried meditating, but his mind was too clouded with drugs to achieve any insight.

Frustrated, he took a deep breath and dragged his fingers through his hair. It was the same hair that he had been dying black since he was a young man in order to look more threatening, all the while concealing the sandy blond hair that was his true color. Such was Elvis, a contradiction, a carefully constructed image of suaveness and masculinity, concealing the shy, insecure child who hid beneath the sequined suits.

Failing in his introspection, he stripped down and jumped into his pool, backstroking across the water and staring up at the starry sky for guidance.

Instead of finding it, he slipped back into his own private hell that was his mind.

"Mama, why did my brother have to die?" The boy asked.

"Elvis, he died because God wanted Jesse to be with Him in heaven."

"But why him, and not me?"

"Elvis, no one knows why God does the things he does, but it's all part of His plan."

"Will you ever die, Mama?"

"Yes, honey. We will all die someday," she said softly.

"I don't want you to die, Mama," he stated, fighting back the tears.

"Don't worry, Elvis. I'll never leave you," she promised, the reassuring lie spilling from her kind, round face.

"You promise?"

"Yes. I promise," she said with a smile as she squeezed his hand.

On the somber day of her funeral, Elvis stared down at her lifeless body imprisoned in the casket, still in disbelief. A part of him had died as well, and he desperately wanted to climb into the coffin with her and join her in eternity.

"You lied, Mama. You said you'd never leave me," he said quietly as tears rolled down his face.

Elvis saw Jesse standing on the other side of the coffin, tears in his eyes as well. The young boy looked so sad that Elvis wanted to embrace him but knew that he could not.

His mind quickly raced to another painful moment that haunted him.

"Elvis, I'm leaving you," Priscilla blurted out.

Elvis was backstage in his white fringed jumpsuit when Priscilla dropped the bombshell on him. His confident smile disintegrated and fell to the ground as she spoke her words.

"You can't leave me. I love you, baby," he pleaded in his soft Southern drawl.

"I can't continue like this," Priscilla said.

"It'll be different, I swear. I'll cancel my tour. We'll start over."

"It's too late for empty promises, Elvis. I've heard them all before."

Elvis was expressionless as his temper welled up inside him. As he stared into Priscilla's beautiful, dark, doe-like eyes, he morphed his pain into a smoldering, controlled rage.

"Then go! Get out of here!" he yelled coldly.

He turned his back on her and strutted out to the only place he felt loved, onstage.

Sadness and regret tensed up in Elvis' face as he climbed out of the pool and toweled off, slowly putting on his robe as he made the most important decision of his life.

Tom was in the den watching television with members of the Memphis Mafia when Elvis entered the room.

"I've been thinking about what you were saying, and I think we should do it," Elvis announced.

He motioned to the members of his clique to leave the room. Like obedient dogs they obeyed, though puzzled by what Elvis and Tom would be discussing that they couldn't say in front of them.

"Elvis, are you sure?" Tom asked in disbelief.

"As sure as I can be. There's nothing for me here. I've lost my Mama. I've lost Priscilla. I've lost everything I've ever cared about. I just want to be human again, to walk down the street without causing a frenzy, to know that people like me for what I am, not who I am."

"Well, if you're sure that's what you want, then I'll make the arrangements." the Colonel said. "I'll take care of everything. I suggest you use your old traveling alias, Jon Burrows, when flying to Buenos Aires. At least until I find you a new identity."

"How does that work?" Elvis inquired.

"Well, I go to the library and look up old obituary notices and find someone who was born around the same time that you were but died at a young age, before he could get a driver's license or a Social Security number. In light of your accent, he should be someone from the South. Then I would send for a copy of the birth certificate, and from there it's all paperwork."

"You make it sound so easy," Elvis stated in disbelief.

"It is easy, believe me. There are holes in the system that you could fly a plane through."

"I've got a couple of requests, though," Elvis interjected.

"What are they?"

"Call me superstitious, but I don't want my exact name to be on the tombstone. It's bad luck."

"We could have your name misspelled. Maybe spell your middle name, Aron with an extra A," he suggested.

Elvis agreed with a subtle nod and left the room.

The thought of faking his death was like a light at the end of the tunnel for Elvis, but he knew there would be consequences to such a radical deed. He was worried about how this would affect the two women on the planet that he loved the most, Priscilla and Lisa Marie. Though he knew it was over between him and Priscilla, he still couldn't stop thinking about her.

He had met Priscilla while he was stationed in Germany, during his stint in the Army. It was just a few months after he had buried his mother, and he was feeling vulnerable and alone. He was attending a party, and Pricilla Beaulieu was there with her parents. Her father was a Captain in the Air Force and thought his young daughter would be thrilled to meet the famous singer. She immediately caught Elvis' eye as a mutual friend introduced them to each other.

"Elvis, this is Priscilla Beaulieu," he said as he quickly sauntered away.

The two exchanged glances and a handshake before Elvis broke the tension with his boyish smile.

"Do you go to school?" Elvis asked politely.

"Yes."

"I guess you'll be graduating soon, huh?"

Priscilla blushed, remaining silent.

"Well," he asked again.

"I'm in ninth grade."

"Ninth grade," he said with a laugh. "You're just a baby."

"Thanks," Priscilla responded angrily.

"Well. You've got spunk. I like that," he said.

They engaged in small talk breifly then Elvis sat down at a piano and started performing several songs, including "Are You Lonesome Tonight?" all the while staring into her eyes. Needless to say, the girl was flabbergasted as the world's most eligible bachelor sang to her in a desperate attempt to impress her.

They began to have a brief, semi-innocent romance. As they talked incessantly, she discovered that this brash young rock star was actually a shy, soft-spoken gentleman who was very caring and very sensitive. So sensitive, in fact, that he could often be brought to tears, usually when talking about his dead mother.

"I miss her so much," Elvis gasped. "You would have liked my Mama."

"I wish I could have met her," Priscilla said understandingly.

"You have no idea how lucky you are not to have lost a parent."

"Actually, that's not exactly true."

"What do you mean?"

"When I was a little girl I was looking through our family keepsakes, when I found a picture of my mother with a strange man and a baby on her lap. On the back of the photo read 'Mommy, Daddy, Priscilla.' I found out that my real father had been killed in a plane crash."

"I'm sorry, little one. I didn't know."

"Don't be sorry. The father I do have loved me as his own. I am lucky for that."

Elvis consolingly put his arm around her and the two began kissing.

Not long after that, Elvis got his orders to go home.

Despite his reassurances, Priscilla was convinced that she would be forgotten as soon he set foot back in America and was greeted by a throng of adoring women. Then one night, much to her surprise, she received a phonecall from him at three in the morning.

"Hi, baby. How's my little girl?"

"Oh god, Elvis. I've missed you so much. I thought I'd never talk to you again."

"Cilla, I told you I'd call."

"I just thought you had forgotten about me. I read in the papers that you were dating Nancy Sinatra and…"

Elvis interrupted her.

"Now hold it! Slow down. I'm not seeing Nancy Sinatra. We're just friends. I'm appearing on her father's show. That's all," he answered deceptively.

"Oh, okay."

"If you're going to be my girl, you're gonna have to trust me more."

"I'm sorry."

"It's okay, baby. It's just that I've got so many pressures on me right now that I don't want any from you."

"What kind of pressures?"

"They got me doing this film, *GI Blues*. It's just horrible. I spent two years in an Army uniform, now I have to make a movie in one. They got me breaking into song every five minutes in the most ridiculous of places. I just want to make a real movie with no songs, no gimmicks, just me acting in a dramatic role."

"You're Elvis Presley. Just don't do the movie."

"It's not that simple. The Colonel says that I have do these movies or else my fans will forget about me."

"I don't think anyone will ever forget about you, including me."

"Ah, Priscilla. You're so kind, but I see the future of music. It's about crooners and teen idols, and I'm too old to be a teen idol now."

"That's not true. All the teenagers I know adore you."

"Yes, but they will always grow up and reject their teenage crushes. I need to appeal to an older audience. Wouldn't it be funny if my career truly is over and I end up going back to driving a truck for a living," Elvis said with a chuckle.

Eventually Elvis made arrangements for Priscilla to fly to America and spend some time with him, despite the understandable objections of her father.

As the frequency and intensity of her visits increased, Elvis somehow convinced her parents to let Priscilla move into Graceland, a potential scandal completely overlooked by the press. After a very long courtship, Elvis reluctantly agreed to marry Priscilla, and they exchanged vows in a very small, almost shotgun wedding in Las Vegas. Nine months to the day later, she gave birth to Lisa Marie.

As he contemplated faking his own death, Elvis understood that he had never before truly realized how much he loved Priscilla and how much he needed her, but now it was too late. She was gone forever. She had left him for Mike Stone, Elvis' own karate instructor. The event still filled him with feelings of anger and betrayal. In fact, in the darkest of times, he had even considered putting a hit out on Stone.

Tom Parker left Graceland the next morning. There was much work to be done. Parker felt invigorated by his new project. It was more than just the prospect of a major payday that fueled his efforts; it was the challenge of pulling off the biggest hoax the world had ever known. Even in 1977, Elvis was perhaps the most famous person on the planet, so it wouldn't be easy, but Parker had plenty of resources. Besides his own cunning, he possessed millions of dollars, and knew several doctors whom he had already bought and sold. Plus he had strong connections to the Mob, stemming from Elvis' days in the Las Vegas circuit, and he had his favorite ally of all, Lady Luck.

CHAPTER III |

INHERIT THE WIND

Elvis Aron Presley was born on January 8, 1935. The Presleys were a young, newly married couple living in a rundown shack in Tupelo, Mississippi. The family was so poor that the delivery was performed in their home by an obstetrician provided by the state. Gladys and Vernon Presley were not expecting twins, nor could they have afforded them. But it was not until after the firstborn, Jesse Garon, was declared dead, that the doctor realized that Gladys was carrying a second child. Within minutes, Elvis Aron Presley was born into the world.

A few months later, a tornado ripped through Tupelo, destroying almost everything in its path. After the storm had passed, only one house remained standing; it was the small shack belonging to the Presleys.

"You're here for a reason," Gladys Presley whispered to her newborn son.

In July of '77, Elvis had begun taking steps of his own to prepare for the fateful date of his "death," slated for August 16, 1977. Colonel Parker not withstanding, Elvis had some powerful allies as well. Besides his money, he had the undying loyalty of the Memphis Mafia. He was also the most powerful and beloved man in Memphis. He had been in and out of the local hospital several times for drug overdoses and rehabilitation. He knew the staff well, and they had always kept quiet to the press about his forays into drug abuse.

His newest ally was in the form of a woman named Ginger Alden, a 21-year-old, dark-haired beauty to whom Elvis had recently become engaged. She had been the only bright spot in Elvis' life of late, but Elvis knew that one woman's love could not rescue him from his despair, not any more. Ginger had been trying to help Elvis for the past many months, as if on a mission from God. She knew he was deeply troubled, and she put aside her own personal needs in order to support him and try to save his life. This attitude was met with suspicion by Elvis' inner circle. The Memphis Mafia fabricated countless stories of Ginger's infidelity, and nicknamed her the Black Witch of Alden. The truth was, she had been very good for Elvis, even getting him drug-free for brief periods of time.

Elvis snuggled lovingly against her in bed; the side effects of the drugs would not allow him to do much more, but despite their lack of physical intimacy, they were emotionally connected. As he held her in his arms, he confided in her about his plot to fake his death.

"Fake your death? Are you insane?" Ginger gasped.

"Not yet, but I will be soon, if I don't do this," Elvis answered softly.

"Honey, it doesn't make any sense."

"It does to me."

"Is this just an elaborate plan to break our engagement?"

"Of course not, baby. You're the best thing that's happened to me in a very long time. It's like you're an angel or something, sent from the heavens to save me," Elvis whispered.

"I've been trying to save you, despite yourself."

"I know, baby. I know. But it's too big a job for just one person. Faking my death is the only thing that can save me."

"How? How is it going to save you?"

"It's hard to explain. You would have to be me to truly understand the pressures that come with being Elvis Presley. The last twenty years I've been living in a bubble, cut off from everyone except a few close friends. I just want to be real again."

"You are real, honey," she said as she kissed him on the cheek. "You just need to get off the drugs."

"I know, but it's impossible to do, living in this world."

"Running away from your problems isn't going to help," Ginger said. "You can't escape the man in the mirror."

Elvis paused momentarily, trying to find another way to explain his decision.

"Do you think you'll go to heaven when you die?" Elvis asked her.

"Yes. I guess I do."

"Well, Jesus said that it's easier for a camel to pass through the eye of a needle than for a rich man to go to heaven. Going to heaven is more important to me than all of these false riches. My mama's up there waiting for me, and I have to see her again. For her, I would give up everything."

"You're a good, caring, generous man. A much better person than you give yourself credit for. I think Jesus can overlook a few cars and a nice house."

"I can't take that chance. I want to leave it all behind and walk the earth doing the Lord's work."

"But what about us?"

Elvis hesitated for a moment before he said, "Sadly, I'll have to leave you behind as well."

Ginger began crying as Elvis held her closer.

"I'm sorry, Ginger. But there's no other way."

"Look, if this is what you want and what you think you need, I'll be behind you and help you any way I can."

"Thanks, baby. I love you."

"I love you, too," she responded as they kissed and fell asleep in each other's arms.

A few weeks passed, and Elvis had not heard from the Colonel. He wondered if Parker had forgotten or simply given up on the idea. Unbeknownst to Presley, Parker had been extremely busy making the proper arrangements, one of which included pulling strings at RCA to have them mass-produce millions of copies of Elvis' records and merchandise, expecting a large increase in sales. He also secured a deal with NBC to cover the upcoming tour, insisting on getting the money in advance.

Elvis was reclining in his den, eating his favorite treat, fried peanut butter and banana sandwiches, when Tom Parker called him and instructed him to meet him at a warehouse in Memphis. Elvis collected his chauffer and they went to the meeting place. Elvis entered alone and found Tom Parker waiting for him.

Andreas Cornelius van Kuijk, a.k.a. Colonel Tom Parker, was born June 26, 1909 in Breda, Holland. At an early age he spent his days wandering the streets of Holland and learning the art of the hustle.

As a young man, he came to America stowed away on a boat, never even telling his family goodbye. After a brief time in the States, he returned to his family unannounced, refusing to say a word about where he had been or why he had returned. Shortly afterward, he returned to America and began hustling and working odd jobs.

In 1929, he joined the U.S. Army and served under Captain Thomas Parker. The Captain was a mentor to him and would unknowingly provide Andreas with his new American identity. Andreas was stationed in Pearl Harbor and served well and was considered a good soldier.

After completing his time in the Army, he took the name Tom Parker and joined the Johnny J. Jones Exposition, a traveling carnival. Parker had always had a love for the carnival and wanted to break into show business somehow and, for an illegal immigrant, there were not many other choices. He worked as an advance man for the carnival, arriving in town a few weeks before the carnival and promoting it. His skill as a con man and his innovative approach to advertising made him very successful as he refined his talent for hustling and promotion. Parker's promotional abilities caught the eye of the Royal American Shows, the biggest carnival in America, and he began working for them part-time. It was there that he met his future wife, Marie.

Through his job with the Royal American Shows he also met a singer named Gene Austin. Though Gene Austin had been a big star at one time, his star had long since faded. Parker convinced Austin to make him his manager, and soon Austin was playing to packed houses once again. Austin seemed on the verge of a return to Nashville when Parker made another bizarre career move; he quit managing Austin and began working for the Humane Society.

For the Humane Society, Parker was amazingly successful in fund-raising and finding new homes for animals, but he quickly began using the job to scam money for himself.

During World War II, he got a job as the advance man with the Grand Ole Opry tour and reestablished himself as a music promoter. While working for the Opry, he crossed paths with another singer who would become his client, Eddy Arnold.

Eddy Arnold was a young country singer from Tennessee. Parker completely immersed himself in Eddy's career, going so far as to man the souvenir stand himself. Soon, Arnold's career began to take off, with several hits and a successful tour. More importantly to Parker, he began making contacts in the music business, with RCA records, and eventually in Hollywood.

In 1948, Tom Parker was made an honorary colonel by Louisiana Governor Jimmy Davis, and from that point on began insisting that everyone address him as "the Colonel."

Together, the Colonel and Arnold charted a string of hits and made several movie and television appearances. Then in 1953, for reasons that are still not known, Eddy Arnold fired Parker as his manager. Parker struggled briefly without a big-name client, but he had already formed a booking agency, Jamboree Attractions, and a music publishing house, Jamboree Music. In 1954, Parker found a new client named Hank Snow.

Hank Snow was a successful country singer and songwriter who had a desire to start a booking agency of his own. Parker began managing him, and the two soon joined forces and formed Hank Snow Enterprises/Jamboree Attractions. Shortly afterward, the Colonel met the man who would forever alter his destiny, Elvis Presley.

"Elvis, my boy, I have someone I want you to meet," the Colonel said devilishly as he stood next to a large coffin.

Elvis opened the coffin and almost fainted when he saw himself lying inside.

"What do you think?" Parker prodded. "Looks just like you, huh?"

After the initial shock wore off, Elvis began examining the wax dummy for detail. He marveled at the likeness, but couldn't help noticing a few flaws.

"Hmm. Not bad. The nose and eyebrows are wrong, though," he mentioned sheepishly.

"No one's going to notice. We're going to bury you quickly, before your flaky fan club members get a chance to see you," Tom reassured him. "It's made of wax. Just like candles."

"It looks like it's sweating," Presley said respectfully, yet concerned.

"It's a little hot in here. But don't worry. I'm going to put an air-conditioning system inside so it won't melt at the wake. It'll be fine. Trust me."

"So, we're really going to do this, huh?"

"Of course, the wheels are already in motion," the Colonel declared. "You're not having second thoughts are you?"

"No, I have to do this. When I was born, I had a twin brother named Jesse. He died that same day, and all of my life I've been asking myself why. Why did God spare me and not him? Did I have some greater purpose to fulfill? When I got famous, I thought that I found my destiny, to pioneer the great sound of rock and roll. But now I see rock stars on TV wearing pink leather pants and doing all this vile stuff, and I think, my God, what have I created? Suddenly, being the king of rock and roll doesn't seem like such a noble purpose," Elvis expounded.

"Then what is your purpose?" the Colonel asked him, genuinely curious.

"I don't know. But maybe this is the only path to find it."

Elvis reached inside his jacket and pulled out a federal badge.

"I remember when President Nixon gave this to me," Elvis said. "He made me an honorary officer in the DEA. Of course, I was really high on drugs at the time, so it felt like it was an honor that I didn't deserve. Someday though, I'd like to be worthy of this badge."

The Colonel let out a laugh. "What are you saying, Elvis? You want to leave all of this behind to become a cop?"

"I don't know. I've always wanted to work in law enforcement. I guess I just want to stand for something real and noble. Maybe I will become a preacher or something."

Parker rolled his eyes at the thought.

"I just want to make a positive impact on the world," Elvis said somberly as he turned around and headed back to his car.

Parker watched him walk to his car with some sentimentally. He knew that this might be one of the last times that he would ever see him again. Despite what Elvis thought about himself, the Colonel knew that the impact that Elvis had had on his life could not have been more positive.

He remembered the first time he had seen him perform. It was May 13, 1955 at the Gator Bowl in Jacksonville, Florida. At the end of Elvis' set, the women stormed the stage and Elvis barely escaped with his life. That was when Parker knew he had found his next client. He was convinced that he could make Elvis a star while making himself a wealthy man. From that day on, he pursued the young boy tirelessly. There was one thing that stood in his way, however -- Elvis' stubborn and overprotective mother, Gladys. She was highly suspicious of the man, and rightfully so.

Persistence paid off for him however, and six weeks later, he had arranged a meeting with the Presley matriarch. He brought along an insurance policy this time in Hank Snow. Snow was his business partner and a Christian country singer whom Gladys liked and trusted. After the two had worn Gladys down with compliments and half-truths, she reluctantly signed the contract that the Colonel presented her. She had been under the mistaken impression that Elvis' career would be under the guidance of the God-fearing Hank Snow and the truth was, so had Snow. After Gladys signed the contract, the Colonel smiled and made a hasty getaway.

On the drive home, he bragged to Snow about the ridiculous contract that the country bumpkins had just signed, and even admitted that he had had a second, more reasonable contract in his pocket, in case Gladys rejected his first, almost illegal offer.

"If that boy becomes half as successful as I think he'll be, I will become a very rich man," he boasted.

"You mean, *we* will become very rich men," Snow corrected him.

"Guess again, Hank. Read the contract. He's signed to me exclusively," Parker stated triumphantly as Hank read the document in disbelief.

The morning of August 16th, 1977 was about to arrive. It was the day Elvis was to die. Less than a week earlier, the City of New York had breathed a collective sigh of relief when the man calling himself the Son of Sam was apprehended. The killer turned out to be a schizophrenic postal worker named David Berkowitz, a man who claimed that he was told to commit the murders by his neighbor's incessantly barking dog. The nation watched the news compulsively to learn the details, unaware that an even bigger story was lurking on the horizon.

Elvis was scheduled to begin his tour the following day starting in Portland, Maine, so there was no room for error. Any delays would have meant aborting the plan altogether. Faking his death in a hotel room in some strange town would not have been possible. It had to be in Memphis, in his own home, surrounded by his inner circle, for the plan to work. Several non-essential workers at Graceland had already been let go to prevent anyone not in on the hoax from discovering and exposing the truth.

In the confusion of all the planning however, one detail had been overlooked. His daughter, Lisa Marie was scheduled to visit him before he left to go on tour. While he did want to spend some quality time with her before leaving her life, he wanted to protect her from being involved in the hoax and the craziness that would ensue. Elvis' worst fear was that Lisa Marie would see his seemingly lifeless body, but Vernon assured him that he would make sure that she would not be around when Elvis faked his death.

Elvis gave an affectionate goodbye to Ginger, Parker, Vernon, and the Memphis Mafia, all of whom were now in on the plan. He discussed the plan once more with them as they shared supper for the last time. They exchanged kind words and reminisced about the old times as they ate.

"Everything is now in place," Elvis stated as Parker looked away. "You all know what to do and you've all been sworn to secrecy. This will work as long as you all keep silent and no one betrays me,"

Elvis washed down a slice of bread with a sip of wine, excused himself from the table and headed to the music room. He sat at the piano and sang a few final songs as Elvis Presley. He played a haunting rendition of "Unchained Melody" before retiring.

Colonel Parker quickly left Graceland and flew to Portland, Maine, where Elvis' next concert was expected to take place. Once he got to Portland, he went to a hotel room and waited by the phone. He felt like an expectant father, nervously awaiting word from the doctors.

Elvis visited Ginger in his bedroom and they rehearsed the plan together. He was feeling unusually spry, and his goodbye kiss became increasingly passionate as they made love for the final time. After they finished, they held each other lovingly before Elvis had to leave.

"Goodbye, my lovely Ginger. I wish things could have ended differently. I wish we could be married like we had planned, but know that I love you."

"I love you, too," she said. "If given the choice, I would much rather be the women who helped save Elvis Presley than simply the one who married him."

They shared an embrace and he gave her one last kiss before walking away.

"Goodbye, Elvis," she whispered.

Elvis walked into his large, lavish bathroom with a packet of pills. It was a concoction he had put together himself, designed to lower his heart rate to a dangerously low level, but not kill him. Elvis was indeed an expert on pills. As with most things that interested him, he threw himself completely into studying and understanding them. He read countless medical books on prescription pills, learning the effects and dosage of every one of them. Despite his knowledge of them, though, he was blind to the one side effect that they all shared -- addiction.

Elvis stared into the mirror and said a prayer. He had chosen the bathroom as his death suite to make it look more accidental and to prevent anyone in his inner circle from having to give an account of his last moments.

As he took the pills, he suddenly felt the call of nature and sat down on the toilet and began reading a book about Jesus. It was a long process. Due to the endless years of drug abuse, he had been suffering badly from irregularity. As he sat on his porcelain throne, the pills took effect sooner than he had expected. His eyes grew heavy and he slipped into unconsciousness, falling off the toilet and landing face first onto the floor.

As planned, his girlfriend and accomplice Ginger discovered the body and called an ambulance. As the rest of the conspirators entered the bathroom to inspect the body, Lisa Marie ran into the room and saw her father lying motionless on the floor.

"Lisa Marie, get out of here!" Vernon shrieked in horror, realizing that he had screwed up the one thing Elvis had asked him to handle.

The paramedics arrived and whisked the body to the hospital. The doctor took Elvis' body and switched it with the wax dummy. Members of the Memphis Mafia were waiting in the wings and gave the doctor and all of the present staff briefcases filled with money. The doctor injected Elvis with adrenaline and he slowly began to awaken. The Memphis Mafia then put a disguise on Elvis and spirited him out the back door as the doctor called for a press conference to declare Elvis dead.

Elvis was taken to an airport and given a small suitcase filled with a few essential and sentimental items: an assortment of pills, some pictures, a couple of books, as well as a large amount of cash.

Elvis walked into the airport and approached the woman at the ticket counter.

"I need to buy a one-way ticket to Buenos Aires," he said, carefully disguising his voice.

"How would you like to pay?" She asked.

"Cash."

"Your name?" The woman asked.

"Jon Burrows," he answered.

He paid for the ticket and waited for the plane to begin boarding. As news of the apparent death of Elvis began spreading across the airport, sadness fell over everyone. A few people even began crying.

"I can't believe it. Elvis can't die," he overheard.

"What a shame. Poor bastard!" someone else said.

The plane began boarding as Elvis' heart began beating heavily with nervousness.

"Sir!" an airline official called out to him.

Elvis' face flushed with fear, as he thought his plan was about to fall apart. He was so close to making a getaway, but now feared his ruse was about to be discovered. Sweat began dripping from his brow and he almost began hyperventilating.

"You dropped your passport, sir," the official said as he handed it back to Elvis.

"Thank you. Thank you very much," Elvis said nervously, before boarding the plane.

As the plane taxied down the runway, Elvis stared out the window in disbelief. He could not believe that the plan was actually going to work. He and Tom Parker had pulled it off. He took a couple of Valiums to calm himself and to deal with all of the emotions he was experiencing. As the plane leapt into the sky like a giant eagle, Elvis looked back not just on a country, but on the life he was leaving behind.

During the flight, he drifted in and out of consciousness, but kept overhearing passengers talking about Elvis' death. Apparently, most of them had just heard about it, either at the airport or on the way to the airport. Uncharacteristically, the passengers were abuzz and talking between the aisles about his death and what his music had meant to him. He couldn't help but be touched, yet paranoid. What if the one of the passengers recognized him? What if his fake beard was to fall off? An anxiety grew in him and he responded the only way he knew how, by taking more pills.

He was barely conscious as the plane touched down in Buenos Aires. He clumsily grabbed his carry-on and got off the plane. He somehow found a cab driver despite the confusion of being extremely high in a foreign country. He handed the cab driver a card that had the address of his future home on it. The driver quickly drove him to the destination and Elvis tipped him generously.

He walked up the steps and pulled out the keys that the Colonel had given him and tried the door. Much to his relief, the key opened the door. He walked inside and found a gateway to his past, before his great wealth. Of course, this place was much nicer than the shack he grew up in in Tupelo, but it was a far cry from Graceland. It was a modest little house, though fully furnished and stocked with food. The walls were white and bare, almost resembling a mental hospital. It was probably a nice house by most people's standards, but to Elvis it repre-sented a vow of poverty and a commitment to his faith. After twenty years of being one of the wealthiest men on the planet, Elvis had finally come home.

He didn't do much exploration of his new place, though. He set down his bags and collapsed onto the bed, drugged out and exhausted.

Elvis woke up in a strange bed, in a strange country, living a strange, new life. A combination of the drugs, jet lag, and the exhaustion from all that he had just been through had caused him to sleep for almost an entire day.

It was the middle of the night, and he took a few pills as he unpacked them and laid them out in his bathroom. He walked out onto his balcony and stared out over Buenos Aires. He watched the sunrise and witnessed the beginning of a new day, the dawn of a new existence. The warm Argentinean sun began to beam down upon his face with lithium-charged rays. As he breathed in the fresh air, he felt liberated at last from the burden of being Elvis Presley.

CHAPTER IV

SPANISH EYES

Buenos Aires, Spanish for "fair winds," was the capital and largest city of Argentina. Spanish settlers discovered it in 1536, but the native Indians quickly drove them out. In 1580, settlers from Paraguay, led by Juan de Garay, reestablished the city. In 1776, while the United States was gaining its independence, Spain united its South American colonies and named Buenos Aires as their capitol. The city began to grow as a port, and in the early 1800s, local leaders dissatisfied with Spanish rule set up their own government. In 1816, Buenos Aires and other neighboring areas declared their independence from Spain, and would soon become known as Argentina. In the 1850s, European immigrants, mainly from Italy and Germany, began settling in the city in large numbers. The city grew in the coming years and became one of the most modern and beautiful cities in the Western Hemisphere.

"Hello there. You just move in?" a man called out from the balcony next door, startling Elvis at first.

It was his new neighbor, a much older man than he, with a thin build and a thick German accent. His skin was wrinkled and reddened by the sun. His gray hair had thinned on top and he had a subtle smile and a slightly crooked nose.

"Yeah. I'll be here for a few months," Elvis answered cheerfully.

"Well, it's nice to meet you. My name is Frederick Schuller."

"Jon Burrows. It's a pleasure to meet you," Elvis replied as he waved.

"So, are you new to Argentina?"

"Yeah. Just flew in the other day from the States."

"Well, it's a nice place to live. The weather's great and people let you be," the older man said.

"I'm glad to hear that," Elvis replied.

"If you ever have any questions about this area, or need someone to show you around, or maybe just play cards with, give me a visit," he said invitingly.

"Well, thank you. That's mighty hospitable of you," Elvis responded in his Southern drawl.

The man then proceeded to tend to his vegetable garden as Elvis headed inside. There was something on television that he wanted to watch -- his own funeral.

It had been a little more than a day since he'd been declared dead. For obvious reasons, the Colonel made sure the coffin was in the ground as soon as possible. Elvis sat on the couch and turned on the television. He was fascinated by the irony of being able to watch his own funeral. To his surprise, he saw tens of thousands of mourning fans gathered outside Graceland and lining the streets along the funeral procession, many crying or praying, some throwing flowers at the hearse as it slowly drove past them.

Elvis was touched beyond words at this public outpouring of emotions.

"I had no idea how much they cared about me," he sobbed.

He got up and ran to the bathroom, and stared into the mirror.

"Why couldn't I feel their love?" he asked angrily.

He looked down and saw the answer in the numerous bottles of pills. In a fit of rage, Elvis started emptying the bottles into the toilet.

"I want my soul back, you bastards!"

He stared down at the large assortment of multi-colored pills that he had cast into the toilet; Dexedrines, Benzedrines, Valiums, Dilaudids, Valmids, and Demerol, all floating on the water in a circle like a kaleidoscope.

Elvis flushed them down decisively. As he watched his stash swirl down into the sewers of Argentina, fear crept over him.

"My God! What have I done?" he lamented.

He realized that he was now without drugs in a foreign country with no connections, no identity, and not a lot of money. He knew that the days of getting an endless supply of narcotics from bribed doctors were over. He no longer had the Memphis Mafia, fame, millions of dollars, or the Colonel to take care of him. For the first time in his life, he was on his own. He knew that he would now have to rely on his own wits to survive. He said a prayer and made a vow to get off drugs.

The next few weeks were a hellish nightmare for Elvis. The withdrawal from drugs ravaged his body, causing the shakes, loss of appetite, vomiting, insomnia and depression. He spent his days sweating and cold at the same time, all but living in the bathroom because a nearby toilet was always needed. His flesh felt as if it crawled with insects, both on the surface and under his skin. His sleep, long an unpleasant experience that he had medicated to control, had become a house of horrors, exposing every scar on his soul, putting him on trial for sins long forgotten. He contemplated suicide and relived every painful moment of his life.

Huddled in a corner of the bathroom, he cried himself to sleep, but was awoken by the sound of the door slowly creaking open as his daughter, Lisa Marie walked into the room, dressed in black.

"Daddy? There you are, Daddy. I've been looking for you all over. Why did you leave me, Daddy? Don't you love me?"

"You know I love you," Elvis whispered painfully.

"Then why did you leave me?"

"I'm sorry, baby. I had to. I couldn't take the fame anymore."

"Now I have no one to play with," the child stated sadly as she began to walk away.

"No, don't go!" Elvis cried out. "I want you to stay with me and talk. Daddy's in a lot of pain right now, and I need to be with you."

"Then you shouldn't have left me," she said coldly as she disappeared.

Elvis began sobbing, throwing his head down into his hands, wishing for things to be different.

He felt a warm hand stroke his hair. He looked up and saw Priscilla.

"Satnin," he cried out, a pet name that, peculiarly, he had used for both Priscilla and his mother.

"Oh Elvis, where did everything go wrong?"

Her face was just as beautiful and radiant as he remembered, shining from underneath the black veil that thinly covered her lovely features.

"Oh, Cilla. I missed you so much. Why did you leave me?"

"I gave myself to you completely, and still it wasn't enough. All I ever wanted to be was your wife, your lover, and the mother of your children, but that wasn't good enough for you. You had to make me some goddamned shrine to your mother. Sometimes, I wonder if you ever loved me."

"I do. I do love you, baby. I always have," Elvis said as he kissed her hands.

As he caressed and kissed Priscilla's soft, manicured fingers, the skin suddenly turned rough and coarse, callused and scarred from endless years of tedious manual labor. He followed the roughness up her arm and realized it was his mother's.

"Mama!" He gasped in disbelief.

"Elvis, is that you?"

"Yes, Mama, it's me. Don't you recognize me?"

"No, honey. You look sick. What happened to you? What happened to my little boy?"

"Nothing, Mama. It's me. I'm still the same person."

"Elvis, are you a junkie? I don't believe it. My beautiful son is a junkie!" his mother sobbed.

"No, Mama, I ain't no junkie. Don't say that!" he pleaded.

"I've failed as a mother. I raised a junkie..."

"No, it's not true. I'm not a junkie. I'm not a junkie!" he shouted until the sound of his own voice woke him from his nightmare.

He looked around to find himself tragically alone as his eyes welled up with anguish.

"I'm not a junkie!" he gasped, still in denial about his condition.

Elvis wept.

"It's just that I feel so alone sometimes, and I hurt," he said. "Jesus, help me," he pleaded in desperation.

Suddenly, he felt calm in his body and soul. His prayers had been answered. In all of the years of torment and addiction, never once did he dare invoke his Savior's name. Though a very religious person, he had never asked Jesus for His help with his problems, thinking it was unmanly and selfish. He had prayed for his mother, his father, and many other people over the years, but never for himself. For the first time, he felt a torch of power being lit from inside him. Suddenly he knew he had the strength to beat his addiction, defeat his demons, and make sense of his life. He was born again.

He still had the urges and withdrawal symptoms that he had experienced before, but he felt that he now had a great, new ally on his side. His health slowly returned and he felt energized by it. The withdrawal symptoms had shaved almost fifty pounds off him. He started exercising and practicing karate again, finding the discipline and spiritual aspect of the martial arts helpful in defeating his addiction.

Elvis' love for karate started in the military. He loved the spirituality and the feeling of invulnerability it gave him. Long before Bruce Lee brought the martial arts to mainstream America, Elvis was giving karate exhibitions on Hollywood sets and preaching its peaceful discipline. He became a black belt and studied under several great instructors including Kang Rhee and Chuck Norris. His poor health and drug addiction had kept him from reaching his full potential but now he found himself free of such shackles. Ironically, it was karate that led to the break-up of his marriage.

Priscilla began taking karate to appease Elvis and share an interest with him. As she got deeper into the training she too discovered the mental discipline it provided. She gained more self-esteem and become more independent. As Elvis started becoming more secluded and withdrawn from his addiction, Priscilla fell in love with her karate instructor, Mike Stone.

Despite this, Elvis stayed loyal to karate and its Eastern philosophy. Elvis was a sponge for religion, absorbing every creed and belief he encountered. Though a Christian, he delved into other religions freely and was fascinated by numerology and even the Occult.

Several months had passed since his last look in the mirror. Up to that point, he had been ashamed of his reflection, ashamed at what he had let himself become. By the time he finally got the nerve the return to the mirror, he barely recognized the face staring back at him. A real beard had grown in; his hair was longer, and his natural blond color began returning. His face was no longer bloated and pudgy, and his eyes burned with the same flame and fury that he had had as a young kid. He felt that he had finally made peace with the man he saw in the mirror and thanked God for his recovery.

Elvis went out on his balcony to watch the setting sun. There had been a storm earlier, but the storm had passed and he could see the cloud-streaked results in a blazing sunset, rivaling the greatest euphoria that his fame or money had ever brought him. In that moment, he decided to dedicate his remaining years to helping mankind as much as possible, wanting to repay the world, and the Lord, for the love that they had given him.

He was feeling triumphant, like a conquering hero. He had defeated an addiction that had ravaged his mind and body for several years. He felt better than he had in a long time. His sickness and depression had ended at last. His withdrawal had felt like a slow death, as if he had been cast into the deepest layer of hell, but his rebirth had begun. He had shed his skin and emerged a better beast.

His neighbor, Frederick, came out onto his porch and saw him.

"Hello, neighbor. I haven't seen you in a while. And I thought *I* was a recluse," Frederick remarked.

"I've been sick, but I'm better now," Elvis stated confidently.

"Well, you look good, as if you've lost a lot of weight."

"Thanks. I feel good."

"Well, that offer for a game of cards still stands," Frederick reminded him.

"Yeah. That would be fun. I guess I could use the company."

"Great. Come on over," Frederick invited.

Elvis smiled and walked over to Frederick's house. Frederick escorted him to his game room. The room had a friendly and inviting aura to it. It was the kind of place in which any man would feel comfortable watching a football game. It had a large TV, a dartboard, pool table, and a small bar. Elvis was especially glad to see the pool table. He loved playing pool and was quite good at it. He felt right at home in this place, and was glad to have Frederick as a neighbor.

Frederick handed out poker chips and dealt the cards as Elvis practiced his poker face. Then Frederick grabbed two beers from his cooler.

"Do you want a beer, Jon?" He offered.

"No, I shouldn't. I'm trying to stay away from drugs."

"It's just a beer," Frederick laughed.

"Yeah. What the hell? I'll take one."

Frederick handed him a beer and started petting his German shepherd, who had ran into the game room.

"Hello, Schatzi. Have you met Jon?" he asked his dog rhetorically. Then he studied his cards. "So, what have you got?" he asked his neighbor.

"Pair of aces, and a pair of eights. Dead man's hand," Elvis added, noting the irony.

"What does that mean?"

"In the Old West, there was a man named Wild Bill Hickcock," Elvis explained. "He was one of the greatest gunfighters ever. Some man shot him down during a card game, and these were the cards he was holding. Ever since then, eights and aces have been called the dead man's hand."

"Interesting story, but the dead man's hand still loses to three of a kind," Frederick reminded him as he set down his superior poker hand and collected the pot.

Elvis grumbled and began dealing the cards.

"How's the beer?" Frederick asked.

"It's smooth. I was never much of a drinker, but this really hits the spot."

"Yeah. It's good beer. German beer, not that piss-water you Americans call beer," Frederick said proudly.

"Do you miss Germany?" Elvis asked casually.

"Very much. I haven't been there since the Forties," the older man answered, searching Elvis' eyes for a response.

"Did you fight in the war back there?"

"Yes, I was in the German Army, but was a deserter, I am ashamed to say. It was 1944, and obvious at the time that Hitler was insane and the war was lost. I decided that I did not want to be sacrificed to the Russians, so I took what I could, and had a friend spirit me and my wife, may she rest in peace, out to Buenos Aires, where I've remained ever since. This has become my home, but even so, I dream of re-turning to my country someday. Ever been to Germany?"

"Yeah, sure. I was stationed there when I was in the Army. Nice country, nice *frauleins*," Elvis said with a playful smirk. "In fact, those were some of the happiest years of my life," he added, recalling fondly a period from a much simpler time.

They played cards and a couple of games of pool as they drank, and eventually retreated to Frederick's porch. Both men were clearly drunk at that point as they gazed up at the stars.

"What a beautiful night!" Frederick exclaimed.

Elvis nodded. "I love looking at the stars. It's a little comforting to know that the people I miss the most back in the States can look up and see the same stars that I'm looking at. It's almost like we're not so far apart," he said somberly, thinking of Lisa Marie.

"So, why did you leave your country?"

"It's complicated. I needed to get away, get my head together, and get clean."

"Get clean?"

"Yeah. I was doing a lot of pills and got heavily addicted to them. It took over my life."

"I'm sorry. I guess I shouldn't have been offering you alcohol."

"Don't worry. I've never had a problem with alcohol."

"Yes, but an addict is an addict. I don't want you taking up drinking to fill that void that the pills have left."

"It's not the pills that leave a void. It's the loss of loved ones that leave you empty," Elvis mused.

"Don't worry, when you get to be my age, you'll understand it all more clearly," Frederick advised him. "You realize no person can belong to you. We are all just logs drifting on a river. Sometimes these logs touch and float together, but eventually they always drift apart. When I was a young man in the war, I thought that my Army buddies and me would be friends forever. One day, we were in a foxhole making plans for after the war, dreaming about drinking beer together, our kids playing with each other, and looking back on our glorious victory for the Fatherland. Then I crawled out of the foxhole to take a leak, and when I returned, they were all dead. Killed by a mortar shell," he said sadly.

"I'm sorry," Elvis said.

"Me, too. But the point is that people will come and go in and out of your life, and tomorrow is never a guarantee. Don't spend the rest of your life regretting the ones who left you, just cherish the time you were together," Frederick said.

Elvis pondered his words as he took a sip of beer. He could see the pain still lingering in Frederick's eyes.

"That must have been a tough war to fight in."

"Yes, it was. Growing up in Nazi Germany, we all expected to win the war. We were so blinded by our allegiance to the Fatherland and to the Fuhrer that we could not imagine anything else. Blinded we were to everything, the madness of Hitler, our inevitable defeat, and the hatred in our hearts. Now, Germany is disgraced and vilified, occupied by godless Communists who oppress our people. Perhaps it's the fate we deserve for our blindness. Perhaps it's good that I left when I did and was spared the heartbreak of seeing my country destroyed."

Not being used to alcohol, Elvis began feeling drunk and light-headed. He decided to call it a night. He thanked Frederick and retreated to his bed.

Elvis and Frederick became good friends, playing cards and pool, and drinking together often. Elvis was happy to meet someone who liked to talk but didn't ask too many questions. It was the first friendship he had formed in over twenty years that he knew was based on his personality and not his celebrity status.

One day, Elvis ventured out to the marketplace, a section of Buenos Aires bustling with trade and having an almost carnival-like atmosphere. There were people of many cultures and languages selling their goods and sharing their smiles with the community.

After grabbing a bite to eat, Elvis heard the remote sounds of an acoustic guitar echoing in the distance. He followed the lovely melody to a man selling guitars. The man was playing the Spanish folk song "Malaguena" as Elvis approached him. After he finished the song, Elvis applauded and bought an acoustic guitar from him. Elvis had forgotten how much he loved music. In the last few years, music had become more of a chore than a passion, simply a job that he was forced to do. Now he wanted to play music for himself, for the love of music.

As he strolled through the market with his new guitar, he accidentally bumped into an older American woman.

"I'm sorry, ma'am," he apologized.

She gave him a polite nod, then looked into his face. Her eyes lit up with recognition.

"Oh, my God! You're Elvis," she screamed hysterically.

Frantically, Elvis ran off, feeling dozens of Spanish eyes upon him. He blended into a crowd of people before deciding to leave. He wondered if he was still that recognizable to people despite the changes in his appearance. As he walked home, he decided he needed to keep a lower profile.

As time went by, Christmas unexpectedly crept up on Elvis. The warm southern climate of Buenos Aires gave no clues such as snow or cold. With no friends or family around, or the crass commercialization of American television, the holiday approached with little warning. It was a very depressing Christmas Eve for him; his memories were filled with joyous celebrations and bestowing lavish and expensive gifts on his loved ones. This year he was alone.

He began drowning his misery in alcohol, but that brought him no joy. Suddenly, there came a knock on his door. Elvis leapt to his feet, desperate for any company on that night.

He opened the door to see Frederick standing there with a present in his arms.

"Merry Christmas, Jon," he said cheerfully.

Elvis welcomed him inside gleefully and opened the present. It was a nice bottle of vintage wine.

"Frederick, you didn't have to do this."

"Nonsense. It's Christmas, and you're my friend."

"But I didn't get you anything."

"That's okay. Do you want to come over?"

"Oh, no. I don't want to intrude on your holiday. I'm sure you want to spend it with your friends and relatives," he insisted.

"Jon, it's okay. I'm alone on Christmas, too."

"Well, not any more," Elvis said with a friendly smile as he grabbed his guitar and the wine, following Frederick over to his house.

He was surprised to see Frederick's living room decorated for the holidays, despite the lack of guests.

"That's a nice tree," Presley remarked.

"Thanks. Finding a Christmas tree down here wasn't easy, but I did it."

Elvis opened the bottle of wine and started pouring a glass for Frederick and himself. They both toasted to the holiday and drank merrily.

"I'm glad you could come over, Jon. My wife died a few years ago, and I don't really have a family any more. You're the first person I've spent Christmas with in a while."

"I'm glad I could do it. To be honest, I was dreading spending Christmas alone and am so glad you came over."

As the night progressed, the two friends had already emptied the first wine bottle and made a dent in a second one. Elvis, now less than sober, got caught up in the spirit and picked up his guitar. He started playing old Christmas carols and gospel songs as they both sang along drunkenly. It ended up being a very special Christmas for both of them, and one week later Elvis invited Frederick over to his house as they welcomed in 1978. Elvis looked back on the year as one of great change, and anticipated the coming year with much optimism.

CHAPTER V

SKELETONS IN THE CLOSET

As January and February wore on, Elvis had begun to feel homesick, missing America greatly. The months that he had been in Argentina were relaxing and necessary, but he knew it was time to go home. Not that he could ever go home to Graceland, but he yearned to be back in America and be with his fellow Americans. He had been lying low in Buenos Aires while the smoke cleared over his death, but it had been over six months and he felt it was time to move on.

He understood why Frederick missed his native country so much. He had only been away from his country a few months and was already homesick. He couldn't imagine how being away for forty years must feel.

Elvis had mostly fond memories of Germany. It was the country where he had regrouped after his mother's death, a place where he had met his future bride, Priscilla, and a world where he was granted a momentary time-out from his rock star life and the onslaught of the American media.

He'd been stationed in Friedburg, twenty miles from Frankfurt, close to the border of Communist East Germany. The Cold War was heating up at that time, and his arrival had stirred up emotions in the neighboring communist country. In the East German town of Halle, a brutal riot occurred when police unsuccessfully tried to arrest three hundred members of a supposed Elvis Presley cult.

Germany was a country still in disarray. It had been a little over a decade since the allies had defeated them in World War II, and the guilt and stigma of Hitler and the Holocaust still haunted the once-proud nation. As the war ended, Russia took over the Eastern half of the country and declared it a communist state. Families were torn in two, and the country became a tense focal point of the Cold War.

At first, Elvis resided with his fellow soldiers in a barracks that had once housed Hitler's SS troops. He quickly moved to civilian housing, where he arranged for his grandmother Minnie Mae, his father, Red West, and his portly friend Lamar Fike to stay with him.

With the recent passing of his mother, a new Elvis emerged. Gone was the prudish altar boy who practiced sexual abstinence and avidly read the bible. He now felt a freedom and a desire to use his fame and good looks to seduce as many young women as humanly possible. As his extended family from Memphis arrived, wild times quickly ensued.

Elvis and his buddies decided to stay at a hotel suite, but were thrown out of the Hilberts Park Hotel within days, due to their rowdy behavior. Next, they settled into the Hotel Grunewald. While he managed to bed his share of chambermaids, the management were not so easily charmed, and within five months he and his buddies were kicked out of there as well.

Finally, it was decided that they needed to rent a house. They found one in Bad Nauheim and its nearby beer halls became regular spots for Vernon and Red as Elvis indulged in sexual romps with dangerously young girls.

In the Army, he outshone every one else in his platoon, not because of his fame, but due to hard work. He became a great jeep scout, a dangerous job where his duty was to scout enemy tank positions. He became excellent at reading maps and terrain, and mastered the fine art of stealth. Unfortunately, it was also in the Army that he began heavily experimenting with amphetamines, using them to endure the long days of a soldier and the long nights of Europe's most eligible bachelor.

Germany wasn't all fun and games though, and on one freezing cold night, an unimaginable disaster almost occurred. Out on a scouting mission, Elvis and his sergeant were riding through the German countryside in their jeep, when Sgt. Jones made an alarming discovery. Due to a mistake on the map, they had driven off course, and now found themselves in Communist Czechoslovakia.

"Holy shit, Presley! We're in communist territory. Get us the hell out of here and fast!" Sgt. Jones yelled.

Elvis hit the gas and headed back to West Germany along the icy roads.

To say this could have been an international incident was putting it mildly. Any American soldier discovered in Czechoslovakia would have been captured and accused of being a spy. It would have put the United States in a very compromising situation, especially if that soldier happened to be Elvis Presley.

Night fell upon the communist country. The darkness and ever-intensifying snowstorm made it impossible to navigate any further. Still unsure of their location, they reluctantly decided to hide themselves and the jeep inside a thicket of trees. Elvis left the jeep idling for some protection against the frigid temperatures. As the freezing alpine winds pushed the mercury down into the mid-teens, Presley and Jones used their ponchos as tents to shelter them from the cold. The rapidly falling snow piled up to the door of the jeep and Elvis was forced to gun the engine numerous times to melt the snow away from the exhaust pipe.

Though their tent-like ponchos worked well to maintain their warmth, it also trapped dangerously high levels of carbon monoxide. It wasn't long before both men were unconscious from the fumes. Elvis managed to regain consciousness, but found his body to be almost paralyzed. He tried to raise his arms but couldn't; he then began to rock back and forth until he fell out of the front seat and into the snow. He gasped deeply, desperately inhaling the much-needed oxygen until he could feel sensation return to his arms and legs. He slowly crawled back into the jeep and turned off the ignition. Then with all of his might he pushed on the unconscious sergeant until he fell out of the jeep as well. Elvis began vomiting from the poisonous fumes, and realized that Jones still wasn't moving. Pvt. Presley soon regained control of his limbs and began shaking the man and throwing snow in his face, trying to awaken him. When that failed, Elvis began kicking Jones repeatedly until the pain jolted him out of his slumber. As Jones came to, Elvis began feeling the after-effects of the carbon monoxide poisoning and passed out again. Sgt. Jones then returned the life-saving favor by kicking and shaking Presley until he regained consciousness again. Both men eventually recovered and found their way back to their base without being captured by the communist soldiers. Elvis would leave West Germany several more times while in the Army but, unlike his venture into Czechoslovakia, these trips were intentional.

He traveled to Paris numerous times and fell in love with the City of Light, and the city fell in love with him as well. The city of Paris, especially the women, reminded Elvis that he was still a star. While in Friedburg, he was simply Pvt. Presley, but in Paris he was Elvis the Pelvis. His appetite for exotic women was always fulfilled as an endless supply of chorus girls lined up to share his bed.

While Elvis was enjoying the spoils of success in Europe, in America the young art form known as rock and roll was dying. Not only was Elvis overseas in the military, but Jerry Lee Lewis' career was rocked with scandal after it was discovered that he was married to his 13-year-old cousin. Chuck Berry had been sent to jail for transporting a minor across state lines. Little Richard had quit rock and roll to become a minister, and Buddy Holly and Ritchie Valens had been killed in a plane crash. Few thought rock and roll could survive such crushing blows, and moral crusaders heralded the events as God's judgment.

In the absence of the rock stars, a new breed of singers emerged, the teen idols. Pre-fabricated prettyboys such as Frankie Avalon and Fabian were molded in the image of Elvis but lacked the charisma, the sense of danger and, of course, the talent. Overseas, Elvis took notice of the new trend and began to wonder if there would still be an audience for him when he returned.

His reveries about a time long past were interrupted by a knock on the door. Elvis opened it to find Frederick standing there with a handful of tomatoes.

"Hi, Jon. I brought you some tomatoes from my garden."

"Thanks, Freddie. You didn't have to do that."

"Consider it a bribe," Frederick joked as he handed him the tomatoes.

"A bribe for what?"

"I have a favor to ask you."

"Sure. Name it."

"I'm going to the hospital for a few days. I was wondering if you could look after my dog and water my garden while I'm gone."

"Sure. I hope it's nothing serious," Elvis said with concern.

"No. It's just a routine operation. I'll be fine."

"Well, that's a relief. I'd be glad to help out."

"Great! Here are my keys. I'll leave instructions on the refrigerator. I'm going in tomorrow."

"You can count on me."

"Thanks a lot. I guess I should be going. Enjoy the tomatoes, and thanks again," Frederick said as he left the house.

Elvis got up early the next morning and let himself in to Frederick's house as Schatzi greeted him at the door. After petting and playing with the dog for a few minutes, Elvis went to the kitchen and opened a can of dog food. He emptied the contents into the dog dish, and Schatzi began consuming his meal. Elvis decided to stretch out on the sofa and watch some television, but the dog ran to the front door and started barking, interrupting his relaxation.

"Let me guess. You want to go for a walk now?"

The dog confirmed his answer with another bark.

"Well, let me find your leash," Elvis said, as if the dog understood him.

He looked around, but didn't see the leash anywhere. He searched by the door and all around the house, but couldn't find it.

There was a closet by the door; he opened it and looked inside. There was nothing hanging in it but a couple of jackets and some old suits. On the floor was an old box; Elvis decided to open it and look inside for the leash. As he peered into the box, he did not find a leash, just some old mementos. There were a few old pictures of Frederick and some insignia from his days in the German Army. Elvis was about to close the box when he spotted an SS pin. Shocked, he looked further. The deeper he dug into the box, the more dark secrets he uncovered. He founds several medals and commendations, newspaper clippings about a war criminal who had escaped justice and, the most damning of all, a picture of a young Frederick walking side by side with Adolph Hitler. Suddenly, it all made sense -- Frederick's exile and residence in Buenos Aires, his vagueness about his past, and his service in the German Army.

Just then, the door opened and Frederick walked inside. Elvis scrambled to close the box, but it was too late.

"What are you doing here?" Elvis asked nervously.

"My surgery was rescheduled. Why are you looking through my things?"

"I was, uh, looking for, uh...Schatzi's leash."

"So, now you know," Frederick calmly said.

"Is it true? Are you a war criminal?"

"I prefer the term *political scapegoat*, but yes, it's true. My real name is Hans Mueller. Lt. Hans Mueller of the SS," he stated proudly.

"I don't believe it."

"You shouldn't look in a person's closet unless you're prepared to find a few skeletons. I'm sure there are a few in yours. Right, Mr. Presley?"

"You know who I am?" Elvis asked.

"Of course. You show up here in Buenos Aires the day after Elvis dies, looking and talking like him, and expect me not to notice. I am a lot of things, Elvis, but I'm not an idiot."

"Yeah, I know. You're a mass murderer."

"Well, the point is, I came here to start a new life, just as you did. If you expose me, I'll expose you. We can both stop living lies, or we can keep our little secrets and live as neighbors."

"I don't make deals with the devil!" Elvis stated defiantly.

"The devil? You Americans are so quick to judge. I seem to remember your country dropping two atomic bombs on innocent civilians. Then there's the attempted genocide of the Indians, slavery, and countless other atrocities that you Americans have conveniently chosen to forget. You make a deal with the devil every time you wave the American flag."

"I think I should leave," Elvis announced as he walked hurriedly to the door.

"Remember, Elvis, we all have skeletons in our closet!" Mueller yelled as Elvis stormed out of the house.

Elvis went back to his own house and defiantly began packing the few possessions he had remaining. He had been planning to move back to the States soon anyway, and the revelation about his neighbor made it an easy decision. Still, he decided to pray for guidance. When that didn't provide him with any answers, he decided to contact the closest thing to God he knew. He once again called Tom Parker. During their conversation, Elvis avoided telling Tom about his neighbor. Instead, he cited other reasons for his return.

The Colonel advised him that his return may be too soon, but Elvis had already made up his mind. Parker then informed him that he had created a new identity for him, but wouldn't give out any details over the phone. Tom agreed to meet Elvis at the airport in Los Angeles the following day and give him his papers. They exchanged goodbyes and Elvis resumed packing.

Elvis felt conflicted about what to do about his neighbor. As vile a human being as Frederick had turned out to be, he still considered him a friend, and Elvis believed heavily in loyalty. Besides, his neighbor knew of his true identity and ratting Frederick out could backfire.

Then, as he continued to pack, he came upon a picture that gave him the answer for which he had been searching. It was a picture of Richard Nixon presenting him with his DEA badge, a symbol of justice, and all things right to him. It was a badge he felt he didn't deserve, but an honor that he deeply wanted to earn.

The next day, Elvis grabbed his bags and took a taxi to the airport. Once there, he bought a one-way ticket to Los Angeles.

"*Gracias. Muchos gracias*," Elvis said as he took the ticket.

Before boarding the plane, he walked over to a payphone and placed a call.

"Yes. I have an anonymous tip regarding the location of Nazi war criminal Hans Mueller," he stated.

After making the call, he boarded the plane and took a long nap. When he awoke, the plane was about to land.

Elvis got off the plane at LAX. He saw an equally disguised Tom Parker, holding up a sign saying "BURROWS." Elvis walked up to him and gave him a hug.

"It's good to see you again, my boy. Damn, you look like you've lost a lot of weight," the Colonel commented.

"Yeah. I got off the pills, starting doing my karate again, and took the weight off."

"I hope you got the weight of the world off your shoulders as well."

"I'm trying, but sometimes that's the hardest thing to lose," Elvis admitted.

"Well, I guess congratulations are in order. Since your death, you've become a god. Records and memorabilia are flying off the shelves. I'm making a killing. Oh, here's some money for you, five thousand dollars," Parker said as he handed Elvis an envelope.

"Five thousand dollars? Is that all my life is worth to you? I thought you were making a killing."

"Relax, son. Business is business. Five grand is enough for anyone to start a new life in this country. You said yourself that money never bought you happiness. Besides, I have something else for you, something you can't put a price on."

"And what's that?"

"A new life. Here are your papers," Tom proclaimed as he handed Elvis another envelope.

"My papers?"

"Your new identity, a birth certificate, and a Social Security card. You can use this to get a driver's license and a passport. I found someone from your area who died very young, and was even born the same day as you."

Elvis opened it up and saw a familiar name inside.

"Jesse Garon Presley. Very funny!" Elvis grimaced.

"Don't you see? You always felt guilty that you lived and Jesse died. Now, Elvis is dead and Jesse lives. You have the chance to live the life that Jesse never had."

Tom's explanation hit home with Elvis, and he instantly forgave the Colonel's greed and hugged him again. They made their way out of the airport.

On the way, Elvis took a glimpse at a news segment on a small airport television.

"After over thirty years on the lam, alleged Nazi war criminal Hans Mueller was arrested in Buenos Aires after an anonymous tip led authorities to his residence," the news anchor announced as they cut to footage of his arrest.

Before being taken away, Hans Mueller shouted to the reporters.

"I just want to say that Elvis Presley is alive and lives next door to me. He's the one who turned me in!" he raved madly.

As the footage ended, the anchor shook his head smugly, trying not to laugh at the apparent insanity of the exiled Nazi.

"Hans Mueller is facing extradition to the United States, where he will be tried for war crimes."

Elvis' face surrendered to a long-deprived smile as he turned and walked out of the airport with the Colonel.

CHAPTER VI ‖

BRIDGE OVER TROUBLED WATER

After returning to the States, Elvis spent a few months in California drifting from town to town. His beard had grown in fully, and when coupled with sunglasses and a baseball cap, he was virtually unrecognizable. It gave him great pleasure to be among people in crowded malls and parks. It was a simple joy that most could not relate to, but something that he had not been able to do for over twenty years. He began to realize how much he liked people. He liked playing pool in neighborhood bars and discussing music and politics with common folks.

Coming home to America reminded him of when he had finally returned from the Army. He had left America an immoral scoundrel, and returned a national treasure. Frank Sinatra best personified the change in attitude. Just a few years earlier, he referred to Elvis' music quite jealously as "a deplorable, rancid-smelling aphrodisiac." Upon Elvis's return, Sinatra did a complete three-sixty and rolled out the red carpet for him. Sinatra and his Rat Pack buddies hosted the TV special "Welcome Home, Elvis". It featured a less intimidating, more mature, tuxedo-clad Presley crooning and trading off songs with Ole Blue Eyes as teenage girls clamored and screamed. It had been over two years since Elvis' last performance and backstage, butterflies fluttered throughout his stomach as they often did, but once onstage, he reclaimed his splendor and glory. Despite being panned by the critics, the TV show was a great success, and Elvis' comeback had begun.

It wasn't Elvis' greatest comeback, however; that night happened in 1968. "The '68 Comeback Special," as it became known, was yet another turning point in his career. In a time when the radio and the charts were dominated by acid-tinged acts such as the Beatles, Jefferson Airplane, and the Doors, Elvis Presley was largely seen as yesterday's news -- unhip, uncool, and almost part of the Establishment that the youth culture was trying to overthrow. The concept for the new show was a stripped-down, return to his roots variety show that included a sit-down acoustic jam with his band mates, playing the classic songs that had made him a star. Tanned, fit, and dressed in black leather from head to toe, Elvis had never looked better in his life. Broadcast on December 3, 1968, the show was the week's highest-rated show, and garnered a Peabody Award; more importantly, it allowed the King to reclaim his throne.

Elvis still smiled when he recalled that night. He had been smiling often since his return to America. His dependence upon prescription pills had completely waned, something for which he was eternally grateful. Physically and mentally, he felt sharper than he had in years, though he found himself occasionally substituting alcohol for pills. It was a habit he had picked up from Frederick in Buenos Aires, but he decided that he had it under control and allowed himself that one vice. Besides, alcohol was a social drug, and interacting with humans was a new hobby of his.

His new name, Jesse Presley, had become a problem. It was hard enough not raising suspicion about his true identity still looking like Elvis. Having the same last name only made matters worse. He decided to have his name legally changed, and began filling out the required paperwork to do so. After much red tape and standing in endless lines, he had his name changed to one more befitting a man of his stature, Jesse King.

Elvis finally settled in San Francisco; like many people who moved there, he found it a very tranquil and welcoming place.

Located on a peninsula in Northern California, the city was originally occupied by the Coastanoan Indians, and wasn't discovered by Europeans until 1595. Portuguese explorer Cermeno Rodriquez Cabrillo is credited with its discovery, and he named it Puerto de San Francisco, or Port of Saint Francis. However, it wasn't until 1769 that Europeans reached the site by traveling overland, when a Spanish expedition led by Gaspar de Portola climbed the numerous hills and looked down upon the beautiful bay.

In 1769, Captain Juan Bautista de Anza established a military fort there, and in the same year Spanish priests opened a nearby mission. In

1821, Mexico won its independence from Spain and claimed California for its own. Then in 1846 war broke out between Mexico and the United States. A few years later, America won the war and took over the entire California region. That same year, gold was discovered in Sacramento, which led to the 1849 gold rush. San Francisco, with its ideal port location, became a valued harbor and supply center for gold seekers. Within a year, the city's population grew dramatically

Because of the gold strike, San Francisco became the financial and cultural center of the West, and the population grew even larger. In 1869, a railroad was completed that linked the city to the Eastern United States, and many Chinese railroad laborers settled into the Bay Area. A few years later, a San Franciscan cable manufacturer invented the cable car, and it became a favorite mode of transportation in the hilly city.

In 1906, tragedy struck the city when a massive earthquake followed by fires left San Francisco almost in ruins. The city rebuilt itself, however, and rose from the ashes to regain its former grandeur. The Golden Gate Bridge, a marvel of modern construction, was built in 1937, and along with the San Francisco-Oakland Bay Bridge, connected the two neighboring cities.

In 1967, the country's attention turned to San Francisco again, as it became the virtual birthplace of the hippie movement and the so-called Summer of Love. Bands such as the Grateful Dead, Jefferson Airplane, and Janis Joplin, created a new sound, and the corner of Haight-Asbury became the center of the psychedelic movement, fueled by a then-legal drug called LSD.

The movement, however, soon took a turn for the darker as con men and criminals descended upon the area in hopes of exploiting the naïve flower children who lived and loved freely. One of these men was a sociopathic ex-con named Charles Manson. Recently released from a ten-year sentence in prison, he arrived in the Bay Area and convinced several women to follow him down near Los Angeles where he formed a sex-and-drug cult in the desert. These women were the cornerstone of his cult, or family, as he called it. In 1969, his family committed the grisly Tate-LoBianca murders, stealing headlines and effectively pronouncing the end of the hippie movement.

In the decade that followed, San Francisco continued to thrive economically, and the city whose tolerance was a welcoming beacon to the Chinese and the hippies had also become a gathering spot for the country's rapidly growing homosexual community. The city had become a symbol of tolerance and personal freedom throughout the country and the world.

Elvis began renting a small, red-painted Victorian house in the Haight Area of San Francisco, a bohemian-minded community near Golden Gate Park. Though the Sixties had long ended, its remnants were still quite visible along Haight Street, which was lined with head shops and psychedelically painted buildings. Though not a fan of the Sixties counterculture or the psychedelic drug scene, Elvis found the people very nice and unassuming, if not an interesting curiosity. The experience was cathartic, and was conducive to his rejuvenated appreciation of music. On several occasions, he had grabbed his acoustic guitar and jammed with countless street musicians. It was a very happy time for him, and though it was 1978, he felt that he had finally gotten to experience the Sixties' hippie vibe.

He had missed out on the Sixties the first time around. Already a larger than life icon at that point, he was too busy living behind the sheltering walls of Graceland and making bad movies to experience it firsthand. He had grown up in the South, in a fairly conservative environment, and remembered resenting the political climate of that time. He could recall the day the Beatles came to America, and though publicly he appeared gracious and welcoming, deep down he knew it was a changing of the guard, and he hated them for it. He had even met them once, and though they talked and jammed together for hours, he couldn't help feeling contempt for them, especially their opinionated young lead singer, John Lennon.

But this was a period of personal growth for him. He found a Baptist church in nearby Oakland, and though he was only white person in attendance, he did not think twice about attending. He had already broken racial barriers in the world of music and didn't see why church should be any different. At first he got a few strange looks, but was soon accepted as a member of the flock. He admired the style and delivery of the church's minister, Devon Williams, who would routinely break into song and dance in mid-sermon. As was the case with many Baptist churches, the service was more of a celebration of life than a preparation for death, and Elvis was drawn to that. Its raucous and hopping services had the parishioners singing and dancing in the aisles and left him with a song in his heart every Sunday. Soon he decided to join the choir, and it didn't take the Minister long to notice his beautiful voice. On occasion he would let him solo and sing some of his favorite gospel songs, many of which he had recorded in his past life. When the parishioners heard this white boy singing the gospels with such soul and conviction, they were stunned and impressed.

Williams quickly befriended him and took him under his wing. He was a kindly, middle-aged black man with gentle eyes and a large toothy smile. As a kid, he had gotten mixed up with the wrong crowd and been sent to prison for five years on a burglary charge. It was in prison that the young man truly discovered the teachings of the bible, and this compelled him to turn his life around and serve the Lord. He could sense a similar crossroads in his new parishioner, and wanted to help him choose the right path.

"Young man, with a voice like yours, you could convert the masses," Williams decried with passion.

"That's something I've always wanted to do," Elvis replied.

"You may you get your chance," the minister said with a smile.

The minister's words became a self-fulfilling prophecy. The following week, Elvis was performing "Where Could I Go But to the Lord?" with the choir behind him. After the song ended, the minister got the flock's attention and grabbed Elvis.

"Brothers and sisters, would you like to hear our brother, Jesse King tell us about his relationship with the Lord?"

They responded with a loud and undeniable "Yes!"

Elvis composed himself and decided to speak with the same passion and fervor as Minister Williams.

"The man you see before you is a very different man than he was a few years ago," Elvis shouted "I used to lead a sinful life. I had every physical possession a man could have, but I wasn't content," he said, as a man from the pews yelled "Amen!"

"I had beautiful women hanging on me, but I wasn't fulfilled. I used to spend every waking moment high on drugs, but I wasn't happy."

"No sir!" a man shouted out.

"I did not know contentment, fulfillment, or happiness until I felt the hand of the Lord," he called out hoarsely.

The crowd said "Amen!" in unison as the choir began singing the chorus from Handel's "Messiah."

"Hallelujah, Hallelujah…" they sang as the crowd began dancing.

Wearing a childlike smile, Elvis walked off the stage, wondering if preaching was indeed his true calling.

From then on, he would sing and speak more frequently at the church, and became good friends with the Minister. As he studied the passages of the bible, he also got deeper into meditation to help center himself, and even went on a diet to keep off the weight. He worked out regularly and kept practicing karate. His health had greatly improved, and his mind, body and spirit felt better than they ever had.

Elvis tried to keep up his end of his bargain with God by doing good deeds whenever possible, whether it was helping a stranded motorist with a flat tire, or giving a little money to one of the many homeless people in San Francisco. In truth, his heart hadn't grown much bigger than it already was. He had always been a generous, caring man. Aside from the lavish gifts he used to shower upon his friends and family, he had routinely given large donations to various charities throughout his life. He regretted no longer having his fortune, only because he couldn't help people the way he had in the past. Despite all of the good karma he had sent out, he still hadn't freed himself from his demons, however. At night, his sleep was tormented with horrible nightmares. Where he once used to take pills to medicate them away, now he was defenseless against the bullying arms of Morpheus.

He had found it hard not to miss his buddies, collectively known as the Memphis Mafia. For the last twenty years, he and the group had been inseparable. They followed Elvis practically everywhere he went. They lived with him at Graceland and stayed with him in Bel-Air. Together, they terrorized posh hotels, movie sets, and any place else in their path. At Graceland, their wild sex parties had reached almost Caligulan proportions. In Hollywood, no one was safe from their mischief; whether it was firecrackers or water pistol fights, chaos and childish pranks ruled the day on the set of an Elvis Presley film. They were now gone, left behind along with every other remnant of his previous life.

He also missed the company of women, especially Ginger. He reminisced fondly on their loving affair and sometimes longed to back to those days, if just to be with her again. He loved women, and when he had been Elvis Presley he had had his pick of virtually any woman he wanted, a luxury he took for granted. Though drug use had made him impotent in the later years of his former life, his libido had since returned, but now he was alone. He recalled how foolish he had been with women in the past. Romancing beautiful women, such as Priscilla, only to betray their love with his philandering. He vowed that if he ever met another woman that he loved, he would be faithful to her. He realized that it had been a lot easier to get women when he was a rich and famous rock star, as opposed to a poor, scruffy-looking vagabond. He wondered if any woman had ever loved him for who he was.

Money, for the first time in twenty years, was a concern, and though Tom Parker had given him some cash, he still needed to get a job. He wasn't trained for much other than manual labor, so he got a job pumping gas, but eventually quit after a few people thought they recognized him. He then gained employment as a truck driver, a job that suited him perfectly. He had been a truck driver before he became famous as well as in the Army, and now it allowed him to travel freely across the country while maintaining a low profile. San Francisco was a good city for it, too, as the countless shipments coming in to its ports from other countries provided him with steady work.

One night, between jobs, Elvis went for a late night jog across the Golden Gate Bridge. At night, the view from the bridge was as eerie as it was beautiful in the day. As usual, it was a foggy night in San Francisco, especially on the bridge. Perhaps that was why Elvis was about halfway across it before he noticed someone precariously perched on the safety rail.

"Hey, be careful. You don't want to fall in!" Elvis shouted naively.

"Don't tell me what I don't want to do."

As Elvis jogged closer, it dawned on him that this man was about to commit suicide.

"Don't come any closer," he warned.

Elvis stopped in his tracks and then slowly began inching his way closer, getting a better look at the man on the bridge. He was a young, good-looking man in his late teens, clean- shaved and dressed un-usually well, considering what he was planning.

"I said: Don't come any closer."

"I'm just getting closer so I can talk to you."

"I don't want to talk to anyone."

"Are you planning on jumping?"

"What do you think, Einstein?" the young man asked sarcastically.

"I don't know. How long have you been here?"

"About ten minutes."

"Then I would have to say that you're not planning on jumping."

"What the hell is that supposed to mean?"

"If you were planning on jumping, you would've have done it already. I mean, it doesn't take ten minutes to jump off a bridge. You just climb over and let go. Gravity does the rest."

"Maybe I wanted to think about what I was about to do. Is that okay with you?"   "What's to think about? Either you want to do it or you don't. If you're hesitating, then you must not want to do it," Elvis fired back, using reverse psychology.

"Why don't you leave me alone?"

"Are you going to jump?"

"Yes, my mind's made up. There's nothing you can say to change it," he asserted.

"Well, 'bye then," Elvis remarked as he walked away, knowing the boy would not jump.

He could tell the kid just wanted attention. It was a similar ploy used by a young starlet he had dated when he was a young man; her name was Natalie Wood. At a party they were attending together, she had gotten mad that Elvis wasn't paying her enough attention. She then climbed out on a window ledge and announced that she was going to kill herself. Elvis and his friends simply ignored her threat and, after a few minutes, Natalie meekly climbed back into the room.

"You're just going to walk away!" the boy yelled with outrage.

"Yeah. If your mind's made up, then how can I change it?"

"You should at least try," the boy insisted.

"Okay, if you want," Elvis said as he shrugged his shoulders. "Please don't jump, Mister. Think of all the wonderful things there are in life," he said insincerely.

"There's no need to be sarcastic."

"Okay, I'm sorry. If you're going to jump, though, I hope you have some identification tightly secured to you."

"Why?"

"So your family can identify the body."

"I think my parents can recognize their own son."

"Have you ever seen what a person looks like after they drag him out of this bay?"

"No."

"Not a pretty sight. It's usually days before they find you and by that time that body is all swollen and bloated from the water. You'll look like you weigh four hundred pounds. Of course, your skin will be all blue from the cold water and you'll be disfigured from all the fish pecking away at you. Not to mention what will happen if a shark finds you."

"Really?"

"Yeah. It's really gross. So why are committing suicide, anyway?"

"My girlfriend broke up with me," the boy explained as Elvis rolled his eyes at his sheer stupidity.

"That's it? I'm sorry, I thought you had a real problem."

"Shut up! You don't understand. I love her. We were meant to be together."

"How old are you?"

"Eighteen."

"Trust me, by the time you're twenty, you won't even care about her. You'll have met some other woman, fallen in love with her, and she'll have broken your heart, too."

"What are you talking about?"

"Getting your heart broken is part of life. It'll probably happen about five more times before you find the girl that's right for you."

"How do you know?"

"I've lived long enough to see it happen many times to many people. Besides, at your age, you don't want to settle down with one girl. Play the field for a while. Enjoy your youth."

"But it hurts so much!"

"I know, but someday it won't. You'll meet someone even better and be thankful that you're not already married."

"And what if you're wrong? What if I get to be your age and never find love?"

"Well, this bridge will still be here. But if you jump tonight, you'll never find out what life has in store for you."

"If I jump tonight, then Becky will realize what a mistake it was breaking up with me."

"No she won't. She'll think that you were weak and mentally unstable. You'll reinforce any negative opinions she had of you. If you want to make her regret leaving you, then live, and become rich and successful."

The boy was quiet for a minute. Then he said, "Yeah. You're right."

"So, are you going to come off that bridge?"

"Yeah. Sure," he said as he began to climb over the barrier.

Just then, the boy slipped, lost his balance, and fell from the edge. He managed to grab hold of the side with one hand, but his grip was slipping fast.

"Help!" he screamed.

Elvis jumped over the rail and raced to the boy, grabbing hold of his wrist.

"Grab my arm with your other hand," Elvis yelled frantically as his other hand grabbed the railing to prevent him from falling, too.

The boy struggled, and Elvis felt his grip on the boy slipping. At the last moment the boy managed to get his other hand around Elvis' arm, and Presley pulled him up until he was back on the side of the bridge.

"Thanks, man. You saved my life, twice."

"Do me a favor. Shut up and get back over the rail," an exasperated Elvis commanded.

The boy quickly obeyed and climbed to safety with Elvis behind him. The young man put his hands on his knees and gasped for air.

"Thanks, man. Hey, did anyone ever tell you that you look a lot like Elvis..." the teenager began saying as he turned around to discover the man had disappeared into the foggy night.

CHAPTER VII

GO EAST, YOUNG MAN

Elvis had a long drive ahead of him. He had driven all day the day before, trekking down the California Coast and into Arizona, before stopping at a cheap motel for some much-needed sleep. Packed in his white delivery truck was a very valuable cargo, hundreds of boxes of gaudy and cheaply-made bead necklaces from Taiwan. It might not have seemed like a valuable cargo, but in a few days when he arrived in New Orleans for Mardi Gras, it would suddenly become as good as gold.

Every year, New Orleans hosted Mardi Gras or Fat Tuesday, a hedonistic party that preceded the Catholic period of abstinence known as Lent. The festival included parades, lavish costumes, heavy alcohol consumption, and public nudity. The main currency of this party was the beads that people would wear around their necks and trade for such desirable items as a beer, a kiss or, most recently, a half-second flash of a woman's breasts. It was a new tradition, but one that was growing rapidly.

Hitting the lonely road was very cathartic for him. It was a romantic voyage into the soul of America. Staring out upon the endless highway made him feel human again. He moved anonymously from town to town, no one person getting more than a few glimpses of him, and before anyone could realize that he looked like Elvis Presley, he had already driven off into the sunset like the Lone Ranger.

1978 had come and gone in the blink of the eye. It was a mostly uneventful year that he spent getting readjusted to his new life. It had been a lonely year for him, and he hoped that 1979 would be an improvement.

As he drove through New Mexico during a rare rainstorm enroute to New Orleans, the lonesome quiet of the road had put his mind in overdrive, and he began thinking about his mother.

Elvis and his mother had had a bond closer than most people's. As Gladys' only child, he was the sole focal point of her attention. When Elvis was three, his father was arrested for forgery, and was sent away for nine months. To a child, nine months was a lifetime, and Elvis and his mother became inseparable. They even developed their own personal language over the years, almost a baby-talk that only they could understand.

As a young man, Elvis had gone to Sun Records to make a birthday present for his mother. For a small fee, he recorded an old standard "My Happiness," and gave it to her. Ironically, his recording of that song left an impression on the folks at the record company, and not too long afterwards Sun Records called upon him to record for them.

Gladys did not want her son to become a famous singer, however. She wanted him to stay in Memphis and always be by her side. As he began his ascent to fame, she would always plead for him to pull back on the reins of his out-of-control career. But once his career started rolling, there was nothing either of them could do to stop the runaway train. Gladys became horrified when, at an early concert in Jacksonville, dozens of lust-crazed female fans charged the stage and swarmed Elvis, practically tearing him to pieces. While that scenario may have been every man's fantasy, she was worried that Elvis could be seriously hurt, even killed.

She even tried her best to sabotage his early career, refusing to allow Elvis to sign with Tom Parker, but inevitably she gave in and Elvis became a superstar. Her fears were confirmed by Elvis' hectic touring schedule that prevented him from seeing her most of the time. As Elvis' star burned brighter, she felt his need for her grow dimmer, and began drinking heavily to insulate herself from her loss. In 1958, Elvis left for the Army, and Gladys was devastated, feeling that their bond had become completely severed. It was while he was in the service that she eventually drank herself to death.

When his mother died, Elvis became a basket case. At her funeral, he threw himself onto her casket and began sobbing uncontrollably. When he returned to his unit, it was obvious to all that he was a different man. He had become more brooding and introspective.

While the hum of the truck engine sang soothingly to Elvis, he spotted a girl hitchhiking in the rain. As a rule, he didn't pick up hitchhikers, but he decided to help her out, because of the weather and because she was a woman. Besides, he needed the company.

He pulled the truck over to the side of the road. The girl climbed into the truck and thanked him profusely as the rain dripped off her blond hair, dyed green and orange. Elvis quickly realized that the girl was only a teenager.

"How far are you going?"

"New Orleans," she answered as she squeezed the water from her hair.

"Going to Mardi Gras, huh? You've got a ways to go," Elvis commented, knowing that New Orleans was his destination as well, but it was a long drive and he didn't want to commit to anything.

"Yeah, I know. Slowly but surely I'll get there."

A streetlight shone into the truck cab, and he got his first real look at her. She looked to be in her late teens, an attractive and petite girl with a beautiful but tough smile. Elvis began to wonder what on Earth a girl her age would be doing hitchhiking at night, in the rain, on such a deserted stretch of highway.

"So, what's a young girl like you doing hitchhiking out here?"

"I'll be eighteen soon."

"Still, it is kind of dangerous."

"Don't I know it? The last guy I was riding with got the idea that I owed him something for the ride."

"What happened?"

"I set him straight, and then he kicked me out of his car and into the rain, which is where you found me."

"What a jerk!"

"Yeah. You're not like that. Are you?"

"No ma'am," he answered with his Southern drawl.

"Well, good."

"Aren't your parents worried about you?"

"Who cares?"

"Why? What's wrong with your parents?"

"Look," she said. "I've kind of had a bad day. I appreciate you picking me up and all, but I don't feel like being interrogated right now."

"I'm sorry, but I do have one more question."

"What?" she asked, slightly annoyed.

"What's your name?"

"I'm Faith, and you?" she said, becoming embarrassed by her angry tone.

"Jesse."

"Well, nice to meet you, Jesse," she said warmly, finally dropping her guard for a moment.

"Nice to meet you, too. So, besides Mardi Gras, what's in New Orleans?"

"Hey, that's two questions."

"Oh, sorry."

"It's okay. Actually, there's a guy I met down there last summer."

"You're going through all this trouble to see him? He must be a hell of a guy."

"He's okay," she answered diffidently.

"Just okay?"

"Can't we listen to the radio?"

"Sure."

The conversation stopped as the blues-based sounds of an oldies station filled the cabin. Elvis concentrated on the hypnotic curves of the highway as Faith stared out into the night, pensive and silent. Suddenly, the Elvis song "Heartbreak Hotel" came on the radio. A smile spread across Elvis' face as he noticed Faith grooving subtly to the beat.

"You like Elvis?"

"Yeah. He's all right, I guess, for old fart music. Oh, I'm sorry. You probably like this music, huh?" she awkwardly apologized. "It's a shame what happened to him, though. Elvis, I mean."

"Yeah."

"You know, you kind of look like him."

"I get that all the time."

"In fact, if you did your hair differently and shaved off that beard, you could be his twin."

Elvis quickly decided to change the subject.

"So, are you planning on going to college or anything?" He asked.

"No."

"No plans for the future?"

"Something will come up. Maybe I'll be a truck driver like you."

"So now you want to be a truck driver?" He said with a laugh.

"Oh, like it's that hard! I can drive."

"Driving is the easy part; not peeing for hours and hours is the hard part."

"Actually, now that you mention it, I have to go pretty bad," she conceded.

"Real bad?"

"Yes. Since before you picked me up. I didn't want to say anything earlier and inconvenience you." '

"It's no inconvenience. There's a mayonnaise jar under the seat," he answered playfully.

"Hah hah," she laughed sarcastically, not finding it funny at all.

"Okay. We'll make a pit stop as soon as you answer a few questions."

"Or I could just piss all over the seat."

"Go ahead. I won't be sitting in it," Elvis glibly responded.

"Okay, dammit. What do you want to know?"

"Why are you running to New Orleans?"

"It's the only place I can go."

"What's wrong with staying at home with your parents?"

"I've got a problem with my stepdad."

"Really? Like what?"

"He's abusive."

"He hits you?"

"Sometimes. Sometimes...other stuff," Faith revealed uneasily.

"Oh, I see. I'm sorry," Elvis answered apologetically, realizing he had uncovered something tragically personal.

"Don't be. I don't need anyone's sympathy."

Elvis hadn't expected her revelation, and his concern for her was now only rivaled by the realization that he was transporting an underage runaway across state lines. The "Welcome to Texas" sign that had just flashed past him reminded him of that fact.

"Are there any more questions?"

"So, who's this guy you're going to be with?"

"His name's Randy, and he's really cool. I'm going to stay with him. He can get me work."

"Doing what?"

"Dancing."

"What? He owns a ballet company?"

"No. At a club. It's a strip club, okay?"

"But you're so young," he remarked with concern.

"Yeah, and soon I'll be of legal age."

"Isn't that degrading?"

"All work's degrading. Driving this truck's degrading. Staying at home with my stepdad is degrading."

"What else does Randy want you to do for him?"

"What do you mean?"

"Well, how much money do you have to your name?"

"It's none of your business."

"Well, not having much money really limits your options, especially a thousand miles from home."

"Look, I told you my rap. There's a rest stop at the next exit. Can we stop there?"

"Yeah. Okay," he answered as he took the exit and headed to the rest stop.

Elvis pulled into the stop and parked as Faith dashed frantically to the ladies' room. Elvis took a bathroom break of his own, then stopped in an all-night store and picked up a cup of coffee and a couple of sandwiches.

He felt great empathy for Faith and her plight. He hoped that Randy was a good person and not someone who would take advantage of her situation, but he doubted it. Over the time that they'd driven together, Elvis had developed a fondness for her, as well as a concern. His greatest fear was that Randy would exploit her, and she would go from being a stripper into prostitution. She was a very pretty girl, very shapely as well. Having spent a lot of time in Vegas, he had seen more than a few young women go down that path and could not bear to see the same thing happen to Faith. There wasn't much he could do to prevent it, though. If he still had his fortune, he could simply cut her a check to buy her a new life, but now he was powerless. He had a little over a thousand miles of the drive left, and knew that didn't give him enough time to help her.

He climbed into the truck cabin where Faith was waiting.

"Are you all ready to go?" Elvis asked.

"Yes. I feel so much better now."

"Here. Have a sandwich," he offered as he handed one to her.

"Thanks. You're a really good person," she stated graciously as she took the sandwich and started eating it.

"I'm just a good Christian," he said proudly as he started up his truck.

"'Good Christian.' Those are two words that don't always belong together."

"Not a religious person, I take it."

"Hell, no. It's all a bunch of lies designed to make money and keep society in line."

"Well, try not to let the acts of humans jade your opinion of God," he suggested as he pulled back onto the road.

"I'll try."

"I'm heading to New Orleans, too," he noted, now feeling comfortable committing to the drive.

"Really? Could you take me there?"

"Sure, I guess."

"Great. Thank you so much!"

"See? Not all Christians are bad," he joked.

"Yeah, you're right. You're one of the good ones, I guess. So, I just bared my soul to you. Now tell me your story."

"My story? Not much to tell," Elvis answered deceptively, trying to figure out what details of his life he could divulge without revealing his true identity.

"Well, have you ever been married?"

"Yes. Once."

"Not anymore?"

"No. We broke up a while ago. To be honest, I haven't really been the same since."

"I'm sorry. Any kids?"

"Yes. A daughter," he conceded as his thoughts drifted to Lisa Marie.

"Do you ever see her?"

"Not in a while."

"Why?"

"It's complicated," he answered.

"Well, I think you should see her sometime. Trust me, not knowing your real father can be tough."

"I'm sure you're right," he sighed as a tear welled up in his eye.

He wiped it away before Faith could notice. Leaving Lisa Marie behind was the greatest regret of his new life, and it was a hurt that was with him everyday. Sadly, he didn't know if he would ever see her again. He tried to reason himself out of his depression with the argument that if he hadn't faked his death when he did, it soon would have been a real one. However, rationalizations could only do so much, and the pain and the loss that his daughter must feel caused great guilt inside him.

Elvis fondly recalled the day he had first received news of his unborn daughter. Priscilla and he had only been married a couple of months when she confessed her suspicions that she was pregnant. He took her to a doctor to be examined while he and Vernon sat nervously in the waiting room anxious and eager for the outcome.

Priscilla came out beaming with joy. "Guess what?"

"What?"

"You're going to be a daddy," she declared with glee.

He smiled with excitement and engulfed her with a hug.

"This is such great news," he proclaimed. "Hey daddy, Cilla's going to have a baby. You're going to be a granddaddy."

The three of them reveled together, enraptured by the prospect of a new addition to the family. It was one of the happiest moments of his life.

Overcome by nostalgia and the desire to talk to someone, he began rambling on about his life, or at least the parts that he could talk about. Countless miles of conquered highway fell behind them as the night surrendered to the morning. Elvis looked over to Faith in mid-sentence and realized that she was fast asleep.

CHAPTER VIII

NEW ORLEANS

Hours later, Elvis was still driving to his destination, fighting off the fatigueof a long drive when Faith woke up.

"We're getting close to New Orleans," he announced.

"Really?"

"Yeah. It won't be long now."

It was bittersweet news for Faith because she knew she was going to be with Randy only out of desperation. She had no illusions of a happy ending. Living simply meant surviving to her. It had always been that way.

The illegitimate child of an alcoholic mother, she had been forced to take care of herself from a young age. In fact, much of her childhood was spent also taking care of her mother, all the while fighting off the sexual advances of her stepfather. She had grown up fast and grown up tough, learning early in life that one does what one has to do to survive.

Despite her parents' immoral behavior, they still considered themselves deeply religious and dolled out strict and sometimes brutal punishment to their daughter whenever she behaved in an "un-Christian" way.

She had met Randy on a rare family vacation to New Orleans. Randy saw her walking down the street and, having a shark-like ability to spot injured prey, he swam straight up to her. He seemed nice and, best of all, he gave her an excuse to ditch her parents. They had a brief but passionate romance, and at the end of the week he gave her his number. They talked on the phone on and off for the next six months; she vaguely described her unhappy home life to him and he promised her a place to stay and a job at his club. She was at first uncomfortable with the idea of dancing nude in a club, but Randy could be very convincing.

She had resigned herself to that fate, but since she'd met Jesse, she had begun to have second thoughts. For the first time that she could remember, a man had treated her with kindness and respect without expecting something sexual in return. He didn't talk down to her or make her feel inferior, and during their trek down the open road, she felt free and alive. She propped her feet up on the dashbord and rolled down the window, feeling the sun shine upon her face and the wind blow through her hair as she secretly hoped that there would be a way for her not to part company with her new friend.

"So, what's up with your hair, anyway?" Elvis teased her.

"What do you mean?"

"It's multi-colored."

"It's a punk-rock thing. You wouldn't understand."

"Don't tell me you listen to that awful music."

"Have you ever sat down and actually listened to it?"

"Not without a gun to my head."

"Then you shouldn't judge."

"It's not even music."

"What makes you an expert on rock and roll?" she asked.

Elvis had to bite his tongue over that question.

"I don't need to be an expert to recognize crap," he stated now, just trying to get a rise out of her.

"Oh, come on. It's better than those moldy oldies you listen to. The Sex Pistols, The Ramones, now that's music."

"You think they're better than Elvis Presley?" he asked, having fun with her.

"The problem with Elvis is the same as the problem with all of rock and roll. They both became old, bloated, and larger than life," Faith said with authority. "It's a new era, and I want my music to be young, lean and real, not some dead, fat guy in a jumpsuit."

Elvis was stung by her inadvertent insult.

"I guess we agree to disagree," he said.

"Well, I'll try not to hold it against you."

The traffic was a nightmare as they entered New Orleans. Thrillseekers from all over the world converged in the city for its once a year carnival. Many of the roads were closed off and overrun by thousands of drunken revelers, many in bizarre, over-the-top outfits and costumes.

There were numerous floats, and people from all walks of life wrapped in beads and wearing purple, green, and gold.

They eventually navigated their way near Randy's house in the French Quarter, home to the rowdiest and raciest parties at Mardi Gras. They had to park the truck at a diner and walk a good portion of the way, crossing the famous Bourbon Street as they went. The French Quarter was a section of the city with heavy European feel, lined with bars and restaurants and, on this night, hundreds of intoxicated youth. Strains of live jazz could occasionally be heard before being drowned out by the loud roar of the crowds.

Elvis and Faith approached Randy's house and he gave her comforting smile, masking his true feelings.

"Well, here we are," he said.

"Thanks again, Jesse. I can't tell you how glad I am to have met you."

"Hey, thanks for the company," he replied as he gave her a hug.

As they shared an embrace, Elvis slyly slipped a hundred-dollar bill into her purse. He wished he could give more, but it was all he could afford at that time.

"I hope you get to see your daughter again soon," she said.

"Me, too. Hey, I'm going to be in town for a few hours. I've got to unload my truck and get a bite to eat. If something happens, I'll be at the diner we parked at down the street."

"Okay," she said as she waved goodbye and walked away.

He watched her enter the house and then sauntered off back the way he came.

After having his truck unloaded and receiving a new shipment, he headed to the diner and had his first real meal in days. He already missed Faith, and as he doused the burnt hamburger they'd served him with Cajun spices, he kept hoping that she would come through the diner doors soon.

The diner was not unlike the numerous truckstops he had eaten at since he became a truck driver, except for the absence of other fellow truckers. Their presence was one of his favorite things about his job. They were a strange fraternity and at countless diners across the country he talked with them and listened as they regaled in endless stories about life on the road. They represented the working man to him, a class of people he had grown up with but became secluded from as the star of Elvis Presley had begun to rise. When he was with them he felt one with the people again and never had to worry about being recognized, as many of the truck drivers sported sideburns and greased back hair, looking more like Elvis Presley than he did.

The Chickasaw, Choctaw, and Natchez Indians originally occupied the area that would become New Orleans. In 1682, French explorer Robert Cavalier sailed down the Mississippi River from the Great Lakes, claiming the entire region for France. The city was founded by Sier de Bienville in 1718, and was made the capital of the French colony of Louisiana in 1722.

King Louis XV gave Louisiana to his cousin, King Charles III of Spain in 1762, but it was secretly transferred back to French hands in 1800. In 1803, needing money to support his war effort, Napoleon Bonaparte sold the colony to the United States in what would be known as the Louisiana Purchase.

During the War of 1812, the British tried to capture the city, but it was defended by General Andrew Jackson's troops with help from Jean Lafitte's band of pirates during the Battle of New Orleans.

After the war, New Orleans thrived as a port and slave-trading center. In 1832, 1853, and 1878, the city suffered from epidemics of yellow fever, spread by mosquitoes inhabiting the numerous swamps in the area. The fever took lives in the tens of thousands over the years.

In 1838, the city celebrated its first Mardi Gras. The holiday carnival would grow to be the occasion for which the city was best known, as well as a great boon to tourism. In the 1920s, black musicians like Louis Armstrong and Jelly Roll Morton pioneered a new sound, and the city also became known as the Birthplace of Jazz. It was an exotic and cultured city also known for its spicy Cajun food and its practice of voodoo and *santeria*.

Back at Randy's, Faith found herself on his bed as they kissed and he tried to remove her blouse. Faith balked at that point and tried to cool his burning desires.

Randy had already begun the Mardi Gras celebration and was quite drunk and belligerent. After a day of drinking beer and seeing an endless sea of women's breasts, he had decided to have sex with Faith, regardless of what she wanted.

"Come on, Faith."

"Randy, I just got in after hitchhiking two thousand miles to see you. Right now, I just want to relax and get settled."

"Well, seeing as how you're going to be staying in my house, I don't think it really matters what you want. Besides, it's a long way back to Reno."

Randy then threw her down on the bed and climbed on top of her. She slapped him on the cheek and he became furious, punching her hard in the face.

"Go to hell! I'm leaving!" she screamed.

"I don't think so," he growled as he pulled her away from the door.

"Randy, stop it!"

"You want me to stop? Then you have two choices. You can either stay here and do what I tell you, or you can sleep on the street."

"Fine. I'd rather sleep with the rats than with you."

She took her purse and ran towards the door. Randy grabbed her again and started pulling her back into the room.

"You're not going anywhere."

She reared back her foot and kicked him squarely in the groin, doubling him over. She ran out the door.

At the diner, Elvis had finished his meal and ordered another cup of coffee. He checked his watch nervously knowing that he really had to leave soon. He had made a reservation at a motel in town and wanted to check in early before the motel might decided to bump him to accommodate the growing swell of tourists.

Just then, Faith stumbled through the door. His eyes lit up until he noticed the bruise on her face and the tears in her eyes.

She ran to him and he met her in a comforting embrace.

"Oh my God, Faith. What happened?"

She was unable to answer.

"Did Randy do this to you?"

She nodded affirmatively.

"He practically tried to rape me, and then he kept hitting me and telling me that I had to listen to him because I had nowhere else to go," she sobbed.

"I'm sorry, baby. If you want, you can head back west with me, and we'll figure out something."

"Really?"

"Yes," he answered as he held her protectively. "Are you hungry?"

Once again, she nodded yes. Elvis ordered her a burger and fries plus an ice pack. Then he settled the bill with the waitress.

"Faith, your food will be here soon. I have a few things I need to take care of before I leave. You just grab a bite and try to calm down a little. I'll be back to pick you up in about fifteen minutes."

"Okay," she mouthed as he kissed her on the forehead and turned for the door. "You're not coming back, are you?"

"What? Why do you think that?"

"Because if I was in your shoes, I wouldn't come back."

"I'll be back and soon, I promise," he stated as he walked out the door.

Elvis had no tolerance for men who hit women. He loved women and thought abusing them was an act of weak, cowardly men. Once, when he was a young man, he saw his father strike his mother Gladys. Elvis had grabbed Vernon and slammed him against the wall.

"You will not hit my mama ever again, you hear?"

His father sheepishly agreed to his terms and never again hit her in his presence, though Elvis suspected that he still had abused her while he was away.

Now he waded through the intoxicated people dancing and flashing each other through the streets and made his way back to Randy's. He knocked on the door. A slight man with brown hair and a perpetual smirk on his face answered the door.

"Randy?" Elvis asked.

"Yeah?"

Having confirmed his identity, Elvis landed a karate kick upside Randy's head, knocking him backwards into his house. Elvis discreetly followed him inside, closing the door and proceeding to beat him unmercifully as the sounds of the Mardi Gras celebration echoed from outside.

"This is for Faith," he announced as he landed a final kick to the face, knocking Randy unconscious. Elvis then left the house and headed back to the diner. He opened the door and saw Faith.

"I can't believe you came back," she gasped.

"I told you I would," he replied with a smile as she greeted him with a hug. "Come on. Let's get out of here," he said as he threw a tip on the table and they walked out together.

CHAPTER IX

RETURN TO SENDER

Faith and Elvis left the diner and fought their way through the drunken crowd. They got to the truck and he pulled out of the parking lot and headed for the motel.

"I have a motel room reserved for the night," he told her.

"Okay."

"It'll be nice to sleep in a bed for a change. I reserved only a single bed, though," he mentioned awkwardly. "I can sleep on the floor or something."

"Always the Southern gentleman."

"Yes, ma'am."

"It's okay. We can share a bed," she responded trustingly.

"Are you sure?"

"Yes, but please let me chip in on the room. You've done so much for me already, at least let me do that."

"No. Keep your money."

"Come on. I've got plenty of money, see?" she claimed as she dug in her purse, surprised to find a hundred-dollar bill. "Where did this come from?"

"What?"

"It's a hundred-dollar bill. Jesse, you did this, didn't you?"

"Well, it might have fallen into your purse when we said goodbye," he answered with a wink.

"What are you, my guardian angel or something?"

"No. I ain't no angel."

She crawled over to his seat and kissed him on the cheek, causing him to smile.

"Thank you, but I can't take this," she said.

"Yes, you can. I insist."

"Tell you what: Let me use this to pay for the room. Please."

"Okay. As long as you keep the change."

"Why are you so good to me?"

"Well, maybe I want to restore your faith in humanity."

"That's a tougher job than you know."

"There's the motel coming up," he said as he pulled into the parking lot.

After checking into the motel, Elvis lay motionless on the bed, trying to soak up as much rest as he possibly could while Faith took a quick shower. She came out of the bathroom as Elvis reanimated himself and dragged his carcass into the shower.

The hot water was invigorating, but just barely enough to keep him awake. After getting out of the shower, he combed his hair and changed into clean shorts and a T-shirt. As he opened the bathroom door, he wanted nothing more than to collapse onto the bed and fall quickly asleep, but it wouldn't be that easy.

Sprawled out seductively on the bed was Faith, wearing just her pink lace bra and panties.

"Hi, Jesse," she said, flashing her best bedroom eyes.

"What's going on?"

"I thought I should repay you for all you've done for me."

"I don't believe this. Why is it that you think every man that is nice to you, just wants to get you into bed?" he asked innocently, though secretly aroused by the sexy young vision.

"Life experience."

"I'm sorry. You're really pretty and I care about you, but I don't want to be just another guy who uses you."

"What? Oh, God! I throw myself at you and you turn me down. I'm so embarrassed!" she cried as she quickly threw her T-shirt back on.

"Don't be."

"You must think I'm a total slut."

"No, I don't. It's just a misunderstanding."

"I hope we can forget about this tomorrow."

"It's already forgotten. I just want to go to sleep. I've got a long day of driving ahead of me," he declared as he fell face first into the bed.

"Good night, Jesse," Faith said meekly.

"Good night," Elvis answered with a yawn as he turned out the light.

Somnolence floated over the room like an invisible mist as Elvis and Faith both succumbed to it, but to Faith, much like Elvis, sleep was a battlefield of nightmares and tormented memories.

"No! Stop! Please don't!" she cried out, shattering the calm of the night.

Elvis was quickly awakened as he turned on the lights to see her twisting and writhing, locked inside her nightmare. He rolled over and tried to wake her.

"Faith, Faith!" he called out as he shook her.

She woke up still in the throes of the nightmare as she blindly punched Elvis hard in the face. The force of the blow woke her up and knocked him off the bed. She opened her eyes and instantly realized what she had done.

"Oh my God! Jesse! I'm sorry. I'm sorry. I thought you were my..."

She stopped before finishing her sentence.

"Punching bag?"

"I'm so sorry. Let me see your eye," she pleaded.

She looked at it as the swelling began rising from under the skin.

"How's it look?"

"It's looks okay," she answered unconvincingly.

"Really?"

"No," she admitted.

Strangely, they both burst into laughter. Elvis looked in the mirror to inspect his wound, then looked back at her to see the similar bruise on her face that Randy had given her.

"Hey," he said. "We match."

Though disarming, his humor didn't help her feel any less guilty.

"Jesse, I am so sorry."

"Stop apologizing. I should have known better than to have jumped into the middle of your nightmare."

"Don't do this. Be mad at me, hit me, force yourself on me, but don't just smile and say it's okay. I don't know how to deal with that."

"It's okay," he said with a smile.

"You jerk."

Elvis wrapped his arms around her, clutching her affectionately as he turned off the lights, and they fell asleep in each other's arms.

Elvis loved sleeping with women, not necessarily having sex, but sharing the bed with them. When he was a child and would have bad dreams, he would crawl into bed with his mother. It was like a security blanket to him, a protector from nightmares. He had even shared a bed with Priscilla countless times before the two of them had ever made love, much to her dismay.

After completing his service to his country, Elvis began calling Priscilla in Germany. He invited the sixteen-year-old Priscilla to visit him in Bel-Air during a school break. Priscilla's stepfather was understandably distrustful of Elvis' intentions, but reluctantly agreed, upon reassurances of the two being chaperoned by Elvis' father.

When she arrived in California, Priscilla was chauffeured to Elvis' rented home, where he paused in his game of pool and greeted her affectionately.

"Oh, Cilla, I've missed you so much, baby. I can't believe you're finally here," he said as he cradled her in his arms.

That night, Elvis took her to one side and ushered her up to his bedroom. Priscilla was head over heels in love, and ready to be taken by Elvis. He took her to the bed and sensually undressed her, kissing her passionately, but then stopped.

"Wait a while, baby. I want it to happen at the right place and at the right time," he said tenderly, though Priscilla was clearly eager and ready at that time.

Instead of consummating their relationship that night, they stopped at heavy foreplay, as they would time and again. Elvis loved foreplay, and even seemed to prefer it to intercourse. He would kiss and caress Priscilla for hours without going all the way, all the while insisting that the time wasn't right.

Faith and Elvis woke up together, still locked in an embrace. She gently caressed his swollen eye as he stroked her cheek, neither of them speaking a word, as no words were needed.

They slowly crawled out of bed and gathered their belongings. Elvis grabbed a cup of coffee at the coffeeshop and met Faith at the truck.

The first hundred miles were silent. Elvis wanted so badly to kiss her, but was afraid to give in to his desires, not wanting to hurt her. The image of her half-naked body posed on the bed was now burned in his mind. The loving moments they had shared that morning bubbled inside him, but still he tried to cast them away. He knew it wasn't her age that bothered him; after all, Priscilla was only fourteen when they started dating, and she wasn't the only underage girl he had bedded in his day. It was Faith's vulnerability that he didn't want to betray. He didn't want to be in love right now, either. Love had always been an emotion that ended up destroying him. Besides, he was no longer Elvis the Pelvis, the sex god who had romanced some of Hollywood's most beautiful women; he was Jesse the truck driver, a phantom who hid from existence, the ghost of a dead twin.

Faith was battling feelings of her own. Aside from his kindness and generosity, there was a smoldering intensity about Jesse, something she couldn't quite put her finger on, an aura of greatness, the presence of royalty, and yet something deeper. He possessed a dark duality; he was a handsome man with an ugly secret. He treated her with such sweetness and affection, but the moment any physicality became involved, he pushed her away. The follies of the previous night saddened her and made her feel unworthy of his attention.

"I was thinking," she said finally. "Maybe you should just drop me off in the nearest big city."

"Why would I want to do that?"

"I've brought you nothing but bad luck."

"You're not bad luck; you're good company, and I'm not dropping you off anywhere. I'm going home and you're coming with me."

"To live with you?" she asked in confusion.

"Here's what I'm thinking: I have a little house in San Francisco. It's not much, but it is a roof over your head. Being on the road all the time, I don't have much use for it; I rarely use it for more than a place to keep my stuff and hang my hat between trucking jobs. If you want, you can stay there for awhile, until you can get a job and get back on your feet."

"Jesse, no. You've done too much for me already."

"It isn't a problem. I'm never home anyway. Somebody might as well stay there. In fact, you'd be doing me a favor, you can house sit for me. All I ask is that you keep the place clean and not have any wild punk rock parties," he said.

"Well, as long as I can cook for you, when you're home." she bargained, trying to find some attribute to offer him.

"It's a deal."

She took his lead and snuggled in cozily against his body as they drove on across the unending highway through the heartland of America.

They conversed for hours during the drive, not so much about each other but about music and film, two passions that they both shared.

"Do you read much?" She asked.

"Mostly stuff on religion. I really liked *Autobiography of a Yogi*," he commented.

"What? Yogi Bear finally published his memoirs?" she joked.

"No, it's a book about Hinduism and meditation."

"I thought you were a Christian," she said, noting the contradiction.

"I am, but I think there's value in all religions. They're just different paths to the same destination."

"I can dig that," she said.

"How about you? Read any good books lately?"

"Yeah. I just finished *The Catcher in the Rye*."

"I've heard of it, but never read it. What's it about?" he asked.

"Oh it's a really good book, a classic, really. It's about this teenager, Holden Caulfield, who feels alienated from the world. He gets kicked out of boarding school and runs off to New York City, then basically has a nervous breakdown. He thinks that the whole world is filled with phonies, and he wants to save the youth from losing their innocence. He has this cap, and when he wears it forward, he imagines himself to be a hunter, killing all the phonies in the world, and when he wears it backwards, he's a catcher, trying to catch children as fall they away from innocence," she explained all in one breath.

"Sounds kind of weird."

"I guess you'd have to be a screwed up teenager like me to understand it."

"You're not screwed up."

"Wait till you get to know me better."

Elvis could relate to Faith's feelings of being an alienated teenager. He had felt like an outcast when he was growing up as well. As a young boy, Elvis and his family moved out of their small shack in Tupelo and, with the help of the government, moved into public housing in Memphis, Tennessee. The family was quickly stigmatized as "poor white trash," a label that Elvis despised and, growing up, his shy, sensitive ways made him a target for all of the bullies in school.

As a teenager, he attended Humes High with his cousin and future member of the Memphis mafia, Billy Smith. In school, Elvis was regarded as a loner, never socializing with other students, devoting most of his free time to his studies and playing guitar.

Music had always been a passion of his. When he was just an infant, his mother would take him along with her when she went to work in the cotton fields. Most of people working with her were black, and Elvis' earliest musical influences were the blues and Negro spirituals that they would sing while doing the backbreaking job of picking cotton. As a young boy, Elvis received a guitar from his parents and began playing and singing. One of his favorites was the sorrowful ballad "Old Shep." In Memphis, he found a wealth of music all around him and absorbed everything he heard, from blues to country. He incorporated all of the sounds into his musical repertoire.

As his musical uniqueness grew, so did the uniqueness of his style. He grew his hair long, darkened it, and began greasing it back, a look he would someday make famous. While other boys were affirming their masculinity with Levis, Elvis dressed in pink and black, and looked more like a pimp than a high school student in Tennessee. His bold, brash look earned him more than his share of beatings in high school, but they never deterred him from dressing so brazenly.

Elvis and Faith drove to the coast, chasing the setting sun. They stopped in Arizona to get some sleep, as Faith was unable to convince him to let her drive. The next morning, they got up and headed into California. They drove to San Diego and headed North up Interstate 5, taking a scenic detour along the Pacific Coast Highway once they got past Los Angeles. Faith's eyes lit up as she saw the California coast for the first time. The beautiful waters of the Pacific Ocean crashed majestically against the shore as Faith watched and took it all in. It was late at night as they made their way up to San Francisco, both starting to get a little restless.

"We're almost there now, just a few more miles," he announced, just relieved to be going home.

"I'm curious to see what your place is like."

"I used to live in a much nicer place," he told her, recalling Graceland and feeling somewhat embarrassed by his current state of wealth.

"I'm sure your house is fine."

"Yeah, but I've got to stop at this convenience store and pick up some supplies, since I have a guest and all. Do you need anything?" Elvis asked as he parked the truck.

"Yeah. Could you pick me up some tampons?" she requested, handing him a few dollars.

"Uh, sure, yeah," he answered, feeling weird and uncomfortable about the task.

He took her money and walked into the store. He shopped quickly, getting some food, and then eventually walking as inconspicuously as possible to where the tampons were and blindly grabbed a box.

All of the sudden, a man ran into the store with a gun and pointed it at the cashier. Elvis saw the man and ducked down in the aisle.

"Empty the register and put all the money in the bag or I'll kill you. Do it, now!" the thief screamed, looking around nervously while keeping the gun pointed at the clerk.

"Okay, okay! Just don't shoot," the cashier pleaded.

Elvis felt compelled to help. He had always seen himself as some sort of protector of the people. One time he and his entourage were riding past a gas station when he noticed that two people were about to get into a fight.

"Pull over," Elvis commanded his driver. "Someone's in trouble."

Elvis jumped out of the limousine and ran up to one of the men.

"If you're looking for trouble, you've found it," Elvis stated as he got into his karate stance.

The man did a double take and realized that Elvis Presley had just challenged him to a fight.

"I don't have a beef with you," the man answered, still confused.

Elvis swung out a karate kick knocking the man's cigarette pack out of his breast pocket.

"I didn't think so," Elvis said as he smiled triumphantly at the man and walked back to his limo.

The same sense of duty was stirred in Elvis again as he charged the gunman from behind. With a swift karate chop to the hand, he knocked the gun out of the assailant's grip and then gave the man a kick to the face. The thief was stunned, but pulled out a switchblade and drove it in to the side of Elvis' abdomen. Knowing when to call it a day, the thief ran hurriedly out of the store. Elvis grabbed the gun off the floor and pointed it at the fleeing criminal, but opted not to shoot. Instead, he threw the gun in his coat pocket.

"Are you okay?" the cashier asked as the robber jumped in the getaway car and sped off.

Elvis, realizing that the police would probably be arriving soon, ran out of the store as well.

"Where are you going? Come back!" the clerk yelled as Elvis charged out the door.

He ran to his truck and hopped inside.

"What's going on?" Faith asked noticing the man that had ran out of the store.

Elvis said nothing. He started up the truck and quickly drove out of the store parking lot. Faith, confused by the urgency, looked down and saw the blood pouring from his side.

"Oh my God! What happened?"

"I got stabbed by some guy trying to rob the store," he said calmly as he headed down the road.

"We have to get you to a hospital."

"No. No hospital," Elvis insisted.

"Why?"

"I want to keep the police out of this."

"Why? What's wrong?"

"It's a long story. I just want to get home. We're almost there."

As they arrived at his apartment, Elvis hastily parked the truck. Faith jumped out and ran over to the driver's side, helping Elvis out of the vehicle and having him lean on her as they walked to the apartment door. Elvis gave her the key, and she opened the door and helped him to his bed. She took off his shirt and inspected the wound.

"Damn, Jesse. That cut doesn't look good," she exclaimed, trying to sop up the blood with his shirt.

"Doesn't feel good either."

She took off her own shirt and wrapped it around his waist, using it as a crude bandage.

"Well, the good news is, it doesn't look real deep. I think it's just a superficial wound," she said optimistically.

"What's the bad news?"

"Well, you're losing a lot of blood. I wish you'd go to a hospital," she pleaded.

Elvis ignored her.

"If you don't want to go to the hospital, at least let me call a doctor."

"No!"

"Why not?"

"He might get the police involved."

"What are you mixed up in?"

"Promise me, you won't call a doctor."

"Okay, okay. I promise."

"Faith, I'm scared."

"Don't worry. It's going to be okay," Faith said, holding his head on her lap and stroking his brow. "I just don't want you to die. You're the only person I've ever known who was ever good to me, and I can't lose you," she said as tears streamed down her face.

"Don't cry, Faith. I'll be okay."

"Don't talk. Save your strength."

She held him close to her as he slowly fell asleep in her arms.

CHAPTER X

DON'T CRY, DADDY

The next morning Elvis woke up alone and in pain, but alive nonetheless. The shirt that was tied around him had been replaced with a real bandage.

"Faith?"

She rushed into his room and kneeled by his side, wearing one of his shirts.

"Hi. How do you feel?"

"Not spectacular," he said as he winced in a tired, hushed voice.

"I checked your wound this morning. I think the bleeding's stopped."

"Thanks to you. You know, you may have saved my life last night."

"You've been saving my life every moment since I met you. Is there anything I can get you?"

"Something to drink, I guess."

"Sure. I went to the store and picked some orange juice; that should help you replenish your blood supply," she informed him as she left to get him a glass of juice.

She returned with a glass and gave it to him.

"Thanks," he said as he drank it down.

"You're welcome."

"Nice job with the bandage," he noted. "You'd make a good nurse."

"Really? You think so?"

"Yeah."

"I wanted to be a nurse when I was a kid," she said with a smile.

"You should still consider it."

"I couldn't be a nurse. It's too much school."

"You could be anything you want to be. You're very smart."

"Really?"

"Yes. Perhaps too smart for your own good," Elvis noted with a laugh.

"Hey! I wanted to tell you, I've decided to get a job here."

"Really?"

"Yeah. I figure I could at least help with the bills and stuff."

"You don't have to do that, I can support us."

"No way! I insist. I guess I'll have to dye my hair back to its original color to get a job, though."

"It's San Francisco. Your hair is fine," he laughed.

"I saw a coffee shop on Haight Street that was hiring."

"You'd be perfect for that job."

"So are you going to tell me what happened at that store last night?"

"Well, I was grabbing a few things when this guy ran in. He pulled a gun on the clerk and tried to rob the place. He didn't see me, so I snuck up behind him and knocked the gun out of his hand. Then he pulled out a knife and stabbed me, then ran out of the store."

"Yeah, I saw him and the getaway driver tear out of there," she acknowledged. "Jesse, I admire your bravery and all, but that was a stupid thing to do. You could have been killed."

"Well, I had to do something."

"No, you didn't. That clerk would have given him the money, and the store would have gotten the money back from their insurance. There was no reason for anyone to be a hero," she lectured him. "Why do you feel compelled to fix every problem you see?"

"I don't know. I guess I've done a lot of things in my life that I'm ashamed of, and now I'm trying to make things right. I'm trying to fix my karma, I guess."

"So what did you do that was so horrible?"

"Can't we talk about this some other time?"

"Sure. Whatever you say. Boy, did I have you pegged wrong."

"What do you mean?"

"Until last night, I thought you were some overgrown Boy Scout, or a Jesus freak or something. Now, you're foiling crimes, and hiding from the cops. My image of you is shattered."

"It's not as seedy as you portray it," Elvis said.

"Don't worry. I find you a hundred times more interesting now."

"Your imagination makes more of me than there is."

"Well, why don't you rest and get your strength back?"

"I can't. I have to go to my boss and have my truck unloaded."

"No. You need to get better," Faith maintained.

"Look. I have a job to do, or else the rent doesn't get paid. I just have to drive a couple of miles and let his grunts unload it. Then I'm off for the next two days."

"Okay. Do what you have to do," she sighed. "Are you hungry?"

"Yeah. Sure."

She left the room and began cooking. Elvis climbed out of bed and looked through his coat pockets, finding and pulling out the gun that he had confiscated the night before. He inspected it and looked in the mirror, waving the gun and doing his best Robert DeNiro impression.

"Are you talking to me? Are you talking to me? I don't see anyone else in here, so you must be talking to me," he hammed.

Faith popped into the room, startling Elvis.

"Are you talking to me?" Faith asked.

"What?" he stammered, caught offguard.

"I thought I heard you talking. What's with the gun?"

"Oh, this? Well, when you're on the road, you can't be too careful. I mean, look what happened to me last night."

"Well, I know that I really don't have any say in the matter, but I'm not real comfortable with the idea of a gun in the house."

"What if someone breaks into the apartment and tries to kill us? This is the city of the Zodiac Killer, after all," he reminded, alluding to a serial killer who had stalked San Francisco several years earlier, but was never apprehended.

"What if you think someone is breaking into the house, but it's just me getting a drink of water or something?"

"That's not going to happen."

"I hope."

"Look, I served in the Army, and have owned guns most of my life."

"Well, it's your place and your gun."

"Don't worry. I'm not trigger-happy."

After lunch, he took his truck in to get it unloaded and quickly returned home. For the next two days, Faith babied him and nursed him back to health. Elvis loved the attention and over the next few months, they grew very close. He showed her around the city, visiting sites such as Fisherman's Wharf and the Golden Gate Bridge. They held hands as they walked like a loving couple, only without kisses or romantic words being exchanged.

As the months wore on, Faith decided to put her romantic feeling aside as well. The household they shared was a loving one; she had a roof over her head, and a good friend as a roommate. She didn't want to risk that for anything else.

It was the happiest time of her life. She felt independent, and yet she had someone to lean on who would take care of her. She had gotten a job at a local coffeehouse and it gave her a sense of pride and self-worth. She also had a lot of time to herself; time in which she reflected and reassessed the direction in her life. Jesse was gone most of the time, but when he did come back from his driving jobs, they were inseparable. Despite her romantic feelings for Jesse, she thought that what they had was more important than romance, and she didn't want to jeopardize it the way she knew sex sometimes can. When he was home, they shared a bed. It wasn't sexual, they both just held each other, both trying to keep away the nightmares.

One day, he was reading the paper and Faith was curled up next to him, staring at the television. Suddenly, Elvis' hands began to tremble as tears silently poured from his eyes. Without explanation, he got up and ran off to another room.

"Jesse, are you okay?"

Confused, she reopened the paper to the page that he was reading, trying to find any news article that could have possibly upset him so. She found a headline that got her attention.

VERNON PRESLEY, FATHER OF ELVIS PRESLEY, DEAD AT 63.

The headline puzzled her, providing more questions than answers. The wheels in her mind started turning.

Elvis had locked himself in the bathroom where he could grieve in private. Losing Vernon felt strange to him, it was not the devastating stab in the heart that he had felt when his Mother died, but still it ripped him up inside. It was more than loss. It was guilt. Perhaps it was because he had always felt resentment toward Vernon, a resentment that he never verbalized, but one his father must have sensed.

Maybe it was an Oedipal reaction to his love for his mother that made him hate Vernon at times. Not that there weren't some good reasons for his resentment. Vernon had been a distant father who drank excessively, abused his wife, and could barely support his family either financially or emotionally.

Shortly after Gladys' death, Vernon married a woman named Dee Stanley. Elvis thought that two years was not a long enough time to mourn before remarrying, and he cringed when Vernon brought his bride back to Graceland and had her sleeping in his mama's bed. Elvis quickly had a house built for Vernon and Dee alongside Graceland, a not-so-subtle eviction.

But now, only after hearing of his father's death in the most impersonal of ways, did he realize that he loved him. Now he cursed himself for not loving him more, for never telling him that he loved him, and for treating him like a second-rate parent, paling against the mystique of Gladys Presley. Despite his flaws, Vernon was his father and he loved him, but now he was gone, leaving Elvis as the sole survivor of his family. He wiped his tears and left the bathroom, deciding to bury the grief inside.

He walked down the hall to find Faith waiting for him.

"Are you okay?" she asked sympathetically, giving him a half embrace.

He returned the embrace but remained silent.

"If you want to talk, I'm here for you. If you don't, I'm still here for you."

"I just need to go for a walk."

"Do you want any company?"

"Actually, that would be nice. Just don't be upset if I don't say much."

"Hey, whatever you want," Faith said.

They strolled down Haight Street, taking in the sight of the numerous hippies who merrily roamed the area. Elvis was quiet and self-absorbed and Faith didn't interfere in his introspection. In fact, there was something that she was analyzing in her mind as well.

They entered Golden Gate Park, a tranquil place they often went to together, soaking up the beauty of nature and the free spirit that inhabited most of the park's visitors. They stood together on a little pond bridge staring into the water when Faith broke the silence.

"We're good friends, right?" she asked innocently.

"Yes, of course. The best of friends."

"Do you trust me?"

"Well sure. Why do you ask?"

"I just want you to know that you can tell me anything, and I wouldn't think any less of you or tell anyone."

"Thanks. That means a lot."

"Well, you mean a lot to me. I know you have a lot of secrets and demons inside you, and I just think you would be happier if you let them out sometimes. Maybe by confiding in a good friend," she proposed, hoping to unravel some of the mysteries that consumed him.

"Maybe I will someday. But don't think that my silence is a rejection of you."

He took her hand and held it gently as he stared lovingly into her eyes.

As Faith heard his words, Elvis was distracted by the vision of his young brother Jesse, clinging to a tree, his eyes red with tears. Apparently he had heard of their father's demise, too.

"What are you looking at?" she asked.

"Nothing," Elvis said as he gave a reassuring smile to his twin brother.

CHAPTER XI

TROUBLE

The next few months were somewhat uneventful; the two friends lived their lives, sometimes separately, sometimes together. Elvis spent a lot of time on the road, and when Faith wasn't working she spent many quiet evenings reading. She had studied for and received her GED, and began reading several medical books, inspired by Elvis' encouragement to become a nurse. There was another book she decided to read. It was *Elvis: What Happened?* the semi-biography of Elvis that cast such a dark light on the Elvis Presley myth. Since the day she saw him cry after reading about the death of Vernon Presley, Faith had begun to wonder if it was possible that Jesse really was Elvis. The physical similarities were undeniable, but still she thought the whole concept of his faking his death seemed far-fetched.

One day she was in a supermarket checkout line when she saw a tabloid magazine claiming to have evidence that Elvis was alive; she put the tabloid in her grocery cart and bought it.

Elvis had left a few days earlier to embark on a grueling cross-country drive to Atlanta. This time, he had the gun with him. It was good for protection, and Faith hated having it in the house.

After several long days of driving across the country, he looked forward to coming home to her. His missed her; he missed her laugh and her smile, and after a long road trip, he missed her home-cooked meals. Food was a big part of Elvis' life, and after living on the road and eating mass-produced cheeseburgers, the food that Faith made was heavenly.

Elvis finally arrived in Atlanta and dropped off his shipment. He was also supposed to pick up a shipment to bring back. Unfortunately, due to some snafu, it hadn't arrived yet and wouldn't be there until the next morning. Well-rested, but forced to spend the night in Atlanta, Elvis decided to slip into a local watering hole for a drink or two. The bar was dank and seedy, filled with a motley assortment of rednecks and derelicts. Elvis sat quietly at the bar sipping on his beer, while watching a pool game almost erupt into a fight.

Atlanta was a very new city, even by American standards. The Creek and Cherokee Indians originally occupied the land, and the first white settlement did not arrive until 1812. In 1825, the Creek Indians ceded their lands to the State of Georgia and, a decade later, the Cherokee were driven out of the area along the Trail of Tears by Andrew Jackson.

The city was named Terminus in 1837, because it was the site of a railroad terminal and, in 1845, the name was changed to Atlanta. Due to the railroads, the city grew rapidly and gained a reputation for being a wild bawdy town where drinking, gambling and prostitution flourished.

During the Civil War, its railroads made it an ideal shipping and supply center for the Confederate Army, prompting Union General William Sherman to invade the city and burn it to the ground.

The Atlantans returned to the still smoldering ruins and rebuilt the city, making it better then before, rapidly expanding its size and population. In 1868, the city became the capital of Georgia, and emerged as one of the South's most prosperous cities as well as a symbol of the Union's under-reported savagery.

While nursing his drink, Elvis' mind wandered back to Faith. He couldn't wait to see her again. Despite his best efforts, he was falling madly in love with her. He started to think that perhaps he should put all of his concerns aside and give in to his desires. Then he realized that the depth of his emotion was what really scared him. This was the most he had felt for a woman since Priscilla, and he couldn't bear to face the pain that could come with it.

Elvis downed his beer and ordered another one as a beautiful woman walked into the bar. She had black hair and a very sexy physique, a detail not lost on the men in the bar. This was not a bar for women, something she realized rather quickly. The men in the saloon grew silent and locked in on her like wolves hungry for their prey. Sensing the sinister vibe in the room, she turned around to leave, but a tall, burly, toothless man blocked her exit.

"Where are you going, baby?"

She stammered out an answer, but he interrupted her.

"You can't leave until you have a dance with ole Smitty," he said with a drunken laugh, referring to himself.

Another guy came up to her, cornering her.

"Yeah, and once Smitty gets his dance, then it's my turn."

A couple of other men crowded around her, each leering, groping and taunting her. Elvis knew he had to do something. He decided to try diplomacy first. He took a swig from his beer and walked over to them.

"Hey, honey, you made it after all," he shouted, as if he knew the woman. "Thanks for coming to pick me up. I thought you'd never get here," he said as he ran up and grabbed her by the arm, trying to lead her out the door.

The men were briefly confused by this, but didn't make any attempt to get out of their way.

"Excuse me," Elvis said. "Me and my girlfriend need to go."

"She ain't going anywhere, boy. Hell, after we finish dancing with her, maybe we'll even take turns with you just for laughs," he threatened as he punched Elvis in the stomach, doubling him over.

Two of the guys started beating on him as two rednecks grabbed the woman and threw her onto a pool table, jumping on top of her. Elvis fought back, landing several fists and karate chops, but the odds were against him, and soon they had him beaten to the ground. Elvis was dazed as he watched them start to tear off the women's clothes, he saw the bar's owner laughing and cheering it on. Several repetitive kicks slammed into his head until he felt as if he was losing consciousness. He knew he had to stop this from happening and remembered the gun in his coat pocket.

He quickly pulled out the firearm and began firing. He shot the two men attacking him, and then shot one of the would-be rapists. Shock and confusion swept over the woman and the others in the bar as Elvis grabbed her and ran out the door. Once outside, he ran to his truck, pulling her with him.

"Get in," he yelled as he hopped in the truck and unlocked the door for her. She climbed into the truck and they sped away into the night.

"Are you okay?" Elvis asked several miles later.

"I'm not hurt or anything," she stuttered, still shaken from the incident.

There was silence, and then suddenly, the woman broke down in tears, dropping her face into her hands.

"I can't believe what just happened. Those sons of bitches!" she yelled. Then she grew quiet. "You're not one of them, are you?" she asked suspiciously.

"No, ma'am."

"I guess I should thank you. I mean, who knows what would've happened if you weren't there. Thanks."

"It's no problem, ma'am. I can drop you off at your house if you want."

"That'd be nice of you. I just live a couple of miles away."

As she gave him directions to her house, Elvis began to think about what he just done. He had shot several people in that bar; any one of them could easily be dead. He would be a murderer, and he didn't know if he could live with that guilt. He might have saved a life doing it, though. He had at least prevented the woman from being raped. He decided that the crime justified the action, and there was nothing else he could have done. He just hoped his conscience would buy it.

He pulled up in front of her house and stopped the truck.

"Well, here we are. I hope you can call a friend or something. If you call the police, please don't identify me or my truck," Elvis said.

"Why? You're a hero."

"Well, they might not see it that way."

"Your secret identity is safe with me," she promised. "Do you want to come in?"

"No. I've got to get out of here. I don't want someone to spot the truck."

"Please. Just for a minute. I'm feeling a little weird about walking into an empty, dark house right now," she pleaded.

"Sure. I'll make sure it's safe."

She entered the house and turned on the lights. Elvis then walked through the house making sure no one was hiding, mainly for her benefit.

"The house checks out, ma'am."

She moved toward him and gave him a big hug.

"Thanks for everything."

As she hugged him, she couldn't help staring at the Elvis painting that she had on her wall. She had a revelation, and looked into her hero's face.

"Oh, my God! You're Elvis Presley!"

"No, ma'am, I'm not. That's ridiculous."

Her somber mood quickly took an upswing, as she began jumping up and down.

"I'm your biggest fan. Oh, my God! Elvis Presley in my house!"

"Ma'am, I assure you, I'm not Elvis Presley. Elvis is dead, remember?"

"You faked your death. I knew it!" she said gleefully. "Wait till I tell my friends."

"Wait. Stop!" Elvis barked, deciding he needed to take a different course of action.

"Okay. I am Elvis Presley," he admitted as she began jumping up and down again. "But it's important that no one finds out. Understand?"

She nodded her head affirmatively.

"What you know about me will be our little secret. Just between me and you," Elvis said as he pulled her closer and planted a sizzling kiss on her lips.

After he pulled his lips away, she gave him a smile and promptly fainted.

"I still got it," he declared proudly as he carried her into the bedroom and set her down on her bed.

His ego soaring, he took a rose from a vase on her nightstand and laid it beside her on the bed. Then he let himself out.

The police had gathered at Carl's Saloon. Ambulances had already taken the three men who were shot to the hospital, but one had died on the way. The police began questioning the patrons and ended up with several conflicting reports. A young officer named James Browning decided to have a talk with the owner.

"The guy came running in here, fired a bunch of shots, and then ran off," the owner claimed.

A drunken patron interrupted.

"That was the beer he was drinking. I bet his prints are on that."

"Was he drinking this beer?" Officer Browning asked the owner.

"He may have been. I don't know."

"But didn't you just say he ran in here, fired, and ran out?"

"I don't know. It happened so fast."

"And yet he still had time to order and drink a beer," Browning demanded, smelling a lie.

"Look, I didn't see him until the shots were fired. All right?"

"Well, who was working the bar?"

"I was."

"So, you sold him a beer, yet didn't see him?"

"I don't remember. It was really busy."

"Okay. We'll be in touch," Officer Browning said suspiciously. "Someone have this bottle checked for prints," he ordered one of the other officers.

The next morning Elvis woke up in a cheap motel, recalling his adventure on the previous night. He wondered about the people he had shot. He hoped that they would all live, but he also knew it was wise to get out of town, and out of the state. He stopped back at the supplier's and they loaded up his truck. He then headed straight for the state line. He had the radio on and was trying to find some news about the previous night. After he had waited through commercials and sports scores, the news came on, but the events of the previous night had been overshadowed by a bigger story.

"In Tehran, an angry mob of Iranian protestors have seized the United States embassy. About an estimated ninety embassy workers have been taken hostage by followers of a radical Islamic movement led by the country's new leader, the Ayatollah Khomeini. President Carter is expected to speak soon on this crisis. We will give you more details as they are reported."

As he digested the lead story, his worst fears were confirmed by the next report.

"One dead and two wounded in a late night shooting at a downtown Saloon…"

The rest of the news went through him as he shook his head in disgust.

"Damn!" he shouted as he pounded on the steering wheel.

Now he was a murderer. Now he was wanted for murder.

Elvis pushed the gas a little harder, wanting to get out of Georgia, wanting to get back home. An hour later, he breathed a sigh of relief as he left Georgia behind, but there was still a long way to go.

The Atlanta police department was bustling as usual, even in the early morning. A tired Officer Browning rubbed his eyes drowsily and ran his fingers through his black hair. He had been up all night investigating the bar shooting. He had gotten several eyewitness accounts, most of which contradicted each other, and the fingerprint check had returned from the FBI computer with a very baffling answer.

He walked into the Chief's office, with quite a strange finding.

"Sir, about the Carl's Saloon shooting..." He hesitated.

"Yes. Go on," replied Chief Warren.

"Well, it appears that it wasn't a random shooting, as the owner maintained."

"Really?"

"Yes. According to a few witnesses, the shooter was just drinking at the bar when some woman walked in. A few of the locals started harassing her, and then they threw her down and attempted to rape her. The assailant tried to stop them, but they turned on him, so he started shooting. He then grabbed the woman, and they escaped from the bar."

"So, is this guy a vigilante?"

"I don't know."

"A vigilante..." the Chief muttered. "God, the press is going to have a field day with this!"

"Well, it gets worse," Browning remarked.

"How?"

"I took the shooter's fingerprints off the beer bottle, and ran them through the computer."

"And?"

"Take a look." He showed the Chief the assailant's profile.

"Elvis Presley? Jim, I'm in no mood for jokes."

"I wish it were a joke. I ran it through again, and it checks out."

"But that's impossible."

"Evidently not."

"So, you're telling me that Elvis Presley is alive, and now he's a vigilante."

"Looks that way."

"Who else knows about this?" the Chief asked.

"Aside from me and you, no one."

"Good. Let's keep it that way, and don't let on about the vigilante angle either. Lots of murders go unsolved and nobody asks questions. Vigilantes, however, attract a lot of questions, and I don't want to have to admit our prime suspect is a dead rock star."

"Yes, sir," Browning said soberly, suppressing a grin.

"I want you to see what else you can find out about this case," the Chief was saying. "I want proof he's alive before I let the media in on this."

"You can count on me, sir," Browning said as he left the office.

Elvis began to rest easier as he made his trek across the country, but still the presence of the murder weapon kept him on edge. He had put it under his seat, but it pulsated in his conscience like the telltale heart. The guilt of the man's death and his fear of being arrested double-teamed his psyche and distracted him from the road. Elvis had always been fascinated with guns. He had had a very impressive gun collection in the past and had been quite the marksman in the Army. But he had never fired at a human being before, and now the reality of what a gun could do had radically changed his opinion of them.

Before stopping at a motel in Texas to catch some much-needed rest, he found the nearest bridge and walked across it with the gun in his pocket. The sun had begun setting in a beautiful yet eerie display of colors. He peered out over the side of the bridge and into the rapidly churning river below. Unceremoniously, he took the gun from his pocket and cast it into the river. He watched it fall to its watery death, and become engulfed in the cold, raging waters. As he walked back to his truck, he vowed never to fire a gun again. It was a vow that fate would force him to break.

CHAPTER XII

CAN'T HELP FALLING IN LOVE

While Elvis was out of town, Faith had begun an investigation of her own. She had already read the book by Red and Sonny West, and had noted some starling similarities between Elvis Presley and Jesse King. She was also shocked to discover the troubling personal life of the man she remembered as Elvis, and possibly the man she knew as Jesse.

She had brought home a tabloid magazine with an article about the possibility of Elvis being alive. She had briefly heard that conspiracy theory before, but basically shrugged it off as wishful thinking by a few obsessed fans. She had never heard the details of the theory, but now they spilled off the pages before her.

Aside from claims that Elvis had been growing disillusioned and disappointed with his fame, there were some interesting facts concerning the man and his death. Faith discovered that RCA had greatly boosted production of Elvis albums weeks before his death, and that the name on his grave was misspelled. She read that he would often use the alias Jon Burrows when traveling, and that a man by that name had paid in cash for a one-way flight to Buenos Aires hours after Elvis was reported dead. She read about the numerous mistakes and odd conclusions on the autopsy report. She wondered if it was possible for a man of Elvis' fame and wealth to pull off such a hoax, and if that same man was the person with whom she found herself falling in love.

She read the article over and over, memorizing every detail, but wondered if it was any of her business anyway. Jesse had been nothing but good to her, and if he wanted to live a double life, then maybe that was his prerogative. Sure, they were roommates and good friends, but if he didn't want to tell her, then she should respect wishes. Despite all of those arguments, she decided to keep investigating.

Elvis was making good time on his way home. It was Faith's eighteenth birthday, and he had promised her that he would be there for it. He couldn't wait to see her again. In his mind, he fantasized about giving her a prolonged birthday kiss, but then he told himself that it would be wrong. The Elvis of old wouldn't have thought twice about kissing her and then whisking her off to his bedroom, but he wanted to change. In light of the shooting death in Atlanta, he decided to become more focused on his spiritual side and not give in to temptation. Actually, he had done a pretty good job of it so far, not just with Faith, but also with drugs and his greatest temptation of all, food.

At one hundred and eighty pounds, he was proud of all the weight he had lost and didn't want to put it all back on. Food to him was about more than just pleasure; it was a subconscious link to his mother. As a child, his mother always cooked for him and, growing up poor, it had been her ultimate gift of love for him. He remembered how unhappy she was when they moved into Graceland. He had servants there who could prepare any meal Elvis desired, and suddenly his mother felt useless and unneeded, which added to the downward spiral that ended her life. It was no coincidence that, after his mother's death, his appetite and consequentially his waistline grew dramatically. It was as if by bingeing on food he could somehow get back in touch with his mother's love.

He wasn't completely victorious over temptation, though. Alcohol had become his newest vice. Not that he had become a drunk, but he did find himself using it to fill a void in his life. Ever since he had started drinking beer with Frederick back in Argentina, he had acquired a taste for it. He never used to be a drinker; in fact he was turned off by the whole concept due to his parent's drinking problems.

His father Vernon had the most visible drinking problem of the two. He remembered Vernon always being drunk when he was growing up. Vernon was the worst kind of drunk, the kind who became violent and abusive. His mother Gladys was the one who kept her drinking concealed from him, hiding beers behind the couch and in other places. It wasn't until he was an adult that he caught on to her drinking, but by that time it was too late. When he left for the Army, her drinking escalated, a habit fueled by her loneliness and her worry over her beloved son. Though reported otherwise, it was her alcoholism that eventually caused her death.

Despite his intentions, Elvis had been slowly drifting away from his religious ways. He had been going to church much less frequently and hadn't read from the bible in weeks. There was no dramatic reason for it. It was just something that happened.

Before returning home to the Bay Area, Elvis made a couple of stops. One was to get a birthday cake, and the other was to buy a present for Faith. He had always loved giving people gifts, especially when he was at the top of his wealth. It was not unusual for him to reward his friends' loyalty with expensive Cadillacs and jewelry. Now his budget was a little more humble, but his heart was still as big. He bought Faith a pretty necklace he had spotted. It wasn't made of gold or diamonds, but his intentions were.

As he rested one hand on the steering wheel and stared out at the highway disappearing into a point on the horizon, he continued to think about Faith. He noted some similarities between his relationship with Faith and his relationship with his ex-wife. While he and Faith were not lovers, both she and Priscilla had moved in with him in their teenage years.

Inexplicably, Elvis had managed to talk Priscilla's parents into letting her leave Germany and come to live with him while she finished school. He had promised Captain Beaulieu that his daughter would actually be staying with his father and his second wife, Dee.

In reality, she would spend most of her nights sleeping in Elvis' bed. The living arrangements raised more than a few eyebrows at Immaculate Conception, the Catholic School she attended. For two years, she lived at Graceland in secrecy, becoming a virtual prisoner at the mansion. Elvis picked out her wardrobe and dictated to her how to wear her makeup and hair. She had become Elvis' human Barbie doll.

But this time Elvis didn't want that any more. He had grown bored with everybody doing everything to please him. The past year and a half had made him realize that life was more stimulating when things weren't predictable and customized to his desires. He remembered how he used to tell members of the Memphis Mafia that he was godlike and that he could move clouds with his mind. They would sit outside and watch him appear to move the clouds as if they were chess pieces. They would agree with him, and shower praise upon him and his powers to the point where he began to believe it himself. Now all he wanted was someone who would tell him the truth.

After Elvis arrived in San Francisco, he stopped at his employer's and unloaded his cargo before heading home. Faith greeted him at the door with a hug; he countered with a happy birthday wish and the necklace. She gushed and thanked him profusely, and then he went to the truck and brought in the cake as she shook her head in disbelief.

"You didn't have to do all this for me," she insisted as Elvis set up eighteen candles on the cake and lit them.

"Nonsense. You only turn eighteen once."

To Elvis, she looked more beautiful than ever, partly due to the fact that she had dyed her hair back to its original blond color and gotten rid of the punk-rock streaks of orange and green.

Elvis turned off the lights and went into a soulful rendition of "Happy Birthday," eliciting a strange, confused look from her. When he finished, she made a wish and blew out the candles.

"Since it's your birthday, I think I should take you out somewhere."

"That's not necessary."

"Come on. Indulge me. I've been cooped up in a truck for the last week. I need to go out and have some fun."

"Okay, but since it's my eighteenth birthday, I want to go to a bar."

"Sure. Whatever you want."

"Cool."

"Will this be the first time you've ever drunk alcohol?" Elvis asked, hopelessly naïve.

Faith answered only with ringing laughter.

"The second time?" Elvis playfully asked, realizing he was the butt of the joke.

As promised, Elvis took her to a bar. It was a bar that he had never been to, but its name sounded chic and European, and its marquee promised dancing. They walked into the bar and disco music was playing. "YMCA" blared through the sound system, and the male dancers on the floor were bumping and grinding against each other. Other than that, it looked like any hopping disco, complete with a mirrored ball and flashing lights accentuating the dance music.

"Wait a minute, is this a gay bar?" Elvis gasped.

"Yeah," Faith declared as she began doubling over with laughter.

"Let's get out of here!"

"No way. This is too funny. Besides, it's my birthday; you have to do what I say."

He bought Faith a drink and brought it over to their table. They toasted to her birthday, as they both took a healthy sip.

"Not that I'm not amused, but why did you take me to a gay bar?" she finally asked.

"I heard they played disco. I thought all you teenagers liked disco," Elvis stated defensively.

"Jesse, I'm into punk rock. I hate disco more than menstrual cramps," she joked, causing Elvis to blush. "Besides, disco's been dead for awhile. All the same, do you want to dance?"

"I can't dance," he lied as he looked nervously around at all the gay men dancing together.

"Jesse, shut the hell up!" Faith said suddenly, laughing.

"What? What did I do?"

She took a sip from her drink and stared into his sullen eyes.

"I know who you are."

"That makes one of us," he joked.

"You're Elvis Presley. Aren't you?" she interrogated as the smile left his face.

"What are talking about?"

"Come on. At least Clark Kent wore glasses. You just have a beard. You look like him. You talk like him. You are him. Admit it."

"You're forgetting one thing," he said. "Elvis died. Maybe you read about it. It was in all the papers."

"Well, the only paper I've read recently was a tabloid, and it claimed to have evidence that Elvis faked his death. But I didn't know for sure until today, when you sang 'Happy Birthday' to me."

"Faith, come on. Talk about grasping for straws -!"

"I did some research. I bought the book *Elvis: What Happened?* and everything you told me about yourself fits perfectly. I put the pieces together, and it all adds up to Elvis."

"Kids today, you all have such active imaginations," he muttered dismissively as he gazed out to the dance floor.

She grabbed his jaw and turned his face towards her, forcing him to stare into her eyes.

"Look, whatever you did, I'm sure you had your reasons, and I don't want to expose you or anything. I just want the truth. We're friends. I think you owe me that much."

Elvis' mind spun in circles for many moments as he downed his drink.

"Okay, you want the truth? I am Elvis Presley. So, now what do you want from me?" He asked with defeat in his voice.

She gave him a quick kiss on the lips.

"I want to go out on the dance floor and boogie with Elvis Presley."

She grabbed his hand and dragged him out to the floor, and they danced together surrounded by a roomful of gay men. Elvis shook his moneymaker and swiveled his hips as he hadn't done in years, though still holding back, freaked out by a couple of lustful glances from some of the men dancing. After several up-tempo disco songs, Elvis and Faith embraced and swayed together in an emotional slow dance as "How Deep Is Your Love?" echoed romantically through the hall and multi-colored lights bounced off the spinning disco ball above their heads.

They arrived home hours later, both more than a little buzzed as they embraced, slightly giving in to their pent-up desires.

"I'd love to you hear you sing one of your songs to me."

Elvis started singing a drunken, yet beautiful *a cappella* version of "Are You Lonesome Tonight?". As soon as he finished singing, she grabbed him and planted a passionate kiss on his lips. He returned the favor as they groped each other and began madly tearing off each other's clothes. He picked her up and carried her to his bed, kissing her softly but forcefully, his lips traveling up and down her young naked body, gently caressing her skin as she ran her fingers through his hair.

He stroked her breasts as they kissed, fulfilling both of their long dormant fantasies. He entered her swiftly and forcefully as the experienced and passionate lover that he was worked his magic. Her mind reeled with passion. Two lost souls merged in flesh and became bound by affection. They climaxed together in an intermingling of love and lust that caused them both to cry out in ecstasy. They paused briefly to hold each other and gaze into each other's eyes, and then reconvened in their lovemaking, lasting into the night.

It had been a busy day at the Atlanta Police Department; Officer Browning had spent the past few days investigating the shooting at the local bar. He questioned some of the witnesses in more detail. One saw the assailant and the woman drive away in a white commercial truck with California plates. Browning was reporting his findings to the chief when a man in a black suit entered his office.

"I'm Special Agent Jericho, from the FBI. I need to speak with Police Chief Kroeger."

The chief simply nodded, and Browning excused himself.

"A few days ago," Jericho began without formalities, "one of your officers accessed our computer and matched fingerprints belonging to this man." He showed the Chief a dossier belonging to Elvis Presley.

"Elvis Presley? You must be joking," the Chief said, playing dumb.

"The FBI doesn't joke," Jericho said bluntly. "Look, we know you have information on this. So stop playing games and tell me what you know. One lawman to another."

The Chief took a deep breath and decided to cooperate.

"Okay. Here is what we know…" he said.

Elvis woke up with Faith in his arms. She was still asleep. As he stared into her beautiful young face, he knew that he was in love. Love scared Elvis. He had loved his mother, he had loved Priscilla, and they had both left him; the pain still festered in his heart. This girl was different, he thought, a troubled angel, a woman who would need him as much as he needed her.

She awoke as he began stroking her hair. He kissed Faith gently on her lips and she smiled.

"Good morning…Elvis," she said with a gleeful giggle.

"Did you have a happy birthday?"

"The best ever." She yawned and stretched. "So tell me, why did you do it? Fake your death, I mean."

Elvis took a deep breath and pondered his next words.

"I guess I couldn't take being that thing called Elvis Presley, the rock star, the icon, the commodity. I weighed over three hundred pounds, and was addicted to a smorgasbord of prescription pills. I just needed to be a real person for a change, and if I hadn't done what I did, believe me, I'd be dead by now."

"Well, somehow I think you made the right decision, as crazy a decision as it was. I mean, you've gotten off the pills, lost a ton of weight, and best of all you're alive and with me," she told him with a smile.

"So, are you ever going to come forward and tell the world?"

"No, I can't. It wasn't a publicity stunt. It was a choice I had to make."

"That's too bad. You could really shock the world if you were to show up on *The Tonight Show* or *Saturday Night Live*."

"I think I've shocked the world enough for one man."

Faith smiled and gave him a playful kiss.

"So, what are we now, boyfriend-girlfriend?" he wondered.

"I don't know. We're two people who live together, like each other, and have sex. That's good enough for me, for now, at least. I'm perfectly content being Elvis' little Lolita," she joked as she kissed him seductively.

"I guess I can't argue that," Elvis whispered as he kissed her back.

Emotions and lust brewed up as they kissed and caressed each other. He climbed on top of her and they made passionate love again.

CHAPTER XIII

HOLLY LEAVES AND CHRISTMAS TREES

Christmas Eve quickly arrived, and Elvis had a song in his heart. He loved Christmas, he loved giving presents, and most of all he loved Faith. He hadn't told her that yet; he was unsure how those words would affect their relationship. He was happy with the way things were and didn't want anything to change, and those words had a way of changing everything.

He had bought a tree, and took great care in grooming it, making it sparkle the way his trees had in Christmases passed. He wished he had the money to buy Faith a mountain of gifts, but still he couldn't wait until Faith opened her presents.

Faith, on the other hand, hated Christmas. Cynical beyond her years, Faith loathed the holidays with a passion. Elvis wasn't sure why, but he desperately wanted to change her opinion of the Yuletide season.

He remembered his first Christmas with Priscilla. Still a teenager, Elvis had made arrangements with her parents, who begrudgingly allowed her to visit Elvis in America for the second time. This time she would stay at Graceland.

After leaving Germany, she met Vernon and his new wife in New York, where they caught a connecting flight to Memphis. Elvis had pulled out all the stops for her visit, stringing miles of Christmas lights all over Graceland, and putting up a life-sized nativity scene in the yard.

The visit got off to a shaky start, however, as Elvis, sensing anxiety in Priscilla, very irresponsibly gave the teenager some pills to relax her. She quickly fell unconscious and didn't wake for two days. When she awoke, she was heartbroken to learn that a large portion of her trip was already over. Elvis vowed to make it up to her, and on Christmas morning, as snow fell on Memphis, Elvis buried her in an avalanche of gifts.

She was nervous as Elvis opened his gift from her. She doubted that she could ever give this man who could buy anything he desired something that he could cherish. She succeeded, though, with a beautiful music box cigarette case that was rigged to play "Love Me Tender" as he opened it.

"Oh, baby, I love it," he had gushed, genuinely pleased by her taste in gifts.

Elvis hoped that this Christmas could be as special.

When Faith arrived home, Elvis sprang into action. He greeted her as she walked through the door, stopping her and pointing out the mistletoe that hung above their heads. After giving her the mandatory holiday kiss, he sat her down in front of the tree and brought her a drink. Elvis grabbed his guitar and began playing a medley of his favorite Christmas songs, many of which he had once recorded -- "White Christmas", "I'll be Home for Christmas", "Merry Christmas Baby" and, of course, "Blue Christmas," playfully wearing a Santa hat as he sang to her. Once he finished singing, he took off the hat and placed it on her head.

"Tonight, you can be Santa Claus."

"Oh, boy," she said sarcastically, while looking adorable with the red cap hanging off to the side of her head.

"Come on. Don't be a scrooge."

"Okay. So what do I have to do?"

"Just grab gifts from under the tree and hand them out."

"Okay, here. This is to you from me," she said as she handed a thin, rectangular present to Elvis.

Elvis tore off the wrapping paper to reveal a book on transcendental meditation.   "Wow thanks, baby."

"I figure you're into all those books about eastern religions," she began to say.

"Okay, my turn," she interrupted as she began opening a gift from Elvis.

Faith unwrapped the gift; it was a medium-sized brown teddy bear. She smiled warmly as she hugged it.

"Aww, it's so cute! It'll always remind me of you. Hey, don't you have a song called 'Teddy Bear'?"

"As a matter of fact, I do," he whispered as he began singing the song's refrain while inching over and kissing her.

They resumed trading gifts. He had gotten her some jewelry, clothes, and perfume, and she gave him some books, a sweater, and a capo for his guitar.

"I hope your opinion about Christmas has changed a little," Elvis remarked.

"Oh, it has. This is the best Christmas ever, though that isn't saying much."

"Why? What was wrong with your Christmases?"

"Christmas Eve, my parents would always get rip-roaring drunk and then start fighting. It never failed. Of course, I never got anything good, or anything I wanted. There was no money to buy me anything. They spent it all on booze. So, here I am, some kid who had been told that if you were good all year, then Santa would bring you nice presents. So all year I'd be good, and on Christmas morning, I'd get some cheap, crappy gifts while my bratty neighbors would get every toy imaginable."

"I'm sorry. I guess I assumed that everyone had a happy childhood."

"Happy childhood? My God, Elvis, you've had a happy life. Your entire existence has been a fairy tale."

"I know it may seem that way, but I've had my crosses to bear."

"Come on. For twenty years, you were insanely rich, famous, and beloved. There was nothing you've ever wanted that you couldn't buy, or snap your fingers and have given to you."

"That's not fair. I grew up in a shack in Mississippi during the Depression. My parents drank and I never got any good presents as a child, either."

"But at least you liked your parents. I saw you cry the day you read about your dad. I know how you feel about your mother, and you're lucky to have that bond. It's something I'll never have, and on Christmas I miss it the most."

"I'm sorry to hear that," he said softly as he put his arm around her.

"It's okay, and thank you. It means a lot to at least have one enjoyable Christmas," she said as she laid her head upon his shoulder.

They began kissing as they heard the first of twelve chimes sound from the clock.

"It's midnight. It's now officially Christmas," she noted.

"Merry Christmas, baby," he responded, as they continued with their kisses. The emotions of the night quickly spilled over into passion as they made love on the living room floor by the Christmas tree.

The next morning, Elvis awoke in bed with Faith. He looked over at his sleeping angel. The teddy bear that he had given her was clutched tightly in her arms. It was then that Elvis realized that for all of her toughness and street smarts, she was still just an insecure little girl, desperately in need of something to cling to, something to hold on to, in a world where she had never been allowed to be a child.

A week later, they celebrated the coming of a new year and the end of a decade as they watched Dick Clark welcome in 1980.

"The seventies are almost over. Thank God!" Faith declared. "No more disco, no more smiley faces, no more polyester leisure suits."

They watched the ball drop in Times Square and marked midnight with a kiss once more. That was how the Eighties began for Elvis, a picture perfect moment, tasting the lips of his beautiful young lover. He hoped that the rest of the decade would be as blissful, but deep in his heart he knew that there was nowhere to go but down.

The next few weeks were filled with romance and lovemaking, as they both threw themselves fearlessly into each other's arms. The apartment was a comfortable little love nest built for two, and they indulged each other's fantasies and desires. They went out to romantic dinners, and walked along the piers of San Francisco. He told her stories about his life, the fame, the wealth, the people he met, and the things he had experienced. He serenaded her with his music, playing his guitar and singing love songs to her. He explained how he had faked his death, and told her about his exile in Argentina, his encounter with Hans Mueller, even the shooting in Atlanta.

One night, they were sleeping in bed together, when Elvis woke up screaming; his cries woke up Faith as well.

"What's wrong?" she asked, hugging him.

Elvis began to realize his horror was just a dream as he caught his breath.

"It was just a nightmare."

"I know. You've had a lot of them. What are they about?"

"Nothing. I don't want to talk about it," he stated sheepishly as he threw the covers over his head.

Faith had hoped that he would tell her about his nightmares. They happened frequently and she knew that they always upset him. It was a missing piece of the puzzle that would have helped explain the enigma that was Elvis Presley, the most guarded secret of a man defined by secrets. She of all people knew how haunting nightmares could be. It was a nightly war that she fought as well. Since she had moved in with him, though, her nightmares had gone away, as if he were some great protector who shielded her from bad dreams. She wished that she could have the same power over his demons.

The next day, they were gazing out over the Golden Gate Bridge, when he confessed something he had longed to tell her.

"Faith, I love you."

Her eyes lit up and she kissed him.

"Oh Elvis, I love you too. I always have, even when I thought you were just a truck driver named Jesse."

They kissed passionately on the bridge as her blond hair twisted and swirled in the cold wind coming off the bay. When they arrived home, he threw her on the bed and ravished her, much to her delight. They had a great sex life. Elvis always had a kinky side to him, a side that Faith gladly indulged. But at the end of the day, they were still friends, cosmic twins who lived for each other.

It was the happiest time in Elvis' life since he had faked his death, perhaps ever. However, something seemed amiss, not with Faith, but with the world, a strange feeling, as if he was being watched. His suspicions were heightened when he went out to get the mail. Across the road he noticed a mover's truck. There was nothing odd about it, until he remembered that it had been there for several days.

He walked across the street to inspect it; he didn't notice anything out of the ordinary, except for a very low buzzing sound from the inside, like some kind of electronics. Unsure of what was going on, he decided to go back in his apartment and forget about it.

As he crossed over to his side of the street, a small black car pulled up next to him. The back door flew open as a man dressed in a black suit grabbed Elvis and pointed a gun at him.

"Get in or die," he ordered.

Elvis reluctantly climbed into the car, and it quickly sped away.

CHAPTER XIV

CAUGHT IN A TRAP

As the car sped off, the man in the back seat handcuffed Elvis' hands behind his back.

"What is this about?" Elvis shouted.

There was no answer, as a gag was put in his mouth and a black hood was placed over his head.

Elvis struggled, but to no avail. He didn't know who this man was, or what he wanted with him, but he was certain he was about to die.

The car eventually came to a stop, and Elvis was escorted out of the car and into a building, where he was led down a long hallway. He was then placed into a chair as the hood and gag were removed, but the handcuffs remained.

Elvis got his first view of his surroundings as his eyes readjusted to the brightness. He was in a plain, empty, dark room with a cheap table in front of him, and a bright light shining from above the table. Across the table stood the man who had pointed the gun at him. He was a tall, rigid looking man in his late thirties, wearing a black suit and sunglasses. His hair was black and greased back, and his face was cold and expressionless.

"Elvis Aron Presley? Hi, I'm Special Agent Jericho, with the FBI. I'm pleased to meet you. Big fan," he stated insincerely. "We here at the FBI have been following you very closely of late. Let's see, first-degree murder and fraud, for starters. I don't think your fans would like the new direction your career has taken. However, obtaining a false Social Security number is the charge that concerns the FBI the most. It's a federal offense, you know. You're looking at twenty years in jail, easy. Of course, I could make those charges disappear with one stroke of a pen. Come to think of it, I could make you disappear with one stroke of a pen. Which action I take depends on you."

"What do I have to do?"

"Play ball."

"How do I do that?"

"Actually, if I'm not mistaken about you, it's something you might actually enjoy. It might even fulfill a lifelong dream of yours."

"What is it?"

"I want you to join the FBI."

"Be serious. Why would you want me?"

"I think you'd be a natural. You've served valiantly in the Army. You're proficient with firearms, a black-belt in karate, and best of all, you're expendable."

"What do you mean, expendable?"

"To put it bluntly, you're already dead."

"Look, you can't treat me this way. I'm a personal friend of former President Nixon," Elvis boasted.

"Funny thing, ever since Watergate, that doesn't mean a whole hell of a lot. In December of 1970, you met with officials of the FBI volunteering your services to destroy the anti-establishment movement in the entertainment world. You professed a belief that the Smothers Borothers and Jane Fonda were responsible for poisoning the minds of young people, and that the Beatles were responsible for social unrest with their unkept appearance and suggestive music."

"So?"

"Well, the FBI has decided to take you up on your offer."

"That was a long time ago. The times have changed."

"The more things change the more they stay the same. Since the end of World War II there has been one movement that has threatened this nation more than any other. Do you know what it is?"

"Communism?" Elvis guessed.

"No. It's rock and roll."

"You're not serious."

"I'm dead serious. Haven't you ever wondered why you were drafted into the Army at the peak of your career? It was because you were a threat to the establishment. Your Negro music and your suggestive gyrations had begun to turn an entire generation against us. So we drafted you and sent you overseas. We thought we could make the American youth forget about you. Of course, we were wrong. We underestimated our enemy. You did your service like a man and became a top-notch soldier, and returned to America an even bigger star than when you left."

"I'm sorry that I disappointed you."

"Don't worry. Now you can make it up to us. There is an underground terrorist faction masquerading as a musical and political organization, determined to destroy the government, and the military. It wears the mask of liberal activism, spreading its message through music, concealing the face of violent revolution."

"You're kidding, right? The Sixties are over buddy. You're about a decade too late," Elvis laughed.

"Sure, the hippie movement is over. People have traded their LSD for cocaine, and their rock music for new wave, but the Eighties will be a new day. The message is still out there and so are the messengers. We have reason to believe that there is an underground plot in the world of music to give rebirth to that shameful decade. Instead of peaceful protest, though, they want achieve their goals through anarchy and murder, and with that peanut farmer of a President in office, there's no telling how far it could go.

"Mr. Presley. I know you've always been a patriotic, God-fearing, Southern boy who gladly served his country when asked. Hell, I want to personally shake your hand for giving us Hans Mueller. But there are others in rock music who are not as loyal to the American way. Their subversive messages have already caused us to lose Vietnam. How many more wars can we afford to lose? There are factions in the music world that wish to attempt a violent overthrow of our government."

"So what do you want me to do?" Elvis asked, befuddled.

"Infiltrate the scene. It's strange, you know. I can train a man to hit a bull's eye from five hundred feet away. I can train a man to live off insects and grub worms, to withstand pain and torture, but I can't train someone to sing and play guitar with soul and passion."

"And that's where I come in."

"Exactly."

"You're forgetting one thing. I am Elvis Presley. I think most musicians would recognize me."

"Of course, but we have a great plastic surgeon for that."

"You want to carve up my face?" Elvis asked with outrage.

"How long do you think having a beard is going to conceal your identity from the world? You have one of the most recognizable faces on the planet. A beard isn't going to hide you for long. You want anonymity? I can give it to you. Then, after you complete this mission, you'll be free to live out your life however you desire. So what will it be, Mr. Presley?"

"Do I have a choice?"

"Yes. Death, prison, many choices indeed."

"Well, gee, in that case, my answer is yes, but you have some choices to make, too."

"Such as?" the agent asked.

"What kind of agent do you want for this job? A reluctant slave with a gun to his head, or a grateful and loyal servant who's behind your cause?"

"What do you want?"

"It's my roommate, Faith. No harm can come to her," he insisted.

"Don't worry. We're the FBI. We're not monsters."

"That remains to be seen. However, if I disappear without a trace, she might report it. Let me send a Dear Jane letter to her, telling her how I have to go away or something. Of course, you would be free to inspect it before it's sent," he proposed.

"Is that all?"

"No. I also want ten thousand dollars. Not for me, but for her."

"Why?"

"She's down on her luck. Ten grand could get her pointed in the right direction," he argued.

"I'm so touched, but no deal."

"Look, You guys spend ten thousand dollars on paper clips. I think it's a reasonable fee for all that you're asking me to do."

"Very well. She can have the money."

"And there's one more thing I want."

"What is it, Mr. Presley?" the agent demanded angrily.

"An FBI badge."

A smile cracked Jericho's face.

"Why do you want a badge?" Jericho asked, somewhat amused.

"I collect them. I've got several police badges from across the country and a DEA badge from Nixon. Now I want an FBI badge."

"No problem. By the time I'm through with you, you'll have earned it."

Jericho grabbed a pen and notebook, and laid it on the table. Then he proceeded to remove the handcuffs from Elvis' wrists and put them away.

"Now write that letter," Jericho instructed as he left the room.

Elvis sorted the details out in his mind. He felt his heart break as he realized that he would probably never see Faith again. That was probably the least of his worries, though. Elvis cleared his mind of his current danger, and concentrated on Faith. It was such a shame that their relationship would have to end so prematurely. As he felt the pains of heartbreak burn in his chest, he cursed himself for falling in love again. He hoped that Faith would be spared the pain that he was feeling. He penned his letter to her, in hopes that it would somehow soften the blow.

> Dearest Faith,
> My heart aches with this news, but I have to go away for a while. Please understand that this is something I have to do, and not a rejection of you. I hope that our friendship has restored your faith in people. In case it hasn't, I've also enclosed a check for ten thousand dollars. Please use it to better your life and to help others. I hope somehow we can meet again, as I will love and miss you forever.
> Love always,
> Jesse

His eyes watered as he wrote his goodbyes, then he collected himself and gave the letter to the agent. Elvis was then taken to a locked room where he was told to wait until further instruction. Alone in his cell, Elvis lamented sadly about Faith, then decided to bury his feelings and help complete his mission.

The next morning, Faith heard a knock on the door. She was very fearful of what news waited on the other side. Elvis had disappeared the day before without a trace. She had debated calling the police, but knew that she couldn't, for fear of exposing his identity.

She opened the door with great trepidation, but was greeted by a courier on the other side.

"Hello. I have a letter for Faith Rogers," the man announced.

"That's me," she stated nervously.

He handed her the letter and made her sign for it before leaving. She opened the letter and immediately recognized the handwriting. She cried as she read the heartfelt words, and was confused by the check that fell into her lap. The money was a small consolation, the greater gift was the knowledge that Elvis was alive somewhere.

Nonetheless, she was heartbroken. She was also scared. Knowing his secret identity, she began to wonder what forces had caused him to do something so rash. The vagueness of the letter was a flashing red light to her. She knew he was a good man who cared for her and would have given a better explanation for his disappearance. It was obvious to her that he had been forced to leave, and that the letter had been written under duress. Whoever had abducted Elvis might soon come back for her. The following morning she cashed the check, grabbed her belongings and got on a train, determined to disappear into the anonymous underbelly of America.

CHAPTER XV

THE WALLS OF JERICHO

In 1957, Elvis Presley ruled the world. He was the biggest and brightest star in the universe. He was loved by women, envied by men, and hated by parents. He had seduced a nation of young teenage girls with his brooding good looks and scandalous gyrations. All of that was threatening to come to an end however, when Elvis received his draft notice from the Army. Parents, preachers, and demagogues alike rejoiced when they heard the news. Finally, this young brash singer who had brought evil Negro music to Middle America would get his comeuppance from the United States military. To his credit, Elvis took the news in stride and did not use his celebrity to get a cushy stint entertaining troops and making appearances on behalf of the Army. Instead, he insisted upon being treated the same as any other person drafted by the military. Nonetheless, his critics salivated at the assumption that Pvt. Presley would fall flat on his face, proving to the world that Elvis the Pelvis was nothing more than an effeminate tenderfoot. But Elvis wouldn't give them the satisfaction.

Once in the Army, Elvis dedicated all of his energy to becoming the best soldier he could be. Knowing the eyes of the world were upon him, he strove to outshine every soldier in his squad, quickly gaining the hard-earned respect of his instructor, Sgt. Norwood, and soon the world. He became an expert marksman and a diligent overachiever, causing his sergeant to once remark, "Boy, if that music career of yours doesn't work out, the Army would love to have you back."

It was this same commitment to excellence that possessed Presley again, this time as a prospective FBI agent. Elvis had always longed to work in law enforcement. He had already used his power and fame to acquire police badges from numerous counties across the nation. In some of his stranger moments, he would sometimes pull over traffic violators, flash his badge and let them off with a warning, causing many a perplexed driver to scratch their head and wonder, "Wasn't that Elvis Presley?"

The badge that Nixon had given him was one that he had acquired on a drug-inspired whim one day. He and the Memphis Mafia were flying to Washington. On the plane he began having a conversation with a Vietnam veteran returning home from battle. Elvis became by the young soldier's story and pulled out a wad of cash and gave it to him. After having his sense of patriotism stirred, the desire to have a federal badge suddenly came over him.

"When we get to Washington, let's go to the White House. I want a DEA badge," Elvis coolly commanded.

Once they got to the White House, Elvis and his buddies strolled in as if they were simply going to a local tavern to get a drink.

"I'm Elvis Presley. I'm here to see President Nixon," Elvis told White House aide Dwight Chapin, as if Nixon had been eagerly waiting for him.

Confused, the president's people scrambled to find Nixon, reaching one of his personal assistants.

"The King is here to see the President," the aide announced.

"The King? Of what country?" Nixon's handler naively asked.

"The king of rock and roll, Elvis Presley," the aide clarified, and went on to relay a message that Elvis was here to lend his services in the war against drugs.

The staffers hastily assembled a meeting between Elvis and the President. Elvis was then shown into the befuddled President's office. Elvis volunteered his support, offering to be an anti-drug spokesman and possibly even an undercover agent.

"Yes, that would be very helpful," a confused Nixon replied, not knowing what to make of this man wearing a purple crushed velvet suit with a cape and a giant gold belt, looking like a gay superhero.

As they talked and shook hands, Elvis quickly cut to the chase.

"Mr. President, I was wondering if you could get me a badge from the Narcotics Bureau? I collect badges."

Nixon quickly agreed, named Elvis a "special assistant," and then presented him with a badge. Elvis was so happy and so high that he broke all White House protocol and gave Nixon a gracious bear hug as his astonished aides looked on. From that moment on, the badge served as an inspiration to him.

The next morning, Agent Jericho was surprised to find a completely different man than the one he had encountered only a dozen hours earlier. Obedient, disciplined, and eager to serve, Elvis slipped on the mask of super-soldier once more. The first day however, he was treated more like a lab rat than a G-man, being poked and prodded with needles and questions. After he had taken a battery of tests and physical examinations, Jericho handed him two books that were a study in contrasts. One was on FBI procedures and the other a compilation of left-wing manifestos and propaganda.

"I expect you to read and study both books, especially this communist-loving book of lies," Jericho instructed. "If you're going to go undercover, you need to know how your enemy thinks. In fact, in that book I've also included a number of anti-war and anti-establishment folk-rock songs that I want you to learn," Jericho continued.

Elvis flipped through the book as Jericho got up and left the room. He returned with an acoustic guitar.

"This will be your weapon of choice," Jericho stated as he set the guitar down at Presley's side. "You have a lot to do, and not much time. So I suggest you get to work while we await the results of your tests."

Elvis spent the next few days sitting in his room studying the books and learning the songs as Jericho watched him through a two-way mirror. Elvis was a very focused person. When he set his mind to something new, he excelled at it, just as he had done with music, the military, and karate.

The next day, Jericho entered Elvis' room with a rare smile on his face.

"Good news, Mr. Presley. You've passed all of our examinations and I shall now begin your training. From now on, you will be referred to only as Jesse King," he informed him.

Elvis nodded in acceptance.

"Now get your things and follow me. We have a plane to catch," he instructed.

Jericho and Presley were chauffeured to a clandestine airport, where they boarded a private FBI jet headed for Washington D.C., to a secret training center. As the plane lifted off, Jericho handed Elvis a stack of song lyrics.

"If you're going to infiltrate the underground world of subversive music, it will be necessary to have a collection of original protest music. We've compiled an assortment of anti-establishment lyrics for you to perform. They're just lyrics, though. How they are sung and what chords you play are up to you," he said.

"Okay," Elvis conceded, "but I was never much of a songwriter."

"I think you'll do fine. Folk-rock-is more about lyrics than melody, anyway," Jericho reassured him, as if he was a music expert.

Elvis skimmed through the lyrics and was surprised by their quality.

"These are really good lyrics. Who wrote them?"

"Who knows? I'm sure you've seen ads in the paper asking people for lyrics to be set to music."

"Yes."

"Well, we placed some similar ads in magazines like *Rolling Stone,* and papers like *The Village Voice,* asking for political lyrics. Of the hundreds we received, there were about twenty that were actually good. Those are the lyrics that you now possess."

"Sounds pretty sneaky."

"Here's the funny part. Thanks to those ads, we now have the names and addresses of hundreds of subversive songwriters in the country that we can now investigate."

"I think you and my buddy, Nixon could have been good friends," Elvis remarked.

"Actually, I knew Nixon," Agent Jericho said.

"Really?"

"Yes. Who do you think Deep Throat really was?" he asked with a smile.

"You were Deep Throat?"

Jericho simply responded with a devilish grin.

"But why? Why would you of all people want to bring down the Nixon presidency?"

"He was getting too powerful. He needed to be put in his place. Besides, I was personally insulted that he would break into the Democratic headquarters and not invite me," he quipped, sounding like a jealous lover.

After he had studied the mountain of material he was given, Elvis' vigor gave way to exhaustion and he drifted off to sleep. Jericho awakened him as they approached Washington. After getting off the plane, they were then shuttled to a secret base, where Elvis was given a room and then taken on a brief tour of the area in which he would be training. Then he was fed and sent back to his room to study, sleep and await further instructions.

The following day, Elvis began a course of intense physical training, including obstacle courses, jogging and weight training. The first couple of days were rough on him, but he endured, and was soon becoming a lean, mean, spying machine. At the end of the week, Elvis was taken to a shooting range.

"According to your military records, you were a very good shot. Let's see if that is still the case," Jericho said as he handed Elvis a gun.

"I can't shoot a gun anymore."

"Would you mind telling me why?"

"After I killed that man in Atlanta, I made a promise to myself that I would never fire a gun again."

"Promises are made to be broken, Mr. King. Now shoot the target, or I'll shoot you," Jericho told him dryly as he walked away.

Elvis looked down at the gun and contemplated putting a bullet in Agent Jericho, but knew that wouldn't be wise. He then stared at the target, pointed the gun and started firing, shredding the target with a series of heart shots.

After seeing the results, Jericho was mildly impressed. More targets were set up and shot by Elvis with similar results.

"Damn, son. I think you missed your calling in life. Instead of singing, you should have been working for us," Jericho praised him.

Elvis just gave him a cocky sneer and put the gun down.

The training continued as weeks turned into months, taking Elvis through a crash course on becoming an undercover agent. He learned surveillance techniques, practiced karate as well as conventional hand-to-hand combat, and became a master of disguises. Elvis' progress had surpassed Jericho's expectations, and by the time he was scheduled for plastic surgery, he had written music for all of the lyrics given to him.

Jericho was more than pleased with Elvis' development. As a hardened veteran of Vietnam, he had seen soldiers of all types come and go, and he could tell that Presley was a man that he would have liked to have had in his foxhole.

Jericho's service in Vietnam had taken its toll on him physically and emotionally, though, from the shrapnel wound that still scarred his leg, to the mental wounds that still scarred his mind.

Vietnam had defined him more than any other experience in his life, and turned him from an innocent boy from Philadelphia into world-class killing machine. He had proven himself on the battlefield numerous times, and his fearlessness and ruthlessness in combat got him promoted to an elite and secret squadron of death-defying saboteurs. Assassinations, demolitions, and other covert activities were his specialties. After serving in the war, his stellar military record caught the eye of officials in the Nixon Administration. They hired him to run clandestine operations, and he was given an unofficial post in the FBI, despite his lack of a college education. He was placed in a secret covert group with only a handful of members. His real name was Nick Black, but he was given the name Jake Jericho to preserve his anonymity and place him above the law as he performed unethical and sometimes illegal activities in the name of national security. Much like Jesse King, he was a phantom with no identity, a man made of flesh and blood who technically didn't exist.

It was Christmas, 1967, and Pvt. Black was stationed in Vietnam. It was his first Christmas away from home, and home had never seemed more far away. He had not been in country very long, and there was a lull in the fighting. He had not seen any real combat, but he was fearful of what lay ahead of him.

Vietnam. Only a few years earlier, Nick Black had not even heard of the country; now he was living in it, and fighting a war for its freedom, or so he was told. In reality, the Vietnamese were a people who didn't need anyone to fight for their freedom, a people whose culture and history were as old and turbulent as war itself.

During the first millennium B.C., the Vietnamese were a farming people living humbly off the land and the rice produced in the Red River delta of Southeast Asia. In the second century B.C., Vietnam was conquered and absorbed into the rapidly expanding Chinese empire. The Chinese were one of the world's first great societies, and for the thousand years that Vietnam was part of their empire, the Vietnamese people adopted their culture and language. During the tenth century A.D., as the Chinese empire began to crumble, Vietnamese rebels rose up and drove the Chinese out of Vietnam, reclaiming its independence.

Though the people formed a new state, the influence of Chinese culture and Confucian philosophy remained interwoven into the nation's fabric. Despite the Chinese influence, Vietnamese culture and art reemerged in the centuries of its independence under the Ly Dynasty.

In 1284, Kublai Kahn led a 500,000-man attack from China, but guerrilla resistance led by Tran Hung Dao eventually drove the Mongols out of their land. After their victory against the Chinese

Empire, the Vietnamese soon turned their attention to the South, and the Kingdom of Champa. After numerous battles with the Champa, the Vietnamese captured their capitol and virtually destroyed the kingdom. As the Vietnamese continued to expand their border to the south, they were confronted with a new enemy, the Khmer, a powerful but declining empire in the Mekong Delta that was easily conquered and absorbed into Vietnam.

In 1407, China again conquered the country, during the Ming dynasty. But in 1428, a rebel leader named Le Loi led the Vietnamese to a decisive victory, driving out the Chinese once again, and restoring Vietnamese independence. Le Loi then took the throne and declared himself the first emperor of the Le Dynasty.

In the 16th century, the Le dynasty began to decline, and power became split between two rival clans, the Trinh and the Nguyen. Soon the country became separated between the two factions. As this friction led to the collapse of the Le dynasty, the peasants revolted, and in 1789 Hguyen Hue took the throne as emperor and briefly united the country of Vietnam. After the emperor died, Nguyen Anh inherited the throne and defeated opposing armies and established the Nguyen dynasty in 1802.

During this time, French missionaries began arriving and tried to convert the Vietnamese to Roman Catholicism, but their attempts were met with suspicion and persecution, and many missionaries were executed. This led to outrage on the part of French religious leaders and military attacks by the government of France. In 1861, the French seized control of Saigon and established a colonial government in Vietnam, and eventually controlled all of the country as well as Cambodia and Laos.

Under French rule, the people of Vietnam grew angry and restless; low wages and poor living conditions led to the formation of several nationalist parties in the 1920s. One of these parties was the Indochinese Communist party, led by a revolutionary named Ho Chi Minh.

In 1940, the Japanese Empire was given the right to place Vietnam under military control, and Communist leaders formed the Viet Minh, with plans to start an uprising at the end of World War II. When the Japanese surrendered to the United States in 1945, the Viet Minh rose up and declared independence. The French still had control of the country, however, and refused to concede its colony, and a year later war broke out again. After an eight-year war, the Viet Minh were driven into hiding, where they regrouped and plotted to regain control as the French named a sympathetic ally, Bao Dai, as the new emperor. The Viet Minh began resistance with guerrilla warfare, and the resulting high casualties forced the French government to withdraw. In 1954, at negotiations in Geneva, the two sides agreed to split the country at the seventeenth parallel, between the Viet Minh in the North and the French and their supporters in the South.

In 1957, North Vietnamese guerillas calling themselves the Viet Cong, led several attacks against South Vietnam, prompting the United States to place a military presence in the country. Seven years later, the North Vietnamese attacked a U.S. destroyer in the Gulf of Tonkin. President Lyndon Johnson was granted wartime powers by Congress to fight the Communist guerillas, and a massive deployment of U.S. troops to Vietnam began.

Thousands of years of history and strife had now conspired to place Nick Black in that strange, foreign land. He, like many of the other soldiers, was ignorant of the country's history and its unending determination to repel foreign invaders, and believed that the war would soon be won. They were unaware of the people's fighting spirit and their philosophical unity, and were ill-prepared to fight guerilla combat against a people who had used it to defeat many an empire.

Nick and his buddy Dan were both profoundly moved by the poverty and suffering of the Vietnamese people, especially the children. They had both written home and requested some things be sent to them in lieu of their own Christmas presents, small gifts for the children of the war who had broken childhoods and no concept of Christmas. Between him and Dan they had received a nice assortment of candy and simple toys such as tops, balls, yo-yos and puppets.

During the week of Christmas, their platoon crossed paths with a caravan of refugees, and he and Dan sought out the children in the group. At first, the children were scared and apprehensive, but their trepidation turned to smiles when the two soldiers presented them with the toys. Their eyes lit up as the sounds of children's laughter wafted through the downtrodden crowd, bringing smiles to the parents as well. Nick knelt down before one of the children and pretended to pull a red ball out of his ear, and then bounced it on the ground. The child smiled with glee as Nick handed him the ball. The kid bounced the ball and then hugged the soldier.

As the platoon parted ways with the band of refugees, Nick and Dan marched together, basking together in the glow of the Christmas spirit.

"You know, as much as I hate being here, today made it all worthwhile," Nick said warmly.

"I know what you mean," Dan agreed. "This was the best Christmas ever. I'll never forget today as long as I live."

The two friends smiled as they walked into the night, but their experiences in Vietnam would soon take a tragic turn.

The upcoming plastic surgery weighed heavily on Elvis' mind, as it would on anyone's. Elvis' good looks had always been an asset. They had helped make him a star, and they always helped with the women. Now his looks would be taken away from him. What if something went wrong, and he ended up disfigured and ugly? It was a long shot, but still it was a possibility. It was not just the loss of his looks, but also the loss of his identity that concerned him. For over forty years, he had looked in the mirror and seen the same face. Was he emotionally equipped to handle the sight of a stranger looking back at him in the mirror?

In the past year and a half, he had lost so much that was his -- his money, his fame, his family, and his name. Now he was about to lose his face. Logically, he knew that this was necessary if he was to continue his ruse. Since his death, numerous people had recognized him -- Hans Muller, the boy on the bridge, Faith, the girl in Atlanta, and countless people on the street. If he truly wanted a new life and a new identity, this surgery was a must. Besides, he didn't have much of a choice in the matter.

He had met with the surgeon several times and was confident that he was a skilled professional, and that the changes would not be drastic.

The day of the surgery had arrived, and after being shaved, prepped and sedated, Elvis quickly began losing his grip on consciousness. His last blurred thoughts were ones of terror and anxiety, fearing that he would awake a completely different person, as if the surgeons would give him a lobotomy as well, taking from him the last piece of Elvis Presley.

CHAPTER XVI |

PUPPET ON A STRING

As Elvis slowly regained consciousness and his eyes flickered open, he found himself alone. His hands reached up and felt the bandages wrapped around his face like a mummy dressed for the tomb. It shouldn't have been such a surprise to him; he knew that due to the swelling and stitches from the surgery, he would need a few days of recovery. Elvis realized that it was probably for the best that he couldn't see his face at this point, anyway. He looked in the mirror but could only see his blue eyes staring out from the bandages. He then noticed that the tips of his fingers were also bandaged; he sat and pondered how his life had come to this.

In a strange way, he was getting everything he wanted -- a new identity, a job in law enforcement and above all, a good acting role at last. Ever since Elvis was a child, he had wanted to be an actor. He idolized the people on the big screen even more than his musical heroes. Actors like James Dean, Tony Curtis and Marlon Brando were his role models. His entire persona was a child of these fathers. He dyed his hair jet black to resemble Tony Curtis, and adopted his brooding sneer from Dean and Brando. He recalled one of his first jobs fondly; it was as an usher at a movie theater. Sure, the job itself wasn't very exciting, but once everyone was seated and the lights dimmed, he was a spectator of pure magic. He didn't mind seeing some of the same movies over and over again. In fact, it gave him a chance to memorize all of the dialogue.

Years later when he became a major music star, he used his fame to get into movies. Over the course of his life, he starred in over thirty films, some good, but most of them bad. He had desperately wanted to be taken seriously as an actor, but kept getting cast in third-rate musical comedies. Though at times he was the highest paid actor in Hollywood, he would have sacrificed millions to be in just one great, breakthrough role.

Colonel Parker had no such ambition for him, though. He had been in complete control of Elvis' career, and took an incredibly high percentage of every dollar he made. As a result, Parker turned down lesser paying roles in movies such as *Thunder Road* and *A Star is Born* so Elvis could make more money in cinematic train wrecks like *Harum Scarum* and *Clambake*.

On several occasions Elvis tried to convince the Colonel to get him better movie roles but to no avail.

"I'm not going to do another cornball movie," Elvis yelled at Tom Parker.

"We had an agreement. You do the singing and I take care of the business side of things," Parker reminded him.

"Well, maybe it's time to change the agreement. Maybe it's time to change my manager," Elvis threatened.

"Are you firing me? After all I've done for you. You were a nobody when I met you. I took you out of the beer halls and put you on Ed Sullivan. You were a penniless truck driver when I met you and I turned you into one of the richest men in the world."

"Making yourself rich as well."

"I'm your manager. I'm entitled to my cut."

"Yeah, but everyone I've talked to says your percentage is way too high."

"Elvis, if you're going to fire me, you better do it to my face."

He stared into Parker's eyes determined to end their business relationship. Then Elvis looked away as his head drooped to his shoulders.

"No, forget about it. I'll do the movie," he said passively.

The colonel smiled and took a puff off of his cigar.

Elvis reluctantly resigned himself to starring in these movies but felt that the world had never gotten to see what a great actor he could be, but now he had a chance to at least prove it to himself. Going undercover as an anti-establishment singer would be challenging and dangerous, but he didn't care. It was the role of lifetime, one that the critics would never see, but one in which a bad performance could bring him death instead of a scathing review.

Soon the doctor came in and asked how he was feeling, but Elvis didn't feel like talking. Sensing this, the doctor simply smiled politely and monitored his vitals before leaving the room. Twenty minutes later, Agent Jericho paid Elvis a visit.

"Hello, Mr. King," the agent said.

Elvis was silent.

"The doctor tells me that the operation was a success and you should have those bandages off in a couple of days."

"What happened to my fingers?"

"Oh, those. We decided that since we had you under, we might as well alter your fingerprints, too. But don't worry, it won't effect your guitar playing."

"You didn't ask me if you could do that."

"Why would I ask? The choice was never yours to make."

"You son of a bitch!" Elvis screamed as he started throwing anything he could find at Jericho. The agent casually ducked and side-stepped the items until Elvis was through.

"Now that your temper tantrum is over, perhaps we can get back to work."

"Go to hell!" Elvis screamed.

Elvis silently fumed for a few minutes as Jericho patiently waited.

"How did you find me?" Presley asked out of the blue.

"What do you mean?"

"When I was in San Francisco, living under an assumed name, how did you find me?"

"Hans Mueller. You know, that Nazi war criminal you turned in. When they brought him in, I was assigned to question him and find out what he knew about the location of any other escaped war criminals. He kept insisting that Elvis Presley was his neighbor and was also the man who made the anonymous tip. Naturally, I thought he was just a crazy old man, but I gave him a lie detector test anyway.

"He passed. Not that it meant anything. Delusional people can usually pass the test if they believe in the lie, but the details intrigued me, so I decided to investigate. He told me you went by the name of Jon Burrows. I did some research on you, and found out that Jon Burrows was a traveling alias that you had often used before your untimely death. In fact, it was the name you gave the FBI to contact you, when you wanted to work for us about a decade ago. I also found out that a man using that name took a one way flight to Buenos Aires on the day of your death. In fact, he rented an apartment next to Mr. Mueller and flew back to the States on the day Mueller was turned in to us.

"After reading everything about you I could find, I realized that you would make the perfect mole for the FBI, and began a quest to find you. After you arrived in Los Angeles, however, your trail went cold, as if Jon Burrows had also died. Every lead and sighting I pursued led to a dead end. There were numerous sightings, but they were randomly reported all over the country. However, the greatest concentration was in San Francisco. Then one day an officer from Atlanta accessed the FBI's fingerprint database and ran prints that matched the ones collected from you when you joined the Army. Upon this discovery, I questioned the Atlanta Police Department. The Chief told me everything he knew, including a witness' report that you drove off in a white commercial truck with California plates.

"Suddenly, it all made sense. You were a truck driver from San Fran. That's why you were spotted in so many different cities, and also why San Francisco was the most common place. I obtained the records of all registered truck drivers in the Bay area, and then narrowed the search down by age, gender, and so on. I came up with a short list with one name of particular interest, Jesse King, a.k.a. Jesse Presley. From there, I simply bugged your house, then made my move."

"But why did you care so much about finding me?" Elvis asked.

"As I said, I thought you'd make a great agent, and watching you train, I know I was right," Jericho complimented him. "My question for you is, why have you been so cooperative?"

"Well, if what you say is true, then I want to help my country, and save lives. I've always wanted to be some type of law officer, and the FBI is as big as it gets. I love my country and would do anything for it. I've always hated how rock stars used their fame to deride this country and our government, and I want to put a stop to it. I feel as if I've squandered all the gifts that God has bestowed upon me, and now is my chance to truly make a difference."

"Good, because this is an important mission. In fact, now I think you're ready to learn the details. Less than a year ago, we received intelligence reports that some subversive factions in the music/political underground had regrouped and were planning some kind of attack on the government."

"Like what?"

"We don't know yet, but we think it'll be something catastrophic. It appears that the hippies have grown up and realized that you can't change the world by simply having sit-ins and smoking pot. They've given up on the tired notion of civil disobedience, and have finally decided that only violence causes change. Instead of protests and food co-ops, we think they're planning assassinations and terrorist bombings. It's your job to find out the details for us. The movement is largely based in New York City. They are well financed and poised to strike. We already have a mole in their midst, Lacey Lewis, one of our top agents."

"A woman?" Elvis asked with surprise.

"Yes. In fact, she's a very beautiful woman, our very own Mata Hari. She's been posing as a girlfriend to one of the organizers of the group. Her beauty and charm have gotten us deep into their lair, but there still some things men don't tell their girlfriends. But if you were to infiltrate their group with Lacey's help, you just might be able to uncover the truth before any innocent lives are lost. Basically, we need to know who's financing them, and what they're planning."

"I hope I don't disappoint you."

"For the sake of our country, I hope you don't, either."

Jericho left the room, leaving Elvis to himself. He began thinking about Faith, wishing they were still together. Things had been going so well between them, not unlike a specific time in his relationship with Priscilla.

It was the mid-sixties, and Elvis had grown dissatisfied with his playboy lifestyle in Hollywood and decided to return to Graceland, where he knew he had a loving woman waiting for him.

He and Priscilla spent treasured moments together, reconciling a love that he had long taken for granted. They took a long drive together one weekend, and while speeding through Mississippi, they passed a large ranch with grazing cattle.

"Look at that house, Elvis. It's beautiful. It's my dream house," Priscilla said warmly.

"You like it? Well then, I'm buying it. I don't care what it costs."

She snuggled up next to Elvis in the car, comforted by the thought of the two of them living together on a ranch.

It ended up costing Elvis half a million dollars, but he bought the ranch, and within days the two lovebirds began moving into Priscilla's dream house.

Elvis and Priscilla spent a few blissful, quiet days alone together on the ranch. Priscilla was in heaven, living out her old-fashioned fantasy of being a housewife, but Elvis grew restless. He had his friends from the Memphis Mafia come down to keep him company. Much to Priscilla's dismay, Elvis decided he wanted to keep his buddies around all the time, and days later Elvis had trailers put in on the ranch for his friends. Priscilla's dreams of having a secluded getaway from Graceland were shattered, but Elvis was now in love with the idea of being a cowboy.

Every morning, he got dressed up in a cowboy outfit and rode his horse around the grounds with his friends, looking for chores to do and playing cowboy. It was while living on the ranch that Elvis met Dr. Nichopoulos or Dr. Nick, as he would call him.

Dr. Nick soon became Elvis' chief physician, and would be instrumental in accommodating, and later failing to control, Elvis' ever-growing addiction to pills.

The day came when the bandages on Elvis' face were to be removed. The doctor slowly unwrapped the bandages and gave him a mirror. Elvis gazed at his reflection as a stranger looked back. He could still see his essence in the mirror, but his eyebrows and nose were different, almost like those of the wax dummy that was buried in his coffin. After the initial shock wore off, he realized he was still a handsome man. In fact, thanks to a facelift, he looked ten years younger. His new appearance put some closure on his previous life and allowed him to begin a new one. Finally, he thought to himself, Elvis Presley was truly dead.

CHAPTER XVII

SUSPICIOUS MINDS

Several days had passed since he had removed his bandages, and Elvis' beard was beginning to grow back, giving him an earthy, Renaissance man look. His hair, which had already grown long, was slightly trimmed and styled. He was given a very exquisite wardrobe of vintage hippie and bohemian clothes. He was then presented with two biographies. One was for Special Agent Jesse King, the fictitious life story of an FBI agent, and one for Jesse Hope, a cover story detailing the life of a politically active folk-rock singer. He was instructed to memorize both. With all the small details taken care of, Elvis and Jericho boarded an FBI jet and flew to New York City.

Europeans first discovered the area that was to become New York City in 1609, when Henry Hudson sailed up the river that now bears his name. It was soon inhabited by Dutch settlers in 1624, and named New Amsterdam. One of the settlers, Peter Minuit, is said to have purchased the island of Manhattan from the Indians for a handful of beads.

In 1664, Great Britain's Duke of York seized the city from the Dutch in a bloodless coup and renamed the city New York. The fledgling United States of America took control of the city as a result of the Revolutionary War. George Washington was sworn in as President at its city hall, and for a brief time it was considered the nation's capitol.

In 1898, the city's borders were expanded to include an additional four boroughs: Brooklyn, the Bronx, Queens, and Staten Island. The port city quickly grew to become one of the largest and most famous cities in the world, as well as one of the world's greatest centers of business, culture, and trade. It was also known for its famous landmarks and skyscrapers such as the Empire State building, the

Statue of Liberty, and the newly built twin towers of the World Trade Center.

After arriving in New York, Jericho took Elvis to a secret FBI safe house, where he unpacked and settled into his new quarters. After getting his things together, Elvis was led to a presentation room.

"Are you ready to meet your new partner?" Jericho asked.

"Yeah. I guess."

"First, I have a gift for you. Actually, it's not really a gift. You've earned it," Jericho praised him as he presented Elvis with an FBI badge.

"Wow! This is great."

"Congratulations, Mr. King. You're now a part of the greatest law enforcement organization in the world," Jericho exclaimed. "Now remember, Lacey doesn't know anything about your real identity. I'd like to keep it that way. You are Jesse King. You always were Jesse King. I want you to stick to that biography I wrote for you. Lacey is a very clever woman, and you two will be working very closely together. If there is any contradiction in your story, she'll catch it."

Suddenly, she entered the room. Elvis felt an immediate attraction to her. Lacey Lewis was a beautiful creature; her long black hair bounced with every step she took, and her dark brown eyes sparkled and slanted upward seductively in a cat-like way. Her cheekbones were high and well defined; she had a natural radiance, a hue that did not require makeup. Her body had more curves than the roads in San Francisco. Her delicate features suggested a feminine and demure woman who could melt any man's heart.

"Who the hell is this?" she sneered, looking at Elvis.

"This is Special Agent King," Jericho said.

Elvis' extended hand was left high and dry as the undercover diva marched toward Jericho.

"Is this the best you've got?" she asked aggressively.

"Give him a chance. You may be surprised."

She finally shook his hand, but as a matter of protocol only.

"He's green. I can smell it. Look, I didn't spend the past four months screwing some hairball so that this rookie could come in and blow my cover."

"Jesse, play a song for her," Jericho commanded.

Insulted and caught off-guard, Elvis meekly picked up his guitar and played a folk-rock song he had helped write called "Going Away."

After finishing the song, he laid the guitar down and looked to Lacey for approval.

She tilted her head in indifference. "He sings okay, but can he fight?"

"Sure. He's a black belt in karate," Jericho insisted.

"I'll be the judge of that," she stated bluntly, challenging Jesse.

"I'm not fighting a girl."

"Don't worry. I have orders not to kill you," she hissed as she accentuated her statement with a roundhouse kick to his face.

"Hey, don't hit the face!" Jericho shouted, concerned about the plastic surgery. "We don't want our golden boy looking like he just fought Ali."

"Fine," she said as she kicked him in the crotch, doubling Elvis over in pain.

"Are you through assaulting your partner?" Jericho asked, shaking his head.

"I'm just making a point."

Elvis' temper was quickly lost as he jumped up and tackled her.

"The gloves are off now," he growled as he pinned her down, poised to punch her in the face, but unable to bring himself to punch a woman.

She responded with a knee to his groin.

"Somebody's watched *Rocky* one too many times," she taunted him as she got on top of him and paintbrush-slapped him in the face.

"Stop it, both of you!" growled Jericho.

"Sorry, I just want to know if I can count on him when things get crazy, and I'm guessing no."

"You know, this isn't how I envisioned your first meeting," Jericho declared in disgust.

Lacey turned to Jericho and began speaking in Russian. Jericho responded in the same language.

"Why do I get the feeling that you two are talking about me?" Elvis asked haplessly, picking himself up from the floor.

"I'm sorry, Mr. King. I just wanted you to know that I'm not some helpless damsel that you'll have to protect," Lacey said as she extended her hand in friendship.

Elvis stared at her hand and began to walk away before Jericho stopped him.

"Look, Jesse. I know your pride is bruised, but if you two can't get along, this mission is dead in the water."

Elvis reluctantly agreed and shook her hand. They stared into each other's eyes as it soon became a contest of who could squeeze harder.

"Well, at least I don't have to worry about you two sleeping together," Jericho remarked sarcastically, and not without a little frustration. "Now, let's play nice, and Special Agent Lewis, please brief Special Agent King."

Agent Lewis pulled down a projection screen as Jericho produced a projector and turned off the lights. Lewis advanced the first slide. It was a picture of a brown-haired, bearded man with long hippie dreadlocks.

"This is Julius Wolfe, a.k.a. Wolfgang; he is a lifelong activist, musician, and former member of the Weathermen. In 1968, he was arrested for detonating a bomb at the campaign headquarters of a Republican State Senator. Though numerous injuries occurred, no one was killed, and Wolfgang ended up only serving seven years of a ten-year sentence. He is one of the charter members of the group we have infiltrated. This group calls itself New Aquarius, and though we have no proof of any violent crimes being committed by them yet, we have reason to believe they are planning something big and horrific for the beginning of 1981. They have been masquerading as a grass-roots political organization, handing out manifestos and organizing concerts and protests in the New York City area."

She paused and clicked forward to the next slide, which showed a very large, rotund man with a bald head and black beard.

"This is Christopher Thorne, a.k.a. Thorny, a former Hell's Angel and Manson family hanger-on. He wisely quit the Manson family just months before the Tate-LoBianca murders, after having a lover's quarrel with fellow family member Squeaky Fromme who, as you may remember, recently attempted to assassinate former President Gerald Ford. Thorne is the enforcer of the group and is very dangerous."

Then she clicked to the next frame, showing a large, muscular black man.

"This is Theodore Cassidy, a.k.a. Abdul Zahid Muhammad, a member of the Nation of Islam and former Black Panther. He is a trained in explosives and is an associate of PLO leader Yasser Arafat."

Special Agent Cambell paused briefly and clicked once more to an attractive man with long, blond hair.

"This is Robert Walker, a.k.a. Zeus; he is my boyfriend, or so he thinks. Walker is the leader of the group on this level. He answers only to the ringleader, whose identity, of course, is unknown. Aside from being a folk-rock singer, Zeus is a great speaker and organizer. In the Sixties, he had ties to the Chicago Seven as well as being a sympathizer of the Black Panthers. He is very intelligent and is believed to be the only member of New Aquarius to know the identity of the ringleader. These four men are the backbone of the organization; there are dozens of other members and supporters, but it is believed that they are all merely pawns, as you will be, peace-loving activists and musicians who are unaware of the secret, violent agenda of this group."

On that note, Special Agent Lewis turned on the lights and asked: "Any questions?"

Elvis raised his hand as Lewis looked around at the almost empty room.

"This isn't school; just ask your question," she chided.

"If you're working undercover as Zeus' girlfriend, why haven't you been able to find out the identity of the ringleader?"

"Hey, I've tried, but he's very tight-lipped," she said. "I've bugged their headquarters and taken fingerprint samples. That's how we know as much as we do. However, when it comes to the ringleader, he is referred to only as The Benefactor. We believe he is the mastermind behind the upcoming attacks."

"So exactly how do I fit in?" Elvis inquired.

"I'm going to introduce you to the group in the next few days. I will tell them that I saw you playing at a coffeehouse, and that your talent and political lyrics made me think you would be good for an upcoming folk-rock concert. Hopefully they'll let you work for them. They'll probably start you out by doing all types of odd jobs like handing out pamphlets, attending protests, and probably even making coffee. There is a shortage these days of people who are willing to work for free, so it shouldn't be a problem. With a little luck and a little talent, they'll let you play at an upcoming rally, but it's important for now for you to just do what you're told and not ask too many questions. Just a warning, if you screw up and blow your cover, I will not jeopardize my own cover to save you. So don't screw up."

Jericho could sense that there was still some animosity between the two of them and decided that it would be a good thing if his agents spent some time together, just to move beyond their initial hostility.

"I think we should all go out for drinks," Jericho suggested. "I'm buying."

They all agreed, and Jericho took them to a remote bar that was darkly lit and only had a handful of patrons. They selected a small table away from most of the people. Jericho ordered a pitcher of beer and poured them all a glass.

"To our mission," he proposed.

Presley and Lewis repeated his toast and clinked their glasses together before drinking.

"So, Mr. King, tell me how you became an FBI agent," Lacey suggested.

Elvis knew he was being tested, and in his mind he scrambled to recall the details of his cover story.

"Well, I've always had two loves in my life, music and the law; growing up in Tennessee, there was a strong sense of both. When I turned eighteen, I joined the Army and began taking my guitar playing more seriously. When I got out of the service, I went to college for forensics. This was the mid-Sixties; there was a growing revolution of the mind and in the country going on there, and I was caught in the middle. While I was disgusted by some of the Anti-American sentiments brewing, I fell in love with the new psychedelic and folk-rock sound emerging.

"I started playing and writing my own folk-rock music. My peers seemed to like my playing and singing, but were turned off by my pro-American, pro-military lyrics. After graduating, I went back home and joined the local police force, all the while sending applications to the FBI, in hopes they'd accept me. One day they did, and here I am," he said with a grin, as Jericho gave him a wink of approval, countered by Lewis's leer of suspicion.

"Okay, your turn, Miss Lewis. How did you get into the FBI?" Elvis asked, trying to deflect some of the attention away from himself.

"I grew up a Navy brat in San Diego and went to college at USC, studying criminology and foreign languages," she said. "I then joined the LAPD and worked there for a few years when I heard the FBI was looking for applicants. I sent mine in and was accepted."

Jericho left the table, ostensibly to make a phone call to headquarters; he returned with some news.

"I'm needed at headquarters. I'll be back in an hour or two to pick you two up. In the meantime, you two relax, have a few drinks, talk, and try not to kill each other," Jericho instructed them before leaving the bar.

It was all part of his ploy to have the two agents bond and trust each other. The mission would require a certain amount of kinship between them, and it had gotten off to a rocky beginning. In fact, Jericho didn't go anywhere. He merely got in his car and sat in the parking lot, monitoring their conversation from a bug he had planted at the table.

"So where do you live?" Elvis asked, making smalltalk.

"They set me up at a efficiency apartment in the Village. They'll probably do the same for you," she answered, her mind obviously elsewhere. She got up and whispered in Elvis' ear, "Why don't we change tables?"

"Why?"

"Trust me."

He agreed and they moved over to a different table.

"So why did we move tables?"

"That table was bugged."

"How do you know?"

"I know Jericho. I swear to God, the guy probably bugs his own house just to make sure that he's not the enemy. Which is why I need to talk to you in private. How well do you know him?"

"Not real well. Just a couple of months."

"Well, let me let you in a little secret; he's not all there. He spent too much time in Vietnam, I guess. But if you haven't noticed, he's a little psychotic."

"Well, that I have noticed."

"Psychotic enough to get us both killed. So we'll have to depend on each other."

"Aren't you the same woman who tried to kick in my manhood a few hours ago?"

"Yes, and I'm sorry. But that was done mainly for effect. Jericho is crazy, and he expects the same in his agents. But I did find out something during our scuffle."

"What's that?"

"You're not with the FBI."

"Why do you say that?"

"The way you fought. Besides, I'm trained to know when people are lying, and you haven't said a truthful thing all evening. Let me guess. You're a musician who got in some trouble with the law and Jericho offered to drop the charges if you went undercover."

"You know what I think? I think you're both crazy. Maybe you and Jericho should run off together have some psycho Nazi children and live happily ever after. I'm through with all of this," Elvis proclaimed as he got up, eyeing the back door and contemplating a daring escape.

Lacey grabbed his hand.

"You can't get away. You think he's not waiting outside that door? Guess again. Maybe you're doing this just to save your ass, but I actually care about my country and I know something horrible will happen if we don't..."

Her sentence was interrupted when Jericho entered the back door.

"Gee, Jericho that was quick," she said knowingly.

"It turns out they didn't need me after all. How come you changed tables?" he asked suspiciously, alarmed by the silence of his surveillance device.

"We decided to get a table with a little more privacy," she responded as Jericho glared silently at her.

"Well, I'm back. Did you two make up while I was gone?"

"Yes. I think we understand each other," Lacey said.

"Glad to hear it."

Jericho sat at the table and poured himself a drink.

"So, what were you two kids talking about?" he asked with an evil smile.

CHAPTER XVIII

NEW AQUARIUS

Special Agent Lacey Lewis was born in 1950, the daughter of Sharon and Captain Stephen Lewis, a career officer in the Navy. She spent most of her formative years moving around the country as her father was repeatedly transferred from one naval base to another. At age eleven, the family moved to San Diego where they finally established a long-term residence. Growing up a Navy brat had been difficult for Lacey, though. Early friendships that she made were quickly severed whenever her father got his transfer orders. Eventually she stopped making friends altogether, knowing her family might be quickly uprooted the following year.

Growing up in a military family and having two older brothers, she inevitably became a tomboy, and she excelled in sports and martial arts. Though blossoming with great natural beauty, she turned down opportunities to be a cheerleader, wanting instead to be an athlete. In the early Sixties however, there weren't many opportunities for females in sports, so she threw herself into her studies.

Her father, though a good, caring man, was often distant, if at home at all. Lacey craved his attention and developed an interest in law enforcement, perhaps to gain his favor. In 1966, her father became even more distant when he was forced to say goodbye to the family and was shipped off to Vietnam to fight in the war. Two years later, tragedy struck when the family received a letter notifying them that Stephen had been killed in action. Lacey was devastated by the news and wept for days. Shortly after her father's death, she began classes at USC. It was a difficult time for her; the anti-war movement was in full swing, and it seemed as if the protesters were spitting on her father's grave.

She was openly hostile to the offending hippies. Needless to say, she wasn't the most popular girl on campus, and her isolation grew deeper.

Upon graduation, she joined the Los Angeles Police Department. She liked the work, but felt she didn't get any respect from the male officers. One day she overheard two of the officers talking about sending an application to the FBI. When she mentioned to the others that she was interested in joining, they laughed at her, but that only made her more determined to join. The men stopped laughing when she was offered a position and they were not. When she was sworn into the FBI, it was a proudest day of her life. She dedicated her success to her father's memory, and vowed to eliminate the factions that she believed brought down the country and tarnished the honor of the Vietnam veteran.

Ironically, years later, she was now in the lair of an anti-establishment organization, snug in the arms of the same kind of man she wanted to destroy.

"So what did you do last night, Lacey?" Zeus asked as he stroked the side of her face.

"Actually, I went to a coffeehouse and saw this great folk-rock singer there."

"Really? What's his name?"

"Jesse Hope," she answered with yet another alias for Elvis.

"Never heard of him."

"He's new to the area. He just moved here from San Francisco," she informed Zeus.

"How do you know that?"

"I talked to him after his set. He's a nice guy. He's a political activist, an old hippie just like us. I told him what we're into. He seemed interested in volunteering."

"Really? So how do I reach this guy?" Zeus asked.

"He gave me his phone number."

"Yeah. I bet he did," Zeus remarked with a touch of suspicious jealousy.

She handed him a napkin with Elvis' number scrawled on it.

"Well, I do have a need for some volunteers right now," Zeus admitted.

With the number in hand, he walked over to the phone. He cleared some pamphlets out of the way, and picked up the phone and dialed.

The phone rang in the FBI outpost. Jericho and Presley had both been listening to the goings on at New Aquarius headquarters via surveillance equipment, so the phone call was not unexpected.

"It's show time, Jesse," Jericho announced.

Elvis picked up the phone and greeted Zeus on the other end. They engaged in some informal talk before Elvis agreed to come down to the office to meet Zeus. After getting directions that he already had, they both said goodbye and hung up the phone.

"Well, I'm in," Elvis announced with a smile. "He wants me to meet him at their headquarters at six o'clock tonight."

"Good job, Jesse."

Lacey had spent some time with Elvis over the past few days, training him on how to convincingly act like a hippie, all under Jericho's watchful eye, of course. She taught him subtle but important things like the handshake, a knowledge of Sixties music, hippie and drug lingo, and of course, how to roll and smoke a joint. She made him roll a marijuana cigarette over and over until he got it right. When he finally rolled a good one, she lit it up and handed it too him.

"You've smoked pot before, right?" she asked.

"A few times, in the Sixties mainly," he confessed as he awkwardly took the joint from her hand.

"No. Hold the joint like this," she corrected him.

Elvis took a deep puff and promptly coughed until his lungs almost popped out of his mouth.

"Okay, that's not good," Lacey said. "Nothing says narc like coughing on the first hit. We're going to keep smoking this until you get it right."

Unfortunately, Elvis could sometimes be a slow learner, but by the third joint he finally got it right.

"Oh my God! I'm so stoned!" Elvis proclaimed as Lacey just burst into laughter.

"After three joints, you ought to be."

She tried quizzing him some more on lingo, but it was no use, they were both wrecked.

"Weird way to make a living, huh?" she joked.

"Yeah. I know what you mean. It's really uh...what were we talking about?" he asked cluelessly.

"Never mind, Jesse."

"Hey, I have a question," he said slowly.

"Okay. Go ahead."

"It's kind of personal and all, but it's relevant to the mission."

"Just ask already."

"I know you're pretending to be Zeus' boyfriend, but do you two actually, you know, have sex?"

"Of course," she laughed. "I wouldn't be a very convincing girl-friend if I didn't."

"No offense, but doesn't that make you feel like a, well, like a whore," Elvis asked, wincing as he said it.

"It feels weird, but I'm not a whore. I'm not doing it for money. Most women do it for very shallow reasons: for love, for pleasure, sometimes even for a steak dinner. I do it for my country and I can live with that," she stated somberly. "Hell, if it weren't for undercover sex, I'd have no sex life at all," she joked somewhat awkwardly.

"I find that hard to believe."

"Well, believe it. I'm married to my job and don't have time for much else. Besides, most guys don't want a woman with my qualities."

"Yeah. Smart, beautiful and sexy; guys hate that."

"Well, thanks for the compliment, but I meant strong and inde-pendent."

There was a time when those qualities would have turned him off as well, but after all the changes he had undergone in the past few years, his opinions regarding working women had evolved.

"They don't seem like such bad qualities to me," he assured her as he stared into her warm brown eyes.

"Really?" she asked as their lips started gravitating together.

She quickly broke the trance and looked away.

"Anyway," she quipped, not knowing what she was going to say next, but wanting to change the topic and the tone.

"Pop question," she shot at him. "All Along the Watchtower," who recorded it?"

Elvis quickly got his head out of his heart and into his lesson.

"Bob Dylan originally, and then it was covered by Jimi Hendrix."

"Good answer. I think you're ready."

"I hope so."

"Me, too. Because if you're not, it's both our asses."

Jericho had given Elvis a small, cheap apartment located next to the undercover headquarters, in case Zeus asked for a place of residence. Elvis rightly assumed that the apartment was bugged and that he was being monitored by Jericho, so he knew that an escape attempt was ill advised. His new place was considerably smaller than the houses he had been used to, even the ones in Buenos Aires and San Francisco. It was an efficiency apartment that contained only a bedroom and bathroom. The claustrophobia it inspired reminded him of his family's home in Memphis, not Graceland of course, but the public housing unit the state had provided the Presleys almost a lifetime ago. It was a poverty that he had vowed to escape. A big home for himself and his family had been the dream that had consumed him in his teenage years, a dream that he reflected upon every time he had picked up a guitar in his small, cramped Memphis home.

Elvis' rise to stardom was not exactly a quick one. While driving delivery trucks around Memphis for the Crown Electric Company by day, he was playing numerous bars in the area at night.

Sam Phillips was the founder of Sun Records, and had gained a reputation for recording blues with many great black musicians whom most labels were afraid to sign. One day he was recording a ballad and decided he needed a vocalist with a lighter touch than the average Memphis blues singer. He recalled a good-looking young man who had paid to record a song at his studio a year earlier.

"Get me the kid with the sideburns," he said, unable to remember Elvis' name.

His secretary grabbed the phone and called Presley.

"Can you get here in three hours?" she asked the young singer.

Within a half hour, Presley showed up at Sun Records gasping for air.

"Don't tell me you ran the whole way," she said with a laugh.

It was during that session that Phillips teamed Elvis with guitarist Scotty Moore and Bill Black, musicians who would remain in his band for the next twenty years. That night, a new sound was invented as well, as they recorded an off-the-cuff version of "That's All Right."

Quickly Sam Phillips gave the single to a disc jockey of no relation named Dewey Phillips. The DJ loved the song and gave it immediate airplay. The song became a hit in Memphis, and Elvis was soon a local celebrity. Sam Phillips saw big things for Presley, and booked him at the biggest event in country music, the Grand Ole Opry.

Elvis was extremely nervous before the big country show. As a kid, he used to listen to the Grand Ole Opry on the radio, but didn't think his brand of music would go over well with the older country music crowd. Elvis was right about that. While he didn't bomb, his performance left the audience at the Ryman Auditorium completely underwhelmed.

After playing the Opry, he began touring the country relentlessly, slowly converting the masses to his original look and sound. One of those people was Colonel Tom Parker. The Colonel met with Presley backstage, but Elvis found him aloof. In truth, Parker was planning a strategy to sign the superstar to-be. Though the meeting seemed inconsequential at the time, it was the beginning of one of the most lucrative partnerships in music history.

Jericho dropped Elvis off several blocks away from the New Aquarius headquarters, wanting him to walk the rest of the way in case there were lookouts inspecting him.

"Now remember, be natural, but stay in character. I've got my eyes and ears on you in case there's trouble. And no snooping, just get them to trust you and take the job with them."

Elvis casually sauntered down the street to the address he was given. He knocked on the door.

A large man whom Elvis recognized from the briefing as Thorny answered the door.

"Can I help you?" the Hell's Angel asked in a gruff, intimidating voice.

"Yes. I'm Jesse Hope. I'm here to see Zeus."

"Yeah. Come on in."

Elvis entered the main room of the compound. The room was in a state of archaic disarray. On the walls were several posters toting causes like nuclear disarmament, saving the whales, and other assorted left-wing issues. There were desks and telephones scattered around the room, as well as typewriters and ditto machines. Sprawled out on a tripped-out looking couch were Lacey and Zeus.

"Hi, Jesse," Lacey said warmly as she waved.

Elvis waved back and walked over to Zeus.

"Jesse Hope, I take it. Hi, I'm Zeus," he said as he extended his hand, Elvis shook it with his newly-learned handshake.

"Lacey tells me you're a good singer. I hope you're a good worker, too."

"For the right cause, you bet, man."

"This is the only cause, brother. Come on, have a seat," Zeus offered.

Elvis plopped down next to him as Zeus lit up a joint and handed it to Elvis.

Elvis took the hit the way that he was taught and handed it to Lacey.

"So, tell me, Jesse. Where are you from?"

"The South originally, as you can probably tell by my accent. Tennessee, to be exact."

"Not too many folk-rock singers down there, I imagine," Zeus pondered.

"No, not really. The good ole boys there didn't really get my music or my message. That's why I moved to Frisco."

"So what did you do during the Sixties?" Zeus asked as he took another hit off the joint.

"Well, you know what they say. If you remember the Sixties, you weren't there," Elvis joked as both men laughed.

"I don't get it," Lacey said in character, portraying the dumb bimbo that Zeus had grown to love.

"I'll explain it to you later, honey."

"But seriously, in the Sixties, I bounced around. Did a lot of drugs, sang a lot of songs, and went to a lot of protests."

"Right on," said Zeus. "Well, right now, we're not just looking for musicians, we're looking for soldiers, soldiers who are hard-working and dedicated to the cause. We need someone who can beat the street, hand out flyers, collect signatures, and hold up signs. You dig?"

"Yeah man, I know what you mean."

"Why don't you come into my office? I have some questions I need to ask you in private," Zeus suggested.

Elvis followed him into the office, and Zeus closed the door behind him. His office was as organized as the other room was disheveled. On the walls were pictures of Che Guevara, Bobby Kennedy and Jerry Rubin.

"Cool pictures, man," Presley complimented him, starting to feel a little high.

"Look, cut the bullshit, man. I know the real reason you're here."

Elvis' heart skipped a beat. "You do?"

"Yeah. You're just trying to get my old lady into bed, aren't you?"

A wave of relief washed over Elvis.

"No man, not at all."

"Hey, I see the way you've been looking at her. She's a sexy girl, but she's my girl. You got it?"

"Look, man. She is a beautiful woman and all, but I wouldn't stand a chance. You should have the seen way her eyes lit up the other night when she was talking about you. Besides, I don't believe in moving in on another man's old lady. That's not my thing, man."

"Well, good. Keep it that way, and we'll have no problems."

"Sure, man. Whatever you say."

"So, Jesse do you want to help us out with our cause or what?" Zeus asked.

"Yeah. Any way I can help, man."

"Good, glad to hear it. Welcome aboard. Maybe after you've been here a while, I'll let you play for me, and I'll see if I can use you in one of our shows."

"Cool!" Elvis said with a stoned nod.

"As you know, I am a man of peace," Zeus claimed.

Suddenly Zeus forcibly pushed Elvis to the wall and put a knife against his throat.

"But if you betray me, you'll end up in pieces."

CHAPTER XIX

DISARMING CONVERSATION

Despite having his life threatened, Elvis' meeting went well and Zeus offered him an assignment for the very next day. That morning, Lacey arrived at the secret outpost to congratulate him. Elvis was comparing notes with Jericho when she arrived.

"Good job, Jesse. You're in," she said with a smile. "You should have seen him, Jericho. He did great."

"I know. I was listening."

"Did he say anything to you about me?" Elvis asked.

"Not too much, but that's not unusual," Lacey said. "With Zeus, though, it's not what he says, it's what he doesn't say."

"I got a little nervous in his office, though; he put a knife to my throat and said he knew the real reason I was there," Elvis said to Lacey.

"Did he suspect you were a Fed?"

"No. He thought I was trying to get you into bed."

"Well, aren't you?" she teased playfully.

"Honey, if I was trying, it would've happened already," Elvis boasted flirtatiously.

"Oh, really?"

Jericho interrupted their conversation. "Kids, let's stay focused here. We've got another agent on the inside, and that's great, but we still need to find out who the Benefactor is, and what they're planning."

"Well, what do we know about the Benefactor?" Elvis asked.

"Not much. He or she is wealthy, lives in New York City, and is very liberal."

"A liberal in New York, that really narrows it down," Lacey quipped.

"I never said it would be easy."

"Don't worry. Things are looking up. I'm on the job now," Elvis said arrogantly.

"Just remember to keep your mouth shut and your eyes open," Jericho warned him.

"Well, I'd love to stay and chat, but I have to get ready. I'm supposed to meet Zeus at noon," Elvis informed them.

A few hours later, Elvis went to the New Aquarius' headquarters to meet with the leader.

Zeus greeted him and passed him off to Wolfgang, who had a sign-up sheet and a box full of pamphlets and brochures.

"Jesse, nice to meet you. My name is Wolfgang. I've got an interesting job for you. We're gearing up for the '80 election, but there's more at stake than just the presidency; there are several local offices up for grabs. There is a socialist candidate that we want to get on the ballot, but we need signatures from registered voters. We're going to send you to Central Park to collect signatures. Ask people if they're registered voters. If they say yes, ask them to sign your petition. If they say no, ask them if they'd like to register. If they ask what our candidate stands for, tell them he's for the rights of the people and the rights of the workers, then give them a pamphlet. You got all that?" Wolfgang asked.

"Yeah, piece of cake."

"Well, not really. Most people equate socialism with communism, so you may get some insults hurled your way. If that happens, just smile and say democracy is about freedom of choice, and the more choices we have, the freer we are," Wolfgang instructed him.

Zeus gave Elvis the needed supplies and left. The first hour did not go very well for Elvis. His shy nature made approaching strangers awkward, but eventually his inner charisma emerged as slowly but surely he began charming the passersby, especially the women.

A few hours later, Wolfgang returned.

"So how did you do?"

"Not too good. I only got about fifty signatures."

"Fifty isn't bad at all, especially for a beginner," Wolfgang insisted, trying to build his confidence.

Over the next few months, Elvis became the group's workhorse as he spent long hours doing everything from collecting signatures to marching in protests. Elvis was getting a little frustrated, though. He knew the clock was ticking, and he hadn't gotten any closer to finding out anything. His long hours kept him away from Lacey, and he desperately needed to talk to her. She had raised some important questions on the night of their first meeting, and he hadn't been able to talk to her privately since. Strangely, he had begun to feel a strong attraction to her as well, but it was difficult for him to tell who the real Lacey Lewis was. She was a woman who wore many masks, and he wondered if he had ever seen her true face. Still, she had an effect on him only be rivaled by Ann-Margret, the sexy redhead he had met while filming *Viva Las Vegas*.

Ann-Margret was a vivacious, young starlet with whom Elvis had had a smoldering affair while making the movie. Though Elvis had made a habit of bedding the leading ladies in most of his films, famous Hollywood beauties such as Juliet Prowse and Tuesday Weld, there was something special about this one. She was a very talented dancer, and sometimes made Elvis afraid that she would upstage him on the big screen. Their competitiveness, mixed with an intense chemistry, had made for some fiery lovemaking, as well as some tantalizing headlines.

These headlines did not sit too well with young Priscilla, whom he still had secretly stashed away at Graceland. She had long suspected Elvis' infidelity, and getting confirmation on the front page of the tabloids hurt her deeply. Eventually, the romance between him and Ann-Margret fizzled out, mostly to appease Priscilla, but many times he looked back on Ann-Margret as the one who got away.

While Elvis hadn't find out any information about the Benefactor, he couldn't help but notice some strange goings on. Thorny, Wolfgang, and Abdul were constantly in and out of Zeus' office, many times with envelopes in their hands. He often saw them coming out of the basement with large rectangular packages wrapped in brown paper. He wondered if they could be explosives. One day, he was asked to go down to the basement to get some supplies, and decided to do some investigating. In one room he found a large, heavily locked cabinet. He knew there was no way to get inside it without breaking the locks. He grasped it and could tell it was very heavy. Just then he heard someone coming down the stairs. He quickly grabbed what he had come for and headed back upstairs.

A few days after that, he was in Zeus' office stuffing envelopes with some other volunteers when Zeus and Lacey came bursting through the door.

"Hey, folks, I have some great news!" Zeus announced. "There's a march in D.C. against nuclear proliferation. We're marching on the White House, and we need as many people there as possible. We're flying you all to D.C. for the weekend."

The mood in the room turned jovial at the prospect of spending a few days in the Washington; the volunteers buzzed with excitement. They were an eclectic bunch of personalities, mostly young, artistic types who had the passion to want to make a difference and the youthful naiveté to think that they could. The free-flowing rap sessions they shared in the office often brought great laughs, and gave Elvis an insight into a generation from whom he had grown increasingly estranged over the years.

The rest of the day was spent making protest signs espousing the need for nuclear disarmament that they would display as they made their trek through the streets of Washington.

"Your sign looks good, Jesse," Lacey warmly complimented him as she sat down next to Elvis and began making some signs of her own.

"Thanks, Lacey. So, are you going to D.C. with us?" Elvis inquired.

"Of course. Zeus needs as many people as possible to attend. Besides, I'm his girlfriend."

"I suppose you two will be marching together," he remarked, trying not to seem too concerned.

"No. He'll be too busy leading and organizing the thing. Why? Do you want to march with me?"

"Sure, if you'd like."

"I'd like," she said with a smile.

Just then Zeus walked past and began rubbing her shoulders.

"Helping out with the signs, honey?"

"Yeah. How do you spell the word 'bomb'?" she asked him as she twirled her hair around her finger.

"B-O-M-B," Zeus answered.

"Thanks, I'm such a bad speller," she giggled as Zeus rolled his eyes and walked away.

Elvis talked casually as they made their signs, careful not too arouse any suspicion amongst the volunteers who were subtly eavesdropping. Some of them resented Lacey. To them, she was just an airhead who happened to be sleeping with the boss. Lacey would have it no other way. By playing dumb, she got many people including Zeus to let their guard down around her and let certain information slip that they ordinarily wouldn't. Nobody saw her as a threat, nobody saw her as a risk.

Around this time, Elvis had read some sad news in the paper. John Bonham, the drummer for the hard rock band Led Zeppelin, had died from a drug overdose. Led Zeppelin, along with Black Sabbath, had changed the musical landscape in the Seventies, transforming the happy, peace-loving sound of the Sixties to an edgier, darker, and more dangerous form of music called heavy metal. Elvis had met the band once, inviting the new pioneers of rock and roll to visit him. Unlike the Beatles, Elvis liked these bawdy young rockers, and when lead singer Robert Plant was in a near-fatal car accident, Elvis made sure to send him a get-well card.

The day of the political pilgrimage arrived and the New Aquarius faction, about twenty-five in all, noisily boarded the plane for Washington.

The stewardesses had their hands full on that flight with a rowdy collection of hippies, artists, and activists letting loose as if they were going on spring break. Zeus and Lacey were secluded up in first class, unaware of their behavior, and unable to supervise their group as they all blew off some steam in an alcohol-induced celebration. Many make-out sessions erupted and, led by Thorny, loud boisterous sing-a-longs, as the usual passengers, comprised of businessmen and government workers, shook their heads in disgust.

For his part, Elvis was somewhat subdued compared to the rest, but he still took part in some of the mischief, encouraging some of the women to flash their chests, which many did. Finally, Zeus was alerted and came out of first class at the urging of the flight crew to settle his group down.

Mercifully, it was a short flight and, once off the plane, Zeus gathered his inebriated troops and gave them a firm lecture about acting like professionals before corralling them onto a bus and getting them to their hotel. For a slice of delicious irony, he had chosen the Watergate for his group to stay in. That night the hotel was rocked with scandal once more as the party continued, monopolizing an entire floor, going from room to room. It took a threat from the management to finally pull the plug on the wild night.

Back in New York, Agent Jericho was performing his own homage to Watergate with a late night break-in at the now-deserted New Aquarius headquarters. He rifled through their files and rummaged through the garbage for any type of clue, but couldn't find anything incriminating. However, he did discover one thing of interest, a permit to hold an event in Central Park on January 20, 1981, the date of the upcoming presidential inauguration.

It was late 1980, but the office was still somewhat up for grabs. The incumbent President, Jimmy Carter, had pulled away from Ted Kennedy in the primaries to win his party's nomination, and on the Republican side, Ronald Reagan had defeated George Bush, but made him his running mate. Though the election was over a month away, the smart money was on Reagan to walk away with it all.

The Carter Administration had been taking a beating of late. Inflation, the Iranian hostage situation, an energy crisis, and the Russian invasion of Afghanistan had made Carter look like an ineffectual leader in many people's eyes. He had recently tried a daring helicopter rescue of the hostages in Tehran, but poor planning and a horrendous sandstorm caused the mission to fail and left eight soldiers dead. The country was now looking for strong Republican leadership to restore their sagging sense of national pride, and Reagan with his tough talk and John Wayne-like swagger seemed to fit the bill. The times, they were a changing.

Jericho began putting some pieces of the puzzle together in his mind. He photographed the document and vacated the building, deciding to keep the permit's discovery under wraps for the time being.

The next morning, Zeus assembled his troops and led their march, all the while barking commands and rallying cries over his megaphone like a general leading his troops into battle. They met up with other protesters from various parts of the country, combining forces for a very impressive army.

While Elvis was romancing Ann-Margret, back at Graceland, Priscilla had been growing increasingly restless and unhappy. She had tried on numerous occasions to come to Los Angeles and visit him, but each time Elvis had come up with an excuse for her not to come. Elvis continually denied he was having an affair with Ann-Margret, but Priscilla's suspicions remained.

At Graceland, Priscilla began to feel like a well-pampered prisoner, locked away in a mansion, away from friends and family. Out of boredom she had decided to explore more of the house. The attic was a room that piqued her curiousity. It was a room that she had never been in, and much of the hired help had claimed to hear strange noises eminiating from it. Her young imagination had caused her to wonder if it was in fact, haunted.

One day Priscilla's curiosity got the best of her and she ventured up into the attic, not knowing what to expect. To her relief, it appeared to be only a storage area for the Presley clan. Old televisions, boxes and furniture were strewn across the room, looking no different than most attics. As she looked through the boxes, she was delighted to find several of Elvis' old outfits, including his Army uniform. She pulled his uniform out of the box and pressed it against her skin, reliving old memories. In the corner she saw a clothing rack with several large dresses hanging upon it. She knew that they must have belongeded to Elvis' mother. Knowing the mystique that Gladys held over Elvis, she could not help trying on one of the dresses. She put the dress on over her clothes, realizing it was much too big for her. Nonetheless, she sauntered over to a full-length mirror to take a look. She clasped the excess material back for a tighter fit as she modeled majestically in front of the mirror. As she gazed at her reflection, she could have sworn that she saw Gladys' image momentarily appear in the mirror. Unnerved, Priscilla quickly removed the dress and placed it back on the rack as she felt a cold chill go up her spine. Sensing the presence of Gladys' spirit, Priscilla decided to retreat from the attic, when she saw a box of opened letters on the floor. She quickly glanced through the letters to Elvis and recognized the name on the return address as one of the many women Elvis was rumored to have had an affair with, a rumor that Elvis emphatically denied. As she began reading one of the letters, it was obvious by the tone and content of the words that the rumors were true. Tears streamed Priscilla's cheek as she read the love letter, confirming her suspiscions.

Suddenly the attic door creaked open, making Priscilla jump nervously. It was the maid, Hattie.

"Come out of the attic, child. There's nothing up there but old memories."

Priscilla forced a fake smile and tucked the letter back in the box and joined Hattie downstairs.

Washington D.C., the nation's capitol, had been founded on the banks of the Potomac River. The Piscataway Indians originally occupied the land, but in 1634 Lord Cecil Calvert, an English colonist, claimed the land for Catholic settlers. After unsuccessfully attempting to convert the Indians to Catholicism, the English forced the Piscataways to leave in 1697, and they eventually disappeared altogether.

After America declared and won its independence, the new nation's capitol was moved from New York City and Philadelphia to its current location. A ten square-mile area was designated for the capitol, and architect Charles L'Enfant was hired to design the city. In 1793, work began on the Capitol, but as it neared completion, it was burned to the ground in the War of 1812.

As the city slowly rebuilt itself, the Civil War broke out and the city found itself practically on the border of the warring North and South. In 1865, in the days after the South surrendered, the city and the nation were tested and plunged into mourning when President Lincoln was assassinated at Ford's Theater.

In the 1870s, Alexander Shepherd was hired to overhaul the town's sagging infrastructure; his aggressive use of federal funds led to the federalization of the city. However, it was not until a beautification plan at the turn of the century took effect that the city gained the monuments, parks, and landscaping for which it is now known. In the 1960s, the city began to grow not just as a cultural center, but as a lightning rod for political protest and assembly.

Elvis met up with Lacey and they marched together, holding their protest signs high above their heads. It was the first time in over a month they had been able to freely talk without the surveillance of Jericho or Zeus. They managed to break away from the large crowd and talk privately while they marched.

"So how's Zeus?" Elvis asked teasingly.

"Well, he's a little ticked off at you and the volunteers for the drunken debauchery yesterday."

"They're just kids blowing off a little steam."

"Then what was your excuse?"

"Hey, when in Rome..."

"That isn't funny," Lacey answered.

"Well, tell your boyfriend that I'm sorry," he remarked sharply.

"He's not my boyfriend, not really."

"Then what is he?"

"He's my assignment; you know that."

"So all the time that you've spent with him, all the sex you've had with him, you haven't developed any feelings for him?"

"Are you jealous?"

"Jealous? Why would I be jealous?"

"I don't know, but you are."

"No offense, but you're not my type," Elvis quipped.

"Good. Keep it that way. Feelings between us would only jeopardize our mission."

"I'm just curious if posing as his girlfriend long enough could make you develop feelings for him, also jeopardizing our mission."

"Don't worry. I'm as professional as they come," she declared. "But to answer your question, I have not developed any feelings for him. He's a hippie and a hypocrite; I hate both."

"He's also a left-wing terrorist," Elvis added.

"Well, we don't know that."

"We don't? Then why the hell are we here?"

"We're finding out if he is one or not."

"Gee, during your presentation, it sounded like a foregone conclusion."

"That's one of the things I wanted to explain to you that night at the bar. You see, Agent Jericho isn't a real FBI agent.""What do you mean?"

"He's Black Ops."

"Black Ops?"

"Black Operations. An elite covert organization that's above the law and carries out the government's secret agenda."

"And what's that?"

"To win at all costs. He has complete access to the FBI and CIA and works above the law to destroy any faction that he deems a threat to national security."

"Like what?" Elvis asked.

"Like the sixties' counterculture, for instance."

"So we're doing all this just to jail a bunch of hippies?"

"No, I don't think so. Jericho received an intelligence report stating that something big was going down at the beginning of next year. It was something being orchestrated by New Aquarius and their Benefactor. What that is, we don't know, but I can tell that the threat is real. He wouldn't be going through all this trouble if it wasn't."

"But what about the rap sheet on Zeus and his henchmen?" Elvis wanted to know.

"That's one of the things I have my doubts about."

"What do you mean?"

"I went undercover and lifted their fingerprints; Jericho came back with the dossier on them and quite frankly, it seemed a little over the top," Lacey explained. "I'm sure they're no angels, but the file claims that one guy was a member of the Manson family and Zeus had links to the Chicago Seven. It sounds a little far-fetched to me. As if Jericho was writing the dossier from a Sixties history book and throwing in every left-wing group and unsavory event he could find."

"Then why am I doing this?" Elvis asked.

"Actually, I was about to ask you the same question. Was I right about you being a musician forced into this to avoid jail?"

"Well, yeah. That's about it. Though I do care about my country, and I want to stop any terrorist attack before it happens."

"I can't imagine a gentle guy like you committing a crime," Lacey said sincerely. "Hell, a couple of months ago you didn't even know how to smoke a joint. So what was the crime? Did you double-park in a no parking zone?"

"No. I killed somebody," he said bluntly.

"Get out of here. You're a murderer? I don't believe it."

"Well, it's true. Though there were special circumstances."

"Like what?"

"I was in a bar in Atlanta when a bunch of locals attempted to gang-rape a girl. I tried to stop them, but they beat me to the ground. I had a gun in my pocket, so I used it to shoot our way out of there, but one of the guys I shot died from his wounds."

"My God, Jesse. That's horrible."

"Hey, it was self-defense, and in the defense of a helpless woman."

"No, I mean it's horrible that Jericho would use an incident like that to extort you," she explained.

"Well, that's how I got here."

"Well anyway, I'm glad we're marching together. There's a lot we need to talk about, away from prying ears."

"So okay, what's your story?" Elvis asked.

"My story?"

"Yeah. How did you end up in the FBI?" Elvis clarified as they marched alongside the Reflecting Pool.

"I don't know. I was a Navy brat and wanted to serve my country the way my father did. Make him proud, you know."

"So, is he proud?"

"I don't know. He died in Vietnam."

"I'm sorry, Lacey."

"So am I. There's not a day that goes by that I don't ponder that same question. To be honest, I don't know if he would be proud of me," she said.

"That's crazy. Of course he would be proud of you."

"Really? Why? Because I'm sleeping with a man I don't love, marching for a cause I don't believe in, fighting for a truth I'm unsure of? What's to be proud of?"

"Because you're doing what you're doing for the good of your country. Don't you think your father encountered some gray areas in Vietnam? That whole war was a gray area."

"Thanks. I never thought of it like that," she gushed as she stopped and hugged him under the shadow of the Washington Monument.

She broke the embrace, not wanting to start rumors amongst the volunteers. Discreetly, Elvis put his hand in hers.

"You know, sometimes I think I should just quit this crazy FBI stuff, settle down, get married, and have children," she confessed.

"So why don't you?"

"After this mission is over, maybe I will."

"You know, I lied earlier," Elvis confessed. "You are my type."

"I know," Lacey smiled. "Like I said, I can tell when you lie."

"Uh oh. That's not good," he said with a laugh.

"I think it is. It means you're not comfortable being deceptive, that your heart is pure. Jericho and Zeus, they're good liars. I think it comes with practice," she said as the wind blew her black hair over her face.

He subtly pulled her out of the march and away from public view.

"You're so beautiful," he said as he gently tucked his hand under her chin and pressed his lips against hers.

She returned the favor as they shared a passionate kiss. Then they snuck back into the protest and walked hand in hand to the White House. In the distance, Elvis saw his brother, Jesse standing on top of a wall, looking down upon the crowd and giving the piece sign with his hand.

CHAPTER XX

GUITAR MAN

The march on Washington was a success by almost any standard, and despite the drunken melee on the first night, Zeus was very pleased with the outcome. The flight back to New York was the opposite of the flight to D.C., very uneventful and subdued.

Elvis and Lacey had had very few chances to speak freely since the day they kissed, but their eyes had met flirtatiously numerous times. They did have a brief conversation, where they both confessed having feelings for each other, but agreed for the sake of the mission to not act further on them until its completion.

A few days after their return, Zeus approached Elvis with a guitar in his hand.

"Hey, Jesse, I just wanted to thank you for all the work you've been doing for us, and to say I'm curious to hear you play," he said as he handed him the guitar.

Elvis nodded in appreciation as he strapped on the guitar and grabbed a pick.

"This is a song I wrote called 'Going Away'."

He took a deep breath and began playing and singing.

His singing and the lyrics of the song immediately impressed Zeus. He knew that he had found the man he'd been looking for.

Elvis finished playing and looked to Zeus for his reaction.

"Wow, Jesse, that song was really cool. You've got a good voice too, man. You kind of sound like Elvis or something."

"Thanks, man. I get that a lot. Elvis was a big influence on me."

"Obviously."

Zeus then sprang out of his seat and ran to his office, returning with his guitar.

"Wanna jam?" he asked excitedly.

"Sure."

Zeus sat down and they began playing around, jamming a few Dylan tunes, before Zeus started playing some of his own songs.

"Hey, Zeus, you're pretty good," Elvis told him.

"Thanks. You know, I'm organizing a big music festival, and I'd like you to be on the lineup."

"Hey, I'd be honored, man. When is it?"

"It's on the twentieth of October. It's not a paying gig or anything; it's a rally and fundraiser," Zeus clarified.

"That's fine. I think playing for money can cheapen music anyway."

"Right on, man. I'll put you on the list, then. It should be a cool night. There'll be a lot of good local talent playing, including me."

"Well, count me in."

Zeus and Elvis bonded that night, united by their passion for music. Elvis felt a little strange, though, becoming friends with a man whose organization he was infiltrating, and whose girlfriend he was secretly romancing.

The next few weeks at Zeus' headquarters were buzzing with excitement as they rallied to put the show together. Elvis' mission objective was put on the back-burner as he prepared for his onstage return. It was his first performance in nearly three years, and though nobody else understood the significance of what they were about to witness, Elvis saw it as one of the most important performances of his lifetime. He wouldn't be able to fall back on his reputation or the Presley mystique; he would sink or swim entirely based on his talent. He wouldn't be wearing a sequined jumpsuit, or have an accomplished band behind him; he would be on stage alone, just a man and his guitar, and his fear of failure had begun to unnerve him. For the first time since Argentina, he began taking pills again, pills provided to him by Zeus. He rationalized that he needed them to handle the pressure, not just of his upcoming performance, but the pressure of working undercover. In truth, most people would have had a hard time dealing with all of the hurdles thrown in his way in the last year. He was still heartbroken over Faith even though new feelings for Lacey had emerged and, to make matters worse, because of the their situation, they were feelings neither of them could act upon. The pressure had been building up inside him and he felt as if he was about to crack.

The effects of the drugs started to become visible to Lacey. A few days before the concert, Elvis walked into the New Aquarius headquarters in a complete fog.

"Jesse, are you okay?" she asked.

"Yeah. I just haven't gotten much sleep lately."

She pulled him closely to her and whispered in his ear.

"What are you on?"

Elvis just shook his head and walked away. Lacey let him go, knowing that this was not the time to confront him. Things had been going so well between them and on the mission, but she feared his behavior could soon be a liability. His being added to the lineup of the festival was a major victory for them, and now she was watching it begin to fall apart. She would not let that happen.

The next day, she saw Jesse at the FBI briefing; his eyes were barely open and he seemed somewhat intoxicated. Jericho was running late and that gave her a few moments to speak to her partner.

"Jesse, what is wrong with you?"

"What do you mean?"

"You've been as high as a kite for the past few days."

"I'm just staying in character," he joked.

"This isn't funny, Jesse. You're not in control of your faculties, and that could get us killed."

"It'll be okay."

"I have to tell Jericho about this," she warned.

"Hey, I've been under a lot of stress lately. It just takes the edge off."

"What are you taking?"

"A few Percodans. That's all."

"Let me guess, compliments of Zeus?"

"I've been having trouble sleeping. Zeus gave me some pills to help me out."

Just then, Jericho entered the room. He smiled insincerely and sat down at his desk.

"Hello, Jesse, Lacey. Anything new to report?"

Lacey glanced over at Jesse, and knew she had to act.

"Jesse's been abusing drugs."

"Is this true, Jesse?" Jericho asked sternly.

Before Elvis could speak, Jericho took one look into his glazed-over eyes and knew the answer.

Elvis gave Lacey a cold look and responded, "No, I've just been taking some pills to help me sleep."

Jericho stared intently at Elvis for a few seconds, deciding what his next course of action should be.

"Lacey, will you please excuse yourself for a few minutes? I need to talk to Jesse alone."

Lacey nodded and left the room.

"What do you think you're doing?" Jericho asked in a scolding tone.

"I've just been taking a few pills. It's no big deal."

"Look, unlike Lacey, I know who you really are. I know what problems you've had in the past. You're an addict, Elvis. A few years ago your addiction almost killed you. Now you're playing with the same fire again," Jericho said.

"It's not really any of your business," Elvis replied belligerantly.

"The hell it isn't. There's a lot at stake right now, and I've invested a lot of time and money in you. Until this mission's completed, I own you. We're on the brink of blowing this case wide open, and you want to piss it all away. Well, I can't have that."

"I'm under a lot of pressure right now," Elvis argued. "I have a lot of things to deal with."

"Like what? Let's hear them," Jericho demanded.

"Well, let's see. About three years ago, I had to leave everything I had behind: my little girl, my home, my fame, my fortune, even my identity. I was forced to leave my country to live in seclusion. I made one friend at that time, and he turned out to be a Nazi in hiding. I returned to America, where I lived as a drifter and not so accidentally killed someone. I had no money and no life, and had to find out about my father's death in a newspaper. Finally, I met someone I loved and began to feel some sense of happiness, and you came into my life and tore me away from it.

"I've spent the last several months living like a caged animal, made to obey your every command, even having my face surgically altered. I'm forced to work undercover in some hippie haven with what you would have me believe is the fate of the free world hanging in the balance. Now I have a concert coming up where I have to play in a style and manner that I'm not used to at all. Any person on the planet would need a release from all of that."

"So, it's the concert that's really causing this," Jericho deduced.

"Have you been listening to me? Can you comprehend all the crap I've had to deal with recently?"

"That's just an excuse. Look, I know enough about you to write your biography. I know about your acute stage-fright, and I imagine taking three years off between performances would only intensify it. This isn't a game, though; I need a sober agent for this mission, not some pill-popping zombie."

"I'm afraid," Elvis confessed.

"What's to be afraid of? You're Elvis Presley, the king of rock and roll. You're going onstage with a bunch of amateurs. Even if you have the worst performance of your life, you'll still blow away everyone else at that concert, unless you go on stage all doped up. If that's the case, then a bunch of two-bit folk-rock singing hacks will make you look like a fool. Do you want that?"

"No," he muttered.

"It's time to grow up and start facing your problems. All your life you've tried to medicate your problems and run away from them. You've even faked your own death to avoiding facing your life, but you can't run away from me. I'm your shadow. So get your head together and fulfill your destiny."

Elvis took Jericho's words to heart as Lacey was waved back into the room. She came in and sat down next to her partner.

"Is this matter taken care of?" she asked.

"Yes," Elvis answered, feeling somewhat ashamed.

She gave him a big hug as he clung to her like a lifesaver in a stormy sea.

The day of the concert arrived. Zeus had rented a decent sized theater and was pleased that everything had come together smoothly. The volunteers had placed ads on almost every phone pole in the city, distributing flyers at every coffeehouse, even placing ads in the newspaper. Zeus had gathered some very talented musicians and respected speakers for the show. In the lobby, there were booths set up where people could register to vote, gather pamphlets, and sign petitions for numerous causes. Zeus was in his element, using his great organizational skills and attention to detail to produce a very professional show. He was buzzing with nervous excitement, anxiously awaiting any problem that might arise so he could tackle it to the ground. He knew that the Benefactor would be at the show watching from a private booth, and badly wanted to impress him to prove that he was the right man for the job. A week earlier, his girlfriend had approached him and asked him not to supply Jesse Hope with any more drugs, warning that his performance would suffer if he did. Zeus was wise enough to heed her request.

Backstage, Elvis was a nervous wreck. He had stop using drugs as ordered, but the pre-concert jitters made him feel as if he was going to throw up. Elvis was always nervous before a concert, especially in the early days. He'd always thought his first appearance on the Ed Sullivan show had aged him a few years. Not that any of the millions who saw him on that historic night would have known it.

Elvis had performed on television before. He had appeared on *Stage Show*, a variety show produced by Jackie Gleason, and *The Milton Berle Show*. That appearance had created a buzz in the music industry, and among teenage girls, who saw him as a dangerous, sexy rebel. That image took two steps back when he made an appearance on *The Steve Allen Show*. Steve Allen made Elvis perform in a tuxedo, and in one of the lamest attempts to be funny in television history, sing "Hound Dog" to an actual hound dog. As much as Elvis hated that performance, it routed Steve Allen's competition in the ratings, including the television juggernaut, *The Ed Sullivan Show*.

Ed Sullivan's executives then decided it was time to get this young kid to perform on their show. September 9, 1956 became an early milestone not only in rock and roll history, but also in television history, as eighty percent of the country crowded around their small, grainy, black and white television sets to watch a legend being born.

He sang and gyrated like a man possessed, causing both scandal and adulation across the nation, so much scandal that, in a later Sullivan appearance, television executives made sure that he was only filmed from the waist up.

Lacey went backstage to comfort him and build up his confidence, but even so he had a tough battle with anxiety.

Zeus opened the show with a speech on political involvement and played a very nice three-song set before bringing the next act onstage. Several other acts came on and played their sets as, in between, Zeus and other speakers gave political speeches.

All had gone well so far; there was a good crowd for the show and they responded well to both the speakers and the performers. Elvis was due up next. Onstage, Zeus announced him, as Elvis waited nervously in the wings.

"Ladies and gentlemen, our next performer is here all the way from San Francisco. Please welcome Jesse Hope!" Zeus shouted as the crowd applauded and Elvis took the stage.

He took a seat on the stool next to the microphone and opened his set with the Bob Dylan song "Blowin' in the Wind," to which the crowd responded nicely. After that, he did two of his originals to finish out his three-song set. He had done a marvelous job and the crowd roared with approval; it was the loudest response of the night.

He got up and bowed as he began to walk offstage, but a surge of adrenaline hit him. The crowd wanted more and he knew he had one more to give them, a final Elvis Presley song for old time's sake. He kicked over the stool and dove into a fevered rendition of "That's All Right (Mama)," bringing the previously subdued crowd to their feet. He danced and swayed with his guitar like the young man he had been when he recorded the song. He pulled out every trick and move he had, as the crowd swooned at his dead-on Elvis impersonation. They cheered in delight as he held onto the last note, got down on one knee, threw his hands in the air and stared triumphantly into the audience.

"Thank you. Thank you very much," he snarled as his lip curled, almost mocking his true identity.

It was evident to everyone in the venue that this unknown singer had just stolen the show.

He strutted off the stage and lay the guitar down as Lacey greeted him with a passionate kiss.

"You were great!" she gasped, excited as a schoolgirl.

The concert continued and was a total success, and the name Jesse Hope was burned into everyone's brain, including that of the man who watched it all from a private booth. He knew he had just seen greatness, and wanted to meet this Jesse Hope. He was the Benefactor.

CHAPTER XXI

BURNING LOVE

The concert had met and surpassed everyone's expectations, including Zeus'. Backstage, there was much celebrating and high-fiving as the musicians rejoiced and basked in the glow of an all-around great show. There were two stars that shined the brightest however -- Zeus, not just for his great opening set, but the flawlessness of his organization and promotion, and Jesse Hope, whose charisma and showmanship had made it a must-see concert.

Zeus rushed to congratulate Jesse Hope after the show, but couldn't find him. He searched throughout the backstage area, but he was not there either. Now on a mission, Zeus threw open the door to the green room and saw Jesse passionately kissing Lacey. They both turned to see his shocked and hurt expression at their mutual betrayal as Zeus stormed off.

Elvis and Lacey both stared at each other in disbelief and disappointment in each other and themselves, realizing that their lust and emotions had probably destroyed everything that they had tried to accomplish.

"Damn! I need to go talk to him," Lacey said as she pushed Elvis away and chased after Zeus.

As she ran to find him, she sifted through her mind to find the right words that would keep them together. She found him weeping in his makeshift office as she humbly tiptoed into the room. She had never seen Zeus so vulnerable. For a man who had the gall to nickname himself after the God of Gods, he now seemed weak and beautifully human.

"Zeus, I'm so sorry," she sobbed, partly acting, but still sincere.

"This was the greatest night of my life, until I opened that door."

"Oh, God, I'm sorry. It just happened. I don't know what to tell you."

"Do you love him?"

"Love him? I hardly know him, honey. I love you. You just haven't been around very much lately. One day you're organizing a march on Washington, and the next it's a big music festival. You're spread so thin lately, I guess I was just lonely."

"Maybe you should leave. I need to think about some things," he responded.

"Okay, if that's what you want. I'll see you tomorrow. We'll talk more then."

He nodded and she lightly kissed him and gave him a hug that he didn't return.

"I really am sorry," she restated as she got up and walked slowly out the door.

The next morning, Lacey and Elvis met up before their briefing with Jericho. They knew they had to tell him about what had happened, and they knew he would be furious. The results of their indiscretion could very easily get both of them banished from New Aquarius, and all of their hard work would be lost.

They sat in their chairs as Jericho arrived in an unusually good mood, a mood that they knew was about to change.

"Hey, Jesse, great show last night," Jericho complimented him.

"You were there?"

"Of course. I have to keep an eye on all New Aquarius activities. And besides, I didn't want to miss a performance by the legendary Jesse Hope," he said with a knowing wink. "What did Zeus think of your performance?"

"I don't know, actually. There's something we need to tell you," Elvis confessed.

"What's that?"

"Last night, after my set, something happened between me and Lacey."

"Come on," Jericho said, being particularly dense. "Out with it. I don't have all day."

"Jesse and I started kissing, and Zeus caught us," Lacey blurted out.

"You're kidding, right? Please tell me you're kidding."

"We're sorry. It just happened," Elvis said sheepishly.

"I don't believe this!" Jericho exploded. "That is the most irresponsible thing I've ever heard of!"

"I know. We just got caught up in the moment," Lacey added.

"So let me guess. Zeus doesn't want anything to do with either of you, and everything is ruined."

"We don't know yet. We're going to see him today," Elvis answered.

"You know I might expect something like this from you, Jesse, but Lacey, I thought you were a professional."

"I am a professional."

"A professional what? That's the question."

"Don't talk to her that way!" Elvis shouted.

"Oh, I see. Now your new boyfriend's going to defend you honor. Well, listen to me: I want the two of you to go to Zeus and beg, grovel, and kiss his ass if necessary until he lets both of you stay onboard. If you don't, you'll both have me to deal with, and if you thought I was a prick before, you aint seen nothing yet. Now get the hell out of here."

Elvis and Lacey hurried out of his office and tried to devise a strategy to get back in Zeus' favor. Lacey went to New Aquarius' headquarters first. Zeus greeted her coldly at the door.

"What do you want?" he asked.

"A second chance."

Zeus was silent as he led her back to his office. Once inside, Zeus just stared at her pensively with his arms defiantly crossed.

"So what do you have to say for yourself?"

"I told you before, but I'll say it again. I'm sorry. He means nothing to me. It was a one-time thing, I swear. Please forgive me."

"So just like that, I'm supposed to take you back?"

"I'll do anything you want. Just take me back."

"Anything?"

"Yes, of course, honey. There isn't anything that I wouldn't do for you."

"Marry me," he said.

"Sure, I'll...wait. What did you just say?" she asked disbelief.

"Marry me, Lacey. I never realized how much I loved you until I considered the thought of losing you. You're everything to me. You're the only person who understands me. Prove your love and devotion to me, and take my hand in marriage."

Lacey was stunned. She didn't know what to say. She knew she definitely did not want to marry Zeus, but still, she needed to get back into his good graces.

"Why would you want to marry me? You saw me kiss another man last night," she reminded him.

"All the more reason to make you mine. I've taken you for granted for too long. I want us to be together forever. Just you and me."

She was dumbfounded by his proposal, and caught up in the rush of the moment; she gave him an answer she would immediately regret.

"Yes, I'll marry you."

"Great! You just made me the happiest man on the planet. I'll make sure you won't regret this. You'll see," he gushed as he gave her a big hug.

Lacey knew she had just made a major mistake, but didn't have the heart to change her answer at that moment.

"Let's get married on my birthday, October 30th," Zeus suggested.

"Okay," she meekly responded, knowing the date wasn't that far away.

The phone rang and Zeus answered as Lacey retreated out of the office, knowing that she had to figure out a way out of the wedding. Just then, Elvis arrived and was met by Wolfgang.

"Jesse, the boss would like to see you in his office."

Elvis followed Wolfgang's lead and passed Lacey in the hall as they exchanged awkward smiles. Wolfgang opened the door and Elvis marched into Zeus' office. Zeus looked up and saw him as Wolfgang left the room. Zeus promptly ended the phone call and rose from his desk, making his way over to Elvis.

"Zeus, I just want you to know that I'm really sorry about what happened last night. It will never happen again. It was just one of those..."

A left hook to the jaw interrupted Elvis' apology. It caught him by surprise and knocked him to the floor.

"You're through here!" Zeus yelled as he started kicking Elvis in the ribs.

Elvis rose to his feet and got into a karate stance.

"Okay, I probably deserved that, but I didn't come here to fight."

"Too bad. You should have," Zeus said as he punched again.

Elvis' temper would not allow him to take any more abuse as he attacked Zeus with a series of karate chops.

There was a knock on the door as Wolfgang peeked in.

"I hope I'm not interrupting…" he said as witnessed the brawl and pulled Elvis off of Zeus.

Wolgang stood between the two combatants, ready to defend Zeus.

"Do you want me to take care of him, boss?"

"No. He was just leaving," Zeus instructed.

Knowing that his days in New Aquarius were over, Elvis turned and headed for the door.

As Wolfgang flexed his bravado, he handed Zeus a plain, white envelope. It was a letter from the Benefactor, hand-delivered as usual to prevent any interception.

"This just came for you."

Zeus stepped back and began reading the letter.

It was obvious by the look on Zeus' face that it was news that he didn't want. "Jesse, wait!" Zeus said.

Elvis turned around and waited for Zeus' words.

"This is from the Benefactor; apparently he really liked your performance last night, and wants to meet you," he said in disgust.

"Really?"

"Yeah, and as much as I'd like to ignore this message, he pays the bills around here and what he wants, he gets."

"Where is he?"

"He's at a hotel room waiting for us. You have no idea how privileged you are to meet him. I don't know why he has chosen to reveal himself to you, but you are not to tell anyone who he is, or even that you've met him, not even Lacey."

"Okay sure. Damn, I feel like I'm about to meet Jesus."

"No, this man is bigger than Jesus," Zeus said cryptically as they headed out the door together.

The two men got into a taxi and headed for their destination. Zeus and Elvis sat in the backseat of the cab enduring a uncomfortable silence until Elvis spoke.

"For the record, I meant it when I said I was sorry about Lacey. It's not going to happen again," Elvis said.

"Damn right, it's not. We're getting married at the end of this month."

"What? Since when?" Elvis asked with surprise.

"Since today. I proposed, and she said yes. I guess I should thank you. In a strange way, you've made it possible. If last night hadn't happened, I might never have asked her."

"That's okay. The punch in the face was thanks enough," Elvis said sarcastically.

Elvis' heart felt as if it was being torn from his chest. He didn't know if what Zeus said was true, but he had a feeling it was. He stared out the car window, trying not to let Zeus see his pain. He gazed at the city's majestic skyline, the Empire State Building and World Trade Center towered triumphantly over him, making him feel even more insignificant.

It was hard for Elvis to believe that he had fallen so far to the ground. Twenty years earlier, he had been on top of the world. After his triumphant performance on *The Ed Sullivan Show*, his already-rising star had reached its zenith, and Elvismania had begun. Almost overnight, screaming legions of young females began following his every step and turning his concerts into near-riots. Having the conquered the world of popular music, he turned his sights to his next target, Hollywood.

Elvis signed with producer Hal Willis and began filming a movie that would be named *Love Me Tender.* Both the movie and the title track became big hits, and Elvis began working on his next two films, *Loving You* and *Jailhouse Rock.*

Jailhouse Rock went on to become a movie classic, bolstered by the song of the same name and the dance sequence that accompanied it.

Around this time, Elvis fulfilled another lifelong dream by buying his mother a house. Graceland, as it was called, was an eighteen-room, Georgian colonial-style house built on thirteen acres of land, and would become the home for the entire Presley clan, as well as his close friends.

"We're here," Zeus informed him as the cab driver pulled over and Zeus paid the fare.

They got out in front of the famous Waldorf-Astoria Hotel, and took the elevator to the top floor. Zeus walked up to a hotel room door and knocked.

"Come in," a distinct voice instructed.

Zeus opened the door as they walked inside. Sitting on a plush sofa in the luxurious penthouse suite was the Benefactor, a man with a familiar face, a person Elvis had met once before. It was John Lennon.

CHAPTER XXII

ENTER THE WALRUS

John Winston Lennon was born on October 9, 1940, in Liverpool, England, while the city was being bombed by Hitler's Luftwaffe in a fierce air raid. The rest of his life would be just as turbulent.

His father Fred was a merchant seaman who was at sea for much of the first five years of John's life. John's mother Julia wasn't much better of a parent, leaving him with his Aunt Mimi to raise while she ran around and had numerous affairs.

A gifted and sensitive child, he was also very creative and given much encouragement by his loving aunt. The pain of being abandoned by his parents was channeled into his art and his love of music. As a child in England, he was mesmerized by the new rock and roll sounds he heard from across the ocean in the United States. He loved the black musicians such as Chuck Berry and Little Richard, but his true idol was Elvis Presley.

His aunt bought him a guitar, and he practiced it day and night, replicating his favorite licks of the American rock and rollers. He then formed a band called the Quarry Men. While in the band, he met fellow musician, Paul McCartney, who soon joined the band, along with George Harrison.

Around this time, John's mother came back into his life. Lennon was filled with glee as he felt a great void in his soul being filled. The happiness was short-lived, however, as, tragically, his mother was soon killed in an automobile accident. Much like Elvis, Lennon's mother's death was a life-shattering event from which his psyche still hadn't recovered.

Within a few years, the band's name evolved into the Beatles, and drummer Pete Best and John's long-time friend and fellow art student Stu Sutcliffe joined them. The band toured West Germany, where a disgruntled Stu got into a heated argument with John, who was drunk at the time. They began to brawl, and John kicked Stu several times in the head. Shortly afterward, Stu died of a brain hemorrhage, and John held himself responsible. Through the years, he was heard to say that it was now his karma to die a violent death.

Not too long after this tragedy, Brian Epstein discovered the Beatles and the rest, as they say, is history.

"Jesse Hope, meet John Lennon," Zeus begrudgingly introduced as John smiled and shook Elvis' hand.

"It's great to meet you. I'm a big fan," Elvis said with a degree of insincerity.

"Thanks. I'm actually a fan of yours, too. I caught your set last night and was blown away by it," Lennon complimented him, studying him from behind his moon-shaped glasses. "You were really good too, Zeus. You did a great job of organizing the show as well. It's obvious that I chose my right-hand man wisely," Lennon gushed as he pulled out an envelope and handed it to Zeus. "Here. It's a little contribution to the cause."

"Thanks."

"No. Thank you for bringing your friend over. If you don't mind, though, I'd like you to leave us. There is much we need to discuss," John said with his Liverpudlian accent.

Zeus was caught offguard by the request, but had no choice but to honor it. He reluctantly walked toward the door.

"Well, Jesse, I guess I'll see you back at headquarters," Zeus said with a fading smile as he left the room.

"I have to say, Mr. Lennon," Elvis began as soon as Zeus was gone. "You were the last person I thought I'd meet today."

"Please call me John. May I call you Jesse?"

"Yes, of course."

"So Jesse, tell me a little bit about yourself."

"There's not much to tell. I'm just musician who's been playing for a long time. I bounced around California for a while, playing gigs and writing songs. Then a few months ago I moved East and met Zeus, and he got me to play at last night's concert. What else do you want to know?"

"How come a man of your talent hasn't become a big star by now?"

"I don't know. I guess I was never interested in fame and fortune, I just wanted to play my music."

"Good answer. I respect that. So, I suppose you're wondering why I wanted to see you?"

"Yes. I am a bit perplexed."

"Well, let me explain. You see, in the early Seventies, I was making music and was very politically active. Then the FBI started harassing me, tapping my phones, having me followed, even trying to get me deported. Hell, they even planted some drugs on me once and had Yoko and me arrested. So I decided to lay low for a while. You know, drop out of the scene and raise my son, Sean. That's why I've been secretly funding New Aquarius, to keep the cause alive without getting my name involved. Now I'm a citizen of this country, the political climate has changed, and it's time for a comeback. Yoko and I have been writing and recording songs for a new album, but that's only the beginning. I want to return to the world of politics as well."

"Great, but what does that have to do with me?" Presley asked.

"Nothing, really. I'm just letting you know where my head's at right now. You see, after I release my new album, I want to start my own record label, and release something different than all the big-label bullshit. I want to make and distribute music for the people. Nothing trendy, just good musicians making good music with lyrics that have social importance. Like your music," John said. "That's part of the reason I've been funding these concerts. I'm looking for some like-minded talent to record on my label, and I think you would make a great first signee."

"Wow, I don't know what to say," Elvis said.

"Say you're interested," Lennon replied.

"I'm interested, definitely."

"Wonderful," Lennon smiled and went across the room to grab two acoustic guitars.

"Would you like to jam for a couple of songs?" John asked.

"Sure, I'd love it."

It was a truly ironic moment for Elvis. Decades earlier, Elvis had been the iconic superstar and John Lennon the young up-and-coming musician, when a similar meeting had occurred.

It was August 27, 1965 when musical superpowers collided, but if Elvis had had his way, the meeting would never have taken place. As usual, Tom Parker was the man who arranged the rock and roll summit, after hearing the Beatles state that Elvis was their idol.

"I don't want to meet those sons of bitches," Elvis angrily barked when Parker proposed the idea.

Elvis felt insecure about the British Invasion, particularly the Beatles. He watched their equally historic appearance on Ed Sullivan and seethed with jealousy as the young teenage girls now screamed for the mop-topped marvels. After their performance, Ed Sullivan conveyed good wishes to them from Elvis Presley, once again the work of Puppeteer Parker. After much pleading and negotiating, Elvis finally agreed to meet the Fab Four, but only if they came to Graceland. Unaware of the primadonna politics, the Beatles enthusiastically agreed.

As John, Paul, George, and Ringo entered the hallowed halls of Graceland, Parker made the introductions. The Beatles, still somewhat new to the fame game, were completely awestruck, nervous, and at a loss for words in the presence of their hero. The silence and tension in the room was thicker than both parties' accents, until Elvis finally spoke out.

"If you guys are gonna sit and stare at me all night, then I'm going to bed."

The Beatles scrambled to appease the King, until Elvis suggested they jam on a few songs. The young Liverpudlians almost wet themselves in their enthusiasm. The musical icons jammed together and talked about the fun and perils of superstardom as Colonel Parker, the consummate gambler, took Brian Epstein for thousands at roulette. As the night ended, John invited Elvis to visit them at their hotel the following night, but Elvis politely declined.

Now, fifteen years later, Elvis and John had met again; this time Lennon was the host and Elvis was his somewhat less than starstruck guest.

John grabbed two guitars, handing one to Elvis, and they started playing, at first trading licks, and then doing some old rock standards and even a few of the Beatles' songs "Come Together" and "I Am The Walrus."

Lennon was quite impressed with his new friend, not just by his musical talent, but also by the fact that he didn't make too big a deal of meeting and playing with John Lennon. It was as if they were equal. John hated all of the ass-kissing and celebrity worship that most people showered on him, but this man above all of that. It was almost as if he had somehow tasted the same level of fame as Lennon. An instant bond formed between the two of them. To John, it was almost as if they had met before.

"I like your voice," Lennon remarked. "It reminds me a lot of Elvis."

"I get that all the time. He's a big influence."

"Yeah, me too. I loved the impersonation you did of him last night. You know, I actually met him once."

"Really?"

"Yeah. When me and the Beatles were together, we all got together at Graceland and jammed."

"Wow! What was that like?" Elvis asked, loving the irony.

"It was great. It was probably the greatest thrill of my life."

Elvis was greatly touched by those words, he then felt bad when he remembered how secretly annoyed he had been at the time by the meeting and by Lennon himself.

"I just wish I could have jammed with him one more time, but now it's too late."

"You never know," Elvis answered with a smile.

"Yeah. Maybe in the afterlife or something, but I don't plan on dying any time soon. Hey, let's play some Elvis songs," Lennon suggested.

Elvis smiled, feeling quite confident in his ability to do so as they played a bunch of his music.

A couple of hours had passed since they first began playing, and John decided to call it a day, but not before giving Elvis his home phone number and inviting him to meet him at the same hotel room in a few days.

"It's been a blast, Jesse. Do me a favor, though. Don't tell anyone about my plans to sign you to my label, especially Zeus. I think he'd be hurt that I didn't ask him first," John said.

Elvis agreed, and they said goodbye. John was in great spirits. At forty, he felt more optimistic about the future than he ever had before. He had just released his first single, "(Just Like) Starting Over," from his soon-to-be-released album *Double Fantasy*, and the response to it had been very positive. The title of his first single was quite appropriate, because in many ways he was starting over.

After a 1962 marriage to Cynthia Powell, John Lennon's career began to take off. The Beatles had just been signed to a record deal, and they had decided to replace their drummer, Pete Best, with a flashy young skins player named Richard Starkey, a.k.a. Ringo Starr. Shortly after John's wedding, the group recorded and released "Love Me Do" and "Please Please Me," which become hits in England. In the interim, Cynthia gave birth to John's first child, Julian.

News of the Beatles' greatness traveled quickly across the pond and, in America, a country still grieving over the assassination of John F. Kennedy, "I Wanna Hold Your Hand" went straight to Number 1 on the Billboard Charts. On February 7, 1964, the first shot of the British Invasion was fired, as the Beatles arrived in America at Kennedy Airport to mass hysteria on the part of their mostly female idolaters.

Two days later, they inspired a generation of would-be musicians and made history with their appearance on Ed Sullivan, viewed by seventy-three million people. It was the beginning of a string of hits and groundbreaking albums by the band that John had formed.

Ironically, it was Lennon who almost destroyed the group's popularity by stating in 1966 that the Beatles were "bigger than Jesus." This caused a more than minor outcry in most of America, even inciting some Naziesque record-burnings in a few cities. John quickly quelled the flames with an apology and a claim that his words had been taken out of context. The Beatles were quickly forgiven, but it was only an omen for the changes yet to come.

Later in the year, John met an Asian avant-garde artist named Yoko Ono. Though he didn't know it then, she would soon change his life. In June of 1967, the Beatles released, to mixed reviews, their most ambitious album to date, *Sgt. Pepper's Lonely Hearts Club Band.*

With what is now considered the Holy Grail of rock and roll, the Beatles changed the entire face of music with one album. They changed their image as well, from clean-cut mod-rockers to psychedelic evangelists of the new Age of Aquarius. The album brought the old sounds of the sitar and the new sounds of the moog synthesizer to the forefront of Western consciousness, packaged in a non-linear conceptual album that revolutionized the world.

For their next trick, the Beatles popularized Eastern religion by traveling to India to meet the Maharishi Mahesh Yogi. During their visit, however, tragedy struck when Brian Epstein was found dead in London. Though his death was emotionally devastating to the band, it allowed John and the Beatles to escape his tight control of their image, and they began to express their political beliefs and their opposition to the Vietnam War.

Around this time, John ended his marriage to Cynthia and began dating Yoko Ono. Shortly thereafter, John and Yoko recorded and released an album together entitled *Two Virgins;* the controversial album featured the couple nude on the cover, and was banned by many record stores.

John quickly immersed himself in political causes, especially the anti-war movement, After John and Yoko wed, they staged a bed-in, a seven-day publicity stunt/honeymoon in the name of peace. From their bed, they recorded the song "Give Peace A Chance" with several friends. As harmonious as his relationship with Yoko had become, John's relationship with the Beatles was another story, and they soon began falling apart. In April of 1970, the band shocked the world by calling it quits.

Elvis arrived back at the FBI outpost to brief Jericho on his very eventful day. He barged into the office and proudly approached Jericho.

"I just met the Benefactor."

"Yes, congratulations. I heard you were going to meet him. So who is he?"

"Get ready. You won't believe this. The Benefactor is none other than...John Lennon."

"John Lennon? Interesting," Jericho said, putting a puzzle together in his mind. "Very good work."

"So I guess the whole mission was a false alarm," Elvis volunteered.

"How do you figure?"

"Don't you find it a little strange that the man you thought was planning a terrorist attack is a leader of the peace movement?"

"No, not at all. One man's peace is another man's holocaust."

"But John Lennon is about non-violence."

"People change, Jesse. He's been a recluse for the past five years, doing God knows how many drugs. Hell, living in seclusion with Yoko Ono for five years would turn anyone violent."

"I spent four hours with the guy today; there's not a violent bone in his body."

Just then, Lacey walked into the office, looking upset and frazzled.

"Hey Lacey. Zeus tells me you two are engaged to be married," Elvis mentioned, trying to mask his pain.

"Oh, God! Don't remind me."

"So, it's true?"

"Yeah, but he cornered me. I begged him to take me back and he said that the only way he would was if I married him."

"And you said yes?"

"What choice did I have?"

"You could have said no."

"Then our mission would be over."

"This mission is over, as far as I'm concerned."

"It's not over until I say it's over," Jericho barked.

"Hey, I met the Benefactor today. He's not your man."

"You met the Benefactor?" Lacey asked with surprise.

"Yeah. I hung out with him all day."

"Well, who is he?" Lacey queried.

"John Lennon."

"No, seriously. Who is he?"

"I'm telling you the truth; it's John Lennon."

"The guy from the Beatles?"

"It's true, Lacey," Jericho interrupted.

Lacey began laughing. "So, what's his big plan?"

"He's coming out with a new album," Elvis answered.

"And how is that a terrorist act?"

"Well, Yoko will be singing on it," Elvis joked as he began laughing with Lacey.

"You two can laugh it up all you want, but nothing's changed," Jericho stated. "Something big is still going down. In fact, new intelligence reports claim that it will happen on January 20th, the day of the Presidential Inauguration. It is known that John Lennon attended Jimmy Carter's inauguration four years ago."

"So what?" Lacey said.

"Did it occur to you that perhaps he attended the ceremony to scout it for future attacks?"

"You're not serious," Elvis said.

"If there was a terrorist attack during the inauguration, think of the consequences. Not only could the President and top U.S. leaders be killed, but foreign heads of state as well."

"Come to think of it," Elvis said, deadpan. "He did play a new song that was kind of strange. He called it 'Give Blowing Up the Inauguration a Chance'." He began to snicker as Lacey laughed with him again.

"Will you two be laughing when World War III breaks out?" Jericho sneered.

"Okay, I'm sorry." Elvis said. "Let me give you the details of our meeting, anyway. He plans on releasing a new album and becoming politically active again. He also wants to start his own record label, and he wants me to be the first person signed to it."

"Really? Cool. You're going to be a rock star," Lacey beamed.

"Did you agree?" Jericho asked.

"Yeah, sure. Then we jammed and got along famously. In fact, he wants to get together again."

"Good. Then you're definitely on the inside now," Jericho said.

"So how does this affect my upcoming wedding?" Lacey asked, trying to remind everyone of her plight.

"Tell Zeus to go to hell. We don't need him anymore," Elvis declared.

"My hero!" Lacey said as she gave him a big hug.

"Let's not be premature about this," Jericho said. "We still don't know what the plans are, and until we do, we need to keep every option open."

"So you want me to marry him?" Lacey asked in disbelief.

"Possibly, yes."

"Okay. This is going too far. This is marriage. This is my life we're talking about."

"Don't worry. Even if you have to go through with it, you will be getting married under a false name. It wouldn't be legally binding," Jericho promised.

"I don't care. We'll still be exchanging vows and performing the ceremony. Call me old-fashioned, but I only plan on doing that once."

"Well, we'll see. Anyway, Jesse, good work. We may crack this case sooner than expected. Perhaps you should head back over to New Aquarius; I'm sure Zeus is curious about your meeting with John Lennon."

"Yeah. You're right," Elvis said as he headed for the door.

"Lacey, I need you to stay for a while," Jericho said meaningfully. "There are some things we need to talk about."

"Okay."

"Well, I'll see you two later," Elvis said as he left.

"So, Miss Lewis, alone at last," Jericho said as the door closed behind him. "Perhaps we should roll the film and refresh your memory as to why you will do precisely what I tell you."

Lacey sighed. "How long are you going to blackmail me with those movies?"

"As long as it takes."

"You know what? Go ahead. Send them to my mother. I'm sure she would rather know the truth than have me forced into marriage under false pretenses."

"Don't tempt me."

"Look, I was young and needed the money to get through college. I think my mother will accept that."

"Perhaps she can, but can Jesse?" Jericho wondered.

"Leave him out of this, you bastard!"

"Oh, I've struck a nerve. You love him, don't you? I'm willing to bet he loves you, too. That is, until he sees your little foray into adult films. You see, he's a little old-fashioned himself. He may be able to overlook your having sex for your country, but for college money? Probably not," Jericho taunted her.

"What do you want from me?"

"Go through with the wedding. Hey, you never know, maybe we'll solve the case before then, and you'll be off the hook. Then again, maybe not."

Lacey gave him an angry look and stormed out of his office. She knew that at any moment she would break down and cry, and she did not want to show him any weakness.

The rain beat down on the jungles of Vietnam, bringing mosquitoes and dysentery. Pvt. Black's platoon had been engaged in a deadly stalemate with the Viet Cong. It was an ugly, unromantic type of combat, not like the John Wayne movies Nick had watched as a kid. The battles he had been in weren't about courage or valor; they were about survival and clinging to a thin thread of sanity. He had already watched a few of his buddies die. He had seen the cold pall of death and it no longer held any mystique; it was all too real. Death was everywhere. It was a smell that permeated the air, like pollen on a warm, spring day. It was a menacing threat that laughed and cackled with each bullet that ricocheted through the dense jungle.

Tet, the Chinese lunar New Year, had recently taken place and was commemorated with a vast military attack by the North Vietnamese that violated a cease-fire that they themselves had requested. The Tet Offensive, as it would be called, was heralded by the American media as a major victory and morale booster for the enemy, but nothing could have been further from the truth. The surprise attack was a surprise to no one on the battlefield; they knew that cease-fires were nothing more than strategic ploys by the enemy to regroup and restrengthen their troops. In reality, the Tet Offensive had been a miserable defeat for the Viet Cong. They lost over 45,000 soldiers, as opposed to just over a thousand American casualties. Truth be told, the greatest offensive and morale breaker to the U.S. troops was news of the opposition to the war and the lack of support for the soldiers back in their own home country.

The media and the American people weren't the only forces who left the soldiers high and dry. The politicians, determined to wage a war that they had no intention of winning, handcuffed the war effort by prohibiting the troops from attacking the enemy within the borders of North Vietnam and Cambodia. As a consequence, American GIs became sitting ducks for the Viet Cong guerillas who would attack and then retreat behind the borders.

The battling had become fierce, and sporadic firefights had been breaking out more and more frequently. Nick and his platoon had been pinned down by enemy fire for several days, unable to advance through the jungle that concealed their enemy. Nick had seen an area of tall grass in the distance that shook and moved periodically during the most recent exchanges. Convinced that it was a Viet Cong outpost and tired of the stalemate, he grabbed his M-16 and ran out from behind the rock that had been his shelter. He fired shots wildly around him as he charged up the hill. Bullets zinged past his head as he ran up to the outpost and threw a grenade. Cries of human pain accompanied the grenade blast, and he could tell his aim had been true. Nick hurdled over a fallen trunk tree and pounced upon the enemy.

There were several Viet Cong soldiers lying dead in front of the well-camouflaged entrance to one of the countless networks of underground tunnels in Vietnam. Those who weren't killed by the grenade were finished off by Black's gunfire. He cleared the bodies out of the way and hurled a grenade into the tunnel, followed by a spray of fire from his M-16. Determined to flush the Cong out of the tunnel, he fearlessly crawled inside, firing his gun into the dark cave ahead of him. Sliding on his belly like a snake, he slithered through the tunnels until he saw a light. He crawled toward the light and fired as he saw human outlines approaching him.

After shooting his way to the light and crawling over dead bodies, he rolled another grenade out the opening, killing several more of the enemy. He cautiously climbed out of the hole to see the Viet Cong soldiers that he had wasted. He had fought through two of the enemy's outposts, and could feel that the stalemate was broken as he heard his platoon advancing. He fell back into ranks as they approached.

With most of the obstacles now out of their way, they advanced forward and happened upon a small village. As the rest of the platoon moved with trepidation through the village, Dan left Nick's side and approached one of the children. He extended his hand and offered the child a candy bar. The child took the chocolate and reached into a pocket in his tattered pants. Dan looked into his eyes, but only saw cold, emotionless darkness staring back. The child turned his hand upward and opened his palm to reveal a hand grenade with a missing pin.

"Oh, shit!" Dan cried.

They were his last words. The explosion killed both Dan and the boy instantly. It knocked Nick off his feet as he looked up to see his friend blown to bloody fragments.

"Danny!" he screamed.

He tried to get to his feet, but felt a massive stabbing pain in one of his legs, as if he'd taken shrapnel in one of his quadriceps. He crawled over to Dan's bloody body, but it was obvious that he was dead. Nick sobbed as he held Dan's ruptured torso. The "shrapnel" in his leg turned out to be a fragment of one of Dan's ribs.

CHAPTER XXIII

HARBOR LIGHTS

Elvis arrived at New Aquarius headquarters; Abdul Zahir Muhammad strutted past him and gave him an icy stare as Elvis continued into Zeus' office.

"Hello, Jesse. I bet we have some things to talk about."

"Yes, we do."

Zeus took a seat at his desk and stared intently at Elvis before asking, "So, what did you and Mr. Lennon talk about?"

"Well, he told me he's going to make a comeback, both musically and politically. He's a real nice guy. We jammed for a while; he reminisced a little. He wants to see me again on Wednesday."

"Well, I'm happy for you. It's a big week for both of us, actually. Thursday, I'm marrying Lacey. You're not invited. In fact, you're no longer welcome here, and I don't want you two to ever see each other again."

"Isn't that her decision to make?"

"From now on, I'll be making the decisions for her. Maybe you haven't noticed, but she's not the sharpest knife in the drawer," Zeus said with a sneer. "Don't worry though, Jesse. I'll take care of you. Here you go. Two tickets to see the Grateful Dead on Thursday. They'll be playing at Radio City Music Hall all week. I suggest you go and make a day of it. It'll take your mind off the wedding. You don't have to thank me. Consider it a gift from your old pal Zeus."

"Go to hell!" Elvis snarled as he threw the tickets back in his face and stormed out of the office, making a hasty exit from New Aquarius.

Zeus grimaced coldly. He had quickly grown to hate Jesse and had become very insecure about his relationship with Lacey. Though initially attracted to her merely for her looks, he fell in love with her easy-going attitude and her willingness to do whatever he told her. It was as if she wanted nothing else but to please him and stay by his side. He expected blind obedience in his workers and loved the trait in women.

He had met her after playing a set at a local coffeehouse in the Village. She came up to him and praised his music. The two talked and soon began dating. He believed her to have below average intelligence, which suited him just fine. There were many underhanded goings on in both his personal and professional life, and a woman who didn't ask too many questions and lacked the ability to connect the dots was a perfect match for him. There were many times that he had been unfaithful to her, and yet she never seemed to notice even the most obvious of clues. Once they were married, he believed her obedience would then be absolute.

The next morning, Jesse arrived at Jericho's office, anxiously waiting for Lacey to arrive. Jericho had confirmed what Zeus had told him, that the two of them would be married unless Lennon's plans were discovered.

She finally entered the office. Elvis welcomed her with an embrace. As they hugged, she slipped a note to him.

"So it's true? You and Zeus are still getting married?"

She nodded her head as she stared ruefully into his eyes. Their silent communication was interrupted by Jericho.

"There is a way to stop the wedding, Jesse. Find out what John Lennon is planning. You're meeting him Wednesday; that will give you an opportunity to find out what he knows."

"I've only met him once; do you expect him to bare his soul to me and tell me all about his terrorist plot?"

"Well, yes."

"So if I find out what his plans are for January 20th, you'll let Lacey back out of the wedding?" Elvis asked, not fully trusting him.

"Of course, and the mission will be over. I'll fly you both back to D.C., and you two will never have to see me again. But don't try to make up some story. I know more about the plans than I've told either of you, so I'll know if you're lying."

"Okay. It's a deal."

"Well, if you two will excuse me, I have to meet Zeus and get fitted for a wedding dress," Lacey remarked with a sorrowful tone in her voice as she left.

Elvis grabbed a pen and a piece of paper and began jotting down a list and then handed it to Jericho.

"Get me one of each, and I'll have Lennon telling me if he wets the bed," Elvis stated.

Jericho read the list and gave Elvis a complicitous smile before dismissing him. There was nowhere he had to go, and he couldn't face cramped up solitude of his apartment so he just wandered the streets of New York, peering out over the Harbor, watching as the lights of the skyline shimmered off the water. He remembered the note that Lacey had given him. He opened it up and read it.

Dear Jesse,

I need to talk to you away from prying eyes. Neither of our apartments is safe. Meet me Tuesday night at nine o'clock, on the Manhattan side of the Brooklyn Bridge.

Love,
Lacey

He smiled and tucked the letter away. He ventured to a bar with the goal of drowning his sorrows late into the night.

The next night, Jesse went to the bridge to meet Lacey. She had come straight from New Aquarius headquarters and was waiting against the railing as the cool October air blew through her dark hair. They exchanged hugs and hellos before walking together.

"So, are you all ready for the wedding?" Elvis asked sarcastically with pain evident in his voice.

"No, not at all. I don't want to do this."

"Then why are you?"

"I have no choice," she said.

"Everyone has a choice. You could quit the FBI."

"There are things you don't understand. I can't quit any more than you can."

"Why? Why can't you quit?"

"It's something I can't talk about."

"I see," Elvis muttered, hurt by her inability to open up to him.

"Jesse, do you believe a person is defined by their past?"

"What do you mean?"

"Is it possible to be a good person when you've done bad things?"

"Yes. I'm a firm believer in redemption. It's not who we were, but who we are that matters," he answered.

"I'd like to believe that," Lacey said wistfully.

"I have to believe that. Trust me, for the last couple of years, I've done nothing but run from my past," he said.

"You can't run forever."

"Why not? Why can't we run away from all of this? Me and you, we'll just hop on a train tonight and disappear."

"Jericho would find us, and then he would kill us."

"He can't kill us."

"Don't be so sure. The FBI has ways of making people disappear."

"That's crazy. This is America," he proclaimed.

"There are two Americas. Don't you realize that? There's the warm, compassionate beacon of liberty that we all want to believe in, and then there's its dark underside that cuts deals with dictators and assassinates anyone they deem dangerous. Being in the FBI, I've seen a lot of the darkness."

"I thought you were Miss gung-ho FBI agent," Elvis said.

"I used to be, but over the years I've seen and heard so many things that I can't rationalize it anymore. In fact, after this mission, I'm quitting the agency."

"Really? Well, look me up when you do."

"I will. If I'm not already married," she said with disgust.

"I don't even want to think about that."

"Neither do I, but I have to. It is this Thursday at three o'clock," she said.

"Where at?"

"The Fellowship of Christ Church on Fortieth Street. Are you coming?"

"No. Zeus made it quite clear that I wasn't invited. In fact, he doesn't want me to ever talk to you again."

"I'm not surprised. He always was the jealous type. God, how did I get into this mess?"

"Don't worry. I'm meeting John Lennon tomorrow, and I have a plan."

"I hope it's a good one. If you succeed, I'll be forever grateful," she said seductively.

"Well, I don't want this wedding to happen any more than you do."

"Why do you say that?" she asked.

"Because," he said with a pause, trying to find the right words. "I love you, Lacey."

"I love you, too," she responded as they embraced each other and started kissing.

Meanwhile, someone was watching them from the shadows across the street. It was Thorny. He had been following Lacey since she'd left the New Aquarius headquarters. After seeing her kissing Jesse, he retreated to a nearby pay phone and called Zeus.

"Zeus, it's me, Thorny. I followed her, and guess who she's with?"

"Jesse?"

"Yep. They were even making out. Do you want me to take care of him?"

"No. Not right now. I don't want her to be around when you do. I know exactly where he'll be tomorrow. We'll get him then."

The following day, Elvis walked to the hotel to meet John Lennon. John greeted him graciously as he let him into the room. They chatted briefly while Lennon sat down on the floor, strumming his guitar.

"Mind if I fix myself a drink?" Elvis asked.

"Not at all. Help yourself."

"Thanks. Can I make you something?"

"I don't know. I don't drink that much anymore."

"Come on. Drink with me. It'll be fun."

"Oh, all right, maybe one or two. Make me a scotch and soda," Lennon said.

Elvis mixed them both a drink from the fully-stocked bar in the plush penthouse suite. While mixing Lennon's drink, he pulled out the small capsule that Jericho had given him and poured the contents into the glass.

After the breakup of the Beatles, John continued with his political causes and his solo career. He had undergone the controversial primal scream therapy to confront some of his demons, and the pain came out musically in his first post-Beatles album *John Lennon – Plastic Ono Band*. The following year, he released *Imagine*, and the title track from the album soon became a universal anti-war anthem.

Around this time, the FBI became deeply concerned about Lennon's subversive political activities and began investigating him; they even tried to deport him. He would have to fight a long, legal battle with the U.S. government to stay in the country. The pressures of deportation and his growing drug use caused a split between him and Yoko, causing him to go on what would be known as his lost weekend. The weekend actually lasted about a year and a half. It was a non-stop indulgence of drugs and alcohol with rocker Harry Nilson, Who drummer Keith Moon, and his former band-mate, Ringo Starr.

In 1975, he got back together with Yoko and, on his thirty-fifth birthday, he received the greatest birthday present he could imagine when she gave birth to his son, Sean.

The next five years were spent out of the spotlight, as John retired from music and politics, and became a full-time father to his son. In early 1980, John decided to sail to Bermuda on his yacht. The trip was cathartic for him and he began writing music again. After his return, a recharged and rejuvenated Lennon decided to make a musical and political comeback and recorded *Double Fantasy*.

Elvis and Lennnon started playing a few songs together, and when they were done he got them both another strong drink. They jammed a little while longer before putting the guitars down. Elvis could tell John was feeling the effects of the drug and the alcohol; they chatted a while longer, until Presley decided to make his move.

"So what do you think of this upcoming election?" Elvis asked.

"I want Carter to win," Lennon said, "but I have a strong feeling that he won't."

"Somehow I didn't peg you as a Reaganite."

"No. I'm definitely not. I met Reagan once, though."

"Oh, yeah?"

"Believe it or not, I thought he was a really nice chap. It was during a Monday night football game. I went up to the announcer's booth to talk to Howard Cosell, and Reagan was there. He was really cool to me, especially considering what I stood for. But he and I talked, and he taught me all of the nuances of American football. It was kind of beautiful that two people from two different generations with such different beliefs could get along and talk cordially about something as trivial as football. It gave me hope for all of us. Then again, he is so out of touch, he probably thought I was Elvis Presley," John conceded, slurring his words.

"It's good to know he's a nice guy, because I think he will be our next President."

"Well I have antidote for that."

"What do you mean?" Elvis asked, hoping Lennon would reveal his plans.

"Well, I probably shouldn't say anything, but if he wins, I'm planning a big anti-Reagan rally on his inauguration day."

"Really?"

"Yes, in Central Park. It'll be a huge all-day concert and political rally. I'm going to announce it on Christmas Day and invite all the media. My hope is to upstage him on his biggest day, and make sure that no one watches his inauguration. I want put a spike in the conservative movement that's sweeping the nation."

"How are you going to do that?"

"I'm going to perform. I'm going to make speeches and play all of my solo hits and songs from my new album, and then a couple of old friends will join me on stage to play. Their name's are Paul, George and Ringo," John proclaimed proudly.

"A Beatles reunion. Is that it?"

"Is that it? I think a Beatles reunion is enough," Lennon said, slightly offended.

"I mean, isn't there anything else planned? A bombing or assassination or something?" Elvis asked, instantly knowing how stupid he sounded.

"What are you talking about? A bombing? Do you even know who I am? I'm against violence and murder. Read my lyrics sometime," an irate Lennon answered.

"I'm sorry. I just thought you were going to do something more radical."

"I can't believe you would think that I would try to resort to murder to make my point. That's their gig."

"Well, good. I'm glad to see you're still a pacifist."

"You're with them aren't you?" John accused him.

"Them?"

"The government. You guys just can't leave me alone, can you? That's why you're asking all these questions, isn't it?"

"That's crazy."

"You drugged me, didn't you? I was wondering why I was feeling funny and telling you everything."

"I think you're being a little paranoid, John."

"I'll show you paranoid," John yelled as he threw his drink in Elvis' face, baptizing him with his scotch. "I think you should leave."

"Okay. If that's what you want," Elvis retreated, wiping the alcohol off his face, knowing that he had the information he wanted.

"I'll see you, John," he said as he walked out of the hotel room.

As he made his way out of the hotel, Elvis was practically skipping for joy, despite the ugly scene with John. Not only did he find out Lennon's plans and complete the mission, he discovered that the big plan would not be jeopardizing any lives after all. He couldn't wait to tell Jericho how wrong he had been, and tell Lacey that she could call off the wedding.

He walked out of the hotel and down the street. Night had fallen over New York City, but the darkness had been removed from his life. He and Lacey would soon be free again. As he sauntered around the corner, a man stepped out of the shadows and smashed him over the head with a pool cue. Elvis fell to the ground in pain. He looked up to see Zeus and Thorny standing over him.

"I thought I told you not to see her again!" Zeus yelled as he kicked Elvis in the ribs.

As he gasped for air, the two men picked him up and threw him into the trunk of a car. They closed the trunk and sped away.

CHAPTER XXIV

CRYING IN THE CHAPEL

Zeus drove the car into his garage in upstate New York. Thorny helped him remove Elvis from the trunk, taping his wrists behind his back. They then carried him into Zeus' house and sat him down in a chair. Thorny left the room and Zeus decided to have a little chat with Elvis.

"You try to be nice to some people," he was saying. "I took you into our group, I gave you a stage to play on, I even introduced you to John Lennon, and this is how you repay me. I warned you, Jesse. I told you to stay away from her, but you wouldn't listen. Now it's come to this."

"What are you going to do to me?"

"What am I going to do to you? Hmm, let me think. Oh yeah. I'm going to kill you," Zeus said as he pulled out a gun and pointed it at Elvis' face.

Elvis jerked violently, awaiting a fatal gunshot that never arrived. Zeus simply laughed.

"Don't worry Jesse. I'm not going to shoot you now. Do you have any idea how hard it is to get blood and brain matter out of a carpet?"

"What kind of hippie are you?"

"Me, a hippie? No, that's just my cover. New Aquarius is just a front for my drug ring, and a good one at that. You'd be surprised how many musicians and peace activists do drugs. You see, I used to be a hippie back in the Sixties, but there's no money in peace and love, only in drugs. Over the years, I've become one of the biggest suppliers of narcotics in New York City, while Thorny, Abdul and Wolfgang do the distributing," Zeus bragged.

"What about John Lennon?"

"Actually, he knows nothing about it. He came into my office one day praising our group's work. Imagine my surprise. He gave us a generous donation and asked if he could be our silent partner, footing the bill for different political activities," Zeus said before doing his best John Lennon impersonation. "Hey, Zeus, here's ten thousand dollars, mate. Attend a no-nukes rally in Washington."

"'No problem, John.' Apparently he'd had some trouble with the FBI before and didn't want to get his hands dirty. So we staged rallies, protests, concerts, whatever he wanted, and he paid us well for it. All the while my boys were selling dope to the crowd. But enough about Lennon; let's talk about you. Tomorrow morning you're going to die a very painful death. Consider it a little wedding gift from me to myself."

"I've got news for you, Zeus. You're not the only one living a lie. My real name is Jesse King, Special Agent Jesse King with the FBI. We've been monitoring your headquarters for some time now, and if I disappear my men are going to move in."

"Do you really expect me to believe that?"

"I don't really care what you believe, but know that murdering a federal agent carries a lot more jail time than dealing drugs."

"Jesse, I'd love to sit and chat with you all night, but I have busy day tomorrow. I hope you understand," Zeus said as he put a piece of duct tape over Elvis' mouth, and taped his arms and feet to the chair.

Zeus left the room as Elvis struggled futilely to get loose.

The next morning, Zeus and Thorny removed Elvis from the chair, taping his ankles together, and his wrists behind his back. The tape on his mouth muted a hundred curse words as they threw him back in the trunk and drove off.

They arrived at an auto-wrecking yard, one of their favorite places for tidily disposing of their enemies. As massive machinery grabbed cars in its metal claws before noisily crushing them and compacting them into small cubes, they removed Elvis from the trunk. They carried him to a junked brown Chevy Cavalier, and threw him in the back seat.

"We're not going to put him in the trunk?" Thorny asked.

"No. I want him to see his death approaching. Don't worry, Jesse. I'll give Lacey your best," Zeus sneered as he slammed the car door shut and walked away.

Zeus and Thorny got in their car and drove off to get ready for the wedding.

Lacey arrived at the church in her wedding gown, not knowing what was going to happen. Jesse was supposed to meet with her and Jericho the night before and tell them what he found out from Lennon, but he never arrived. She feared not only having to go through with the wedding, but that something terrible might have happened to Jesse. Welling up with emotions, she burst into tears and ran into the bathroom to recompose herself. She thought of her father and how ashamed he would be of her. This was not how she had imagined her wedding day.

She remembered her older brother Ronnie's wedding. It was a beautiful July day, shortly before her father was to be shipped off to Vietnam. It was a lavish wedding in a large cathedral. Bouquets of flowers lined the aisles, and Lacey had felt pristine and regal in her pink bridesmaid dress. The bride, Jennifer, wore a long, flowing wedding dress, and Ronnie looked handsome and mature in the Navy uniform that he, like his father, chose to wear instead of a tuxedo. Ronnie was also headed to Vietnam and he had wanted to get married before he left. In the back of everyone's mind, including Ronnie's, was the fear that he might not make it back. To everyone's relief he did return, but his father would not be as lucky.

As the metallic screams of dying cars sounded around him, Elvis closed his eyes and remembered his martial arts training. Focusing all of his energy into his legs, with one quick thrust he smashed his bound feet into the car window, spidering it. He recoiled his legs and thrust them forward again, breaking through the window. He wriggled over to the broken window and tried to squeeze through it. Just then the massive forklift jaws closed in on the car.

He frantically slid through the window as the machinery began lifting the car. Diligently he inched forward as the shards of broken glass dug into his skin. As he managed to get his body halfway out, a piece of broken glass cut into the tape around his wrists; he quickly moved his hands back and forth until the glass had sawed a tear in the tape. With a burst of strength he broke the tape and freed his arms. He pushed himself out of the window and fell to hard ground ten feet below.

He momentarily writhed in pain, and then undid the tape on his ankles and mouth. He got to his feet as he watched the car he had just escaped from get crushed into a block smaller than three feet square. He ran out of the lot, found a pay phone, and placed an urgent call to Jericho.

"Jesse, where have you been?"

"Zeus and his goons kidnapped me and tried to kill me. They're not activists, they're major drug dealers. I need you to pick me up so we can stop the wedding," Elvis insisted.

"What did you find out about Lennon's plans?"

"I found out everything. I'll explain it all when I see you. Pick me up. I'm at Joe's Auto Wreckage Yard. Bring guns."

After he had waited for what felt like an eternity, Jericho finally arrived. Elvis jumped into the car.

"We need to get to Fortieth Street by three o'clock," Elvis barked as they raced away.

During the course of the drive, Elvis told Jericho about his recent ordeal and Zeus' drug dealing operation.

"What about Lennon?" Jericho asked.

"He doesn't know anything about it."

"What about January 20th?"

"It's not a terrorist act. He's planning a free concert in Central Park, where he's going to reunite with the Beatles and try to resurrect the Sixties movement."

"That's interesting,"

"So, that's it right? The mission's over?" Elvis asked urgently.

"Yeah. I guess so. As soon as we grab Agent Lewis, and arrest Zeus and his henchmen."

"I'm all for that. So after we do that, we're free to go?"

"Yes. If nothing else, I am a man of my word."

Time was not on their side, however. Three o'clock was drawing near and they were still some distance from the church.

The wedding began as panic swept over Lacey. She gazed over at the small wedding party and back at the church doors, contemplating an escape, hoping for a miracle. As she plodded down the aisle, she felt instead as if she was walking the plank. Zeus was waiting at the altar like a hungry shark.

Jericho and Presley were getting close to the church until they got caught in a traffic jam.

"Dammit!" Elvis exclaimed.

"Let's get out and go by foot, it'll be quicker," Jericho said.

"Yeah. You're right. Let's go."

"Here. Take this," Jericho said as he handed Elvis a firearm. "We may need it."

Elvis tucked the gun away as Jericho pulled the car over to the side of the road and they began running.

Meanwhile, at the church, the minister had finished making his speech and the rings were given. Lacey felt nauseous as the ceremony neared completion.

"Do you Robert George Walker, take this woman to be your lawfully wedded wife?"

"I do," Zeus said with a smile.

"And do you, Lacey Mary Taylor, take this man to be your lawfully wedded husband?"

Before she could answer, the church doors were kicked open as Jericho and Elvis ran in with guns drawn and their badges displayed.

"Freeze, FBI!" Jericho shouted as Lacey's eyes lit up.

The stunned wedding party gasped in disbelief. Thorny pulled a gun out of his vest, but Lacey kicked it out of his hand.

"Lacey, what are you doing?" Zeus demanded angrily.

"Oh, yeah. Did I mention I'm with the FBI?" she quipped innocently as she gave a ditzy laugh.

The four men reluctantly surrendered as Jericho put them in cuffs. Elvis grabbed Lacey and gave her an impassioned kiss.

The police arrived as Special Agent Jericho informed them of the charges against the four, and they took the drug dealers away.

"So is the mission over?" Lacey asked, still in the dark about many of the details.

"Yes. It's all over," Elvis said.

She hugged him joyously and asked: "What now?"

"We're going home."

CHAPTER XXV

HEARTBREAK HOTEL

As Jericho gave the proper information to the local authorities regarding the arrest of the New Aquarius members, Elvis took Lacey aside and explained the goings-on of the past forty-eight hours. He told her about the terrorist threat that turned out to be a Beatles reunion, about his abduction and Zeus' admitting to being a drug lord, as well as his attempt to kill him, and his harrowing escape from the jaws of death.

"Wow! And you still made time to crash my wedding," she joked playfully.

Jericho approached them, full of warmth and joy, an apparently changed man from the evil fascist they had grown to hate.

"The mission was a success, and it's all thanks to you two."

"We didn't exactly save the world, you know," Lacey pointed out. "All we did was unwittingly break up a local drug ring. There never was a terrorist threat."

"That's not the point," Jericho said. "The mission's over, and no one was killed. We can all relax and enjoy ourselves now, and to show my appreciation, I have something special planned for both of you. I've arranged for a car to drive you both off at your respective apartments. I want you to pack, because in a few hours a limo will bring you to the Iroquois Hotel for the night. Tomorrow, we'll fly you both back to Washington D.C. for debriefing, and then you'll be rid of me forever."

"What's the catch?" Lacey asked suspiciously.

"There is one catch. After you've checked in at the Iroquois, I want you two to join me for dinner to celebrate."

"Since when did you become Santa Claus?" Elvis inquired.

"Come on, cut me a break, guys. I know I've been a real prick during this mission, but that's how I do things, and that's how I get results. This is the FBI, not the Cub Scouts. But the mission is over, and it was a success. Now I want to bask in our success as the team we have become. Is that so wrong?"

Lacey rolled her eyes at his speech as the car pulled up to take them to their respective apartments. .

After Lacey got into her apartment, her first move was to get out of the wedding gown that she had quickly grown to despise. She didn't pack it with her belongings. Instead, she left it on the floor, not wanting any reminder of the terrible corner into which she had painted herself. By reflex, she put her gun and three hundred dollars in cash into her purse. She gathered her clothes and a few trinkets she owned into a suitcase and awaited the limo.

The limousine arrived and took all three agents to the Iroquois Hotel, where Lacey and Elvis checked into adjoining rooms and met Jericho in the lobby. They all went to the very elegant Triomphe, a high-class restaurant next to the lobby to have dinner.

They ordered their drinks and their dinner, and began chatting, not unlike war veterans fondly recalling a horrible battle.

"So what was it like meeting John Lennon?" Jericho asked.

"Hard to describe," Elvis said. "I'm not that impressed with celebrity, but I thought he was a good person, much wiser than when I first met him."

Too late, he realized what he'd just let slip.

"When you first met him?" Lacey asked in confusion.

Jericho also realized his gaffe and tried to cover it up.

"I want to propose a toast," Jericho announced as he raised his glass.

Elvis quickly raised his glass, and Lacey followed suit.

"To a damn good team that I hate to see break up," Jericho announced.

They clinked their glasses together and drank, and Elvis' revelation was soon forgotten.

"So what part of the ceremony were you up to when we interrupted?" Elvis asked.

"Actually, the reverand had just asked me if 'I do'."

"Damn, I knew we were cutting it close!" Jericho laughed.

"What would your answer have been?" Elvis teased.

"I don't know. I felt like I was about to throw up," she said. She gave Elvis her full attention. "What did you and Lennon talk about?"

"He told me how thrilled he had been to meet and play with Elvis Presley," he said, secretly bragging.

"Mmmm, I love Elvis Presley," Lacey admitted.

"You hate rock music," Jericho said.

"Yeah, but I liked Elvis. I grew up with him. He was a rock star before they got all hairy and wimpy; I mean, he got drafted and served his country without any complaints. He was a real man, and a sexy one at that."

Elvis couldn't help but give Jericho an arrogant smile.

Soon their dinner arrived, and they all dug in to their meal as the drinks kept flowing; everyone was feeling good, even Special Agent Jericho.

"Tell me, Lacey, what are your plans after tomorrow?" Jericho asked casually.

"To be honest, I think I'm quitting the Agency."

"What? Why?"

"I don't believe in it anymore. Take today, for instance. I almost ended up married to a drug dealer just to prevent a rock concert. The FBI is a dinosaur that needs to evolve or become extinct. I don't know that it can evolve, and I don't want to drown in the tar pits with it."

"Okay. I have a question for you, Jericho," Elvis announced.

"Sure. What is it?"

"Why are you such an asshole?"

Lacey howled with laughter as Jericho struggled to explain himself.

"I know you both must hate me, and I can't blame you. I'd hate me, too, if I were you," he said, slightly slurring his words. "But neither of you has been in a war. I have. It's easy to be kind when you haven't seen the crap I've seen. I had a buddy, Danny. He used to play with all the Vietnamese kids whenever he got the chance. He'd give them toys and make them laugh. I can still remember seeing the smile on one kid's face as Danny gave him a candy bar. Seconds later, the little bastard pulled out a grenade and killed both of them."

The other two were silent for a moment. Then Lacey spoke:

"My Dad was killed in that war, so don't tell me I don't know what you're talking about. But sometimes you have to let go of the hate."

"Oh, look who's talking!" Jericho growled. "The main reason you went through with this mission was to get back at all the hippies who protested the war. Admit it."

Elvis interrupted.

"Look, it's been a helluva day and we've all had a lot to drink. I think Lacey and I need to go back to our rooms and get some sleep. We'll see you tomorrow," he told Jericho with a fake smile. He escorted Lacey upstairs, ending the post-mission celebration.

"I hate him so much," Lacey raged in the elevator.

"Don't give him any more power over you," Elvis suggested. "Let's think about how much worse our night could have been. You could have been on your honeymoon with Zeus. I could have been a cute red stain inside small cube of steel, and the country could have been facing a terrorist attack, but we're not. Instead, we're together, we're drunk, our mission is over, and we have adjoining rooms in a very nice hotel. What could be more perfect?"

Lacey smiled as they both unlocked their doors and went into their rooms. Then she opened the adjoining door and said, "That's what's wrong. It's all too perfect."

"Yes, isn't it?" Elvis said seductively as he took her in his arms and began kissing her.

"Jericho knows our weaknesses," she protested between kisses, "and he doesn't want us thinking things through tonight."

"Look, earlier today, when I was trapped in a car about to be smashed into a large brick, all I could think about was you and how much I regretted that I could never be with you. I don't know what tomorrow holds, but I want to spend tonight with you," he whispered as he kissed her neck.

"Oh, God!" she moaned as he kissed his way down to her chest.

He ran his fingers through her hair as he slid the straps of her sexy black gown off her shoulders, and it fell to the ground with no resistance. Her breasts were bare; as he pinned her arms against the wall, his lips made a path down her body. He cupped her beautiful breasts in his hands as he kissed her lips again, tasting the wine that they had earlier consumed. He slowly pulled off his shirt, revealing his now toned physique as he tossed it carelessly on the carpet. He removed the rest of his clothes, picked Lacey up effortlessly and carried her to the bed with authority.

Lowering her onto the mattress, he continued kissing her body. Their hot, naked flesh melded together in the heat of their passion. She sighed with contentment as she laced her fingers in his hair and felt his kisses dance all over her body. He drove deep inside her as she let out a loud moan that he silenced with his lips. They made wild, passionate love, clinging to each other.

"You're so beautiful. I love you!" he cried out as their love reached a climax.

He collapsed upon her as he kissed her tenderly and stroked her hair. They made love again late into the burning night, falling asleep in each other's arms.

They woke up late in the afternoon, still locked in an embrace, smiling with the glow of rapturous love.

"Last night was perfect," he sighed.

"Too perfect."

"Why do you keep saying that?"

"Everything was in place for us. A lovely dinner, adjoining rooms and flowing alcohol, all set up by Agent Jericho."

"So what's your point?" he asked as he kissed her neck.

"He made sure that our minds were on things other than our mission."

"Our mission's over."

"Yes. Quite abruptly, I might add."

"I still don't get what you're saying," Elvis admitted.

"After all the work the three of us did on this case, Jericho seemed quite content that the terrorist act was merely a rock concert. He was so convinced that something horrible was going to happen, and yet you tell him something completely different and he accepts it immediately."

"Why wouldn't he? What else do you think is going on?"

"I think he knew that there never was a terrorist attack being planned, that it was something political all along, and he used you and me to find out what it was."

"Why would he care about some political movement or John Lennon?"

"John Lennon engaged in a lot of subversive political activities in the Sixties and early Seventies." Lacey sat up in bed now, deadly serious. "Enough to get the FBI to aggressively investigate him, even try to get him deported. Lennon got the hint and laid low for a few years, but now he's back, both musically and politically, and just as a deeply conservative, pro-military candidate is poised to take the White House."

"But they can't deport him now. He's a naturalized citizen."

"Exactly. But they can kill him."

"Come on, Lacey. You're being paranoid. The government can't just kill someone like John Lennon."

"They've done it before. John F. Kennedy, Bobby Kennedy, and Martin Luther King, all dangerous, left-wing political figures taken out by an assassin's bullet."

"The government didn't kill them, a bunch of nut-jobs did," Elvis countered, rejecting her conspiracy theories.

"Strange coincidence, don't you think? The fact that all three of them were killed by deranged loners. The public dismisses the assassins as lone nuts, while the puppet masters simply walk away. I'm convinced a lone nut will kill Lennon as well, and before Reagan takes office," Lacey predicted.

"How would they get some person off the street to go and kill a political figure?" Elvis asked, beginning to wonder if there could be some truth to her theory.

"You program him to kill, like a Manchurian Candidate. The FBI and the CIA have been researching methods of mind control for decades. They've done countless experiments using everything from hypnosis to LSD. It was part of a top-secret program called Operation: Artichoke. Perhaps their research has paid off."

"My God! Do you really think they can do this?"

"I've been in the Agency for a number of years, and I've seen a lot of things," Lacey said balefully. "Not only do I think they can, I think they have."

"But if they kill John Lennon, it'll be my fault!" Elvis gasped in horror.

"You've got it. You led them right to him."

"We've got to stop them!"

"Negative. We're in way over our heads. We're going to fly back to D.C., quit the Agency and live out our lives, or else be killed ourselves."

"What about John Lennon?"

"Screw John Lennon. When my father was risking his life over in Vietnam, John Lennon was protesting him, and lending morale to the enemy. That son of a bitch helped kill my father."

"Did you ever think that maybe he was trying to save your father?"

"I don't care what his intentions were, it's the results that I have to live with."

"We at least have to warn him."

"It figures!" Lacey said bitterly. "I had to go and fall in love with a crusader. You do what you have to do. I'm catching a flight back to Washington. Now, if you don't mind, I'm going back to my room and get ready."

As she left, she slammed the door loud enough to be heard on the listening device hidden on the lamp in Elvis' room.

CHAPTER XXVI ‖

DEVIL IN DISGUISE

The cold autumn wind whistled through the trees, taking dead leaves as doomed prisoners, as adults and children alike dressed like devils and ghouls to ward off spirits looking for bodies to inhabit. It was Halloween, or Samhain as the Druids had called it, a day when front yards became cemeteries, and jack-o-lanterns smiled wickedly upon the living, in homage of the dying season. It was the day of the dead.

In one section of town, people were celebrating the dead in a different way. They were called Deadheads, rabid fans of the band the Grateful Dead. They traveled loyally cross-country to follow the band and see their concerts. That night was the final show of a week-long engagement at Radio City Music Hall. The Deadheads sometimes dressed in bright swirling psychedelic colors and tie-dyed T-shirts adorned with decals ranging from skulls to dancing bears. They grooved on a vibe of love and joy, immune to the corrupt and insidious world around them, locked inside a never-ending acid trip, becoming living time capsules of Sixties' counterculture.

In a van outside the Iroquois Hotel, Agent Jericho listened in on the conversation between his agents through a bug he had planted in their rooms the day before. He silently cursed Jesse and Lacey for being too smart for their own good. He wanted nothing more than to fly them back to Washington D.C. and free them from his captivity. Now his plans had been altered and they would have to die.

Lacey retreated to her room and got dressed. Groggy and still upset, she grabbed her purse and went to get a cup of coffee and a breath of fresh air.

Elvis had just finished getting dressed when he heard a knock on the door.

"Who is it?" Elvis asked as he put his wallet in his back pocket.

"Room service."

"I didn't order room service," he muttered. Nevertheless, he unwisely opened the door, only to see Agent Jericho.

"Compliments of the house. Our special today is dead duck," Jericho stated as he pulled out his gun and forced his way into the room.

"What are you doing?" Elvis demanded.

"You couldn't just get on that plane and forget about what happened, could you? You and Lacey had to get to the bottom of it all, didn't you? Now you'll both have to pay the price. Get on the floor, now!" Jericho commanded as Presley obeyed.

Keeping his gun pointed at Elvis, Jericho opened the connecting door to Lacey's room and peered inside.

"Lacey?" he called out. When he didn't get an answer, he demanded: "Where did she go?"

"I don't know," Elvis said. "She stormed out of my room and I haven't seen her since."

Meanwhile, Lacey had returned from downstairs and was walking down the hall to her room, sipping her hot coffee, when she passed Elvis' room and heard Jericho's voice. She stopped and listened in on the conversation.

"So, you two geniuses figured out that I'm going to kill John Lennon. Bravo! What was your next move, try to save his life? Elvis Presley saves John Lennon -- what a great story, but it's not going to happen. Here's what is going to happen: You're going to walk out of this hotel nice and quietly, and I'll be behind you, deciding whether to shoot you in the back of the head or not. What I decide depends on how well you behave on the way to my van. Got it?"

Elvis nodded and moved to the door with Jericho behind him. Lacey grabbed her gun out of her purse and tucked it into the front of her jeans. She lingered by the hinge side of the door, waiting for the two men to enter the hall.

The door opened and Elvis walked out, staring straight ahead; Jericho's gun-hand followed. Quickly Lacey grabbed Elvis by the arm and pulled him back towards her as, in the same motion, she kicked the door, slamming it on Jericho's wrist and knocking the gun out of his hand. Jericho pushed the door back toward her, and she threw the coffee in his face, kicking his gun down the hall before running in the opposite direction, pulling Elvis behind her. They ran into the stairwell and hurried down the steps. Jericho scrambled to retrieve his gun, then chased after them.

He looked down the stairwell and saw them several flights below. He fired a couple of shots at them and Lacey fired back, none of the bullets hitting their mark. Lacey and Elvis ran down several more flights with Jericho right behind them. Lacey saw a mop and bucket; she grabbed it, and overturned it on the steps as they continued down the stairs. When Jericho hit the wet steps he slipped and fell, buying the fugitives some time as they raced out of the hotel. They ran down the street trying to flag a taxi, to no avail. Two young children in Halloween masks walked past them; one was dressed as Frankenstein and the other as Batman. Elvis and Lacey grabbed their masks and put them on, still running as the children screamed in fright and began to cry.

After two blocks, the couple ran into a large group of Deadheads wandering the streets, gathered around Radio City Music Hall, blocking traffic and causing headaches for commuters. The deadheads were out in full force; milling around in a disorderly crowd along the sidewalk selling assorted clothing and trinkets. Lacey had an idea. She approached one of the merchants and started buying several tied-dyed items. She and Elvis quickly dressed in the hippie clothes. Because it was also Halloween, many of the Deadheads were also wearing campy Halloween masks for a laugh, so Elvis and Lacey actually blended in with the crowd. Hidden in their disguises, they watched as Jericho stalked past them, frantically looking through the crowd for his escaped agents.

"Hey, man, wanna buy a flower?" one Deadhead asked Jericho.

"Get out of my way!" he barked as he continued pushing his way through the human sea.

Still catching their breath, Elvis and Lacey felt slightly relieved as they watched Jericho disappear in the distance.

"Thanks. You saved my life," Elvis said.

"We're not safe yet," Lacey pointed out. "He's not going to stop looking until he finds us."

"What do you suggest?"

"It's a Grateful Dead show. There are bound to be vans or buses that brought the Deadheads here. We'll pay someone to let us hang out in their bus for the next few hours."

"Good idea."

They went and found the underground parking lot for the Music Hall, where groups of Deadheads were dancing in circles like shamans, women in flower print dresses twirling with their arms wildly gyrating in an exaggerated sign language. The music was a cacophony of a hundred different Grateful Dead songs playing at once as others beat on tribal drums. The sweet smell of marijuana filled the air, along with enough bubbles to make Lawrence Welk jealous.

"Toto, we're not in Kansas any more," Elvis joked.

They spotted a particularly eclectic group of 'heads in their twenties, laughing and dancing in front of their Day-glo painted bus. There were four of them; one had long, scraggly brown hair and was wearing a bluish tie-dye shirt. He was grooving next to a beautiful blonde girl who had a flower in her hair and was twirling around and around.

Elvis and Lacey took off their Halloween masks and approached them.

"Hey, how's it going?" Lacey asked, trying to sound hip.

"I'm feeling groovy. How about you?" The brown-haired Deadhead grinned.

"I'm, uh, groovy, too. Look, I have a question. Me and my old man here have been hiking all day and need a place to crash out before the concert. If we paid you fifty bucks, would you let us crash in your bus until the show?"

"Fifty bucks? Really?"

Lacey pulled out a fifty-dollar bill to confirm the deal.

"Sure. Hop in," the Deadhead told them as a broad grin stretched across his face.

"Great!" Elvis said. Lacey paid the 'head and they began boarding the bus, when suddenly the blonde and another male Deadhead approached them.

"Hi!" the blonde-haired girl said as she blew bubbles into the wind. "Who are you?"

"I'm Sunflower, and this is my old man, Pimento-loaf," Lacey said, ad-libbing horribly.

"They gave us fifty bucks to let them crash in our bus," the deadhead said.

"Cool. I'm Linda," the girl stated as she danced away.

Lacey and Elvis both got on the bus and sat down. Elvis stared at Lacey for a moment.

"Pimento-loaf?" he asked in amazement.

"Hey, I made up a hippie name off the top of my head. I didn't hear you make any suggestions."

"I could have come up with something better than Pimento-loaf."

"Well, it's too late now, Pimento-loaf," Lacey teased him.

"So, what do we do next?"

"It would be a good idea if we got tickets for the show. This lot is going empty out once the show starts."

"You're the boss."

The Deadhead Lacey had given the money to climbed aboard the bus.

"By the way, my name's Mushroom," he told them.

"Good to meet you, Mushroom," Lacey said. "Could you do us a favor? If anyone comes around looking for us, tell him you haven't seen us, okay?"

"You got it, Sunflower."

"Oh, and I hate to ask, but do you have anything to drink? We're dying of thirst," she said politely.

"Sure, there are drinks in the cooler. Help yourself," Mushroom offered as he grabbed a pair of roach clips and got off the bus.

"Nice people," Elvis noticed.

"Whatever!" Lacey said, opening the cooler. "No matter what I do, it seems like I always end up surrounded by goddamned hippies."

"Maybe it's karma," Elvis suggested.

She rolled her eyes and muttered, "Now don't you start with all that hippie talk."

"I'm just saying that if you spend years in the FBI trying to put hippies behind bars, don't be surprised if you end up trapped on a hippie bus."

Lacey found a big container of orange juice and some paper cups and poured a cup for Elvis and one for herself.

As they drank down the orange juice, they began plotting their next move.

"Okay, after the concert, what do we do?" Lacey wondered aloud.

"Get out of this city," Elvis suggested.

"Definitely. Maybe we can take a train somewhere. Do you have any money on you?"

"No. Not a dime."

"That's okay. I've got over two hundred dollars left. Of course, I doubt if that's going to be enough for two train tickets."

"Hey, these Deadheads travel from city to city following the Grateful Dead. Why don't we just pay them to take us to the next show or something?" Elvis suggested as he poured Lacey and himself another cup of orange juice.

"Yeah, that's good thinking. There'd be no paper trail to worry about, either."

"But I think we should get off the bus in a city that the Grateful Dead aren't playing, in case Jericho decides to follow the band in search of us," he amended the plan.

"Then what?"

"I don't know. Get to a phone and warn John Lennon."

"If you insist."

Lacey's ears pricked up as she heard someone from outside announcing that they had extra tickets for sale. She grabbed her purse and jumped off the bus, buying two tickets from the man.

"Hey, I got tickets," she announced proudly as she got back on the bus.

Mushroom and the girl climbed on the bus as well, with a lit joint in their hand.

"Hey, you two want a hit?" Mushroom asked graciously.

"No, thanks," Elvis said.

Suddenly, a strange look crept over Mushroom's face.

"You didn't drink that orange juice, did you?"

"Yeah, why?" Lacey asked with concern.

Mushroom burst out laughing.

"What's so funny?" Elvis demanded to know.

"You guys just drank some serious acid."

"We did what?" Lacey screeched.

"Yeah," Mushroom said. "We mixed our acid in the orange juice. Don't worry. It's good stuff."

Lacey began having a panic attack as Elvis tried to comfort her.

"How long before it takes effect?" Elvis asked.

"Oh, about forty minutes. It's okay. We took some, too. We'll all trip together."

"Oh, my God, Jesse! What are we going to do?"

"Don't worry. It'll be okay. Haven't you ever tripped before?"

"No. Have you?"

"Yeah. Once back in the Sixties," he answered.

"What was it like?"

"Actually, it was pretty freaky."

"Oh, God! I don't believe this," Lacey cried.

"Look, don't get too upset," Elvis told her. "If you get all worked up about it, you'll have a bad trip."

He hugged her and tried consoling her as time ticked away.

He had experimented once with LSD in the sixties. He and Priscilla, along some members of his inner circle all took the acid together, and while he found it enlightening, he and Priscilla decided it just too powerful and dangerous to ever try again.

As Elvis tried to comfort Lacey they were both distracted by a scene unfolding just outside of the bus. A young Deadhead in a bad way became overwhelmed by the otherworldly sensations in his head. He sat down on the pavement and rocked back and forth.

"Get out of the way! Get out of the way!" he bellowed, apparently to no one, as he stared down at the ground with his head in his hands. "Do you realize? Do you realize?" he screamed. "Anything. Anything," his cryptic drug-induced rant continued.

Elvis and the rest of the people on the bus stared out at this strange event, slightly amused yet concerned.

"What's wrong with him?" Lacey asked fearfully.

"Either he did some bad acid, or he did some terribly good acid," Mushroom joked.

"Is that going to happen to us?" Lacey asked Elvis frantically.

"God, I hope not," Elvis answered, unable to take his eyes off the troubled kid.

Several Deadheads crowded around the young man and tried to soothe and comfort him. He eventually decided to lie down on the pavement and began motioning as if he was swimming the backstroke in an imaginary sea.

"Now, there's something you don't see every day," Elvis joked, caught up in the bizarreness of the moment.

"He's okay now," Linda said reassuringly.

"Oh, sure," Elvis answered sarcastically.

The boy sat up again; this time he had a very angry look in his eyes. He got to his feet and pounded on his chest as he let out an anguished scream and ran blindly, hurling himself into a group of people. He rolled on the ground and began letting out primal apelike grunts as the tackled Deadheads got to their feet.

Suddenly a police car pulled up and two cops got out. They ran over to the boy and apprehended him, hog-tying him as he screamed incoherently.

"Jesse, I'm scared," Lacey whispered to him.

"Don't be."

"What if something like that happens to me?"

"I don't think *that* will happen," Elvis said as the red flashing lights of the police car suddenly distracted him.

He looked around and it seemed as if every molecule on the bus was vibrating at a super-high speed, and he noticed vapor trails coming off his hands.

"I'm tripping," he proclaimed.

Lacey looked up at him and noticed that his face was melting.

"Me too," she gasped.

CHAPTER XXVII

ON THE BUS

The Grateful Dead were formed in San Francisco in 1965; their original name was the Warlocks. Ken Kesey, the eccentric author of *One Flew Over the Cuckoo's Nest*, soon hired the band. He had been using the money he made from the book to finance what he called acid tests. It was a new, experimental type of event where people would get together in strangely-lit, Day-glo painted rooms, and take a powerful, yet still legal drug known as LSD. Kesey decided to use the Warlocks as the acid test's house band. Shortly afterward, the Warlocks changed their name to The Grateful Dead and the long, strange trip had begun.

As the counterculture revolution grew from the seeds planted in San Francisco, the Grateful Dead became the symbol of this new consciousness. In 1967, the Summer of Love began, and as the Beatles brought the sensation to the mainstream, the Age of Aquarius was born. The Dead, as they were also called, performed concerts across the land, including Woodstock and the infamous Altamont Festival. Soon the Grateful Dead had acquired a legion of loyal fans, known as "Deadheads," who would follow them across the country and even to exotic locations in Europe and at the foot of the pyramids in Egypt. Fronted by Jerry Garcia and Bob Weir, the cult following had grown into a cultural phenomenon as the Dead became a traveling embodiment of the Sixties movement.

Lacey was mesmerized by the strange new sensation buzzing through her body. She began staring intently at her hands and at everything around her, as if she was seeing the world with brand new eyes.

"How do you feel?" Elvis asked.

"Weird. Like my soul is trying to escape my body," she answered in a slow monotone.

Suddenly two other Deadheads jumped on the bus. One was a tall, thin man with straight blond hair and a beard, the other was a short woman wearing a long flowing flower-print dress.

"These are our buddies, Steve and Moon. They share the bus with us," Mushroom announced.

Elvis and Lacey just waved robotically and smiled.

"This is Sunflower and, Pimento-loaf, is it?" Mushroom recalled.

"You can call me Jesse. In fact, please call me Jesse."

"They gave us fifty dollars to crash in our bus before the show, then accidentally drank some of the special orange juice."

"I guess they're not going to be taking a nap after all," Moon said with an insidious laugh.

Elvis and Lacey just stared at them and smiled. Suddenly, Lacey burst into spontaneous laughter, almost falling over from it.

"I was gonna ask if the acid had kicked in yet, but I guess we have our answer," Linda said.

As the Deadheads danced and frolicked in the warming rays of acid joy, Lacey and Elvis were laid out in the throes of pure intoxication, zonked and clinging to each other on a bed in the bus. They had closed their eyes and were in a cosmic flight through the universe of their minds, soaring through pulsating rainbows and swirling neon stars.

They opened their eyes and gazed into each other's.

"You've never looked as beautiful as you do right now," Elvis plainly stated as he slowly moved his hands through her hair, immersed in its tactile sensation as much as its beauty.

She softly caressed his beard, fascinated by its fullness as they began kissing, softly and timidly, like two virgins on their first date.

All sense of time was distorted and after what seemed like only a few minutes, it was suddenly time to go to the concert. Elvis was less looped than Lacey, so he appointed himself her caretaker. He made arrangements with his new friends on the bus to take them out of town and to the next big city along the way to their destination, paying them an additional fifty dollars out of Lacey's purse. It was a task that the Deadheads would have done for free, but since he offered to pay them, they decided not to refuse. Elvis convinced Lacey to leave her purse and the gun inside it on the bus, and they put their Halloween masks back on, in case Jericho was still roaming the vicinity.

They followed the masses to the Music Hall's entrance. Elvis saw his twin brother in the distance, playing merrily in the parking lot, chasing the bubbles without a care in the world as Lacey clung to Elvis like a child, laughing and giggling at the bright, vibrant colors that swirled around her and distorted beautifully in her kaleidoscope eyes. Elvis saw Jericho standing by the door. Jericho had adopted a Deadhead disguise of his own, trying to look inconspicuous as he stared at the crowd looking for his rogue agents. A wave of paranoia swept over Elvis, even though their identities were carefully concealed. He decided not to alert Lacey to Jericho's presence, not wanting to trigger any fear or paranoia in her, not wanting her to overreact and attract any attention to them.

They inched their way past Jericho and through the throbbing, multi-legged beast that was the line of people. They took off their masks, presented their tickets, and went into the concert hall. A wave of relief swept over Elvis as he now felt free inside the hall.

"I'm starving," Lacey whispered, realizing that they hadn't eaten all day.

"Me, too, and yet the thought of eating repulses me."

"I know what you mean."

Food was not something they desired. It was fuel for a human organism, and they had evolved into beautiful spirits, sharing a universal consciousness with the cosmos, no longer made of flesh and blood. They had become an atom in the eyelash of God. However, they opted to eat nonetheless, still enslaved to their fleshy prisons, not knowing how long it would be until they would eat again.

After consuming some concession-stand food, they made their way to their seats. The concert hall was an exercise in contrasts. Counterculture soldiers dressed in denim and tie-dye uniforms now overran this classy and expensively ornate hall, best known for hosting the world famous Rockettes. The mood exploded as the Grateful Dead took the stage. Multi-colored lights splashed over the crowd as the band opened with "Heaven Help the Fool." The fans cooed in delight.

Perhaps it was the energy of the crowd, the deftness of the band, or even the acid, but Elvis and Lacey lost themselves in the music. All of the pressures and craziness of the past few months broke loose and escaped through the electric tones that ricocheted off the walls and slithered up their spines. They found themselves caught up in a spiritual dance that had already consumed the rest of the crowd. The rich sounds of Jerry Garcia's guitar battled beautifully with the syncopation, creating a musical mist that danced through the air and blew over the acid-drenched audience. The energy of the performance kept building until it seemed as if a riot or a mass spontaneous combustion would break out, but just in the nick of time the musical alchemists somehow cooled the vibe down and lowered the audience safely to the ground.

Like skilled magicians, the band cast musical spells into the crowd until all members of the audience were sharing universal thoughts of perpetual joy. They conjured up songs like "Fire On the Mountain" and "Not Fade Away," as the spiraling light show fed the grooves of their long improvised solos.

By the time the Grateful Dead finished with "Uncle's John's Band," Elvis and Lacey felt as if a mass exorcism had occurred, removing all their demons and anxieties.

They stumbled slowly back to the bus, holding each other lovingly, feeling a closeness that only comes from surviving an ordeal together.

Back on the bus, they were reunited with their new friends, all sharing a common, sacred experience. As they reminisced about the concert, the bus pulled out of the parking lot and began its trek to the next destination. As they left New York City and got on the interstate, Lacey and Elvis looked into each other's eyes, both expressing the silent knowledge that they had escaped the wrath of Jericho, at least for the time being.

As the bus drove south into the night, Steve pulled out his acoustic guitar and started playing a collection of songs, mostly by the Grateful Dead, as Moon and Linda sang along. Elvis then borrowed the guitar and put on a show of his own. He didn't know any Grateful Dead songs, but instead played a number of rock standards, including many of his own; his musicality won instant favor with the Deadheads and he sensed that in an unconscious, unspoken sense he had gained acceptance into the group.

"So where are we headed?" Lacey asked, realizing that the destination was still a mystery to her and Elvis.

"Well, the next show isn't until about a month from now in Florida, so we're going to drive down to the Smoky Mountains where we have a cabin, hang out for the next week, and then we're gonna bum around for awhile and meet up with some friends," Steve answered.

"Oh, I see," Lacey responded, not sure of what their next move should be.

"Since you two paid us a hundred dollars for doing stuff we would have done anyway, you're welcome to camp with us up in the mountains," Steve offered.

Elvis and Lacey looked at each other and knew that it was a good plan.

"Yeah. That'd be great. Thanks a lot," Elvis said.

"No sweat. Us Deadheads have got to stick together, man. Besides, the money you gave us will really help us out."

"Thanks, nonetheless," Elvis said, amazed at their generosity.

"Maybe you can repay us with some songs later."

Elvis smiled and withdrew into Lacey's arms; both of their brains were still flying from the effects of the drug, but now at a more comfortable pace. Elvis couldn't help looking back on the very weird day, on the events of the last few months, his journey since his faked death, and all that he had seen and experienced in his crazy life. It reminded him of some Grateful Dead lyrics he had heard several times throughout the day which were still echoing through his mind.

"What a long, strange trip it's been."

CHAPTER XXVIII

FIRE ON THE MOUNTAIN

Elvis awoke after a long sleep to see the familiar, lush, green meadows of Tennessee outside the bus window. A wholesome sense of joy filled him. He was back in his home state.

"It's alive," Mushroom joked as Elvis yawned and stirred.

"Wow! The two of you slept like logs," Moon added.

"Where are we? Tennessee?" Elvis asked still feeling disoriented.

"Good guess."

"It wasn't a guess. I grew up in these parts," he stated proudly as he put his arm around Lacey, who seemed equally groggy.

"We should be there soon," Steve announced from the driver's seat.

"Is there any coffee, by any chance?" Lacey murmured.

"No. We don't drink coffee. It's unhealthy for the body," Linda stated.

"Oh, okay," Lacey responded, finding it ironic that they viewed coffee as bad, but LSD-laced orange juice was acceptable.

The previous night had been an eye-opening experience for her. The acid trip had turned her on to a world she had never known. In one night, the phenomenon of the Sixties had finally made sense to her. From the tie-dye to the music to the need to get closer to Nature, she suddenly understood it.

The acid had had a much different effect on Elvis, however. Messianic complexes of old had resurfaced, and sometime during the Grateful Dead concert he had come upon the realization that he was a messenger of God. It was a belief that he decided not to share with anyone, wondering if it was more of a drug-induced psychosis than a revelation.

"So when did you two start following the Dead?" Mushroom inquired.

Elvis and Lacey looked at each other and tried to think of answer.

"It seems like only yesterday," Elvis wisely volunteered, dodging a bullet.

"Yeah. I know what you mean, man."

"Why do you have such a big bus for only four people?" Lacey asked, trying to change the subject.

"Well, it's not usually just four people," Mushroom explained. "We get a lot of stragglers like you. We have some friends we're meeting down in Florida before the next show, too. They usually travel with us. Besides, this bus is basically our home."

"So why do you do it? Why do you devote your lives to following the Grateful Dead?" Lacey inquired.

"Hell, why not? It's a chance to be part of something greater than ourselves, to be part of a tribe. Why do you two do it?" Moon answered, lobbing the question back to Lacey.

"Pretty much the same reason," Lacey responded vaguely.

"Why should I spend the best years of my life trapped in some office running around like a rat in a maze to attain possessions that I don't really need?" Linda said.

"Yeah. All we need are the stars in the sky and the songs in our heart," Mushroom added philosophically.

"I can dig that," Lacey agreed sincerely.

The bus made its way up the winding mountain road, through beautiful forest with mist all around it that gave the Smoky Mountains their name. The bus reached the National Park office; Steve got out to fill out the proper paperwork, and then they drove to their lodge.

"We're here," Steve happily announced.

The merry travelers got out of the bus, stretching their limbs and inhaling the rich scent of evergreen. Autumn had hit the trees of Smoky Mountains like the tasteful stroke of a painter's brush, adding reds, oranges, and golden browns to the green foliage.

The lodge was nothing but a modest log cabin. It looked pretty small, considering there were now six people in the party, but nobody was complaining. They quickly unpacked the bus and brought their things into the cabin. Shortly after they got settled in, it was time to eat. It was a vegetarian meal, much to Elvis' chagrin, but it was still food, and he wasn't turning down any meals.

"I don't suppose there's a telephone here, by any chance?" Elvis asked anxiously.

"No. No phones and no electricity. Isn't it great?" Steve proclaimed.

Elvis didn't answer.

After dinner, Elvis and Lacey snuck off into the forest to have a talk. There were many things they couldn't discuss in front of the Deadheads.

The cool, fresh November air blew through their hair as they strolled along a foot-worn path underneath the green canopy, walking hand in hand over the freshly-dewed earth.

"It's really beautiful up here, isn't it?" Lacey mused.

"Yeah. Quite a contrast to New York City. And the best part is there is no way Jericho could have tracked us up here."

"Don't say that. He has ways."

"No, I think we're safe here. It's a good place to lay low and figure out what we're going to do next."

"So what exactly happened yesterday at the hotel?" Lacey wanted to know.

"Shortly after you stormed out of my room, Jericho forced his way in. He must have had our rooms bugged."

"Yeah. It was stupid of us to think he didn't."

"He basically confessed he was planning to kill Lennon, and then said that now he was going to kill us for figuring it out. That's when he led me out of the room and you saved me. By the way, thanks again."

"Don't thank me. We're in this together. That being said, there was something I overheard that I didn't understand."

"What's that?"

"Why did he refer to you as Elvis Presley?"

Elvis stopped in his tracks and inhaled the cool air deeply.

"Well, I guess it is time to tell you. There isn't any reason not to."

"Tell me what?"

"I am Elvis Presley."

"Come on. Be serious."

"Hey, you asked."

"I know, but it seems pretty hard to believe. I mean, how is it possible?"

"I faked my death to escape my fame. Jericho tracked me down and forced me to join the FBI and have plastic surgery on my face to go undercover."

"That's completely crazy. I don't believe it."

Elvis grabbed her and pulled her towards him, gazing deeply into her eyes.

"Remember when you said that you could tell when I was lying?"

She nodded.

"Look into my eyes, honey. Am I lying?"

"Oh God! I believe you," she said, impulsively hugging him tightly. "I don't know why, but I do."

"Because it's true. I'm sorry I didn't tell you sooner, but things have been so crazy that I had no choice or chance."

"I thought I was in love with you, but now I don't even know who you are."

"I'm me. I've always been me. No plastic surgery or alias can change that. I don't even think I realized it until last night, when my brain was swimming in acid. For the last three years, I've been running from myself, but I'm tired of running. You can't escape your own shadow."

"Is that why you faked your death? To escape?"

"I don't know. Do you know what the really ironic thing is? Part of the reason I faked my death was so my life would be simple again. Now here I am, hiding in the mountains from the FBI with a group of Deadheads, trying to save John Lennon's life."

"You've saved me," Lacey replied.

"How do you figure?"

"I've been a fool for so long. I thought I had all the answers and knew who the bad guys were. Hate and bitterness have a way of blinding a person. For years, I hated everyone who held certain beliefs, and blamed the world for my father's death. Thanks to you, though, I can see again. I don't need hate to preserve my father's memory. I can do it with love. I've never loved anyone since my father died. I wouldn't allow it, but now I find myself in love with you."

"I love you, too," Elvis said as he kissed her and they held each other.

Lacey broke the embrace first. "I have a question, since I'm kind of new to this whole love thing."

"What's the question?"

"Is love as scary as it seems?"

"It's scarier."

"Then why does anyone do it?"

"For moments like this," he whispered in her ear.

For a while they didn't speak, but walked until they came to a waterfall, and stood watching it in silence, mesmerized by its beauty.

Finally Lacey asked, "Have you ever lost someone you loved?"

"I've lost everyone I've ever loved," he stated with regret as a light rain began to fall on the mountain. "My mother died many years ago, my father more recently. My wife left me for another man, and I'll probably never see my daughter Lisa Marie again. Then there's Faith."

"Who's Faith?" Lacey asked.

"A girl I met a couple of years ago. She was a teenage runaway I picked up when she was hitchhiking. She is a really sweet girl, very nice, very vulnerable. We were friends. I took care of her and let her stay with me. Then one night, we become lovers."

"What happened to her?"

"I don't know, actually. I was kidnapped by Jericho and never saw her again."

"I'm sorry. I didn't know."

"I'm just worried about her now. I hope she's okay."

"Did she know who you really were?"

"Yeah. She deduced it. Of course, it was before my plastic surgery, so it was a little more obvious," he said. "Come to think of it, you're the first woman to ever fall in love with me without knowing I was a famous rock star. That means a lot. Before I used to wonder if any woman could ever really love me for who I was."

"How could I not?" Lacey asked as they began kissing heatedly.

They pulled each other to the grass as the rain began to fall hard on the mountainside, drenching them as they tore each other's clothes off. The cold beating rain could not dowse their passion as they made hot, frenzied love amidst the downpour. The storm climaxed with them, then began to let up as they rested gently within each other's embrace.

They reluctantly put their cold, wet clothes back on and decided to head back to the campgrounds, following a rainbow that had emerged in the post-storm sky.

"We still haven't talked about what our next move is," Lacey reminded him.

"I guess we're stuck up here for now, but at the end of the week when we leave the mountains, we'll find a phone and I'll call John and warn him," he suggested. "Who knows? Maybe Carter will win the election and everything will be called off."

"Don't bet on it," Lacey said grimly. "Besides, who wins the election won't change our circumstances. We know too much. Jericho won't rest until we're dead and John's head is on a plate."

"What do you suggest?"

"We need new identities and some serious cash. We have less than a hundred dollars to our name."

"I know just the person who can help us," Elvis proclaimed with a smile.

They returned to the cabin, their wet clothes sticking to their skin as the Deadheads playfully teased them and ushered them to the campfire to warm up and dry out.

The next few days were spent hiking with the group, exploring the subtle beauty of the mountains. The evenings were spent around the campfire telling stories and singing along as Elvis and Steve took turns with the guitar. The fourth night in the mountains was more serious, as they stayed close to the radio listening to the incoming tallies of the Presidential election. Much to the Deadheads' dismay, Reagan defeated Carter in a landslide. Even Elvis and Lacey, who would ordinarily be rooting for the Republican Governor, were saddened, knowing that a sequence of events had begun that could lead to the death of John Lennon.

Back in Washington D.C., a town that was now gearing up towards a peaceful transition of power, Special Agent Jericho was preparing for his next course of action. Only a few days earlier, he had been responsible for leading the New York City police on a large drug bust, bringing down the New Aquarius drug ring. He had declined the honors and the publicity, instead immediately flying back to the capitol. He sat at his desk, watching the election coverage wind down as he placed a call to one of his operatives.

"This is Special Agent Jericho. The Walrus has resurfaced. Prepare the harpoon," he said cryptically, then he hung up the phone without waiting for an answer.

CHAPTER XXIX

FRIEND OF THE DEVIL

The next day was unusually warm for Autumn, especially in the mountains, and the Deadheads used the weather as an excuse to strip off their clothes and bathe in a nearby stream. The four of them cavorted around naked in the cold water, as if there was nothing unusual about this activity. It was the off-season and there was very little chance of anyone outside the tribe approaching them; nonetheless Elvis and Lacey balked at the idea.

"Come on, you two. Free yourselves from society's rules," Mushroom shouted.

Lacey looked over at Elvis, gauging his reaction.

"What the hell? I almost died twice last week," Elvis philosophized as he stripped down and jumped into the icy waters. "What's a little nakedness among friends?"

Elvis let out a shriek when he hit the cold water. Now Lacey was left as the lone standout; finally she gave in and removed her clothes, revealing her perfect body. She leapt into the water amidst the cheers of her fellow skinny-dippers.

Elvis swam up to her and joked, "Is the water cold, or are you just happy to see me?"

She reprimanded him with a splash in the face as they playfully wrestled with each other.

Shortly afterwards, the cold set in as the original swimmers scampered out of the stream, frantically getting dry and covered with a blanket as they shivered in the wind.

Lacey decided to get out as well, leaving Elvis alone in the water.

"Now, before I get out, let me just say that cold water has a way of making some things shrink," he announced self-consciously as he climbed out of the water.

They all headed back to camp, where they got a fire going and all agreed to drink a glass of the *special* orange juice. The sun had set into darkness as the acid began taking effect. They shared a joint as Mushroom beat on a drum. Their inner animals emerged as everyone danced around the campfire like shamans. All self-consciousness dissipated into the air like the smoke and embers of the campfire; everyone eventually paired off with their cosmic mate and had amazing sex under the star-filled sky. Elvis and Lacey were now part of the tribe.

That night, as the two other couples snuggled in their bed, Elvis and Lacey shared a sleeping bag once again.

"I just want you to know how brave it was of you to give up your inhibitions and go skinny-dipping today," Elvis whispered.

"What do you mean?"

"I mean, I know you're an old-fashioned girl and all, but I think it was very liberating."

"I'm glad to hear that, but I have a confession to make. I'm not as old-fashioned as you may think."

"What do you mean by that?"

"There are a few things in my past that I'm not real proud of."

"What are you saying?"

"When I was a teenager, I had a tough time getting money together for college," she answered.

"And -?"

"It was the Sixties and all, and some guy convinced me I could make some quick money if I posed for some pictures," she continued.

"What kind of pictures?"

"Well, nude pictures."

"That's not too bad, I guess. I mean, a lot of women have posed nude."

"Well, it still didn't solve my financial woes, so I…also made a few movies," she said slowly, watching his response.

"What kind of movies do you mean?"

"Pornographic movies," she said reluctantly.

Elvis was silent.

"Look, it was a long time ago. I was a dumb kid who needed the money."

"What exactly did you do in the movies?"

"What do you think?"

"Well, was it just you dancing naked or something?"

"No. It was me having sex with men...and a woman."

"Oh, Lord!" Elvis gasped.

"Are you mad?"

"I don't know what I am."

"I'd understand if you were. I've been mad at myself for doing it ever since."

"Does anybody else know?"

"Jericho knows. He blackmailed me with the films. That's why I did some of the things I did on the last mission."

"That son of a bitch!"

"That's why I was willing to go through with that phony marriage. He said that if I didn't, he would show you the films."

"You could have just told me."

"I didn't want to lose you. I didn't think you'd understand."

"So why are you telling me now?"

"I thought you deserved to know."

"Well, thanks for thinking of me," he said sarcastically.

"I can't change the past, Jesse."

"Look. Why don't we just go to sleep? I don't want to talk about it any more," Elvis grunted as he rolled over, turning his back to her.

"I'm sorry," she whispered as she put her arm around him.

Elvis pretended to drift off to sleep, but there was little chance of that. Aside from the fact that the acid was still coursing through his body, his heart was broken. He was an old-fashioned man who expected near-chastity in his lovers. Sexual innocence was a virtue that he held above almost all others, and now he had learned that the women he loved had been in adult films. It was too much for him to comprehend. Not that he really had any right to judge anyone's sexual past. His sexual conquests were legendary, and many times illegal, but he was not immune to double standards, and he believed that women had an obligation to keep themselves pure. For months he had over-looked the fact that Lacey was sleeping with a man she didn't love, because it was out of duty for her country. But despite all the feelings of betrayal and jealousy brewing in him, one emotion still loomed larger, his love for her.

Priscilla posed herself seductively on their bed wearing a black see-through teddy that she desparately hoped could help reignite the passion that had once defined their relationship. Since the birth of Lisa Marie, Elvis had barely touched her and she had begun to blame herself for their dormant love life.

Elvis shuffled into the bedroom, barely noticing his sexy bride's outfit. Visibly high, he plopped down on the bed, oblivious to Priscilla's not so subtle message.

"Elvis?"

"What, Satnin?"

"Do you know long it's been since we have made love?"

"No, but I'm sure you'll tell me."

"It's been too long, honey. I'm just a woman with real needs and emotions and I love you so much that I need to feel your hands caress me, your lips against mine and for you to make love to me."

"You're talking like a harlot, not the mother of my child."

"Can't I be both, just for one night?" Priscilla asked.

"Don't put me through this again. I've got pressures coming at me from every direction. I don't need them in the bedroom, too. What do you want from me, woman?"

"For you to love me as much as you love your fans, your mother, even your pills. It seems like my entire life has been dedicated to pleasing you. I wish that for one night you could try pleasing me for a change. Elvis?"

Priscilla looked up at Elvis and realized he was fast asleep.

The next morning Elvis snuck out of the knapsack before Lacey awoke. He needed some time to think and found a large rock to sit on as he stared out at the mountaineous scenery and sorted through his feelings.

Mushroom approached him from behind, startling Elvis at first.

"What's up, man?" Mushroom asked as he sat down next to Elvis.

Elvis shrugged nonchalantly not saying a word as Mushroom lit up a joint and handed it to him. Elvis declined, already upset with himself for his recent drug use.

"You're not really a Deadhead are you?" Mushroom asked.

"What makes you say that?"

"You and your old lady don't know anything about the Grateful Dead. Of all the songs you know on guitar, none of them are dead tunes," he said. "So, what are you running from?"

"What makes you think I'm running?"

"We're all running from something."

"Oh yeah? What are you running from?" Elvis challenged.

"Adulthood, I guess. You see. My life was all planned out for me before I was even born. I was going to go to the best schools, study business law and make all the right friends. I was going to marry a pretty yet motherly woman, have 2.5 children and live in a nice house with a two-car garage in the middle of white suburbia."

"That doesn't sound too bad."

"Why would I want to spend the rest of my life climbing some imaginary ladder trying to acquire useless possessions and status symbols just so I can be as miserable as everyone else in society," Mushroom preached. "Okay, now it's your turn. What are you running from?"

"The law."

"Really? What did you do?"

"Nothing. I'm a victim of circumstance. It's not my fault," he said before pausing and letting out a deep sigh. "Then again, maybe it's *all* my fault. Maybe I've just been running from myself."

"Well, your secret's safe with me. But after we leave the mountains, we'll have to part ways."

"I understand," Elvis replied as Mushroom got up and walked away.

The week ended as the band of Deadheads left the mountains and dropped Elvis and Lacey off in Knoxville. They exchanged hugs and good wishes, never knowing that they had tripped and jammed with Elvis Presley. After grabbing a couple of cheeseburgers and acquiring quite a bit of change, Lacey and Elvis found a payphone. Elvis dialed up John Lennon's home phone number at the Dakota. John answered.

"John, this is Jesse Hope. I'm calling to..."

"Jesse, you bastard!" Lennon screamed. "I talked to Zeus at the jail and he told me all about your involvement in the FBI. To think I trusted you!"

"John, I'm truly sorry, but..." Elvis tried to warn him, but Lennon cut him off.

"You Feds need to read your own Bill of Rights someday. I'm going on with the concert. You pigs do whatever you have to do!" John growled as he slammed down the phone.

Elvis looked at Lacey. "That went well."

"What now?"

"Don't worry. I have an ace up my sleeve," Elvis reassured her as he dialed Tom Parker's number.

The phone rang at the Parker estate in Las Vegas, and Tom Parker picked up the phone.

"Ya?" The Colonel answered.

"Tom, it's Jesse."

"Jesse, my boy. How are you doing?" Parker asked.

"Not too good, old buddy. That's why I'm calling you. I'm in a serious jam right now. I need to cash in some favors."

"Anything. Name it."

"I need two new identities, one for me, one for a woman about thirty years old. Plus I need ten thousand dollars in cash."

"Well sure, Jesse, anything for an old friend. It will take some time for me to get those new identities though, maybe about a month. Bureaucracy takes time. I tell you what, today's the seventh. You give me a month, and on the seventh of December go to Las Vegas, to the Hilton. I'll have everything you want in a safety deposit box under your name. Just show them your ID, and they'll give you the package."

"Okay, I go by the name Jesse King, now."

"Consider it done."

"Thanks, Tom, but I have one more favor to ask," Elvis added.

"Go ahead, I'm listening."

"Grab a pen and write down what I say."

"Okay. I got one," Parker answered.

"Give this message to John Lennon in New York City as soon as possible."

"John Lennon?"

"Yes, John Lennon."

"Okay. What's the message?"

"John, this is Jesse Hope. I know you hate me and think I'm in cahoots with the FBI, but I just want to warn you that there's an FBI agent named Jake Jericho who is planning to kill you before Reagan's inauguration. Watch your back."

"Is that it?"

"Yes, and thank you, Tom. You're a lifesaver. More than you know," Elvis added.

"Okay, Jesse. Good talking to you again. Take care of yourself."

"You too, Colonel," Elvis responded as he hung up the phone.

As Tom Parker put the phone down, he heard a loud, slow, sarcastic applause from Agent Jericho, who had been listening in on the conversation, and sat on Parker's couch with a devilish grin and a loaded gun.

"Well done, Mr. Van Kuijk. I'm very pleased that I didn't have to shoot you in the head," Jericho remarked. "Now, just forget everything that has happened in the past week and you'll be okay. Just a reminder: if things don't go as planned for me, I'll have to raise a major stink over your illegal immigration and send your fat ass back to Holland, minus the millions of dollars of course. Or maybe I'll just kill you and your wife. It depends on my mood that day." Jericho placed his gun to Parker's temple and stared menacingly into his eyes. "But we don't want that to happen, do we?"

Elvis walked away from the phone and smiled at Lacey.

"It's all taken care of," he announced. "All we have to do is go to the Hilton in Las Vegas and there will be new identities for both of us, plus ten thousand dollars in cash in a safety deposit box."

"Wow! You've got some good connections."

"Hey! It's good to be the King," he joked.

"So let's get our butts to Vegas."

"Well, there is one catch."

"What's that?"

"Getting new identities will take some time. We can't pick the stuff up until December seventh."

"Pearl Harbor Day, a day of infamy," Lacey pointed out. "That's not a good omen, Jesse."

"Don't worry about omens. The Colonel will deliver."

"Let's see," Lacey mused, "we have seventy-eight dollars left. That's got to last us a month and get us to Vegas. That's not going to be easy."

"We can do it. We're FBI agents," he said with a smile.

In the near distance, a slow moving freight train rolled down the railroad tracks.

"Let's hop the train," Lacey said as she began running after it.

Elvis didn't have much time to argue, so he ran after the train as well. They ran up just behind the locomotive and raced along beside it until they spotted an open, empty freight car. Elvis caught up to it and jumped in, then reached out his hand and pulled Lacey into the car

Mark David Chapman sat on the floor in an almost fetal position. Sweat poured out from under the baseball cap he wore backwards on his head and dripped onto the rims of his glasses. In his hand, he clutched a copy of *The Catcher in the Rye*. There was madness in his eyes, and sadness in his heart. His mind had been barraged by voices telling him to do bad things, commands from a higher power.

He chewed on his fingernails as he skimmed through the book, re-reading important passages and weeping. The ringing of the telephone interrupted his thoughts as its shrill sound dug into his spine. He wiped the sweat from his brow and got up to answer the phone, fearing the voice on the other end. The voices had been haunting him for some time, ever since he got back from Beirut, Lebanon. His voices had good connections, though. They would often deposit large sums of money into his bank account, financing his trips from Hawaii to New York City. In the last few weeks, the voices had gotten louder, angrier.

"Hello," he said, his voice wavering nervously.

"Holden Caufield?" the voice asked.

"This is him."

"The time has come, Holden. It's time to kill the phony at last. Kill the phony, Holden. Do it," the voice commanded before hanging up on him.

Chapman slowly hung up the phone, and slid his baseball cap around his head until the bill was facing forward. He opened a drawer and pulled out a Charter Undercover .38 Special. He then pointed the gun at the face he saw in the mirror as a deranged but relieved smile crept over his face.

CHAPTER XXX

MYSTERY TRAIN

Elvis and Lacey sat on the floor of the freight car trying to catch their breath as they felt the steel wheels rolling beneath them.

"Any idea where this train is headed?" Elvis asked.

"I don't know. West, I believe."

"Next time, give me a little warning before you bolt off for a train."

"There wasn't any time. Think of the money we're saving; free transportation and free shelter."

"Yeah, but if we made a mistake jumping into the car, it could have cost us an arm and a leg," he joked dryly.

She politely smiled at his bad pun.

"Are you still mad at me?" Lacey asked out of the blue.

"Still? Since when have I been mad at you?"

"Since I told you about those movies."

"Hey, that's your business. It was a long time ago, right?"

"I know, but you've been really distant ever since."

"I wasn't trying to be."

"You haven't tried to be anything. You've been completely cold and business-like. You're usually sweet and caring."

"What do you want from me?"

"Maybe I want you to hold me and tell me that you still love me. It was really hard for me to admit those things to you. I'm embarrassed and ashamed of it. I almost married some idiot, just to prevent you from finding out about it. I was afraid that it would change the way you felt about me, and when I look into your eyes, I can tell that it has." She began to weep.

"What do you want me to say, that I think it's great the woman I love turns out to be a porn star? Well, I don't, and it's tearing me up inside. If it didn't, then it would mean that I don't love you, but I do."

"Really?"

Elvis crawled up beside her and put his arm around her.

"Of course. Did you think I would just stop loving you? Do you think love's that easy?" he asked. "I love you, Lacey, and it would take more than some movies to change that."

"I love you, too."

They hugged and kissed, their passion boiled over as they made love on the floor of the freight car. Houses and scenery sped by at the reckless speed of the locomotive's rhythmic pumping engine. The train entered a mountain tunnel, casting them into total darkness as their intensity detonated like a bullet on the track. When the train emerged from the tunnel and the light shone again through the freight car door, the two of them lay naked and motionless in each other's arms.

The next morning, the slowing churn of the wheels alerted them that the train would soon be pulling into a station. As soon as the train decelerated to a safe speed, Lacey grabbed her purse and the two of them jumped and rolled to the ground. They dusted themselves off, snuck away from the tracks, and happened upon a diner where they stopped for a bite to eat. They could tell they were in Texas from the number of men wearing cowboy hats, and from the strange looks that their dirty tie-dyed clothes garnered.

After they'd eaten, they walked over to the train tracks and waited for another freight train to come their way. They readied themselves as they heard the faint rumbling of the locomotive in the distance. As the train roared past them, they ran along with it and found an open freight car and jumped inside.

As they tumbled onto the floor, Lacey let out a surprised scream as she saw a tall, unkempt man staring down at them.

"Don't be scared of me. I'm just a train hopper like you," the man insisted.

"I'm sorry. You just caught us offguard," Lacey apologized.

"Did you think I was a bull?" The man asked with a thick Southern twang.

"A bull?"

"Yeah. That's what us train hoppers call the railroad police," he explained.

"Hi, I'm Jesse; this is my girlfriend, Lacey."

"My name's Zack," he said as he shook Elvis' hand.

The man's face was tanned and leathery, his beard dirty and unruly; his thinning brown hair hung down around his semi-toothless face in greasy strands.

"Are you two Deadheads?" he asked, noticing their psychedelic clothes.

"Yes, we are," Elvis answered, deciding to keep that as their cover story.

"Yeah. There's a lot of you folks hopping trains."

"Do you do this often?" Lacey asked as they settled down on the floor.

"Yep. I'm a career train hopper. The freight cars are my home."

"Wow! I didn't know that train hoppers still existed," Elvis marveled.

"We're a dying breed, all right."

"How do you get by?" Lacey asked.

"Odd jobs, and the kindness of strangers. A lot of these rails go through farming areas; sometimes I jump off and grab a couple ears of corn or something."

"That's sounds strangely romantic," Elvis commented.

"Yeah, lately it's become a little trendy, though. Lawyers and stock brokers taking a week off, pretending they're hoboes or some shit."

"That's funny," Elvis remarked.

"Yeah. Over the years, I've seen all types riding the rails. Hoboes, tramps, bums, winos, convicts, and Deadheads as well."

"So what are you?" Lacey asked.

"I'm just a traveler."

"I bet you could write a fascinating book," Elvis told him.

"Sure, once I learn me how to read." The other two didn't know what to say to that. "So what about you two? Hop trains often?"

"No. We just started."

"Well, it's a real American adventure, I believe. One of the few things left that technology hasn't totally ruined, though it's trying."

"Why? How has it changed?" Lacey inquired.

"Trains move too damn fast these days; it's hard for an old-timer like me to get on them sometimes. These wheels are like guillotines if you fall under them. I knew an old hobo who got his legs cut off trying to hop these new trains."

"That's horrible!" Lacey gasped.

"It goes with the territory. We used to call him Skip, now we call him Shorty," Zack laughed morosely.

"I hope you don't mind us hopping on your freight car."

"No, not at all. Meeting new people is half the adventure." He opened his duffle bag and pulled out a half-eaten roll. "Never underestimate the greatness of a restaurant's garbage bin," he stated with a grin. "I'd offer you some, but it's all I have."

"That's okay. I had garbage for lunch," Lacey joked callously, causing Elvis to give her a gentle elbow to the ribs.

"You two married?"

"No, just in love," Elvis said sweetly as he stroked Lacey's hair.

"Well, if you want to stay in love, don't get married."

"That's not very nice," Lacey pouted.

"Have you ever been married?" Elvis asked.

"Hell, yeah. Why do you think I first hopped on a train? To get away from her," Zack said with a cackling laugh.

"So do you recommend this life for anyone else?" Elvis questioned, deeply intrigued by this hidden pocket of American culture.

"Yes, if you like to travel, and don't mind giving up the creature comforts. But it can be dangerous."

"Dangerous? How?" Lacey wondered.

"Well, I told you about them train wheels. Then there's the bulls always harassing ya, and there's this legend going around the jungles..."

"What do you mean by 'jungles'?" Elvis interrupted.

"They're little camps by the tracks set up by hoboes. Usually it's just a campfire, maybe an old mattress or something. Anyway, there's a story going around that there's a serial killer that's been riding the rails. They reckon he's killed over a hundred people through the years. He knocks train hoppers unconscious, then robs and kills them and dumps their body in bushes away from the tracks."

"Oh, my God!" Lacey exclaimed.

"I doubt if it's true. I haven't heard anything in the news about it," Elvis rationalized.

"Well, maybe the cops don't know that there's a serial killer. Cops are really funny about jurisdictions, and they don't share information from state to state," Zack pointed out. "Plus most of these guys are drifters and don't have families that report them missing. Besides, if you get dumped off around these parts, the coyotes and buzzards will find you long before the police do."

"I guess it's possible, but I still don't believe it," Elvis responded.

Without warning, Zack pulled a blackjack out of his bag and swung it down on Elvis' head, knocking him out cold. Before Lacey could do anything, he cracked the blackjack against her skull as she slumped over, unconscious as well.

Zack stood up and smiled.

"Believe it!"

CHAPTER XXXI

BLOOD ON THE TRACKS

Elvis slowly regained consciousness; he tried to reach up to feel the damage to his aching head, but his hands were bound behind his back with rope. He saw Lacey lying on the opposite side of the freight car, bound and unconscious. Zack was lurching over her, looking through her purse.

"What the hell are you doing?" Elvis yelled.

Zack ignored him as he found Lacey's money; he grinned with delight as he stuffed the cash in his pocket. He discovered the gun and inspected it.

"Nice gun," he remarked.

"Untie us, you son of a bitch!" Elvis yelled.

Zack dug further into Lacey's purse and pulled out her FBI badge.

"What the hell? Are you two G-men?"

"Yeah, and if you don't let us go, you'll get the chair," Elvis threatened him.

"I never killed a G-man before."

Lacey began coming to; she moaned softly, still unaware of their plight. "What happened?" she asked.

"Hello, little princess. We're going to have some fun," Zack said with an evil smirk.

Lacey began screaming frantically as she realized what was happening.

"Don't scream, baby. No one can hear ya. Save your energy. You're going to need it," Zack growled menacingly as he slid his hand between her legs.

She kicked and jerked spasmodically like a fish on land, as Zack just laughed sadistically.

"Zack!" Elvis shouted, trying to get his attention. "Do what you want with me, just let her go."

"What a good boyfriend you are!" Zack sneered. "But why would I do that, when I can kill you both? You see, normally I would just kill you two and dump you off somewhere, but it's not every day I find women on these rails, especially one as beautiful as your girlfriend here. I think me and her are going to get to know each other a little better. Don't worry, you can watch. Feel free to yell out any suggestions."

"No, don't!" Lacey screamed as he pulled up her shirt and began fondling her breasts.

His hands began exploring her body, his attention diverted away from Elvis. Lacey screamed as he pulled her pants down, but Elvis managed to get to his feet and ran over to Zack and kicked him hard in the side of the head. Then with his hands still bound behind him, he hit the killer with a flurry of kicks to his ribs. Zack grabbed Lacey's gun and pointed it at him. Elvis kicked the gun out of his hand and charged him, knocking him against the wall of the freight car.

Zack landed several punches to his face as Elvis slammed his knee repeatedly into the man's groin until Zack threw him to the floor. Elvis landed in the open doorway, hanging dangerously over the edge. Zack ran towards him, but Elvis tripped him up with his legs and climbed on top of him. They both got to their feet as Zack threw some more punches. Lacey tried to stagger to her feet in the moving car, but her pants were tangled around her legs. She got on her knees and began crawling towards them.

Zack knocked Elvis back against the wall with an uppercut. Elvis fought back tenaciously with a series of kicks to the face until Zack stumbled backwards over Lacey's body. He fell backward out the door, but held on to the edge and tried to pull himself back into the car. Lacey rolled over and thrust-kicked both feet into his face, knocking him loose. He fell under the wheels and was cut to shreds.

They both gasped for air. Blood trickled down Elvis' face.

"Are you okay, Lacey?"

"Yeah. I guess so," she whimpered, still in shock.

"Put your back against mine, and I'll untie you."

They sat back to back as Elvis awkwardly untied the ropes around her wrists. Now free, she spun around and untied Elvis. She straightened her clothes, and then the two of them clutched each other tightly, both thankful to be alive.

"You look horrible," she said, examining his bruised and bloody face.

She pulled some napkins that she had taken from the restaurant in Texas out of her purse and wiped the blood from his face.

"I can't believe what just happened," she said in both relief and disgust.

"I know. I'm so sorry."

"Don't be sorry. You saved our lives."

"What can I say? It was my turn," he joked as they both laughed as only war-hardened veterans could after such a near-disaster.

"I can't tell you how amazed I am at your strength," Elvis whispered into her ear.

"What do you mean?"

"You were almost raped and killed, and minutes later you're tending to me."

"Unlike you, I bleed on the inside," she said. "Though I was really scared."

"God, I love you!"

"I love you, too," she answered.

"After we take care of business in Vegas, what do you say about a nice, calm life behind a white picket fence, where our days are spent fishing and reading the newspaper?" Elvis suggested.

"Sounds like a nice plan." Something occurred to Lacey, and she got up and searched the shadows at the other end of the car. "Hey can you believe it? He left my purse," she said as she opened it. "Dammit. He took our money."

"I know. Look on the bright side, though; he could have taken a lot more."

"You're right, but still, that was all of our money. What are we going to do?"

"Well, he didn't take the gun. We could rob a liquor store," Elvis joked.

"Don't tempt me."

"You could take the money and I'll take a couple bottles of brandy."

"Now you're talking. I could definitely use a couple of shots about now."

"I'll drink to that."

"God, I want to get out of these clothes," she grimaced.

"That I'd be happy to help you with," he teased.

"That's not what I mean. I mean I've been wearing these same stinking tie-dyes for over a week. I'd just like to take a nice, hot bath and shave my legs."

"Me, too. Well, except for the whole leg-shaving thing."

Elvis made his way over to Zack's duffle bag and looked through it, hoping to find some cash, but there was nothing in there but a black jack, a knife and some rope. He took the knife and threw the bag out of the train.

"So, tell me. What was it like being Elvis Presley?" Lacey asked out of the blue, trying to take her mind off their plight.

"It had its moments. There's no better feeling to walking onstage and seeing thousands of people screaming for you. My fans were so good to me. I wish I could have lived every moment of my life onstage. The only mistakes I've ever made have been offstage. The whole celebrity thing messes with your mind, though. Everybody wanted something from me. I lost myself in the shuffle. After twenty years of being this larger than life rock star, I couldn't remember who I was anymore."

"You're Elvis Presley. Isn't that enough."

"I don't know. Sometimes I think the country is in a moral decline, and that I'm to blame for it."

"Why do you say that?"

"When I came on to the scene, it was the Fifties. The nation was filled with respectful, church going families with wholesome values and beliefs. Then I came out and parents and preachers decried both me and my music, claiming that we would destroy the moral fiber of the nation. At the time I thought they were just uptight and paranoid control freaks, but twentysome years later, I look at the world and at music and realize they were right. I did destroy the wholesome values of the fifties. Do you have any idea what it's like to know that you're responsible for the decline of Western civilization?"

"You can't believe that."

"Well, I do. And you know what the funniest thing is? I never intended to be a rock and roll singer. I just wanted to sing country music and gospel. One night, my band and me were in the studio at Sun Records trying to cut a song. Things weren't going well and to blow off some steam in between takes we improvised an up-tempo version of *That's All Right*. Suddenly Sam Phillips came running in saying that that was the sound he wanted. Just like that rock and roll was invented. Now I hear all these idiotic rock journalists preaching about the greatness and integrity of rock and roll, and how it can save the world. The truth is, rock and roll was an accident, a fluke, the bastard child of a one night stand."

"I didn't know that."

"Yeah. And I'm an accident, too."

"What do you mean?"

"I had a twin brother, Jesse that died at birth. My parents weren't expecting twins and didn't even know I existed until after Jesse was declared dead. I wasn't supposed to happen."

"Is that why you took the name Jesse?"

"Actually, that was the Colonel's idea, but I went along with it because I always considered Jesse to be a part of me."

"How's that?"

"Never mind. You'll think I'm crazy."

"No I won't. Tell me."

"Since I was I child I've felt his presence. Sometimes I see him, sometimes I just hear his voice."

"Really? You see him?" she asked with concern.

"From time to time."

"What does he look like?"

"He looks like me, at least the way I used to look, but he's still just a child."

"You don't really think he's real, do you?"

"Actually, I think he's the ghost of Jesse and being his twin brother makes us spiritually linked. Either that or I'm completely insane," Elvis said humorlessly.

"Have you ever told anybody this?"

"No one except my mother. I was always afraid people would think I was crazy."

"Do *you* think you're crazy?" Lacey asked carefully.

"I'm not sure. Ever since I took his name, I've felt different, like I'm becoming him or something. His voice in my head has gotten louder and I can't get him out of my mind. I think faking my death was a mistake, for a lot of reasons."

"Like what?"

"I think I upset the natural order of things. My so-called death was historicial and changed the world in certain ways. I fear that my secret existence may somehow set off a chain reaction of events that could have cataclysmic results."

"Like what?"

"Well, it might cause the death of John Lennon, for starters."

"Don't worry, we'll save Lennon."

"That's the point. Maybe we're not supposed to. Maybe he was meant to die."

"I think you're over estimating your importance to the world. You're not a god."

"Sometimes I think I'm some kind of god," Elvis blurted out, continuing to purge himself of long kept secrets.

"What are you talking about?"

"I think that I'm some kind of savior or something. I know it sounds weird," he said.

"Weird is not the word."

"Look, I've felt this way for a long time, long before I faked my death. When I dropped acid in New York, it all seemed to make sense."

"Acid does funny things to your mind," Lacey pointed out. "Besides, you spent twenty years in a world where you could have any possession or any woman you wanted. The world adored you and showered you with love. You lived high on drugs with a bunch of people always kissing your ass. Who wouldn't have a god complex after that? I've seen you bleed. You're not the messiah."

"So you think I'm crazy?"

"Crazy is a strong word. Let's just say I think you're confused."

"You're probably right," he sighed as he stared out of the freight car door.

Lacey studied him silently, realizing that he had some serious mental issues that he still hid from the world. Years of drug abuse and living the ultimate ego trip had taken a toll on his mind, and she wondered just how delusional he truly was.

"Can I tell you something?" Lacey suggested, hoping to make him feel more comfortable with his confession.

"Of course."

"Since that night in New York when we dropped acid, I've felt different, too."

"How so?"

"As if everything I've ever believed in was wrong."

"In what way wrong?"

"As if I didn't understand. I mean, while we were hiding out at a Grateful Dead concert, there was a member of the government looking for us, wanting to kill us. Is this the country that my father died for?"

"No. Things have gone horribly wrong."

"Suddenly, I have been having thoughts like John Lennon's, and I hate to think that someone could be killed for just having thoughts and expressing them."

"Look, it'll all work out. It has to," Elvis said heatedly. "We've got God in our corner; that counts for a lot."

"Oh, grow up!" Lacey said bitterly. "Since when has God interfered with evil-doings? Where was God during the Holocaust? Where was God during the Spanish Inquisition? Where was God when my father died?"

"God has His reasons."

"Oh, I'm sorry. I forgot. You're the messiah. Well, the next time you see God, ask Him this for me. Where the hell was He?" she screamed as she broke down in tears.

Elvis clutched her and held her closely.

"I don't know," he whispered, unsure of the answer himself.

As night arrived, the two vagabonds reluctantly fell asleep. Their injuries were not helped by the vibrations of the wooden floor as the train bounced along the tracks, carrying them deep into the desert. As they slept, Elvis tossed and turned in anguish as his recurring nightmare visited him once more.

A young Elvis was performing onstage as the crowd cheered with approval. He sang and shook with the groove of the song as women in the audience clamored and screamed for more. Waiting in the wings was his mother, who kept looking at her watch impatiently. Finally the song ended, and the crowd exploded into a deafening roar. Elvis began to walk offstage toward his mother, when the crowd jumped the barriers and charged the stage. Elvis tried to get away. He tried to escape the stage, but couldn't as he became engulfed in a throng of crazed female fans. He tried to fight the waves of people, but the sea of women had caught him in the current as they dragged him away. He reached out to his mother but couldn't reach her.

"Don't leave me, Elvis!" she cried.

"I'm trying, Mama!" he shouted. "I can't get free. They won't let me," he hollered as the fans carried him further away.

"You don't want to get away!" Gladys accused him.

"I'm trying. There's just too many of them."

"You always loved them more than me, didn't you?"

"No. It's not true!" he pleaded.

"You've made your choice!" Gladys Presley shouted.

The women turned violent and began ripping away at his clothes, their nails cutting into his skin, trying to get a piece of him. In the distance, his mother began fading away.

"No, Mama. No!" Elvis gasped as he was rocketed out of his sleep.

He awoke to see Lacey's concerned face.

"Are you okay?" she asked.

"I just had a bad dream."

"Well, after what we've been through, I can't say I blame you. Come on, let's go back to sleep and try to think happy thoughts," she advised him as she hugged him gently.

For Elvis it was a task not easily done. He lay awake wishing he could break free of the never-ending nightmares and the guilt over his mother's death.

Morning arrived, and the train began to slow as it pulled into Flagstaff. They jumped off the train and landed running on the hot sands of Arizona. They brushed themselves off and wandered the desert before finding a road. They traveled along the highway lined with yucca and sage, extending their thumbs, intent on hitchhiking until they decided what they would do next.

Joe Running Wolf was heading back from Flagstaff after dropping his grandson off at the train station. A Navajo traditionalist, he found it tragically ironic that his people rode the train, when it was the same railroad that brought the white man to the West in great numbers, eventually leading to the slaughter, oppression, and near-elimination of his tribe. His children thought that he was old-fashioned and clinging to the past, but he believed that the proud history and culture of the Navajo were all that they had left. It seemed to him that as each year passed, a little more of their culture and language became absorbed by the white man's world.

He still tried to teach his grandchildren the Navajo language, but they had no interest in learning it. It was a poetic language that he had used in the Army as a code-talker during World War II, a code that was unbreakable and very instrumental in America's defeat of the Japanese. But once the war ended Joe, his language, and his people became disposable once more.

Typical of the white man's treatment of all things, he often thought to himself, like the buffalo that were killed by the white hunters, slaughtered for their hides and tongues, while the rest of their bodies were left to rot wastefully in the sun. They were a people who took without asking, who killed without caring, and received without giving thanks.

As he headed back to Navajo land, the reservation that he called home, Joe spotted a ragged couple in tie-dyes hitchhiking down the highway. But what was more significant to him were two birds in the sky above them, mating in mid-air. To Running Wolf it was a sign from a vision he had had while in a peyote trance - a king dressed as a pauper, a holy man who walked the Earth, dead to it in every manner but existence. Without hesitation, Joe Running Wolf pulled his pickup truck to the side of the road in front of the couple and got out.

"Do you two need a ride?" he asked hospitably.

Elvis and Lacey exchanged glances, not sure whether to be grateful or suspicious. Knowing that Lacey still had her gun in her purse, they decided to take the stranger up on his offer. They thanked him and climbed into his truck. Moments later, the three of them drove away, heading north up the hot, desert highway.

CHAPTER XXXII |

PROMISED LAND

The Navajo were a people of great tradition and history. The Dineh, or "The People" as they called themselves, had migrated from the northern part of the continent to the Southwest around the fifteenth century. Once nomadic, they had settled into an area of Arizona and New Mexico between four mountains that they believed to be sacred, and learned farming and weaving from the Pueblos who preceded them.

In the 1600s, the Spaniards arrived, bringing sheep and horses to the area in their failed search for the Seven Cities of Gold. The Navajo soon became herdsman, and enjoyed very prosperous times until the arrival of the Anglos, who began settling on Navajo land. The Dineh reacted with force, leading raids on the white settlers in an attempt to drive them away. Instead, the U.S. Army intervened and, in 1864, led by Kit Carson, U.S. troops destroyed the farms and homes of the Navajo. In what they would call "Long Walk," Carson and his army forced about 8,000 Navajo to march three hundred miles through rough terrain to Fort Sumner.

Along the way, hundreds of Navajo died from fatigue, starvation, and harsh treatment. At Fort Sumner hundreds more died, unable to grow food on the barren land. In 1868, after the government realized it was too expensive to support the Navajo on government land, they were allowed to return to their holy land, only to find all of their crops and farmland had been ruined. For the next few years they were plagued with bad crops and bad weather, and began to believe that the gods had conspired with the white man to destroy their tribe. But the

Dineh were resilient, and eventually prospered once again.

"So where are you two headed?" Running Wolf asked as he drove down the highway.

"Las Vegas...eventually," Elvis answered.

"What do you mean 'eventually'?"

"Well, we're supposed to meet someone in Vegas, but he won't be there until about a month from now," Elvis said.

"I guess that explains why you were walking."

"We hopped a train from Tennessee. We were robbed, so now we have no money, no food, no place to stay, and a month to kill," Lacey explained.

"Is that right?" Joe asked.

"Yes, unfortunately," Elvis answered.

"That's a shame. If you're willing to work though, I think I can help you," Running Wolf said.

"Sure. What are you proposing?"

"I live on the Navajo reservation. I raise crops and sheep, and I could use some extra help. In return, I could give you food and a place to sleep, and in a month I'll ride you into Vegas," he proposed.

"That would be great."

"It's a deal then," Running Wolf said.

"Not that I'm complaining, but why are you being so nice to us?" Lacey asked.

"Let's say I have my reasons."

"And they are -?" Lacey asked suspiciously.

"I have a need for cheap labor."

"If that's all you need, then you have yourself a deal. By the way," Elvis said, "the name's Jesse, and this is Lacey."

"It's good to meet you. I'm Joe Running Wolf," he said as a subtle smile lit his wrinkled face.

They drove up to the Four Corners Navajo reservation. Elvis and Lacey stared out the window at the beautiful assortment of buttes and mesas scattered across the red desert, as if God Himself had carefully placed each one by hand in a brilliant work of art.

Elvis had always felt a kinship with Native Americans; his great-great-great grandmother was a Cherokee named Morning Dove who had left her tribe to marry a white man.

In 1960, Elvis had starred in a movie called *Flaming Star*. It was one of the few good movies of his career. He played Pacer Burton, an Indian half-breed torn between his white and Indian roots when the two cultures clashed in the Old West. The movie garnered him good reviews, and he was inducted into the Los Angeles Indian Tribal council. In a much more light-hearted and lesser quality movie, *Stay Away, Joe*, he had even played a Navajo.

As they drove onto the reservation, Elvis and Lacey marveled at the beautiful scenery and the native houses, or hogans, as they were called, six-sided dwellings made of wood, bark, and earth that were equal parts spiritual center and shelter. The hogan symbolized the Navajo world, the roof representing Father Sky and the floor Mother Earth.

The reservation was a paradox, partly embracing ancient customs and ways, partly embracing the modern world. Even Joe Running Wolf, who fervently held on to the ways of the past, owned and drove a truck. Much like his name, his world was a combination of two separate cultures. While one section of the resevation was a sacred holyland, another was a large souvenier stand, selling tours and trinkets to the same people that drove them to the brink of extinction.

They pulled up to Running Wolf's hogan and got out of the truck. Joe led them inside. His hogan was very basic; there was no electricity or running water, and no furniture. Sadly, he lived there alone. His wife had passed away several years ago, and his son had a family of his own that he had moved off the reservation and into modern housing in Gallup, New Mexico. They had invited Joe to move in with them but he refused, partly out of stubbornness and partly out of tradition. He did not want to leave Navajo land; he felt that such a move would be a betrayal of his people. Besides, there was a custom that a hogan could not be abandoned, unless a member of the family died there of un-natural causes. Joe would stay.

As Elvis and Lacey sat on the floor, Joe prepared food for them. He served them corn and *ai'chee*, which was sheep intestines stuffed with sheep fat and fried over the fire. His guests ate happily and became en-tranced by his stories of Navajo mythology. They talked long into the candle-lit night. Elvis and Lacey slept on the floor wrapped in a wool rug handwoven by Running Wolf's departed wife.

The next morning they began their month-long assignment. They tended to Running Wolf's crops and brought out bales of hay for the sheep to eat, because there wasn't enough grazing land. The work was hard, but Elvis and Lacey didn't mind; they had food to eat and a place to stay, a place where Jericho would have a difficult time finding them. Joe Running Wolf was a very hospitable host. He even gave them new clothes to wear. It was traditional Navajo garb. Elvis wore a velveteen pullover that hung over his pants, a silver concho belt, and moccasins. Lacey's dark hair and eyes made her look like a Navajo princess as she wore a dress made of two Navajo blankets sewn together at the sides and top and brown leather boots that went up to her knees.

A few days after their arrival, Running Wolf's son Sage came to visit as he often did. He was quite surprised to see his father's guests. As he watched them working the land in the distance, he was mystified that his father would do something so out of character as to share his solitude with these strangers, and felt obliged to comment.

"Father, where did they come from?"

"Outside of Flagstaff; they were broke and needed a place to stay."

"You hate the white man. Why are you being so generous to them?"

"That man Jesse is a holy man."

"He told you that?"

"No, he doesn't even know it."

"Then how do you know?" Sage asked.

"It came to me in a vision."

"Let me guess, peyote?"

"Yes."

"Father, when are you going to abandon those ancient super-stitions?"

"Like you've abandoned me?" he demanded bitterly as he retreated into his hogan.

Sage kicked a mound of sand in frustration. They had been es-tranged all of his life, and things didn't seem to be improving. He loved his father, but didn't want to live the life that Running Wolf wanted him to lead. As a child, he had only wanted to live the normal life that he had heard about, a life with electricity, a life with modern conveniences, and a life where he was not held captive by ancient beliefs and rituals. Above all, he wanted his children to live that life as well.

As he walked to his car, he saw Elvis emerge from the fields to talk to with Running Wolf.

"Hi, you must be Jesse. I'm Sage, Joe's son," he said offering to shake hands.

"Pleased to meet you, Sage."

"I guess my father's got you busting your hump," he said with a smile.

"It's okay. Hard work never hurt anyone. I think your father's a fascinating man. He's taught me and my girlfriend a lot about the Navajo."

"Yeah. He's definitely knowledgeable about the ways of our people."

"Are you staying for dinner?" Elvis asked.

"No. I should be going. Tell my father I said goodbye."

"Well, you can tell him yourself, if you want. He's right in there," Elvis said innocently, nodding toward the hogan.

"No. We'd only end up arguing."

Sage got in his car and drove away.

Elvis felt perplexed by the exchange. As he watched Sage drive off into the distance, Running Wolf came out of his hogan.

"Is he gone?" Joe asked.

"Yeah. He just left. He said goodbye."

"Goodbye. That's the only word he ever could say to me," Running Wolf stated sadly as he turned and went back into his home.

A few days later, Running Wolf decided to reward the hard work of his guests by taking them horseback riding. He took his two horses out and they rode into the desert, Running Wolf on one horse and Elvis and Lacey on the other. Running Wolf was surprised by Elvis' ability to ride a horse, not knowing that he had ridden them many times before. They rode off into the arid land away from the beaten path as they got a rare glimpse of some of the amazing rock formations on the reservation.

"This land is the Navajo's homeland, Dineteh," Running Wolf explained. "Many years ago, the white man made us leave this land and walk hundreds of miles to Fort Sumner; hundreds died along the way."

"Yeah. Sorry about that," Elvis awkwardly apologized.

"Apologies are not what I seek. Eventually, we returned to our land and become the wealthiest reservation in the country."

"Well good. Everything worked out then," Elvis said, uncomfortable with the conversation.

"There is nothing good about it. Our people have sold their soul to the white man, making money by allowing them to drill and mine on our sacred land. Their culture has poisoned our minds and turned our people into drunks."

"You know, there comes a point when your people have to take responsibility for their own decisions," Lacey interjected sharply. "Nobody poured the alcohol down your throats."

"You've never allowed us to make our own decisions. You've imprisoned us, stolen our land, and forced us to live under your laws," Running Wolf told her. "We've had to conform to your ways or die. The decision was never ours. Look at my own son; all of his young life I taught him the way of the Navajo, only to have him grow up and reject our ways, reject our religion, and even reject me."

"I'm sorry, Joe," Elvis said humbly.

"Sometimes I wonder if he rejects me because of our beliefs, or rejects our beliefs because of me."

"He's your son. I'm sure he loves you very much," Lacey added reassuringly.

"Then why did he move away from me?"

"Why don't you ask him?"

"Me and my son don't really talk about those things."

"Maybe that's the problem," Elvis suggested.

Running Wolf didn't respond. Instead he turned his horse around and rode off as they followed. The sun was setting on the desert and he wanted to be back before nightfall.

Colonel Parker sat in the backroom of a Vegas casino, playing cards with three old mob friends he had made back in the days when Elvis was headlining the Hilton.

"Bambino" Muccelli, one of the mob's best hit men, threw in a thousand dollar chip. "I call. Whatta you got?"

"Read 'em and weep boys," Parker said triumphantly. "Four aces."

"I thought you were bluffing," Muccelli said as he threw down his two pairs.

As Parked raked forty silver chips over to his pile, mob boss Tony Guardino couldn't help but comment, "Damn, Colonel, you must have a horseshoe up your ass."

"Or a few aces up your sleeve," Muccelli added.

"Perhaps you're both right," Parker declared with a smile as he began dealing.

"So, Colonel, tell us the details of this job," Guardino said.

"It's simple. I want this envelope placed in a safety deposit box at the Hilton under the name Jesse King," he instructed as he pulled out the package.

"Colonel, if that was all you needed, you wouldn't have come to us."

"Oh, there's more. On December 7th, my friend, Jesse King will pick it up," he stated as he pulled out what looked like a police sketch of Jericho.

"This man is going to be there as well. He is going to try to kill Mr. King. I want you to stop him and kill him instead."

"No problem," Muccelli answered. "It's just a matter of the fee, and because we go way back, I'll do it for a mere fifty grand."

"I think we have ourselves a deal," Parker said as he chomped on his cigar.

A feeling of relief swept over Parker. He had regretted betraying Elvis but, at the time, he had had no choice. Agent Jericho had broken into his mansion and held him at gunpoint, demanding that he co-operate. The threat of death or deportation had convinced him to do as Jericho instructed, but he was determined to make things right. He owed a great deal to Elvis Presley. The talented singer had brought him great wealth and fame, and never questioned his decisions.

He just hoped that Muccelli could intercept Jericho in time. He didn't know what kind of mess Presley had gotten himself into, but he knew that if the FBI was involved, it was serious. Parker just prayed that Jericho wouldn't smell the double-cross before Muccelli had the chance to kill him.

Nearly a month had passed since Elvis and Lacey first stepped foot on Navajo land and agreed to work for Joe Running Wolf and despite a very awkward Thanksgiving, the three of them had grown close. Running Wolf decided it was time to tell his guest about his vision.

"Jesse, are you a religious man?"

"Yes, I am," Elvis acknowledged. "I even considered becoming a preacher at one time."

"Why didn't you?"

"I don't know; I guess it wasn't in the cards."

"Do you know why I picked you and Lacey up that day?"

"Not really."

"A few days earlier, I had taken some peyote and had a vision of a holy man, a great spiritual messenger. That messenger was you."

Elvis laughed. "Peyote, huh? That could explain it."

"Your people are too quick to dismiss the spiritual aspects of peyote," Joe told him solemnly. "It isn't a drug. It's a portal to the gods. It allows you to see all. I would like you to take some with me and complete your journey into the ways of the Navajo."

Elvis thought it over and agreed, on one condition.

"Only if your son is there with us."

"I have no control over my son," Running Wolf insisted.

"Well, ask him."

"Okay, I will."

Much to Running Wolf's surprise, his son agreed to attend the ritual. It was a major concession on his part. Sage had always viewed peyote as a dangerous drug that had betrayed his people, making them look foolishly to hallucinations for answers to very real problems. Peyote did not grow their crops, nor did fend off the invading white man. It did not put food on his family's table or prevent his mother's death. It had kept his people in a state of altered perception at a time when much clarity was needed.

Running Wolf was ecstatic that his son would attend the ceremony. He thought that perhaps the ritual would finally enlighten Sage to the ways of his people and show him the evils of the white man's world.

Running Wolf prepared the peyote, gathering the small buttons from several barrel cacti and boiling it into tea. Lacey had heard of their plans and insisted on joining them. After her positive and mind-blowing experiences with acid, she was eager to expand her consciousness into other psychedelics, of which peyote had a reputation for being the ultimate. It was as if she was trying to make up for the years she had lost in college to being angry over Vietnam. Now, ten years later she had found her inner hippie. Running Wolf didn't like the idea of a woman participating in what was usually a male ritual, but her persistence wore him down and he reluctantly agreed.

Running Wolf built a fire, and Elvis and Lacey sat on either side of it. Sage arrived and joined them around the blaze. The four of them talked and exchanged stories. Elvis and Lacey got along well with Sage, but couldn't help noticing some tension between Sage and his father.

Joe served them all the tea that he had made from the peyote, and they drank it down, except for Sage. His father offered him the tea again, but Sage refused.

"No, thanks. I don't do drugs," he maintained.

"Sage, this isn't a drug. It's a gift from God."

"Well, tell God no, thanks."

As Elvis and Lacey stared into the flames of the campfire, Sage and his father began arguing. Suddenly, Sage stood up and stormed away.

Running Wolf was too proud to go after him, instead continuing with the ceremony as if nothing had happened.

He began a special chant for the occasion, and then lit a pipe and passed it his guests as a shooting star fell from the sky. A strange feeling came over Elvis as he gazed into the flames, seeing unfamiliar faces and forms twisted and writhing in the fire. He felt his body floating through a tunnel in his mind; in the distance he heard Running Wolf's dog barking fearfully, as if it sensed an otherworldly spirit blowing through the camp.

Suddenly, the noise was gone and everything turned the brightest of whites. Gradually the vision turned to shades of green, and birdsong could be heard as a lush forest came into focus. Elvis looked around to see himself at home, amongst the rolling green hills of Tennessee. Across the valley, he saw a pond shimmering in the brightness of the morning sun. He walked over to the small body of water and knelt on its bank.

He looked into the water and saw his reflection, a face given to him by Agent Jericho, and one to which he still hadn't grown accustomed. He ran his fingers through the water, causing ripples that folded and twisted his reflection. As the surface of the water returned to its original state, his reflection had now changed. It was his face before the surgery, the face of Elvis Presley, or so he thought.

"It's me, Jesse," the reflection informed him.

"Jesse? How can it be? You're dead."

"I know, dead by your hand. You murdered me in the womb, you bastard! You couldn't bear to share the world with me, so you killed me."

"No, that's impossible. I loved you, Jesse. I always wished you'd lived and been my brother," Elvis insisted.

"You're a liar. You wanted our mother's love all to yourself, didn't you? The fame and fortune you received was meant for me. I was the firstborn; I should have been the king. You killed me and took my destiny, but that wasn't enough. Now you've taken my name as well, my identity, my soul!" the mirage screamed as hands reached out of the water and clutched Elvis' throat.

Elvis struggled to break the grip, but couldn't, as Jesse pulled his face into the pond. Elvis choked on the water and frantically jerked and splashed, trying to resist and break free, but he couldn't. The hands dragged him into the abyss, submerging his body completely. His lungs filled with water, until Elvis thought he was about to die.

Then, another flash of white blasted through his mind as he found himself in an infinite room, devoid of walls or doors, containing only white nothingness, and two coffins. Elvis walked up to the first coffin; he saw a name carved into the pine lid. Gladys Smith Presley, it read. He slowly opened it and peered inside to find his mother. Her eyes were closed and she looked tranquil and at peace.

"Mama, I really miss you," he said, his lips quivering. "Ever since you died, nothing has made sense. You were my soul, my conscience, and I loved you more than you could ever know. When you died, it left a void in me that I could never fill. I tried. I tried with women, drugs, food, and anything else I could think of, but every morning that I awoke to a world without you in it, I felt alone.

"I can't live with this emptiness anymore. I need to put your ghost behind me. I need to say goodbye. Mama, I love you. Please set me free," Elvis said as he kissed her forehead.

Suddenly a feeling of completeness and inner peace came over him.

"Goodbye, Mama," he said as he closed the casket.

Elvis slowly moved toward the second coffin, unsure of its contents. He read the inscription on it: Elvis Aron Presley. He opened it, expecting to see himself; instead he found the dead body of John Lennon lying in his place. He slammed the lid down and ran into the void as he heard a dog barking in the distance.

Elvis came out of the trance and saw Lacey beside him, screaming and writhing with torment. He shook her and called her name; finally she broke free of her vision. She opened her eyes and saw Elvis. With tears in her eyes, she clung to him and tried to regain her calm.

"What happened?" Elvis asked, still traumatized by his own vision.

She didn't answer, just gripped Elvis tighter, trembling in his arms.

The next morning, Elvis and Lacey got ready for their ride to Las Vegas. Dressed in Navajo clothing, they went out by the truck and waited for Joe Running Wolf.

"What did you see last night?" Elvis asked.

"I don't want to talk about it," Lacey said with a shudder.

"I understand. My vision was pretty scary, too. I think that will be my last peyote trip."

While they waited for Running Wolf, Sage pulled up in his car. He got out of his vehicle and approached the two visitors.

"I just came by to see you two off and thank you for all the help you've given my father."

"You don't have to thank us. He's a lifesaver. I don't know how we would have survived this last month without him," Elvis conceded.

"I think he really likes you two. I wish I could get along with him the way you do."

"Sage, your father loves you."

"Yes, but he doesn't like me. We're too different, I guess. I just wish he could accept me for who I am."

"It's not too late. Tell your father you love him. He's not getting any younger, and you don't know how many more chances you're going to get to tell him. My father died before I got the chance to tell him I loved him. Trust me, when he's gone, you'll wish that you had."

"Thanks, Jesse. You're as wise as my father believed you to be," Sage informed him.

Joe Running Wolf emerged from his hogan and Sage went to him to talk. Elvis watched from the truck. He couldn't hear what Sage was saying to his father, but judging by the hug they suddenly gave each other, Elvis guessed that Sage had taken his advice.

Sage got in his car and drove away as Running Wolf wiped a tear from his eye. Then he started up the truck as Elvis and Lacey got in. He gave Elvis a knowing smile and they headed for Las Vegas.

"Did last night provide you with any answers?" Running Wolf asked Elvis.

"No. Only questions. I don't think that I'm the holy man that you believe me to be."

"Why do you say that?"

"There was nothing holy about my vision last night."

"Perhaps your journey still needs completing," Running Wolf countered, refusing to give up on his belief in him.

Elvis just stared pensively out the window, gazing out at the endless desert as his mind sifted through the possible meaning of his peyote trip.

CHAPTER XXXIII

VIVA LAS VEGAS

As Elvis and Lacey approached Las Vegas, the city rose out of the desert like a sinful mirage, an oasis of pleasure where all things have a price and every moment takes a toll. Vegas was a second home to Elvis, a city holding countless memories for him, a mix of heaven and hell.

He had first performed in Las Vegas at the New Frontier Hotel in 1956. The engagement was a disaster. Though he was on top of the entertainment world, his cutting-edge cool went straight over the heads of the Vegas audience, which consisted mainly of silver-haired gamblers who would much rather have seen Perry Como or Frank Sinatra.

Many years later however, Elvis returned to Sin City, but this time he owned the town. It was 1971, and he was on the heels of a great comeback. He triumphed in a multi-night run at the Hilton Hotel, then known as the International Hotel.

Those performances helped enable a great comeback. After Vegas, he began a highly successful tour of the United States, even selling out for four consecutive nights at Madison Square Garden. By now he had adopted the white jumpsuit look onstage, complete with cape and bell-bottoms.

His winning streak continued and, in 1973, he made television history once again with a live satellite telecast called *Aloha from Hawaii.* It was the first concert to use the new satellite technology. It was broadcast all over the world and was seen by 1.5 billion people.

Of course, the most significant day he had spent in Vegas was in 1967. It was the day he took Priscilla to be his bride. It was a very secret and private ceremony at the Aladdin Hotel which only fourteen people attended, a fact that caused much anger among the members of the Memphis Mafia who were not invited. What they didn't know was that Elvis had very little to do with any of the details of his wedding. Tom Parker arranged the wedding, deciding to use the special day as a publicity stunt. As soon as they were wed, they were wisked away to Palm Springs on Frank Sinatra's Learjet. A fleet of reporters who had just learned the news greeted them as they stepped off the plane. Their wedding day quickly turned into a press conference and photo shoot.

Elvis carried Priscilla over the threshold of Graceland as he sang "The Hawaiian Wedding Song" and continued carrying her up the stairs to the bedroom. He set her gently down upon the bed and kissed her slowly. Despite their years together, Priscilla was still a virgin, preserved perfectly for the right moment. Their long pent up passion was finally released as they made gentle but scorching love.

For the longest time, Elvis didn't want to get married. He loved Priscilla dearly, but in many ways he was still a child. He didn't want that to change; being Elvis Presley meant that he didn't have to change, that he could be an adolescent forever. But Elvis had always intended for Priscilla to be his bride, and their honeymoon was made it all the more special. Though frustrating at times, Pricilla was given the climatic ending for the fairy-tale romance that had consumed her life. Cinderella had won her prince, a prince that soon became a king.

Nine months later, Lisa Marie was born. As Priscilla, still aglow with the miracle of childbirth held her daughter, Elvis touched the baby and marveled, "She's perfect," as the infant clutched his finger. Elvis beamed with joy as he kissed Priscilla lovingly. At that moment he was not Elvis Presley or the king of rock and roll. He was simply a daddy and a husband.

In the Seventies, Vegas became Elvis' stomping ground, a much larger version of Graceland, a brightly-lit playground where his inner circle of caretakers expanded from the Memphis Mafia to the real Mafia. That was where his drug addiction began to truly flourish. Elvis was the biggest attraction that the town had ever known, making mountains of cash not only for the Hilton, but the entire city as well. He had the freedom there to do as he pleased and had countless women giving themselves to him backstage. His exhausting two shows a day schedule increased his demand for prescription pills and put strains on his already rocky marriage to Priscilla. As Priscilla mothered his child, Elvis began looking elsewhere for sex and, in Vegas, he didn't have to look far. Priscilla was now untouchable in his eyes, non-sexual, like the Virgin Mary.

Vegas' own history was also filled with seeming contradictions, a vast oasis in the middle of the harsh Mojave Desert. The desert's arid and unforgiving environment sheltered the area and its Paiute Indian inhabitants from European eyes for many years. Spanish for "the meadows," Las Vegas was first discovered by non-Indians in 1829, when a Mexican trader, Antonio Armijo, led his sixty-man party off the accepted route to Los Angeles. The party camped in the desert about one hundred miles northeast of Vegas and sent a scout, Rafael Rivera, off to find water. Within two weeks, Rivera discovered Las Vegas Springs, and the area soon became a pit stop for traders and gold miners enroute to California.

In 1855, Mormon settlers from Salt Lake City traveled to Las Vegas to protect their mail route and build a fort. They also planted fruit trees and vegetables, but abandoned the settlement a few years later due to countless Indian raids.

As the railroads moved West, Las Vegas was chosen to be a stop, and a town began to grow around it as work on the railroad began in 1904.

In 1931, gambling was officially legalized in Nevada; that same year, work began on the nearby Hoover Dam. While the rest of the country was enduring the ravages of the Great Depression, Vegas was experiencing great prosperity.

In 1946, mobster Benjamin "Bugsy" Siegel realized that Las Vegas could hold the future for the Mob, and opened a casino/resort called the Flamingo Hotel. Initially the casino flopped, and Siegel began embezzling money from the Mob to pay for the soaring construction costs. Upon the discovery of his money skimming, his boss "Lucky" Luciano put a hit out on him, and Siegel was gunned down at his girlfriend's mansion in Beverly Hills. Despite his death, the Flamingo began to flourish, and Vegas soon became a hotbed for gambling and entertainment, as well as home of the Mob.

Elvis and Lacey spent the last of their money on a taxi that dropped him off near the Las Vegas Hilton. Elvis calmly ran his hands through his hair, not looking much like the typical Vegas visitor in his Navajo clothing, with his long hair and beard. He made Lacey wait in the cab as he entered The Hilton's lobby. Several sets of eyes were on him as walked up to the front desk. Jericho sat on a bench, pretending to read a newspaper. He had grown a beard as well, and wore a cowboy hat and sunglasses as a disguise. To his left was "Bambino" Muccelli, playing a slot machine as cover while he watched the lobby.

"May I help you?" the woman at the front desk asked.

"Yes, I'm here to pick up the contents of my safety deposit box. The name's Jesse King," he said as he handed her his identification.

She inspected his ID, unlocked the box, and handed him a large envelope.

"Here you are, Mr. King. If you could just sign here."

Elvis signed the form and tucked the large envelope under his arm.

As he walked out the door, Jericho put down his paper and began to follow him outside. That was the cue Muccelli had been waiting for. He whispered a command into his walkie-talkie and quickly moved on Jericho, grabbing him as he walked out the door.

"Bob, how ya been? So good to see you," he said as he put his large arm around Jericho.

"Do I know you?" Jericho asked suspiciously.

"We have a mutual friend," Muccelli insisted as a black limousine began to pull up alongside them. "Get in and we'll talk about it."

Jericho calmly reached inside his vest for the gun with a silencer. He had planned to use it on Elvis and Lacey, but there had just been a change of plans. He pulled the trigger, discreetly shooting Muccelli in the side of the chest. Muccelli fell to his knees.

"Oh, my God! He needs a doctor," Jericho shouted as a crowd quickly formed around him.

As the crowd tried to figure out what had happened to the man, the limousine sped off, and Jericho slipped away in the direction that Elvis had gone. He distanced himself from the scene and looked for Elvis, but he was nowhere to be found. Jericho cursed under his breath as he realized that his prey had gotten away.

Elvis had quickly jumped in the taxi that had been waiting for him, unaware of Jericho or the murdered hit man. As the taxi drove off, Elvis opened the envelope to find ten thousand dollars, birth certificates and Social Security cards for people by the name of Jesse Smith and Rebecca Morrow. He gave Lacey a big smile as he flashed her the money.

"See, I told you I'd take care of everything," he boasted.

"So what now?" she asked with a big grin.

"Tonight, we're going to celebrate," he said. "To the Desert Inn,"

Elvis instructed the driver.

They checked into the hotel under assumed names, and after se-
curing what few possessions they had in their hotel room, they hit the
streets for a night on the town. Elvis had longed to show Lacey a good
time. The entire time they had known each other, they had been too
busy or too poor to let loose and have fun. Now, with ten thousand
dollars in his possession, he decided to show her how Elvis treats his
lady, Vegas style.

His first stop, however, was mostly business. He went into a
pawnshop and purchased a handgun. He knew Jericho was still looking
for them and wouldn't rest until they were dead. Lacey had her gun,
but he felt better having one of his own. At least that was his cover
story. While he did purchase a .45 Colt, he also purchased a diamond
ring that someone had pawned.

After grabbing a quick bite to eat, they took a taxi and went
shopping, shedding their Navajo clothes for a more glamorous look.
Lacey bought a slinky, black dress and shoes while Elvis purchased a
very dapper black suit. Lacey then had her hair done as Elvis got a
shave and a haircut. They were now ready for a night on Vegas.

They headed off to dinner, dining at one of Vegas' famous buffets
featuring all-you-can-eat sirloins and lobster. There had been long
periods of time in the past month when there hadn't been much food to
eat, and now they were making up for it.

"This is way better than sheep intestines," Elvis noted as he dipped
a piece of lobster in melted butter.

"What's the plan after we leave here?" Lacey asked as she cracked
open a lobster claw.

"Tomorrow night, we'll get on a plane and head to Los Angeles.
We'll establish residence and get picture IDs and passports. Then I
suggest we fly away to Europe or somewhere and live out the rest of
our lives together."

"Then what?"

"Then we grow old together," he replied with a loving smile.

"Maybe we should leave tonight."

"No, let's just stay for one night. I want tonight to be special."

"Do I have any say in the matter?" she asked with a mock frown.

"Of course. But I really want to stay. Trust me. You'll be glad we
did."

She reluctantly agreed, and after eating until they could barely move, the two of them lumbered out of the restaurant and went to the casino. The casino was alive with action and sensory overstimulation. Flashing lights, ringing bells, and the sounds of dropped coins hitting metal erupted all around them. They warmed up their luck on the slot machines and then made their way to the blackjack tables, as free drinks flowed like a stream and the dealers ruled the casino.

The dealers were the true magicians of Las Vegas, performing instantaneous calculations in their heads and dealing cards, deftly sliding stacks of multi-colored chips along the green felt, effortlessly keeping track of all bets, while making sure the game moved quickly and smoothly.

After losing at blackjack, Elvis decided to try his luck at the craps table, placing some safe bets until it was his turn to roll the dice. As he blew on the dice for luck, he noticed a fidgety man place a large bet on the Don't Pass bar, essentially betting against Elvis. Presley threw the dice against the wall, rolling a six and establishing his point. He now had to roll another six before rolling a seven. After the stickman slid the dice back to him, Elvis rolled again as another six came up. He had won, and noticed the man who had bet against him curse silently and begin to leave the table. It seemed apparent to Elvis that the man was now broke. He quickly stopped the man and handed him a five-dollar chip.

"Here. Next time, trying betting on me," he told him.

The man smiled and heeded Elvis' advice, placing the chip on the Pass bar. Several other players saw the exchange and decided to bet with the shooter, placing their chips on the Pass bar as well. Elvis rolled a four and several non-seven rolls later, he rolled a four again. The gamblers kept increasing their bets on the Pass bar, and Elvis went on a long hot streak, making point several times in a row. Each time, the players cheered in approval and kept betting with him. Eventually, his winning streak came to an end, but not before making a lot of money for himself and most of the players in the pit. As he handed the dice to the next shooter, many of the players patted him on the back and thanked him for his hot hand.

"Thanks for the chip and the advice," the first man said. "I was completely wiped out until you did that, now I'm in the money," he bragged as he handed a five-dollar chip back to Elvis.

Elvis smiled and decided he had used up all of his good luck at craps; he went looking for Lacey. As the alcohol had taken effect on both of them, they decided to step out of the casino and walk around town, enjoying the warm desert air. As they strolled past one casino, Elvis began laughing as he saw a very strange sight, a group of Elvis impersonators posing in white sequined jumpsuits. He was finally beginning to realize how much of a phenomenon he had become since his death.

The last three years had been such a blur to him, from driving a truck around the country to spying for the FBI, he hadn't had much of a chance to watch TV or talk to many people, and the mass commercialism of his image took him by surprise. It had taken on a life of its own, much as most of the Elvis sightings he had seen on the front pages of the tabloids. A small handful of the early sightings had been legitimate, but he had long since had his face surgically altered and still the sightings continued.

There were other kinds of sightings as well, visions of his ghost, strange tales of his picture's healing power, and his image being seen in strange places once reserved only for Jesus and the Virgin Mary. Not only was he an entertainment icon, but he had become a religious icon as well. He laughed as he looked back at messianic complexes that he sometimes had, heavy drug-induced delusions of godliness that he used to share with the Memphis Mafia; now his beliefs had come to fruition.

"Hey, look, honey. You're everywhere," Lacey joked.

"Yeah. Those guys look more like me than I do."

"That has to mess with your head."

"How come those guys only impersonate my white jumpsuit look? I mean, you never see one in black leather, or dressed like me in my early days."

"What was up with those white jumpsuits anyway? Where you doing a lot of drugs at that time?"

"Yeah. There may have been some connection to the drugs," he admitted.

The streets of Las Vegas jumped with vibrant energy; it was a city where dreams were made, where fortunes were won and lost in a blink of an eye, and on any given night anyone could leave the casino much wealthier than when they entered.

Elvis and Lacey walked past a twenty-four hour wedding chapel, when Elvis suddenly sprang into action. Without warning, he fell down on one knee, pulled out the ring and proposed to Lacey.

"Lacey, I love you. Why don't we start our new life together right and get married?"

Lacey was in shock. A bunch of onlookers overheard his proposal and had gathered around to watch the drama unfold.

"Are you serious?" she asked in disbelief.

"As serious as I can be. We can just go into that chapel right now and get married. What do you say? Will you marry me?"

"Yes!" she cried as they hugged each other and the small crowd rejoiced.

Elvis took her hand and led her into the chapel, where after filling out some paperwork and making a payment, the two of them walked up to the altar. The justice of the peace gave a brief speech about the sanctity of marriage and then proceeded with the ceremony.

"Do you, Jesse Smith, take Rebecca Morrow to be your lawfully wedded wife?"

"I do," Elvis answered.

"Do you, Rebecca Morrow, take this man to be your husband, till death do you part?"

"I do."

"Then by the power vested in me by the State of Nevada, I now pronounce you man and wife. You may kiss the bride."

They engaged in a soulful kiss as the organist played the appropriate wedding music. They thanked the justice of the peace, collected their marriage certificate, and waltzed out of the chapel as husband and wife.

"I can't believe we're married!" Lacey gushed.

"Me, either. I guess it's time for the honeymoon," Elvis suggested playfully.

"What? Do you think you're going to get lucky?" she teased.

"I already am lucky."

They walked back to their hotel and Elvis, being old-fashioned, picked her up and carried her across the threshold before laying her down on the bed. He kissed her gently and the newlyweds began to make love.

CHAPTER XXXIV

HAPPINESS IS A WARM GUN

It was August of 1969. In upstate New York, a massive music festival called Woodstock had just taken place. It was a three-day rock concert fueled by drugs, sex, and opposition to the Vietnam War. As 300,000 young people danced and made love in the rain, many of the day's top musical acts performed their hearts out at the historic show. The Who, the Grateful Dead, Jimi Hendrix and Janis Joplin, to name a few, provided the soundtrack for the definitive moment of the love generation.

Halfway across the world, Nick Black sat in a foxhole with his feet buried in the mud. Giant rats and ten-inch long orange and black-striped centipedes crawled all around him as gunfire and mortar blasts staged a concert of their own.

The sketchy details of Woodstock had reached Black on the front line, but he greeted them only with bitterness and jealousy. If he had been born of privilege, as many of the peace activists were, then perhaps he could have evaded the draft by going to college, but he had been dealt a lesser hand. He was stuck in the rugged jungles of Vietnam, trading shots with the enemy and watching friends die. He would much rather have been back in the States, going to concerts, receiving free love, and preaching against a war he knew nothing about, but he was in Vietnam, enduring sporadic firefights and thanking God for every moment that he stayed alive.

His only momentary break from the war was the few weeks he spent stewing in a military hospital, recovering from his shrapnel wound and blaming himself for what had happened to Dan. He blamed his sensitivity as the weakness that had ultimately caused Dan's death. After all, it was his idea to help the children of the war, and it was trying to help them that had gotten Dan killed.

For all his troubles, Nick was given a Purple Heart and a quick return to the war front before his physical wounds had fully healed and while his mental wounds had just begun to abscess. He returned to his platoon to find several members had been killed in his absence, only to be replaced by fresh, young bodies straight out of high school.

As he and his troops carefully made their way through the mountains, snipers fired unanswered shots at them. One of the shots picked off Jerome Watkins, a black man from Georgia who had been a good friend to everyone in the platoon. The sergeant concluded that the nearby village of Lai-Don had been providing the guerillas with both food and ammunition, and decided to pay them a visit.

The American soldiers attacked the village like a horde of locusts, destroying everything in their path. A cache of weapons found buried in the earth was all the provocation the already bloodthirsty Marines needed. Nick Black and his fellow soldiers went on a rampage to avenge every American soldier's death as far back as the Revolutionary War. A bloodbath ensued, a massacre never reported by the press as they shot up the village and set fire to the thatched huts.

As the wrath of the platoon rained downed upon the hapless villagers, Nick saw a child running wildly towards him, with something tightly clenched in the child's hand. With the memory of Dan's death still fresh in his mind, he didn't hesitate before firing several shots into the boy's chest. The child fell hard to the ground.

Nick waited the allotted time it would have taken a pin-pulled grenade to explode before going near the boy. As he approached him, he saw the child's face. It looked familiar to him. As the boy gasped his last breath, his hand unclenched and a red ball rolled from his fingers and onto the dirt. As Nick put the puzzle together in his mind, a dark realization came over him. All of his emotions poured out of him as he looked up to the sky and let out a loud, anguished scream. It was a final expulsion of guilt and remorse, a blackening of his heart, a declaration of war against his own conscience. At that moment, Jake Jericho was truly born.

Elvis awoke before Lacey, and studied her beautiful face in wonderment. She was his wife. He still felt a sense of disbelief at that fact. They hadn't known each other very long, and hadn't even gotten along at first. Yet there she was, his sleeping bride, her lovely, naked body wrapped in satin sheets by his side. He thought of his first marriage and the pain of the divorce, and hoped that he would never have to experience that again. He truly wanted to spend the rest of his life with Lacey.

Years of infidelity and drug abuse had destroyed his marriage to Priscilla. In the end, she left him for a man who could barely support her, but gave her something Elvis couldn't any longer – love and affection. Elvis had always been too busy to pay her any attention. He had molded her into a pristine mother figure to replace his own deceased matriarch. He demanded virginal purity from her, so pure that Elvis could not bear to taint her with lovemaking. She became a priceless, antique doll to Elvis, placed under glass for him to look at, but too valuable to touch. He realized now that love wasn't something that a person could own. Despite Lacey's less than pure past, he knew that he loved her and that he had to work every day to keep that love alive.

Though he had given up his fortune, he had never felt richer. This moment was a small miracle. Only three years earlier, he had practically been a zombie, living only for his next fix. He had had a network of doctors prescribing him pills at all hours of the day. After Priscilla left him, his drug abuse spiraled madly out of control. His daily Demerol habit turned him into a full-fledged morphine addict. His romance with his live-in lover Linda Thompson had also gone down in flames. Their relationship had deteriorated into a pathetic mother/infant dependency to the point where she sometimes had to physically feed him. He had been in an out of Memphis Baptist Hospital due to several overdoses and despite Dr. Nichopoulos' numerous attempts to wean Elvis off drugs, his addiction remained.

When he was under the influence he became another person: A photo negative of his true self, an angry and violent man with little concern for anyone else.

Priscilla came face to face with that man on a frightful Vegas night that became the final straw in her decision to leave him.

Crazed from amphetamines and feeling his masculinity being threatened by his inabilty to make love to his wife, Elvis summoned Pricilla up to his Hilton hotel suite between shows. She entered the room to find Elvis sprawled out on the bed with an angry look in his eyes. He grabbed her and threw her down on the bed.

"This is how a real man makes love to his woman," he growled as he forced himself on his wife.

His usually gentle lovemaking turned violent and cold. After he finished with her, he calmly got dressed for the next show as Priscilla wept silently.

Lacey awoke and caught Elvis staring at her. She gave him a smile and a kiss.

"Good morning, my beautiful wife," he whispered softly.

"I can't believe I am married to Elvis Presley. I never would have thought it possible."

"Elvis Presley? That fat guy in the jumpsuit? No, honey, you're married to Jesse Smith," he corrected her.

"Hey, don't ruin my fantasy!" she joked. "When I was a little girl, I had such a crush on you. I even had a poster of you on my wall. I can remember staring into your baby-blue eyes and wondering what it must feel like to kiss you."

Elvis pressed his lips against hers.

"Now you know, baby."

It was only a sample of the many kisses he began to shower upon her as he slid down underneath the sheets, kissing every inch of her body. She closed her eyes in rapturous pleasure, hoping that the moment would never end.

John Lennon and Yoko Ono spent the morning at their home in the Dakota in a photo session with renowned photographer Annie Leibowitz, posing for the cover of *Rolling Stone*. Leibowitz's skilled eye was evident as she decided to pose a nude Lennon clinging desperately to a fully-clothed Yoko Ono, who looked aloof and unconcerned. After seeing the picture, John was ecstatic.

"That's great. That sums up our relationship perfectly," he proclaimed.

John was in great spirits. His new album, *Double Fantasy,* was rapidly climbing the charts, and his first single, "(Just Like) Starting Over," was already a big hit. The first phase of his comeback was underway and his political comeback would be next.

John and Yoko had purchased plane tickets to San Francisco for the following week, where they would attend a rally called by the Teamster's Union to march in the streets with striking Japanese-Americans in a wage dispute with the Japan Foods Corporation. It was there that Lennon had decided to announce his reemergence on the political scene. There was another reason for his elation however; he was just a few weeks away from telling the world about his free concert in New York City with the rest of the Beatles.

Later in the day, Dave Sholin, a radio producer from San Francisco, visited the Lennons to conduct an interview promoting the new album. In the interview, John expressed his happiness with *Double Fantasy* and his optimism for the new decade by saying, "I am going into an unknown future, but I'm still all here. And still, while there's life, there's hope."

With his words he smiled regally, proud and confident like a returning king. After finishing the interview, John and Yoko left the Dakota to head to the recording studio where they had been working on tracks for a future release. They walked outside, only to find that their limousine had not yet arrived. While they waited, a number of fans approached them and asked Lennon for his autograph. One of the people there was a strange young man named Mark David Chapman. He nervously handed Lennon a copy of *Double Fantasy*, which John graciously signed. Dave Sholin noticed that their limousine was late and offered the famous couple a ride. Lennon agreed and they all rode off to the studio.

After doing some sightseeing and visiting a few casinos, Elvis and Lacey sat down for dinner, once again taking advantage of Vegas' great buffets.

As they began eating, Lacey was surprised to see Elvis shower pepper onto his charred sirloin until it was almost buried in spice.

"You want some steak with that pepper?" she joked.

"Sorry; I guess I use a lot of pepper."

"Yes, I can see that," she said. "Okay, now that we're getting settled in with our new lives, how we do make a living?"

"A living?"

"Yeah. Ten thousand dollars won't last us very long."

"We can get jobs."

"Doing what?"

"Well, I've worked as a truck driver, and I've heard people say that I'm a pretty good singer. What about you? What are you good at?"

"Spying, killing people, and miscellaneous covert operations. Nothing I can list on a resume."

"You don't have to work. I'll support you."

"Look, I don't plan on being some housewife. You can't expect me to go from spying for the FBI to baking brownies."

"Do we have to figure this out now?"

"Well, I think it's something we have to discuss sooner or later."

"Damn. We haven't been married a day yet and you're already nagging me to get a job."

Lacey angrily tossed the spare rib she'd been eating down on her plate and gave him a cold look.

"I'm just kidding," he said, realizing she was upset.

"Sure you are."

"Honey, what's wrong? You've been cranky ever since we left the reservation."

"I just want to get out of this town."

"We will. There's a train leaving in a couple of hours. We'll be on it in no time."

"He's still out there, you know. Jericho hasn't forgotten about us, and unless we come up with a plan, he'll find us."

"Look, I agree, and after tonight we'll do everything you said, but until then let's relax and enjoy life for five minutes."

"Fine," she sighed as she resumed eating dinner.

The hunter had laid in wait for many hours, loitering by the Dakota, waiting for John Lennon's return. He had had a chance to kill him earlier, but had backed out at the last minute. It was a sin for which the voices in his head now laughed at him. In his hand was a copy of *Double Fantasy.* He had bought it to look like any fan that would be waiting for John Lennon. In his moment of truth, he had pulled the album out instead of the gun. Lennon nonchalantly signed it for him, unaware of the dark intentions brewing in the man's heart. Now, the autograph mocked Chapman as a searing reminder of his cowardice and his failure. He would not fail again.

The wind swept across the street and through Chapman's clothes, freezing him in his stance. Though it was a warm December night by any New Yorker's standard, the Hawaiian resident found it bone-chilling.

The chance for redemption arrived as a limousine pulled up to the curb. Yoko emerged from it, followed by John. The couple merrily walked to the building's door as a voice shouted from behind, "Mr. Lennon!"

John casually began to turn around, only to see Chapman crouched in a combat stance about six yards away. The vicious voice of the .38 Special barked five times into the night as its teeth sank into Lennon's back and left shoulder. Lennon staggered through the door and up five steps before collapsing face-down. Blood was streaming from his wounds and out of his mouth as Yoko screamed frantically.

Chapman made no attempt to leave as he stared at the scene in a blank, trancelike state.

The doorman screamed at Chapman, "Leave! Get out of here!"

No expression registered on the assassin's face.

"Do you realize what you've done?" the doorman yelled as Yoko helplessly cradled John's head.

"I just shot John Lennon," he stated unemotionally as he threw his gun down and calmly began reading *The Catcher in the Rye*.

The casino was bursting with excitement. Elvis was content playing the slot machines, while Lacey tried her luck at some poker. The crowd on the casino floor was smaller than usual; many gamblers were diverted to the sports booth, where they were watching their wagers in progress on *Monday Night Football*. Amidst the ocean of worry-free hedonists betting their money in the ultimate adult playground, a wave of horror began rippling through the casino. A swell of tragic information coming from the football viewers worked like a snake through the room, instantly changing the expressions on people's faces. The constant sounds of the casino became obscured as concerned conversation began to dominate the background.

"What's going on?" Elvis asked, grabbing one of the people in the casino.

"It's John Lennon. He's been murdered," the man answered, still in disbelief at his own words.

Elvis froze with fear as he realized how stupid and childish he had been, running around Vegas like some big shot while he knew lives were at stake, including his own and his wife's. He looked up and almost let out a yell as he saw Agent Jericho watching him from across the casino.

Their eyes locked on each other as Jericho began quickly moving towards him. Elvis hastily retreated and began frantically searching the casino for Lacey.

She was at a poker table. She had just laid down her hand, a pair of aces and eights, as Elvis spotted her.

"Sorry ma'am, you lose," the dealer informed her as Elvis grabbed her by the arm.

"We have to go, now!" Elvis barked urgently.

"Why? What's wrong?"

"Jericho's here."

She immediately understood as she grabbed her purse and went with him. They slipped out the back and into a large parking lot as they tried to make a getaway. Elvis went to the nearest car and smashed out the window with the butt of his gun.

'Can you hotwire a car?" he asked Lacey hurriedly.

"Of course," she answered as she reached through the window and unlocked the door.

She broke open the steering column and went to work as she unlocked the passenger door. The procedure was interrupted by the sound of a familiar voice.

"Jesse, Lacey -- long time, no see!" Agent Jericho shouted arrogantly from across the lot. "What a roll I'm on. I get to murder John Lennon and Elvis Presley all in the same night. Who says you can't kill rock and roll?"

Elvis drew his gun, but not before Jericho fired several shots. Elvis ducked behind the car, but as he got up he could see through the car window that Lacey had been hit and was bleeding badly.

"You son of a bitch!" he screamed as he fired back.

Elvis' marksmanship proved true as two of his bullets hit Jericho in the chest and he slumped to the ground. Elvis jumped into the car to check on Lacey.

"Baby, are you okay?" he asked with trembling lips.

"I'm hurt bad," she confessed, blood forming a spreading stain on the front of her blouse.

"You'll be okay. I'm going to get you to a hospital."

"It's too late for that."

She knew her fate. It was the same as the horrific vision that she had seen at the Indian reservation during the peyote ritual. She had seen her own death that night. The details were frighteningly similar to the ones now swirling into her view.

"I love you, Lacey!" Elvis whispered as tears streamed down his face. "I will save you!"

"You have saved me. In more ways than you will ever know," she gasped. "I love you, Elvis," she said as he kissed her lips. She went limp, and he felt the life escape her body.

"Lacey, no!" he screamed, holding her body close to his. In the distance, he heard sirens echoing towards him, and knew that he had to leave. He kissed her for the final time, memorizing the details of her face before running off into the dark night.

CHAPTER XXXV

STARTING OVER

Elvis had suffered a double dose of death on that dreary December night. With John Lennon's death, the world mourned with him in a touching and overwhelming display of love and affection for the singer not seen since Elvis' own death three years earlier. For Lacey, his lovely bride, he grieved alone. It was the most painful experience of his life, sadder even than his mother's death.

Now, over a month since she had died, the pain had not lessened in the slightest. Since her death, he had crawled deep inside a bottle of whiskey and didn't have any plans to climb out of it, drowning his thoughts and emotions in its poisonous nectar.

Her funeral was held in her hometown of San Diego, but he didn't attend. It would have been too excruciating, and he feared that other FBI agents might be there, still searching for him. He sent a letter of condolence to her mother, even though she didn't know who he was or about the magic time he and Lacey had spent together.

He visited her grave a few days after the funeral. He brought a bouquet of roses and laid them at the base of her headstone.

"Lacey, it's me, Elvis. I really miss you, honey. I wish things could have worked out differently for us. I really wanted to grow old with you, even though I suspect our love could have kept us young. I blame myself for what happened. I am so sorry. You deserved better."

He burst into tears. "I loved you so much and the hurt is so great that sometimes I don't know if I can go on. But I will go on, for you. Know that everyday of my life I will be thinking of you and missing you. Know that I am grateful that you were my wife, even if ever so briefly. I hope things are good up in Heaven, and I hope to see you there someday. Tell my mother that I said hello. I know the two of you will like each other.

"I love you, Lacey. I always will," he rambled as he kissed the headstone and walked away.

His eyes got misty as he thought of his visit to her grave, just as they did whenever he heard the new John Lennon song "(Just Like) Starting Over," which in the wake of his death was being played nonstop.

It was January 20th, and it seemed as if starting over was what the nation was trying to do at the beginning of 1981. Elvis sat in a bar and watched the inauguration of Ronald Reagan. It was a day that gave hope to much of America as a new President took the oath of office, promising to restore the country to its level of previous greatness. The new era got off to a great start as it was announced that the American hostages taken in Iran had been released and would soon arrive home to be reunited with their families after 444 days of captivity.

It was a great day for America, but Elvis knew that it could have been a greater one with Lacey on his arm and John Lennon taking the stage in Central Park, reunited with the Beatles. The world was spared the pain of knowing what could have been, but he, however, was not.

He looked back on the past three years and wondered what good he had actually accomplished. Perhaps the world have been better off if he had lived the rest of his life as Elvis Presley, eventually dying from his addiction to pills. Lacey would still be alive, perhaps John Lennon as well. All Elvis had wanted to do was to live his life anonymously among the people; instead he had changed the course of human history.

He realized that he had no right to do that. He thought about his friends and family who mourned his death, and the fans who had almost made him a messiah. Who was he to play with their heads? He thought of the soul of his dead twin brother Jesse. First he had been cheated of his life, and now of his identity. Elvis felt like a monster who had been given the world but couldn't be satisfied. In life, he was a star, an icon, the king of rock and roll, but that wasn't enough. He had faked his death and became a legend, a mystery, a god.

He didn't feel like a god, though. His days were spent in deep depression, painfully mourning Lacey's death. His nights were spent in some bar, drinking until he could barely walk. He contemplated suicide every day. The money Tom Parker had given him was rapidly running out, and he was too screwed up in the head to earn more.

Ironically, he yearned for the days of old when he was Elvis Presley, when unlimited money was at his disposal, when people would practically fall to their knees in worship of him, when every desire could be satisfied at the snap of a finger, when he could drug himself into such a state of numbness that none of it really mattered. It was too late for wishes, though; he had chosen this alternate reality and there was no going back. Elvis was dead and Jesse was dying, two twins equal in fate.

Even his belief in God, the shining light that had gotten him through some of his toughest times, had been stripped from him. There was no God, he rationalized. How could there be in a world where violence and suffering reigned over the righteous and the peacemakers?

A miracle happened on that day, though, a miracle he could not believe. As he looked up, he saw an angel. It was Faith, to be more exact, an angel who had walked into his life a few years earlier and now appeared to return as she sauntered into the bar. Elvis refocused his eyes in disbelief. She looked even more beautiful than he remembered, but with a sad aura about her.

She glanced over at him, but didn't appear to recognize him. He began to think it was all a hallucination, until he remembered that she knew him before the plastic surgery. He had also shaved off his beard and cut his blond hair short.

He got up from his table and sat down next to her.

"Faith?" he said, wondering if it truly was her.

"That's me. Who are you?" she asked, wondering how this drunken man knew her name.

"It's me baby, Jesse."

"Jesse who?"

"Jesse King. You know, Elvis," he whispered.

"No, it can't be. How is that possible?"

"I was kidnapped by the FBI. They altered my face. Look into my eyes, you'll see it's me," he pleaded.

"Oh, my God!" she whispered. "I don't believe it."

"You have to. You're the only one I have left."

"Oh, Jesse!" she gushed as she hugged him.

"I thought I'd never see you again."

"Me either. Where have you been? What have you been doing?" she asked frantically.

"It's a long story, but I'd love to tell it to you."

"You look ten years younger."

"You look just the way I remember you. What have you been doing?"

"I moved down here to San Diego. I used the money you sent me to go back to school."

"That's great. What are you studying?"

"I'm studying to become a nurse."

"Wow! I always thought you would make a good nurse."

"I know. You were the inspiration."

"Really?"

"Yeah. I shudder to think what would have happened if I hadn't met you. How bad my life probably would have been. I was right. You were my guardian angel."

At those words, Elvis broke into tears, realizing that he had made a difference after all, saving a young girl from a life of degradation and exploitation. He wrapped his arms around her and wept. She was overwhelmed by the outpouring of emotion and realized that the whole bar was staring at them.

"Come on. Let's get out of here," she suggested.

They got up and left the bar together, as they had left a diner in New Orleans some time ago. Faith had returned to Elvis' life.

Bibliography

Bresler, Fenton, *Who Killed John Lennon?* St. Martin's Press, 1989

Brewer-Giorgio, Gail, *Is Elvis Alive?* Tudor Publishing, 1988

Brown, Peter Harry and Pat H. Broeske, *Down at the End of Lonely Street: The Life and Death of Elvis Presley* Signet Books, 1997

Coleman, Ray, *Lennon* McGraw-Hill Book Company 1985

Douglas, John, *Guide to Careers in the FBI* Simon & Schuster 1998

Goldman, Albert, *The Lives of John Lennon* William Morrow and Company, Inc., 1988

Grushkin, Paul, Cynthia Bassett and Jonas Grushkin. *Grateful Dead: The Official Book of the Deadheads* William Morrow and Company, Inc., 1983

O'Neal, Sean, *My Boy Elvis: The Colonel Tom Parker Story* Barricade Books 1998

Presley, Priscilla Beaulieu, *Elvis and Me* Berkley Books 1985

Salinger, J.D., *The Catcher in the Rye* Bantam Books 1964

Turrell, John Upton, *The Navajos* Weybright and Talley 1970

West, Red, Sonny West and Dave Hebler, as Told to Steve Dunleavy. *Elvis: What Happened?* Ballantine Books, 1977

Printed in the United States
15873LVS00001B/157-177